TRIPLE THREAT

Indigo City Darker - Book 1

A.J. DOWNEY &
JARED KINGPACAL LAIN

COPYRIGHT

DEDICATION

To Jared. It's been an absolute pleasure watching you grow as a writer throughout this project. I'm so proud of you. – A.J.

I would like to dedicate this book first and foremost to my wife, Heather, who has constantly had my back through my years of writing, and staying there when I made the unexpected change to romantic literature. Secondly I would like to dedicate this to my co-author A.J. Downey, who helped me make the step up from being a hobby writer to an actual practicing and published one. Thank you, both of you. - Jared

CHAPTER ONE

*L*achlan...

There are skills and abilities that are highly valued in a professional hitman. It's common to assume that these skills are hand-to-hand combat, marksmanship, intimidation, the ability to drive aggressively, and well, the fundamental ability to kill another human being. I'm quite good at all of those things, but that's beside the point. The real things that mark a successful hitman are confidence, competence, and situational awareness.

I will freely admit to having these things in spades, as well as being devilishly handsome. I'm a professional killer, a hitman for hire, and this is no small task in a world where 85 percent of so-called professional hitmen are government sting operations, smoking out people who are attempting to solicit murder. That's an important distinction – I may be an assassin, but I am no murderer. I'm hardly something so mundane.

Thanks to the aforementioned situational awareness, I know that the checkpoint I am approaching has six people monitoring it – two are functional employees, one a supervisor, and the other three are armed security personnel. That's fine, no concern of mine. They aren't my target; they aren't even a speed bump at this point. I flash the pretty one a rakish smile, at about a quarter capacity. I want to come across as casual charming. At half strength, my smile can cause physical changes in a woman's body – flushed cheeks, stiffening nipples, and a certain arousal.

I regularly take advantage of this ability.

At full strength, I've been told it is a thing of terror. My partner, Roan, has told me that it's a lunatic's jeer, like the Joker if he were handsome, not caked in makeup, and just a little saner.

For this application, a quarter will do. She smiled back at me as I place my briefcase, laptop bag, and jacket in two different plastic bins to roll through the x-ray machine.

"Give me ten, mate," Roan whispered through my earpiece.

"Shoes or no shoes?" I asked. There was a bit of generic European in my accent. With the smile, that vaguely cheesy accent was almost guaranteed to slide panties down.

"I'm sorry, sir, but unless you have a premium pass and background check on file, it's no shoes," she said, a hint of a blush coming to her cheeks. I knew what she was thinking about.

"Of course, madame, my apologies." I untied one shoe, then the other, and studiously placed them in another bin.

"You're good," Roan said in my ear.

I stepped through the metal detector which flared red and a tone sounded, planned of course. "I knew I forgot something," I said and pulled a stainless steel and gold pen from my pocket. I dropped it in the bin, and stepped through a second time, no red, no tone. Flawless.

This technological sleight of hand was an integral part of how we worked, Roan and me. He could be a few thousand miles away, sitting at an impressive computer terminal that would seem to emulate the hacker terminals from such movies, but better made – no mess, no scuff.

The amusing thing was that most of his rig was set up for the games he played. He could do almost everything we needed through one computer and two screens.

He linked into the system; something he did through the phone I carried. The trick was that I had to trigger their system before my bags went through the x-ray machine. This lets Roan's electronic fingers slide into their system. As I was dropping the pen back in the tray, the monitor to the x-ray machine was fed a custom feed – swapped pictures of other bags. This sometimes, rarely, caused some raised eyebrows. It was surprising the sort of things that people carried in their luggage.

I carried three pistols and a pair of knives through the airport; no one the wiser. Two Beretta 93R pistols were in concealed holsters, a knife tucked into the elastic band of a sock, the third gun, a Heckler and Koch MP5 submachine gun was in the bag, along with ammo. There were a few other sundry things I might need on this mission that were also included; you would think it would amount to much more than it was, but I was, in actuality, traveling light. One checked bag full of what normal people would travel with, and the briefcase as a carryon.

Flying was still the main method of travel; commercial had just become more tedious to get through. The trick was to stick to smaller terminals, municipal fields, small carriers, and largely avoiding any of the major airports. Roan could get through dated security systems and spoof basic metal detectors and x-ray machines, but some of the big backscatter rigs and protected systems were too actively guarded to even try to spoof.

The flight was pleasant enough, though the drink prices were highway robbery. A few gin and tonics should hardly cost that much. The gin itself wasn't even top shelf. That was almost an abomination.

The job was almost a vacation in and of itself; take a flight out of the Ocean City municipal field, through Miami-Dade, and then on to St. Anne Island. Roan only had to spoof in once. After I was through Ocean City's security, I didn't have to do another security check until I went to re-board on St. Anne. Considering the clientele of the island, wealthy and privileged as they were, that was notoriously lax. No visiting politician or celebrity wanted some security person digging through their overpriced clothing because their new sex toy looked like a pistol.

No, the only security leaving the island was just to make sure that you hadn't forgotten anything you came with.

St. Anne's Island was a monument to wealth and excess, resorts clustered around the beach, a massive golf course, and amenities that were on par with the excess of Persian Gulf states. There was an artificial ski slope, because of course there was, and all the facilities were staffed by young people, attractive, and most only barely dressed.

The first time I had come to the island, I had almost succumbed to exhaustion. The sheer number of women who were there for the exact thing I wanted was breathtaking. Some were guests, others were staff at the resorts. But after that first trip, it wasn't quite so enjoyable. It took me a while to figure out why.

There was no sport in it. They were here to be seduced, or to do the seducing if the visiting guests wanted it. I wasn't some bloated, overweight, balding, boner-pill popping, asshole looking to sweat and wheeze my way through average looking newly single women and painfully inexperienced post-teen girls.

No, thankfully that wasn't why I was at St. Anne's.

I was at St. Anne's because of a nasty breakup between a pair of former business partners, the Verbas. Emil and Radamir weren't brothers, they had been married men. Now, they were divorced men. I had a folder of details about who cheated, and who stole what, but I didn't care about the petty drama, as entertaining as it might be.

All I cared about was that Emil had paid us handsomely to make sure that Radamir didn't enjoy his newfound freedom. More to the point, that he didn't start talking to the wrong people. Emil didn't want his ex spilling the secrets of the Verba business. One of the professional rules was *don't ask* about whatever the business was. That wasn't particularly important, unless the business involved one or more of the black trinities – guns, drugs, or money laundering.

Those three things tended to get even good hitmen killed.

Roan had done his digital snooping, and found out that the Verbas were human traffickers, pulling attractive young women and girls from the streets of Eastern Europe, Russia, and of all places, Ohio.

This made eliminating Radamir easy to rationalize, and I felt like we might have even been overpaid for the job.

I checked into my room, changed into casual clothing, and started stalking. Radamir's profile placed him as a heavy drinker and whatever the proper term was for a womanizer, but for gay men. Roan and I decided to have a race – who could find Rad first. He was off, doing the keyboard warrior thing, and I picked up the phone. I told the receptionist, using a thicker European accent than earlier, that in more words and more polite terms that I was a wild and crazy man looking for other wild and crazy men, and inquiring as to where to find them.

Fifteen minutes later, I was strolling through what was easily the loudest nightclub on the island; a place full of throbbing music and pulsing light. It was also the biggest sausage party I had ever seen. There was more sweaty meat in the club than had been at the Budapest sausage fest. I hadn't seen so many mesh shirts, bare chests, and gold chains in one place. I felt underdressed and subdued. I didn't have much experience playing that level of gay. That might make things difficult.

Radamir appeared, moving in the uneasy and broken gait of a man who was on a cocaine bender and fucking his brains out. A younger looking man was at his side and looked hurt when Rad brushed him away. Once he got what he wanted, he had no further use for a person. I ordered a Negroni and watched him work.

He was a butterfly, no attention span, and only had eyes for the prettiest boys. His hands had tremors as he flirted, joked, and groped through a herd of young men.

I slipped into his outer circle, being charming and chatting. I did my best to look like a first-timer, a man who was flirting with the notion, suppressed urges, and the like. It only took three drinks to move from the edge of his circle to leaning next to him. Getting his attention took bitching about the bathtub gin they were using to make the Negronis and gimlets. When I put my hand on his thigh, I had him hooked on my every word.

Half an hour later, Rad invited me back to his suite where he was having an after-party.

The after-party was the Slavic version of a rap video. The music was too loud, and it was crowded, and everyone was doing drugs. It was a mess, and the music was foreign. I knew more than a few languages but never really managed Russian, so couldn't follow any of the lyrics. The bonus was that if anyone was armed, they had small weapons. I didn't have to worry about rifles, or RPGs. Those made for a rough day.

Rad was going to have a worse day, even if I wasn't there to kill him. Whatever the human body's limit for cocaine and erectile dysfunction pills was, he was trying to find it.

When the two of us were alone, I wasted no time with flirting or playing coy and went straight to business. The struggle was short. I knocked him out with a sleeper hold, then improvised a noose and helped poor distraught Radamir Verba hang himself. Suicide or auto-erotic asphyxiation; either way, it was a good cover and tied up the loose ends well.

I snapped a picture of him, in all of his deceased shame, and sent it to Roan. Roan would make sure that our employer received the proof of death, and we would be wired the remainder of our fee.

I spent two more days on the island, waiting until Rad was finally found. His entourage didn't go looking for him until the hospitality bowls of drugs ran out and their own stashes were exhausted. That's when they found him, dead almost a day and a half at that point. The report was clean and clear – there were no drugs found in his room, though there had been plenty when I left. The toxicology report was expected to show hideous amounts of illegal pharmaceuticals, and the lack of a suicide note leant the impression that his self-termination was likely highly impulsive, and for a man so recently estranged and divorced, this wasn't so unusual.

The flight home was more relaxing. I skipped the gin. That was an important factor. No gin was better than bad gin.

My car, an unimaginative and easily overlooked silver sedan, was waiting at the Ocean City economy parking lot, and the four-day parking fee was just as much robbery like everything else based around aircraft. It was a bit of a drive from Ocean City up to Indigo City, but one of the rules we had was that we never used the nearest airports – Indigo City's airfield or BWI, Baltimore/Washington International. There was a single clause to this, the bug-out rule. If we were in a compromised situation, all of our travel paths and plans ran out of all the other local airports and so if there was a counter-op run against us, they would button down all of those other airfields. There was no reason, other than intuition, for them to even consider the small field there, and they'd most assuredly be looking at BWI.

Roan was anal about contingency plans. He had turned our shared home into a fortress and had plans for a dozen different threats. We had an 'official' bug-out plan that involved scooting over to Dulles as fast as possible for an international flight straight to Mexico City. That one broke so many of our own rules that any competent professional would recognize it for the decoy that it was. We weren't worried about professional hitmen; we were concerned about some blundering governmental task force getting involved. When those dolts stepped in, they would take the bait so hard that they would probably lock down Dulles in the process.

That was one of the reasons we were settled down in Indigo City. It had more exits that almost any other city in the vicinity. Rail ran north and south, so escaping into DC, Boston, NYC, or even Canada would be easy. There were airports everywhere. And there was the actual port in the city; acquiring a boat could be easier than a car in some cases.

A person staggered into the road, a glimpse of pale skin flashed almost flare-like under the glare of the LED headlamps, and I grabbed the brakes.

Fuck, fuck, fuck!

The sedan was heavy, but the brakes were enormous ceramic things, and it had tons of fancy electronics under its hood. As fast as my reflexes were, the car had already spotted her and was braking on its own. I pulled the wheel to the side, and it slid to a stop just a few feet away from her, but not before the car met the guardrail and slid down it a good twenty feet.

Fuck.

She stared at me with big doe eyes, a mane of blue hair around her head. I expected her to bolt, like a wild animal. She had the look of a junkie, maybe a homeless person, maybe someone who brewed their own kombucha. Fucked if I knew.

What I didn't expect was for her eyes to roll up into her head and for her to collapse.

Fuck.

I got out of the car and rushed to check her pulse; it was there. She was breathing too, and nothing really seemed to be broken. She was fairly dirty – clothing worn and ratty, and mismatched running shoes. She definitely looked like a homeless case close-up. Rule one was hitmen didn't call the police. Hitmen also didn't take people to the hospital. Too much security, too many alert eyes, too many *questions.*

I turned her face into the headlights from the car.

"Sadie?" I felt her name clench in my throat when I saw her face. She was older, I was too, but she looked decidedly unhealthy, cheeks gaunt, and her eyes were bruised and sunken in. When I picked her up, she felt light, lighter than a grown woman should, and I could feel her ribs through her clothes. "You're safe now Shady, I won't lose you again," I whispered as I sat her in the back of the car. I felt my voice crack. My common sense said bodies ride in the trunk, but this wasn't a body. This was my long-lost Sadie Brooks. Someone I had known as a child, someone I thought I would never see again.

"What happened to you?" I asked her unconscious body, buckling her into the seat. I was thinking back to when I had lost track of her, when she fell out of the system. I had no idea that she had still been in Indigo City; so close, but still impossibly far away.

The drive back to Bootlegger Head was tense. I tried to do my best impersonation of a chameleon, one eye on the road, and the other on the back seat. My mind raced, trying to plot out what had happened in the years since we last spoke. I hadn't started my career leaning toward becoming a hitman, but what she had talked about; I couldn't really remember. Military for the GI bill, then college; maybe social work. I felt a protective urge that if someone was after her, threatening her, they would be in for – not a world of hurt, just a very sudden end.

I parked the sedan in the garage and carried Sadie up to my bedroom and put her on the bed for now. She was still breathing, but here in the better light, I could see the bruise blooming on her hip and thigh, once I'd dragged her jeans down. I inspected the lump on the side of her head. *Had I clipped her with the front fender? Had she hit her head falling in the road?* She would probably be okay, but would definitely require medical attention far better than I could provide. Still, for right now, she was stable.

Roan was going to be annoyed – no one came to Bootlegger Head, we didn't have guests. We didn't have visitors. Even the rare visits from utility workers and the professionals who handled things like roof damage and landscaping were barely tolerated.

I went down and unloaded the rest of the car, trying to figure out how to break it to him.

Roan was waiting in the walk-through between the kitchen and the solar. When he wasn't at his terminal in the 'Bat Cave' he would be sitting in the glass-walled living room overlooking the Chesapeake, or working out. "Fresh batch of artisanal gin," he said and offered me a glass. "Some startup in New York, they're doing stuff with botanicals you would probably approve of."

"Is that anise?" I asked, after taking a sip. Shit, it was good.

"Good taste, it is. They're doing some absinthe riffs with gin. I thought you would approve. How did it go?" he asked. I jumped a little, and fuck if he didn't notice.

"You know that long stretch, where all the sea grass is?" I asked.

"Yeah, dreary stretch, lots of low-income housing," he said.

"Yeah, I almost hit a woman with the car there. She's in my bedroom. Look after her and make sure she doesn't die," I said. He would have questions, I could see them, but I was in no mood to answer them. I could feel the comedown creeping up on me. I couldn't lie to Roan; he would smell deception. It was better to either divert to a different topic, or to simply be silent.

"The car will need a body shop. I had to put it into the guardrail to avoid running her over. The brakes probably need to be checked too," I said, wrapping that item of discussion up.

"Who is she?" Roan asked, but I saw him make the mental note about the car.

"Someone I used to know. Her name is Sadie, Sadie Brooks," I said. He nodded and added it to his previous note. "And while you're taking care of the rest of her? Get rid of that goddamn blue hair. She looks ridiculous. She's supposed to be a brunette. Make sure to clean her up, and for fuck's sake, don't tell her that we're hitmen." He nodded.

"So, did everything before that go well?" It was a perfunctory question; the job was fine, and he wanted to deflect me from the previous topic.

"Went fine. There was a lot of trash to be taken out, but we were only paid for the one, and that was what we delivered. Nice work as always," I said. I hoped I didn't sound impatient. *What if Sadie woke up in my room, what if she wasn't as stable as I judged her to be, what if she died?*

"Payment has been made in full, and Verba is pleased with the suicidal death of his former partner, said he can't spill anything now," Roan said.

"I never feel bad when it's taking down a trafficker," I said.

"You never feel bad," Roan said. "That's why you make such a good hitman."

"I'm going to shower and shave, is the McLaren ready to go?" I asked.

"It is," Roan said.

"Don't wait up," I said.

CHAPTER TWO

---

*R*oan...

Some jobs were harder than others. The Verba job was easy as far as that word has meaning in the field of being a para-military para-intelligence assassin. The difficult jobs involved either extreme differences in time zones, or heightened security. The first just messed with my sleep patterns – I had to be up when Lach was working, regardless of what time it was at Bootlegger Head. The second made me work much harder and put greater stress on the tech I had. There was no lack on my end. Our budget ensured that I had, not just the best gear money could buy, but that it had redundancy on top of redundancy, and that even the contingency programs had contingency programs.

St. Anne's was in the same time zone as me, just much further south, that made things easier. Our basic plan of using tertiary airports made busting security a piece of cake. Spoofing the archaic systems at Ocean City was so simple that I had macros set up to do it for me, to the point that I could pick how much I wanted them to hassle Lach. Sometimes that pretty head of his got too big for his own good, and he would get too comfortable ghosting though security. It would throw him for a loop if I l gave the TSA people an eyeful of some strange sex toy, or curious thing to get their attention, never enough to get him in serious trouble.

As funny as getting him detained and strip searched would be, dealing with a handful of minimum-wage employees and legal attention was too expensive a joke.

Everything ran smoothly. One of the biggest security weaknesses in the world was the wide-open world of the IoT, the Internet of Things. The IoT was comprised of every piece of technology that was capable of accessing the internet. There was plenty of security and protocols for actual computers and mainframes, but the IoT was made of smart televisions, game consoles, doorbell cameras, and every other dumb gadget smart enough to connect.

Lach had no idea just how powerful a device his phone, with the programs and changes I had made to it, was. Everywhere he went, I had bait in the water, a mobile hotspot ready and eager to grab anything that wanted Bluetooth or internet connectivity. The colloquial term for this was a *Stingray*, a device that law enforcement and others used to hijack cellphones and such during crisis situations. His pocket stingray grabbed game systems, smart thermostats, smart TVs, smart refrigerators, and all the rest. The number of these devices with no protection should be a matter of national security.

It let me hijack computers because unsecured phones connected to the local Wi-Fi, or smart pedometers, or one of my new personal favorite accessories, wireless headphones. Bored TSA agents, low oversight, listening to streaming music. Might as well have the front door wedged open for me.

The backdoors that these created? Well, it was a cyber-disaster in the making.

These back-channel portals were how I handled half of my work in the field. If Lach spent more than a minute near a closed-circuit camera, I could tie into its feed. More than ninety seconds and I could spoof its feedback. It was easy. It was insultingly easy. Known systems were even easier, like Ocean City's security terminal. As long as Lach went through gate two, I didn't have to touch a key. The macros went into action efficiently and silently, I just supervised the scripts running.

A few days in St Anne's with that phone and the scripts I had written into it, I was inside their security system. It was surprisingly primitive. There was CCTV, the links were there, but they were still running what seemed like analog tape machines and not digital. There was no way to link the two. I supposed that was for their security and the privacy of their guests; the people who visited the island to get their rocks off. Lach had confirmed there were people there that most everyone knew, from celebrities to political types and even just top-tier high-money players. The sort of people who would have business with a couple of Adidas-wearing fiends like the Verbas.

While Lach was gallivanting across some unlisted island in the Caribbean, my time was less extravagantly spent. Our highlight reels could not have been more different. While he was rendering Radamir unconscious and staging his naked suicide, I had to deal with changing landscaping companies. To be honest, the thought of hanging the previous company's rep by one of their mower belts was very tempting. Tedious, fucking patronizing asshole.

He was one of those 'thank you for your service' types, support the troops, all that nonsense. I couldn't shake the military, it hung around me like some sort of cloud – my choice in shirts, exercise regimen, even the way I walked – or so I was told. I laughed the first time I was told that one. I absolutely walk like a military man, comes with having half my leg taken off and looking like someone tried to run me through a wood chipper, Fargo style, only getting tired halfway through.

I sighed.

I still felt like half the person, maybe less, than I had been before.

Lach had been a better help with that than any of the shrinks or support groups I went to. I just wasn't that sort of guy, not the big blubbery type to hug and cry it out. Lach pushed, and I pushed back. I was in better shape than when I had two legs. The gym in the house was my support group, and my therapist was the bench-press bar.

'Where did you serve,' they would ask, ready to tie on the yellow ribbon, wave the stars and stripes. 'Oh, the British Royal Marines,' I would tell them. *Oh, that there were Marines and armies that weren't American, how tedious.*

It could have been worse… there were lads that I had done work with, who had the uncommon position of being veterans from armies that had fought the Americans, or the British. One of the best comebacks I could remember was a poet of a man who made no bones about being a veteran and then seeing the shock on people's faces when he told them he wasn't GI Joe US Army, but had been a commander in the Iraqi Republican Guard.

Same went for one of the toughest men I had ever met, a whippet of an Argentinian who remembered the Falklands War.

One of the things I never managed to escape was the order and routine demanded by the regiment. There were no running miles now. I could still run if I fit the prosthetic, but damn the thing, and damn the handful of neighbors, the few that noticed. If I had a mad fit to run, there was a treadmill.

More physical training, exercise in the gym.

Shower.

Breakfast. Six days a week it was protein – eggs, rasher of bacon, steel-cut oatmeal for some carbs. One day a week, on Sunday, I attended my personal church. The Black Watch was one of those faux Irish pubs through the week, but on Sundays the owners did a proper English breakfast, with tea if it was early, Guinness if it was even earlier.

Codger that ran the place was a salted piece of wood that claimed to have been in the Royal Navy back when it had battleships. He came to the States, and found out that Americans loved fake Irish food better than the real thing. But he had his regulars, and he still flew the Union Jack. Proper fellow, him.

The largest source of chaos, Kyle Lachlan, was the only reason I was still alive. After the IED took my leg, I came too close to giving up. My life had been the regiment, and the regiment didn't have many openings for one-legged men. Recovery and PT afterwards had been hard, almost too hard. Then there was this damned American wolf right at my heel.

How I ended up in an American hospital, well that came down to a lot of finger pointing and a lot of higher ups covering their brass. I wanted to call it quits, maybe take up being an alcoholic, a cripple, maybe a beggar. That seemed better than trying to move forward, but the smiling American wouldn't let me.

Then he pitched me. He knew how I worked, and wanted me to come work with him. Independent contractor, picking up the old tools and putting them back to work. The tools, the computers and drones, it didn't matter how many legs I had, they still worked fine.

Fast forward and we're pro. I'm six years sober, and bloody fucking rich.

But Lach is still chaos, crashing through life like the most charming shark, a wolf that was into snatching panties instead of sheep. I needed that chaos, otherwise the routine would overwhelm me, maybe even fall in on myself in a ball of OCD tics and twitches. But the converse is true, my organization, my order, he needs it. Without me, his recklessness and impulsiveness would destroy him. Bond needed M, Frodo needed Sam, and history is full of real mavericks who would have gone off if it wasn't for the bannerman holding them up and together.

I have to remember that chaos is in and of itself neither good nor bad, but necessary. This is harder to keep in mind when Lach shows up with an unconscious woman and a damaged car. I wasn't really surprised when he left. He kept his carnal indulgences to himself when he was working, and St. Anne's had been a buffet of coconut-oiled flesh and decadence. I cerebrally didn't begrudge him his womanizing; it was what he did. But I did envy him, because the thing I really lost wasn't my leg, it was my confidence. And he oozed it.

THE WOMAN BARELY FIT THE DESCRIPTION; SHE HAD MATTED BLUE HAIR, was painfully thin, her face gaunt, and she was absolutely *filthy*. She was small enough, and easy to pick up off the bed and carry to the bathroom. The tub filled while I checked her. She had good pupil reflex when I shined a light in her eyes. She had bruises, scrapes, but no broken bones and nothing life-threatening. Maybe more importantly, there were no track marks on her arm, no necrosis from the more horrific drugs on the street, and her teeth looked fine if in need of a brushing – *no meth use.*

What was concerning was the way her breath rattled in her chest. That sounded bad, like pneumonia, and that wasn't something I could handle. Stitches, treating burns, and the rough and ugly of Marine triage? Splint a leg, set a broken bone, pull bullets out of flesh wounds, that, sure. Internal injuries, serious illness, I wasn't a bloody doctor.

I placed an encrypted phone call to Maxine Rutledge, Doc Max to most everyone. I gave her the short version – skinny Caucasian woman, respiratory distress maybe pneumonia, no apparent drug use. Max said she would be out in the morning, unless it looked like it was life-threatening. I told her she would be expected.

Getting back to Miss Brooks meant addressing the rest of the problems I could deal with, like the unfortunate smell. A bath would set that to rights. I eased her into the tub and started cleaning her up. In the dramas this would be a sensual or erotic thing – soapy water and naked breasts – but there was nothing like that. She was dead weight, and I felt more empathy for her than anything else. She was obviously surviving a hard life, and barely by the looks of it.

The blue hair dye came out fairly easily, though I hoped it would come out of the tub as well. Her hair was bottle bleached under the cheap blue, and it looked pretty rough. We would handle hair dye or a haircut when she woke up. Instead, for now, I let her soak and went through her pockets, looking for something to go on besides Lach telling me what her name was. She had a dollar and change, some random debris that I could only assume was sentimental in nature – a flat polished stone, a guitar pick – and a few other sundry items.

It was a sad accounting, that.

The matter of shaving came to mind.

After a great amount of debate, I opted to split the difference. Shaving legs and armpits was less challenging than shaving someone else's face. A man who wishes to be a hermit or unnoticed learns many small trades, and I could handle a razor or pair of scissors enough to trim a man's hair. I was certainly no cosmetologist where she was concerned, but I could do a little. If she wanted to do more personal landscaping than what I did, it would be on her to handle it when she was awake.

I was tired once she was tucked safely in one of the guests rooms. She would be sore and famished when she woke, but the kitchen was well stocked. Since there *was* a guest, I went room to room and locked the doors that didn't need prying eyes in them – Lach's room, the pantry, certainly the arsenal, and lastly the garage.

After all that, I had another task to look after.

The sedan.

One of the best tools in an operative's tool bag was to remain inconspicuous. Silver was the most common automobile color, and four-door sedans were common to the point that people's eyes slid over them and only noticed them enough to avoid hitting them. There were things more inconspicuous, but no respectable operative would drive a light blue minivan.

A singular piece of the disguise was that the vehicle had to be absolutely nondescript. All the badges on the sedan were interchange-able. Was it an Audi, a Mercedes, a Chrysler? It was all of them, none of them, it didn't matter. With access to the state registry, I could change Lach's car information in less than a minute.

A silver sedan with a banged-up fender was not so nondescript. There was also his vanity to contend with – he liked everything flaw-less and perfect – and a cracked headlamp, a wrinkle in the bonnet, a damaged quarter panel, and he would be in a foul temper. The damage was startling. The front quarter panel was deeply gouged by the rail, the passenger doors were badly scratched, and the rear tail-light hung from a single clip and a length of wiring harness.

Getting the car fixed would be more trouble than it was worth. The sedan was a few years old at this point. A replacement would be the better option. I set up an email query to our automobile people, a clandestine garage out in California. Simple request, replacement sedan with the normal tier-two package – engine upgrade, chassis reinforcement, bullet-resistant glass and armor panels around the body, and self-sealing tires and gas tank. They would get back to me with an invoice and shipping information. The delivery truck would very likely take the old sedan as part of the deal.

That would make Lach happy. He was almost always pleased when we acquired new cars, new guns, or some other new thing that wasn't a piece of electronics that worked for me. With that out of the way, I could focus on our new guest, this woman that he knew.

I had come to accept his chaos.

That didn't make having a guest any easier. I had come to expect and enjoy my solitude.

I still had plenty of time to do the background searches on whomever Sadie bloody Brooks was.

～

Doc Max showed up before Lach turned back up, but that wasn't a real surprise. Doc was punctual and Lach was off duty. He might be MIA for two or three days, blowing off steam. Maxine arrived in a matter of black coupe, wearing a matching matter-of-fact black slacks and white blouse. The black and brass doctor's bag was her one concession to the medical field, and she had mentioned it feeling fitting since she only did house calls and didn't run something as large as an office practice.

"There's bad news, but mostly good," she said, after spending fifteen minutes examining her patient. "Short version is pneumonia, some bronchitis, and a fever. The good news is that all of this can be handled with antibiotics, and a few other things she can take." I nodded appreciatively and offered her a cup of Earl Grey. She accepted with a polite nod of her head. "Thank you, Conan," she replied.

One of my delights from the Doc was that she could properly pronounce my name, with the right inflection. I was British, not Cimmerian. While I might have been a great many things, a sword-swinging barbarian with an atrocious haircut, I was not. She likewise appreciated the simple delight of a properly prepared tea. In our respective professions, civility was often a scarce commodity.

"I have several days' worth of the medication she will need in liquid form. Unconscious people are inconvenient to pill, and I know you can handle a hypodermic." I nodded. "After the vials are out, there is the same medication in pill form, for when your Sleeping Beauty is awake and able to swallow."

"How long will she be unconscious?" I asked.

"A few days if it can be helped; one of the medications is a sedative. She needs serious rest. Considering the experiences that I've had with transient Americans, you should know they like to make a mess and try to run," she said and took a sip of her tea.

"Transient Americans?" I asked.

"I don't know her circumstances. She might have a home, it might be a bad one, but superficially, she looks homeless. I don't want to presume, so transient American. They wake up, in a strange place, with IVs, maybe electrodes, and panic. When they panic, the first general instinct is to escape. They pull the IVs out like they're in a movie and bolt for the nearest door, usually so hopped up on their own adrenaline they ignore how fucking excruciating that actually is, and by the time they reach the door, they pass out," she said.

"People actually do that?" I asked.

"Panicked people, scared people, yes," she said. "After someone pulls an IV out by force, they'll look like a heroin junkie for a few weeks; the bruises are deep and ugly. Sometimes you have to deal with secondary infections from that, or blood-clotting issues. It's messy. We'll keep her asleep for a while, taper off the sedatives, and then let her come up naturally."

"Lucky you had all that in your bag," I said.

"You are a perceptive person, Conan. You said she likely had pneumonia, so I prepped for treating pneumonia and exposure-related diseases. I have what you'll need to run her a saline and a glucose IV, no need for her to dehydrate or completely starve while she's asleep," she said.

"As always, thank you," I said.

"It was nice and easy this time – no blood, no bullet wounds. I appreciate that courtesy." She laughed.

When the good doctor left, I was allowed back to my background searches for the stranger in the guest room. Lach had told me her name was Sadie Brooks, and my web trawlers hadn't come back empty-handed. On the contrary, they had so much it was impossible to sort through all of it. Was Sadie her legal name, just a nickname, her middle name? Was it Brooks, Brookes, Brux? I only had the three syllables he'd said before leaving.

Matching pictures to faces wasn't going well. She wasn't in the best of health, and if she was a *transient American*, chances were that she didn't have a large social media footprint to track. Hopefully when she woke, she would be amenable to answering questions and filling in all the gaps.

Hopefully.

CHAPTER THREE

Sadie...

This was the third, maybe the fourth time, that I'd woken up. It was different in that it was the first time I felt any sort of *with it* when I did. I had vague impressions of the first few times. Of waking up, mouth dry, an arm behind my shoulders lifting me into a sitting position enough to drink. Water, a salty chicken broth, some Gatorade, maybe...

I vaguely remember being helped to the bathroom a time or two, but none of it made sense. None of it looked real. A fever dream of opulent surroundings. A home, a *rich one*, and not a hospital.

I twisted onto my side and huddled in on myself and waited for the dizziness to pass, trying to put the nonsensical images into some sort of comprehensible order. I wasn't having any luck.

I hurt, stiff from lying in bed for too long, aching, tired, my head full of cotton batting rather than the brains I was born with.

I pushed myself up into a sitting position and the room tilted at a crazy angle. I put a hand to my face, the heel of it pressed to my forehead as I winced and waited for the sensation of my brain sloshing around in my skull to dissipate. A rich voice, velveteen and wrapped in a British accent, startled me.

"Here, drink, you're dehydrated, Love. The good doctor cautioned against restarting an IV until I was certain you wouldn't panic."

I looked up sharply and cried out, stilling as everything screamed in protest and star fire erupted at the edges of my vision.

"Who are you? Where am I?" I demanded, voice shaking.

"My mother named me Conan, but you can call me Roan, and you're in my house," he said. The mountain of a man stepped forward, his loafers sinking into the plush carpet, his gait a little uneven. He used a cane, but that didn't seem right. I mean, he was too young to be using one. Probably late thirties? Maybe early forties.

I let my eyes skate over the expensive black slacks and crisp white dress shirt until I looked up into cautious light green eyes. They were made vivid by the fiery orange ginger of his hair and the light dusting of his beard; his pale skin heavily freckled. He had the beginning of crow's feet around his eyes. Not an age thing, and not a smile thing; at least I didn't think. I mean, he wasn't smiling now and with the shuttered and guarded look he gave me, I didn't think he ever did.

He held out a bowl that was gently steaming and said again, "Drink, Sadie."

"How do you know my name?" I demanded. "Where am I?"

"A mutual acquaintance of ours found you and brought you here. Please have a bit more," he urged again, and held out the bowl a bit more for emphasis.

I tried to swallow, but my mouth was too dry and finally, reluctantly, I took the bowl.

I drank, and the motion quickly became greedy because *God, was that good...* A rich chicken broth with vegetable and herbal notes, yet no pieces of either in it.

"Um, thank you," I said and handed the bowl back, wiping my lips with the back of my hand. I looked down and pulled the blanket up over my chest, blushing. "Where are my clothes?" I demanded.

"Does this not suit you?" he asked, setting the bowl aside on the nightstand.

It was actually a nice satin and lace nightgown, but no – not really.

Not when my nipples were on full display pressing against the off-white cloth so thin you could see the shadow of my areola through it.

What the hell? I thought, followed by, *Oh, God... was this guy a human trafficker? What happened, how did I even get here?*

"You're safe here, you have my word," he soothed. "Please don't be upset."

Lord have mercy, there was absolutely nothing that I could keep to myself. Every thought, every feeling, crossed my face as though it were a reader board and no matter how hard I tried, I could never keep it under wraps. I was an open book to anyone who ever looked at me and it got me into more trouble than...

"Miss Brooks." His voice was disapproving and held a note of warning.

I had tried to act fast. Had tried to act before it could show on my face, but no luck. I tried to bolt past him for the door and I almost made it except for that damn cane of his.

He flipped it around and literally hooked my foot, and I went crashing to the floor.

"That would be inadvisable," he said crisply and held down a hand to me. I scooted away from him and looked up into an unreadable face – his expression tight around the edges with something I couldn't define. I just knew it wasn't good.

"What are you going to do to me?" I demanded, and he sighed.

"The worst sort of things," he said flatly. "Nurse you back to health, provide you a warm and safe place to stay, treat you like an honored guest, which you are. There are clothes suitable for you in the armoire and these dressers." He tapped the white lacquered dresser with his cane. "When you are more attired to your liking, I will bring you something more substantial to eat, and antibiotics. The doctor was adamant that you finish your regiment of medications, and now that you are conscious, we can start using the pills."

"What's wrong with me?" I demanded, and trying to breathe too deeply, fell into a fit of coughing.

"Pneumonia, primarily."

"You still haven't said how I got here, why I'm here."

"Lach brought you, and I'm afraid only Lach knows."

"Lock? Who's Lock?"

"I'll be back shortly. I'll answer more of your questions then," he said. He swept up the bowl and went out the door. I leaped up and got to it just in time to hear the click and sure enough, it was locked.

I stood, shaking with weakness and fatigue, chest heaving as panic took over and I didn't know what to do.

I turned slowly, surveying the room, and went back to the bed and sank onto the edge, raising my leg he'd hooked with his cane and pressing my hands over the spot, rubbing it out. It hurt.

My vision blurred and I sniffed. I was tired, so very tired of bad things happening to me. I didn't even know where to begin with it all. From foster care, to a myriad of dead-end jobs barely being able to make ends meet; through crappy apartment after crappy apartment, with even crappier boyfriends or roommates. To being in love with an addict with there being no hope, all the way to the fire burning me out of the last tenement I'd lived in over a year ago, which had been right after losing my job. That had all culminated in leaving me with *nothing*. I was out of ways to cope… all I wanted to do was go 'home.'

'Home' for all intents and purposes, was in a row of abandoned warehouses that I'd been sheltering in with my meager bag of belongings that had somehow been spared from the fire. I'd been there for six months now, and that bag was all I had left.

I crumbled thinking about its contents. All that was left and precious to me in this world, dwindled down from that long-ago trash bag of belongings I'd been allowed to gather before being taken into foster care.

I looked up at the ceiling and around the room I'd been locked in and wondered, *what next?*

CHAPTER FOUR

------

*L*achlan...

"That is going to cost you extra, Lachlan," Svetlana said from where she was still sitting on the floor. Her hair was tousled, her expensive lingerie in need of laundering, and her makeup was a ruin, my last orgasm spent on her chiseled Russian face.

"You know I don't care," I said, with a careless smirk. "And you know I pay my bills." I could see her scowling at me through the mirror of the hotel bathroom. Her lipstick was smeared, and I could see my cum as it dripped from the point of her chin onto her tits. When it came to being a hedonist – one of Roan's words – Radamir had been nothing more than a crude amateur, cowering on an island, hiding behind a wall of bodies, fucking any guy who would turn and drop pants for him, all the while eyes popping out from coke and knockoff blue pills.

That was like picking a used car dealership to steal cars from when the exotic car dealership was across the street. Svetlana – not her real name, her real name was one of the train wrecks of Slavic syllables long enough to require an acronym – was a Ferrari, a Maserati of a woman. Tall, skinny, angular, and there was no doubt that her lingerie was top shelf, expensive. Her makeup was more of the same, probably sold by consultation only at some high-end boutique in DC, or maybe even New York City.

To the average man walking down the street, she was the sort of creature he couldn't even imagine talking to. She was an alien who only lived in underwear commercials and the pages of lingerie catalogs. She wasn't fucking real to them. With the money that Radamir had, he should have had a half dozen male models in his bungalow – sculpted and flawless examples of what a human body could be when its only purpose was perfection.

"Maybe warn me next time if you're in that sort of mood," she said, finally getting up off of the floor. She excused herself to the bathroom and shut the door. I heard her making small noises and then spit into the toilet.

I felt a wicked smile creep onto my face, replacing the smirk.

She might have been a flawless and unapproachable goddess to almost every man on this planet, but for me, she was three holes to fuck and a face to come on. I felt a twitch between my legs at the thought. It was only a twitch though. I didn't snort coke or resort to erectile dysfunction pills like some sort of degenerate, and three rounds was more than satisfying.

The room was in her name, so I didn't worry about leaving while she was still getting cleaned up. That was normal enough. I checked the funds app on my phone and saw that the transaction had been completed. Svet and her people had been paid. I took a bottle of mineral water from the mini-fridge as I was leaving. Considering how long it would take her to shower, and then reapply her face and clothing, I had plenty of time for a drink or two in the hotel bar. She might just end up staying in for the night. I probably got a little carried away when I took her from behind, but either she liked it, or was a good actress about it.

That was why I never minded the higher cost of Svetlana and girls from her service.

The hotel bar was a swanky high-end joint, wood paneling and a faux nautical theme, like a yacht club. I had a couple of gin and tonics, insisting on the best stuff they had. I considered charging them to the room, but that would have been unfair. If I charged a drink back to the room, I would never see that escort again. I only did it sparingly, and when I felt that I had been overcharged for what I was sent.

Roan would be livid if he knew about any of that. He bristled enough about my dalliances with escorts. Not that they were security risks, more that he disagreed with the concept of prostitution. I supposed he couldn't comprehend the pleasures that a professional could provide, and was stuck thinking about the beaten, drug-addicted, down-on-their-luck women who were arrested for hooking on the side of the street.

The thought of the tacky clothing, bruises, and the way that those people smelled and talked finished off whatever interest that might have been rallying in my balls. Shame, the MILF at the other end of the bar could have been carrying a protest sign that she was a lonely horny woman looking to fuck because her husband was a career man who needed pills. I gave her a half-power smile as I walked past and saw her cheeks flush.

It was good to be me.

Roan had sent me a couple of messages – *Sadie was fine, Doc said pneumonia, new car ordered, and finally, when should he expect me home?* Sometimes I felt like a devilishly straight man who was married to a nattering old woman who by odd chance was a large ginger Brit. I replied simply – *Good job, home later.*

CHAPTER FIVE

*R*oan...

Cooking; *proper* cooking, is a lost art these days. Everything is fast food, carry out, or in the instances when someone does cook at home, its heat and eat out of a box, bag, or can. That's no way to live. The Bootlegger Head manse had a full kitchen, almost large enough to be a service kitchen.

The house was an older one, built in a different age. Back then, the Chesapeake had been full of skipjack boats and crab trawlers. Electricity and running water had to be built into it, decades after its last nails were driven into place.

There were a handful of old photos that showed the back lawn, the side facing toward the sweeping grass and sand of the beach, covered in pavilion tents and white wooden folding chairs. Dozens, maybe hundreds of people had routinely attended parties on the Head, but it wasn't Bootlegger then. It had some name that was only left as a faded scrawl of letters in old ledgers and maps. Rich people lived here, watching boat races in the bay, feasting on crabs and wild waterfowl.

Then came Prohibition, and with it the bootleggers. They would come up the bay in pleasure boats with oversized engines, cruising from pier to pier, delivering illegal alcohol to the wealthy people who called the Chesapeake home. The almost squared-off expanse of grass and scattered trees became Bootlegger Head when a particularly infamous local mafia type made it his home, and the base of his operations. The house had kept a distillery running in the basement that a generation before had been used as a wine cellar and pantry for the house.

This speakeasy attitude had given the house a large number of hidden doorways, and more locking doors than most any house would normally have. These doors proved useful for handling our new guest.

The oven chimed, and the chicken inside looked glorious.

Keeping Miss Brooks as healthy as possible while she was in her induced sleep had involved just making chicken stock. That had been good practice making liquid gold, the rendered product of boiling the entire chicken carcass. I basted the spatchcocked bird with some of this dew of the gods and put it back to cooking. Spatchcocking involved cutting the whole bird in half, spreading it out so it cooked more evenly, and then surrounding the whole thing with root vegetables and herbs; very French.

While the bird browned, I took a bowl of basic chicken soup to the guest bedroom. It had a bit of chicken, and finely sliced carrots, parsnips, celery, and most of the same herbs as the spatchcock. Ingredient wise, they were almost the same thing.

She was standing at the window when I let myself into the room, after a pair of curt knocks. "It's good to see you up and about," I said. She turned to face me, her hair a messy halo around her head. Patchy in color now – blonde, gray, and blue… it was dreadful.

"The kidnapper appears," she said. The only thing harder than the tone in her voice was the glint in her eye.

"I'm no kidnapper," I said. "You were brought here unconscious and sick."

"What do you want from me?" she demanded. "I don't have anything. No money. Nothing, not a goddamn thing."

"The only thing I'd like from you is that you give me the benefit of the doubt. Your wellbeing is my paramount concern," I said.

"I don't know you enough to even consider trusting you," she practically hissed, much like a feral cat.

"I figured as much, and that's why you're locked in this room. If you get with the proverbial program and relax, this is a rather large and very nice house. It has quite a few amenities that are rarely, if ever, used. The better your behavior, the more access to the house and the more freedoms will be granted to you," I said. "I know this isn't ideal, but honestly, if Lach hadn't brought you here, you'd very likely be dead right now."

"I thought you said I wasn't a prisoner," she said pointedly.

"You're not," I told her.

"Your terms definitely make it sound like I am," she said and crossing her arms she stood a little straighter. "I want out. You know, since I'm not being held here against my will and all." Her tone was chilly and rife with sarcasm. I had to smile.

"I get that, and I understand." She crossed her arms defensively. "No, no! I do. However, it's not up to me. That will be between you and Lach." She scowled and changed tact slightly.

"Who took my clothes? Who shaved me? What else did they do to me?" She was scared, angry, and her clear frustration had her on the verge of tears.

"How about this," I said gently, setting the tray on the dresser. "I let you eat this chicken soup, and maybe it will calm you a little, and when you have calmed, we shall revisit this conversation."

She screamed and ranted for about an hour. There was a particularly entertaining jag about putting Xanax or Valium in the soup. Then she wept for a time, then finally she quieted, likely purely from being spent. She was still quite ill.

While she was having her fit, I went back to my tasks in the kitchen. I was keen to see how well my chicken would turn out. The bird had to rest before cutting. This typically applied more to roasts and steaks, but it didn't hurt fish or fowl. Anyone else would gladly have served this with a glass of dry oaked Chardonnay, but the only use I had for wine was in the cooking. A glass of water was no French vintage, but six years sober is a long streak to break for a glorified roasted chicken and the pretense of looking and feeling sophisticated. Could I stop after a glass? After a bottle? I honestly didn't know and didn't feel like finding out by waking out of blackout.

I didn't feel like going to weekly meetings and collecting coins.

LACH EVENTUALLY RETURNED SINGLE WORD ANSWERS TO A FEW TEXTED queries. They were annoying, nattering questions. Sometimes finding out where he was, and when he was going to come back to the house made me feel like a peevish mother. I took a breath and remembered that this chaos was vital to his mental health, and in a perverse way, my own.

I checked back in on Miss Brooks.

"How was the soup?" I asked.

"Fine," she said, tersely.

"Wonderful, and how are you feeling?"

"Your concern is heartwarming," she said bitterly. "I'm alive and almost naked."

"Lach wanted me to make sure you didn't die," I said. "He knows you from somewhere but didn't feel it necessary to tell me. Do you recall meeting him on the road?"

"I don't know who you're talking about, and no." She crossed her arms. "I would like my clothes back."

"There are plenty of suitable clothes in the dresser, and the armoire, I told you this earlier," I said.

"There's nothing in there but nightgowns, slips, and fucking lingerie," she snapped.

"What do you want?" I asked.

"Bra, t-shirt, panties that aren't fucking see-through, jeans, socks, a pair of *shoes*, twenty bucks, and you to open the door and not follow me," she said.

"You have spirit, but I'm sorry. I cannot allow you to leave," I said. She was getting angry again and I could see her nipples stiffen under the sheer fabric of the lavender nightgown she was wearing. She adjusted her crossed arms to where they covered her breasts as her face reddened.

"Go fuck yourself, then," she said.

"That won't get you anywhere, Poppet," I said. "Mind your tongue or you could have less clothing made available to you."

"I'm already one piece of clothing away from being naked," she said. "What happens when I'm still not your obedient little pet after that?"

"I could truss you up like a rib roast, or shave you bald." I gave her a shrug.

"You wouldn't dare!" Her mouth dropped open and her outrage was adorable.

"Love, you have no idea what I'm capable of. I happen to be a very good cook, electronics engineer, and a number of other things; I am well versed in first aid, hand-to-hand combat, and demolitions. Play by the rules and be nice, you can have your run of the house, the library, the home theatre, and the services of a first-rate non-professional butler and cook. Test me, and you'll find out how much I know about restraints and attitude adjustments," I said calmly. She seemed mollified by this, and thankfully so. I had no desire to drug her, manually subdue her, or any of the other methods I knew to make people docile.

That wasn't to my tastes.

"Ah, yes, now that that is out of the way," I said, letting my tone lighten, "would you care for some French Provencal chicken with root vegetables?"

"Root vegetables?" she asked.

"Aye, carrots, parsnips, onion and the like," I said. "I assume you know what onions, herbs, and chicken are?" I asked. She nodded. "Would you like a glass of wine with it?"

"A glass of wine?"

"Yes, a small glass shouldn't interfere with any of the medicines you're taking. Think of this as a white-collar prison – the sort where millionaires are sent to spend six months cooling their heels for insider trading or murdering their wives."

"I didn't do anything wrong," she said, face crumbling slightly.

"I assume that's true," I said. "Which is why you are a *guest*, and not an actual prisoner."

She sniffed and shuddered, hugging herself tightly. She pursed her lips, and decision made, asked me, "What kind of wine?"

"I would pair a Chardonnay," I said.

"Is that sweet?" she asked.

I chuckled. "No. There are some sweeter dessert wines, but those go with cheesecake and such, not savory."

"I'll have one of those if you've got it. I don't like fancy wine."

I felt a pang of regret as I poured a bit of a winter Riesling, the sweetest bottle I was willing to surrender to such an ignoble fate. I took her a plate of the chicken and herbs, the heel of a loaf of bread, and a stemless glass with a half pour of the wine. She inspected it, then tore into the food. She didn't taste it, didn't savor it. She ate the chicken with her hands and only picked up the plastic fork when she noticed the look on my face.

"When you're done, you should probably change. You've spilled some on yourself," I said. She didn't seem to notice as she devoured the bread. I left her to her meal; Lord knew when the last time she ate a proper one was.

THE NEXT MORNING, I DELIVERED SADIE A FEW MORE MODEST PIECES OF clothing – a slightly more substantial dress and a pair of thong panties. She held them up and gave me a scathing look.

"They aren't see-through." I shrugged.

It was true, and it was part of how the game would be played. There were two things that I was running with – I would give her what she asked for if she behaved herself, but in the most monkey's paw manner I could. She wanted panties that weren't see-through, and I knew she wanted something plain, something normal and comfortable. But she never said that, so I was under no obligation to oblige.

The second thing was that I knew she was a high flight risk and Lach wanted her to stay; only God knew why. He never did things like this, so this must be very important to him. The last thing that I would allow would be for her to escape. In comfortable clothes she could feel confident and bolt. When her clothing choices were sheer underwear and satin negligees, or a midriff baring hot pink shirt and black thong, she wouldn't be sprinting down Bootlegger Head making for the main road to Indigo City.

We could sport like this for a while.

"So, do they meet your approval or not?" I asked.

"They do not." She scowled.

"My condolences, perhaps better luck next time," I said. "In the meantime, I was going to discuss what was going to be on the menu this evening."

"Dinner?" she asked and her interest looked piqued.

"Are you going to repeat my own words back to me every time I say something? Because honestly, it's getting annoying as all bloody hell," I said politely.

"I'm… sorry, no," she said after a hesitant pause. "What's on the menu? That chicken last night was pretty good."

"If I start it now, I can have a rib roast done for a late supper. There is also a filet of sole that I could do with a lemon and capers pan reduction, fingerling potatoes, and asparagus," I said.

"I've never had sole, what is it?" she asked.

"It's a very tender white fish," I replied.

"That," she said.

"As it pleases you," I said and smiled.

"Can I get some different clothing?" she asked.

"Maybe tomorrow, Poppet, maybe tomorrow," I said. I could feel her staring daggers into my back as I left the room and locked the door behind me.

I BROUGHT HER LUNCH SOMETIME LATER, SWAPPING THE DIRTY DISHES for a sandwich. She had swapped the lavender negligee for a rose colored one, with intricate lace trim above her breasts and around the hem.

"Are you this Lock guy's servant?" she asked.

"Ah, no. We're business partners," I said.

"But you act like one?"

"In some ways, yes, but I could never be a proper butler. I have too keen a tongue and I'm not willing to keep it to myself," I said. "I cook and keep the house, but I would do these things wherever I lived, and I happen to live in a very large, very old, very nice house," I said.

"Do I have to stay in here?" she asked.

"That depends," I said. "If you promise to keep a certain level of decorum, certainly not. If you would rather make a madcap attempt at escape, then, aye. I assure you the latter would be pointless. The doors are double deadbolts and they are all locked. The same goes for the windows. This place is for all intents and purposes, a fortress. The walls are reinforced, the windows are bulletproof, and shatterproof. There isn't a landline phone, so there isn't any way to call for help. Make as much noise as you want. The armor and insulation in the walls render them soundproof. We are also quite remote. The nearest neighbor is almost a mile away," I said. Her eyes seemed to bulge at this.

"You're joking," she said.

"We aren't at the point in our relationship for me to be funny." I smiled.

"Oh, you aren't a comedian, then?" she asked with a pluck that she hadn't had since the morning she woke up.

"What do you do for a living, Sadie?"

"I fucking survive is what I do for a living, Mister Gordon Ramsey," she said.

"That is a profession that I am quite familiar with," I said. She rolled her eyes at me. "I happen to be a veteran, Her Majesty's Royal Marines. I've killed many people, and despite their very best efforts, none of them were able to return the favor." I smiled. Her eyes grew large again. "It's a pickle you're in now. Your keeper, who would much rather cook you nice meals and see you healthy again, is a skilled sniper, trained in interrogation, explosives, and cyber warfare."

She shook her head in disbelief.

"That's just in the movies," she said. "I don't believe you."

"Quite; but they get most of that wrong, and for a purpose. Do you think that the powers that be would allow movies to show people how to kill and for a profit at that? It would be a mess, ruin the entire industry, and then the police departments would be even more useless than they are now. Half the things you see in the movies flags the police to what you're doing faster than a cricket can hop, yeah?" I raised an eyebrow.

"Why should I believe you?" she asked, something a little sincere, a little hesitant in her voice.

"Because I have no reason to lie to you," I said. "Plus, I dropped you rather quickly with an ankle hook the other day, did I not?" She nodded reluctantly. "As long as you play nice, I'll play nice. If we both play nice, there are nice cups of tea, a great lovely kitchen, and there is a ninety-six-inch high-definition television in the home theatre."

"You have a home theater?"

"Of course, I do enjoy movies as much as I loathe going to the actual theatre," I said. "Come, I'll show you a little bit of the house."

"When can I have some clothes?"

"You're clothed now, and you've got nothing I haven't seen before," I said. "You can stay as you are, or you can come as you are, those are the choices."

"Prime rib or sole," she murmured.

"Oh, dear no, that choice is also gone. Rib roast takes time to sit, roast, and rest before serving. It's sole now." She rose from where she sat on the bed and walked slowly toward me. She was skittish, hesitant, like a wild horse. I half expected to see her nostrils flaring, ears flicked forward, tail twitching impatiently, nervously. I gave her the doorway and mocked a bow. She stepped close to me, only as close as she had to, to get through the doorway. When she was out of arm's reach, she bolted.

I sighed and followed after her. She made a mad scramble down the hallway and hit the first door to the right, almost bouncing off of it from the force. "Linens closet, love," I said. She lit off again, hitting a door on the opposite side of the hallway, repeating the nearly comical bouncing action. "Laundry room." She gave a harsh scream and over-shot the archway into the living room to run smack into the wall instead of turning the corner. "Literally just a wall," I said.

"Gah!" she screamed. I waited by the archway and listened to her hit the next four doors.

"Guest bedroom, guest bedroom, second linens closet, servant's stairs," I replied.

"I just want out!" She came back toward me, finding not even windows in what was functionally the guest wing of the house.

"Your behavior," I tsked. "Things would be so much better for us both if you'd stop running around like a bloody chicken." She stared at me, her chest heaving and face tinged with red, eyes brimming with tears. "Now, that's it. Just calm down." I gestured to the archway. "The living room, home theatre, and service kitchen are this way. I wouldn't recommend running, the floor can be slick."

I gestured toward me and she drifted my way sullenly, stopping again out of arms reach. I turned sideways and gestured she should go ahead. She would find the stairs down to the living area past me. She skirted around me as though I would suddenly lunge and bite, hugging herself tightly.

She flew down the curve of the staircase, stopping to survey the sofas and settees in the living room, the shelves of curated books, and illuminated nooks where statues and art pieces were displayed. Her eyes slid over treasures and antiquities with the same flat eye that tourists survey the walls of kitsch in family-style restaurants.

I followed her casually as she found the service kitchen and imme-diately crashed into the door leading out onto the back veranda and grunted with effort. The door didn't budge. She tackled several windows with frantic effort including climbing up on a counter and beating on the window with her fists. It was better to let her wear herself down before the next escalation occurred, and that would be soon. As she tried to pull the window over the sink open, I did get an eyeful of her bottom, and saw she was still wearing the sheer panties.

"It's not glass, it's Lexan," I said. She had started leaving bloody smears against it. "It would take a NATO high explosive or armor-piercing round to get through that." She came off the sink, and I shuddered as my expensive cookware was scattered and the lemon curd and caper jars shattered on the tile floor. She snatched one of the knives from the magnetic latch and brandished it at me.

"I'll cut you. I'll hurt you if you don't let me out," she said, desperation tingeing her voice.

"Put the knife back on the bar there, if you wouldn't mind," I said.

"You're scared, you're no killer." She growled in desperation, and the sound and sight of her conjured images of a frightened feral cat.

"That knife has a blade made from meteoric iron, and the handle is polished fossil. I will be very upset if you damage it," I said. "And if you come after me with that blade, you'll spend the night stripped naked, tied like a hog, and left to contemplate the mistake of your actions."

She flashed the knife at me; her grip was terrible, and when she lunged, it was timid. I swatted the strike away, hitting just inside her wrist with my forearm. She lost the knife and scrambled back, going for another one.

"Oh, you've got spirit," I said with a laugh. She had a knife in each hand now, a mismatched set. The left held the santoku I used for dicing vegetables; the right held my fish boning knife. She came and started slashing, frantic and furious. She was fading though. Days spent asleep, without full and proper nutrition, sick for Lord knows how long, I was honestly surprised she was still on her feet.

Spirit indeed.

I used my cane to disarm her, knocking the santoku to the floor, and then snaring her opposite hand. She gave an indignant noise and then I had her. It was easy to put her right arm in a submission hold. She gave a weak scream and went to her knees. "I told you what was going to happen if you acted up, and I'm a man of my word."

Thoroughly winded from her running and screaming, still with the shadow of pneumonia over her, Sadie was barely able to resist being bound hand and foot. I left her sitting on the floor in the service kitchen while I set to putting it back in order. She glared at me, face flushed and lips pressed thin to vanishing, tears wetting her cheeks, though she didn't sob or weep. She had a level of pride I could appreciate.

She had some struggle when I carried her back to the bedroom. I changed the bindings on her hands and feet, something that would keep her from escaping or causing too much mischief but not completely immobilizing her. "I think that since you are new to this situation, I should be lenient. You'll stay hobbled, but I'll let you keep your modesty and thus your clothing."

"Go fuck yourself!" she screamed, her face sheened with sweat and tears alike.

"As you like," I said flatly, shutting the door to her room behind me and throwing the lock.

CHAPTER SIX

*S*adie...

I jolted awake at a light but stinging dab at my hand. I sucked in a breath and tried to look over my shoulder. A pair of solemn green eyes met mine.

"What are you doing?" I demanded.

"Cleaning your cuts. You've made a mess of your hands."

I turned away, and wouldn't look at him again, balling my hands into fists. He sighed, and it was a slightly frustrated sound.

"You like to be difficult, yeah?"

"Why should I make anything easy for you?" I demanded.

"Because contrary to what you'd like to believe, I'm not trying to hurt you, Poppet." His voice was soothing and held a quality much like regret.

"Then why won't you let me go?" I demanded, tears stinging my eyes. I sniffed.

"And go where?" he asked gently, uncurling my fingers, prying them away from my palms one by one and making a tsking noise. "See, now look what you've done," he said just as gently and dabbed at my palm with what I presumed was a cotton ball soaked with antiseptic. I hissed where it made contact with the spots my own nails had dug into my flesh.

"I didn't ask to be kidnapped," I said through gritted teeth.

"Aye, I know that, but I see it less as 'kidnapped' than I do as 'rescued' which isn't precisely what Lach and I are in the business of doing, I should have you know."

"Right." I rolled my eyes and let the derision creep into my voice. "You kill people, or whatever."

He chuckled lightly and said, "I've taken the liberty of laying out something for you to wear."

"More lingerie?" I demanded.

"A dress," he said. "Silk."

He got up and whatever chair he'd brought into the room and had set by the bed creaked as he rose.

"Are you going to untie me?" I demanded.

"That depends..." he said, trailing off and waiting me out. I rolled my eyes again for him making me ask.

"On what?"

"Are you going to behave, Miss Brooks?"

"Depends," I said with apprehension.

"On what?" he asked, and I could hear the smile curving his lips in his voice.

"Are you going to hurt me?" I asked.

"I have zero desire to harm you, Miss Brooks, but that entirely depends on you."

I closed my eyes, squeezing them shut as my chest grew tight and my throat closed up. It became so very hard to breathe through the crushing panic of *what were they going to do to me?* I sniffed as my sinuses flooded and the snick of what could only be a blade caused me to jump.

My bonds made a snapping or popping noise as he cut through them and he said, tone gentle and more subdued than I'd heard it thus far, "No, don't move just yet." I froze, and he gently massaged my wrists and said, "Gently and carefully, now. Your shoulders may ache. Move them too quickly and it will hurt."

I pulled my arms around and covered my chest as he freed my ankles from their bonds and I immediately drew my knees up and huddled in on myself.

"I do so hate to have to prove my points, Ms. Brooks, however, I find that doing so quickly, in the beginning as I have, does wonders in saving heartache in the end."

"Just get out," I said, and hated how pitiful and mournful it came out.

"As you wish," he said and then added, "You may join me when you're ready. I believe I've proven myself more than capable by now."

"Just go away!" I screamed, and he did. The door gave a soft *whump* as he shut it. There was no click of the lock this time.

I stayed in the room.

~

HE CAME BACK TO FIND ME JUST AS I HAD BEEN, ONLY I'D HUDDLED beneath the blankets this time. He set a tray of food on the bedside table and left as quietly as he came, and I didn't move a muscle. Instead, I closed my eyes again, despaired some more, and slept again. When I woke, the tray was still there, but the room was dark. I pushed myself into a sitting position, ignored the food and pills on the tray, and staggered to the attached bathroom.

I relieved myself, huddled in the shower, and let the hot water pelt my head, shoulders, and back, watching the water, tinged blue by the cheap dye in my hair, run in rivulets over my arm and wisp to the circular drain set in the shower's floor.

I don't know how long I stayed like that, but the hot water never seemed to run out even though it was my intention to just chill there until it did.

Eventually, my vacant staring even got on my own nerves and I got up, leaving the shower and wrapping my hair in one of the big white towels, winding another around my body.

The bathroom was almost as big as the bedroom. It had a big bath-tub, an even bigger glassed-in shower, a long counter with a sink and another, separate lower counter with a big, cushy stool that looked more like an ottoman in front of it. This counter had a big mirror with recessed lighting around it, and I pictured some rich lady sitting at it doing her makeup.

I sat on the stool and stared into the mirror. I wasn't rich, nor did I think I could be considered a lady and I damn sure didn't know why I was here.

The only thing I could think of was that I was here to be trafficked. That I was here to heal up, be fattened up, only to end up fucked and fucked up. Used until I was no longer palatable before I was killed.

I mean, that's what the Brit had said. That he had all these kinds of skills used to kill people… so why not me too?

I covered my face with my hands and tried to breathe around the panic that was threatening to overwhelm me.

"I suppose now is as good a time as any to do something about that dreadful hair."

I jumped and shrieked slightly and looked up in horror at the Brit's reflection in the mirror behind me.

"You haven't eaten." His tone was merely an observation, nothing accusatory or otherwise to it.

"Why? What are you going to do with me?"

"I'm going to see you well, keep you alive," he said. "Nothing more."

"Then what?" I demanded. "Are you going to sell me?"

"Sell you?" he echoed, then laughed as though it was the funniest thing he had ever heard.

"Okay, I get it," I mumbled both embarrassed and a little affronted. "I'm too ugly for that, or something…"

"Now I didn't say that," he said and stared me down in the mirror.

"Then why was that so funny?" I asked.

"Funny? More ironic, and never mind that. May I?" he asked and held out his hands slightly, gesturing at me.

"What?" I asked.

"Your hair," he said. "I was left instruction to fix it; back to your natural color." He took a step, and I flinched.

"You don't know what my natural color is," I said.

"You've enough root showing now, besides that, I was told it's brunette." He pulled the towel from my head and tsked lightly. "You've quite damaged it, now haven't you?" he said, and I held very still as he ran his fingers through it.

"Please don't," I said softly.

"I think it will look better when I'm through," he said.

I shook my head. I mean, it looked like crap but I couldn't find a care for it. I didn't care about anything except not getting raped again… I didn't even care too much about dying next to that. Some things were worse than death and that was honestly one of them. I'd had close calls before at the foster home. It's why I'd left, but my luck had eventually run out in the bottom of a dry, abandoned swimming pool at a defunct YMCA in a sketchy part of Indigo City, shortly after I'd become homeless the first time. I'd been twenty-three.

"What do you say, Miss Brooks? Allow me fix your hair for you?" I shuddered, dragging my eyes up from the counter to meet his in the mirror above my patchy blue, gray, and blonde head and saw… guilt, I think. I don't know. Maybe I was projecting my hopes a little hard onto him.

I bit my lips together and sort of wanted to see if this was a peace offering or what and so I nodded. Once down, once up.

Roan smiled at me, and nodded back, once down, once up and said, "I'll return in a moment. The supplies were delivered today."

"WHO DID THIS TO YOU?" HE DEMANDED, COMBING THROUGH MY WET, damaged hair, sometime later. I'd gotten dressed, if you could call it that, in one of the fluttery, clinging, silk dresses that he provided me, and I hated the things. Not that they weren't pretty, they were, and not that they didn't feel nice against my skin, they did… more that they left little if nothing of my body to the imagination and that disturbed me.

"A girl I met in the soup line," I said. "She paid me twenty dollars to dye my hair so she could take pictures for her cosmetology final."

"A bit exploitive, did she pass?" he asked as he lifted the first section of my long hair and painted on the nearly black goop that would return my hair color to the rich, dark mahogany it'd originally been… maybe. I didn't know what would happen, honestly, mixing so many things on my head.

"Better than some of the other things I could be doing for money," I said softly.

"Have you ever?" he asked pointedly and my gaze flicked up to his in the mirror over my head, his green to my brown. I lost my nerve and looked away first.

"No." It wasn't exactly a lie. I'd done something akin to prostitution once, before I was homeless, a long time ago. I had been in love with an addict, and he'd gone through what little money we'd had and still needed more. He'd brought his dealer home, had begged, and I had loved him so much, had hated how much he was hurting, and I had been weak. I'd let the man sleep with me in exchange for Simon's fix. It was my greatest shame.

"I don't care how hard it gets, that's not me." That was true, now. I'd sworn then, *never again,* and I'd meant it. No matter how hard it got, I would never… and I hadn't, and I wouldn't now.

When I glanced back up there was something like… I don't know, *pride?* on his face, in his expression, as he painted another section of my hair, running it through his gloved hands which were covered in black nitrile gloves, to the ends. I felt sick with shame all over again. I didn't deserve that look.

"You don't look like your average hairdresser," I said of him, his white sleeves rolled above his elbows, a black chef's apron covering his front as he worked the glop through my hair, the acrid tang of professional grade hair dye tickling my nose. I shivered under the hairdresser's drape he'd put over me and clasped my hands in my lap. He'd brought in what looked like a dining room chair for me to sit in, so I at least had the ability to lean back.

"I am a lot of things, Poppet. Whatever the occasion requires sometimes."

"A Jack of all trades, and a master of none?" I murmured.

He chuckled.

"Oh, I've quite mastered a few," he said shamelessly, but it wasn't a boast. Just matter-of-fact.

"What am I doing here?" I asked again.

"Ah, now that would be between you and Lach," he said.

"Who is this Lock and why isn't he here?" I demanded.

"He's off dealing with his comedown. He'll be back when he's ready."

"Comedown?" I asked.

"Aye, love."

"He a druggie?" I asked, apprehensively. That I absolutely *would not* do again. Be at the mercy of any type of addict. Roan laughed, and it was a good sound, surprising in its suddenness; rich and vibrant in tone.

"No, no, he needs time after a job to come down from it. He goes off and does his own thing, comes home when he's ready."

"Oh. Are you, uh, his *partner*, partner?" I asked.

"Yes, but not like that. I'm quite enamored with the fairer sex even though they've little and less use for me," he said mildly but it drew my eyes up to his face in the mirror. It was guarded now, solemn.

"You're not awful to look at," I said. "Not that I want to give you any ideas."

His lips thinned in the frame of his fiery, trim beard and he chuckled slightly. "It's what you haven't seen, Poppet, and never mind all that now."

We lapsed into silence and I didn't really feel the need to make any more small talk.

"How long are you planning on keeping me here?" I finally asked sometime later as he clipped up the last of my hair to cure.

"As long as Lach requires," he said with a shrug.

"You always do what this Lock says?" I demanded.

He limped around me and leaned his butt against the makeup counter in front of me. He folded his gloved hands in his lap and met my eyes and unequivocally said, "Yes."

I shuddered and looked away. I didn't know what to make of his fervent sincerity, I just knew that I had to get out. Somehow, someway. I had this stifling feeling that staying here would not end well for me.

CHAPTER SEVEN

---

*L*achlan...

The house at Bootlegger Head was a very comfortable place. Roan very much loved his creature comforts, the overdone kitchen, the mock tavern bar thing, all the halls and rooms, locked doors, the massive television, and all the rest. He talks about some foreign word that means the longing for home when you're traveling. Maybe that was a thing for someone who didn't travel like I did and who had always had a home to return to... Me? I didn't long for the big house on the head, but I was a creature of comfort, too. I stayed in five-star hotels at exclusive destinations, and everything was the best that could be had.

The Lamborghini gave a contented growl as I pulled into the garage. I had the urge to rev the engine, just to listen to the sound of the Italian V12 echo off the concrete walls. *Fuck it.* I revved the engine, grinning with satisfaction as the tach jumped to 7,000 RPM. After a minute, I cut the car off, and the silence was almost deafening.

I let myself in through the garage access door. The sedan totally looked like shit; the side shredded by the guardrail I'd hit to avoid Sadie. I hadn't thought about it in the last day or so, but that was the point of avoiding the house for a few days, besides the usual post-job cool-off. I knew he had it under control, but it was annoying just the same to see the car was still there.

I deposited my travel bag near the inside door and paused. Roan wasn't clumping up the hallway yet, and I didn't hear anything else. The concealed door to the Bat Cave was a few feet inside, hidden in wood paneling. I pressed in the right place and the latch gave a consenting click and then popped open. One thing I did particularly like about this ancient house was all the secrecy it held, the hidden doors, the spyholes, all of that Prohibition era jazz. I stepped in and then down several steps.

The room was large enough, it had been a private speakeasy, and a place where business deals were done. There were three doors – one led out onto the grounds, an escape tunnel through the boathouse, the second was a winding staircase to the roof, and the last was the door I had just used. The center of the room was dominated by a multi-screen desk, computer monitors, light-up keyboards, and the rest of that hacker business. The Bat Cave, the Roan Corral – he hated that one.

My knuckles cracked and I shook my fingers out, like a concert piano player before playing, and I attacked Roan's keyboards. I shuffled through several significant numbers, guessing at his passwords, and hit the green lights with 1664, the number of his recovery room after he lost his leg. I shook my head, all the times he fussed at me about using predictable passwords and personally significant numbers. *Jeez, man, take your own advice.*

I clicked around until I found the closed-circuit security system. Almost every room in the house had a concealed camera or three. The Bat Cave didn't have any cameras, the closets didn't, but almost everywhere else did. I found both of them. Sadie seemed like she was sulking in her new room. The dress looked like silk, hair was suitably dark, but it looked like an amateur job, no lowlights, no highlights, just monochrome. I didn't like it. It still wasn't her. I bet he'd done it himself, or just gave her a box of dye. Still, I had to give it to him – she looked better now that she was clean.

Roan was sitting in the living room, something playing on the big ninety-six inch television. It was all streaming, and it only took a minute to find that feed. I waited a second before switching whatever western he was watching for something much more suitable, like a home shopping program.

And waited.

I heard Roan come clomping down the hall. The door latch made its little sound, and when the door opened, I was poised in a perfectly disrespectful pose. I saw the indignation tighten around his eyes, his lips. My feet were propped up on his precious workstation, keyboards shoved out of place, and I took a drink of his special alcohol-free botanical whatever.

"What in the, and I cannot stress this enough, actual *fuck*, are you doing, mate?"

"This?" I pointed at the bottle. "This is just awful. Is this cinnamon and orange?"

"It is, and it's mine, and bloody hell, use a glass," he said, and made to snatch the bottle out of my hand.

"Easy there, Admiral," I said and kept him from grabbing it. "Do you seriously drink this?"

"When I feel like it, yes," Roan said. "I would ask when you got back but I'm pretty sure the entire bloody countryside heard you pretending to be a redneck in the garage." I grinned at him, and relented, letting him finally have his bottle of whatever it was. He gripped it tightly, fingers white. *Man, you need to get out, blow off some of this steam.*

"I've taken care of your girl, but she's a bloody wildcat," he complained.

"I saw." I gestured to the bank of monitors.

"How did you get in?" Roan demanded.

"I ran a hacking... subroutine, and it... decrypted... the frag drive..." I said, groping around for whatever the fuck sounded good.

"You bloody ass," Roan hissed.

"Sixteen sixty-four, man, you deserve worse," I said. "You keep anything real hidden around here or do I really have to walk all the way to the Buckingham Bar?"

"It's the Black-Eyed Susan," he said.

"It's the home bar, and no matter how hard you try, Roan, you can't force an American version of the Rose and Crown," I said. He gave me a rude gesture, and I grinned. "And you need to lighten up, just a little bit."

"Lighten up, he says? Lighten up?" he scoffed. "The man with his dirty shoes on my desk, drinking my spiritless spirits, and messing with my spaghetti westerns, and that's not even bringing up the wee lass you deposited on me before taking your weekend on the town; lighten up?"

"Yes, lighten up," I said. "The job went well, they paid us. Verba was so happy with that post-mortem erection, he gave us a bonus. A bonus. How often do our clients give bonuses? You can probably buy the mock distillery that makes your mock juice. But, since you mentioned Sadie, who did that dye job, you or her?" I asked.

"I did," he said, almost defensively.

"It should do until we can get her to a proper salon, or until it can grow back in her natural color," I said.

"Priorities," Roan muttered.

"I'm glad you understand," I said. "So, give me the rest of the details, how is she?"

"She's doing much better. Doc Max gave her some pretty strong meds. She's a fighter, stubborn as a mule," he said.

"And?"

"Aside from being underweight, and lingering upper respiratory issues, she's fine. No sexually transmitted diseases and no drug addictions. She doesn't even smoke," Roan said flatly.

"Fantastic. I hope you've been feeding her well."

"Crust of bread, cup of water," he said sarcastically. "Now who is she?"

"I already told you, Sadie Brooks," I said.

"Who is Sadie blessed Brooks?"

"The girl in the guest bedroom," I said. Didn't he get that I just wanted him to take care of her for now? I would deal with the rest later. I had no desire to lay out the painful and awkward parts of my past.

"Yeah I know that, *Kyle*," he said.

"I don't owe you every chapter of my life, *Conan*," I fired back. "Just fucking take care of her until I'm ready, or is that too much to ask?"

"Just another mess of yours to clean up, is she?" he asked.

"Is that going to be a problem? More than you can handle?" I felt my temper rising. Why couldn't he just do this, just accept it?

"Do you plan on visiting your guest before you leave again?"

"Leave again, where the fuck am I going now?" I asked.

"While you were slagging that five-thousand-dollar-a-night whore, we were offered another job. A certain French ex-pat, likes to call himself *le Generale*, wants to contract us to take care of some problems for him," Roan said. "You have a meeting set up for the day after tomorrow with one of *le Generale's* lieutenants, first impressions and handshakes, all that. I bumped it to the itinerary on your phone. You might know if you ever checked it."

"Are you going to be a little bitch because I won't tell you who she is?" I asked.

"Goddamnit, Lach, you just threw her in my lap and vanished. I don't know who she is, and there is no way I can run a proper search. There are too many variables, too many different ways to spell her name, and that's not even bringing up if Sadie is short for something, a nickname, or if it's even her first name."

"Right now, all you need to know is that she's important to me, and that's all I'm going to say. Just fucking take care of her, for fuck's sake, just fucking do that. Okay?" I felt my nerves going raw, remembering those dark pages of my past.

"Fine," he said. I could see his jaw muscles clenching. "You'll be heading to DC tomorrow to set up for the meeting. Contract looks like it could be big."

"What's big?" I asked, relieved that we'd finally fucking switched back to the upbeat business of killing people.

"Same as we would normally take in two years," he said.

"Nice, that kind of money could get me a really nice car," I said.

Lamborghinis and Ferraris were nice and all, but there were plenty of tools who had those cars. The silver sedan chaffed, with its mediocrity, and even the Aventador was starting to feel stale. Koenigsegg? Those were certainly rare, expensive, and fast. But they were rare enough that most people didn't know what they were. "Maybe a Bugatti, just a super-fast car," I said, mostly to myself.

"Yes, Bugatti money, Lach," Roan said. "Which is why we do it by our books, and we take the job and the money. You should spend a little time with your love in the guest room and figure out what you're going to do with her. Then, tomorrow, off to DC."

"There's nothing to figure out. We're done talking about this subject," I said. "Has she done something to piss you off?"

"She's tried to escape several times, and threatened me with my own knives," Roan said.

"Regular knives, or those fancy ones on the magnetic strip?"

"The expensive ones, with the meteor…"

"The fancy ones, is this why you keep bringing this up?" I asked, grimacing.

"Just slightly miffed," he said.

"So, she needs some more time to cool her heels," I said. "I don't want her to be angry when I do talk to her. I'll grab something from the fridge, grab a shower, a few hours' sleep and then I'll be off to DC to schmooze the general's pets." I eyed Roan's weird alcohol-free spirits and headed to the kitchen for some food and a real drink.

There was no normal food. Everything was in special containers, and it was nothing but all of his fancy-ass shit. He followed me into the kitchen and stopped at the central island. "Would it fucking kill you to keep something normal around here?" I asked.

"Normal?" He snorted a laugh.

"Not pretentious," I said.

"You travel the world and complain that the food here is pretentious?" he asked sharply.

"There is nothing in here that I can just pick up and eat. Everything in this joint has to be opened, plated, sauced, and garnished with parsley," I said. "I just want a fucking sandwich, so I'm gonna jet, and go grab something that comes in a paper wrapper and in a paper bag. Maybe even a cardboard box." He protested, he wanted me to stay and talk more about Sadie, and the jobs, but there was no reason. Sadie wasn't ready for me to talk to her; she certainly wouldn't want me to see her like she was. She needed more time to get settled in, plumped out a little bit.

"Don't wait up," I said, and left him to his simmering fury.

CHAPTER EIGHT

*R*oan...

A decade ago, I would have dealt with Lach with an uppercut to the chin, then probably a few bottles of whiskey, or a few hundred rounds downrange with the rest of the lads. Lighting up the tactical course with live rounds was a hell of a way to blow off steam. Then there would be pints and trying to give cute girls the business at the bar. Old Conan had done that more than once – gotten into fights, blazed away boxes of ammo, drained cases of beer, and easy chavettes.

Old Conan left with two legs. New Conan was a recovering alcoholic, and the urge to go to the bar and drain a bottle was overwhelming. It would be so easy. It would be so goddamn easy. Instead of even walking to the Black-Eyed Susan room, the house bar, I went to the workout room. The new cure for anger was controlled breathing and pushing weight – the ritual of breath versus the movements of the machines, the clank and clang of the plates dropping, the whine of resistance through the gears and wires.

Breathe out, lift, pause and hold, breathe in, lower.

Repeat.

Ten reps, twenty reps.

Breathe out, lift, pause and hold, breathe in, lower.

Change machines.

I was looking for a certain zone where my mind was zeroed out. The only thing that mattered were the internal functions – the smooth movement of muscle, the control of my joints, the flow of air through my body. Old Conan could reach this endorphin Zen fairly easily. Running was the greatest act of homage, but that was so much more difficult now. The missing leg only part of the problem.

The replacement prosthetic wasn't the issue. The highly flexible carbon fiber runner's leg was an amazing piece of engineering, but that flavor of Zen was gone. I couldn't get out of my own head. I couldn't think of anything but how ridiculous it looked, running with a prosthetic that looked like an airplane propeller.

The only time I ran now was on a treadmill, alone.

I pushed myself, grinding out all my frustration with Lach, turning it into sweat and muscular burn.

The shower afterwards almost felt like being reborn. The cooling mint bodywash made my entire body tingle, and I felt myself stiffen. That was unexpected. My mind wandered back to Sadie, her small breasts and how she smelled after she came out of the bath. At the time, my attention had been so focused on the task at hand that I hadn't considered her delicate features. How transformational that bath had been.

I was fully hard.

I stroked myself with a light touch and felt a shudder ripple up through my body, rising from the head of my cock, through my abdomen, and rising through my chest. My breath caught in my throat.

My imagination leaped into action, reminding me of how her cheeks flamed red with indignation, her nipples hard under the silk garments I had provided her. The flash of pubic hair through the sheer panties, the way I could almost make out the cleft down there. I stroked myself.

How long had it been since I'd been with a woman?

Too long it would seem.

What would her lips feel like; what would her kiss taste like? How would her pussy taste? Her lips around my cock. It had been entirely too long since I had a woman go down on me. I stroked faster, squeezed tighter. The shower beat against my back, wreathing me in steam.

I thought of taking her from behind, holding those hips, giving her everything I had. I shuddered again, imagining the sensation against my soapy grip on my shaft. Was she shy? Was she dirty? Would she wrap her legs around me? Would she look up from sucking my cock and tell me to come on her face?

I felt my balls tighten, that tension chasing its way up from the base of my spine.

"Oh God," I grunted and I came. My good knee felt rubbery as my orgasm blew out of me like an exorcism. "Fuck." My voice was thick and raspy. I was glad that no one had seen that, and some of the lingering thoughts I had about Sadie sank a stone of shame in my stomach. She was important to Lach, and we'd never had the same girl. It was an all but unspoken rule between us.

Not a hard rule to keep, considering how little I pursued women these days.

I finished the shower cold. I shaved; taking the red stubble away made me feel younger and more aggressive. Old Conan had a rough beard, didn't keep clean-shaven. He was a different person, he wasn't me. It took me longer than normal to bring myself back to centered. I couldn't hide in my old world forever. Sadie needed to be brought something to eat, and facing her would be arduous as usual. Nothing seemed to damp her ire.

She looked up at me as I entered her room, her gaze tracing my face. "I think I liked you better with a bit of scruff. This makes you seem more civilized."

I felt my lips twist, and I tamped the smile down into a disapproving expression, one that I admit was becoming harder and harder to hold onto.

"What's this?" Sadie asked as I delivered her dinner.

"It's a slice of Alabama prime rib, served en sandwich with fromage Americano and a plain aioli," I said. "With petite salted frites."

"That's a really fancy way of saying 'bologna sandwich,'" she said, looking at it with some mild interest. "At least it's normal and not half moldy out of a trashcan."

I winced inwardly at the images she conjured, but kept my expression stoic.

Sadie glowered at me. "It's bad enough you've kidnapped me, are holding me against my will, dress me up like a Victoria's Secret model, and have been *super* invasive." Her expression softened. "I guess a little normal is… nice."

"Last time I attempted to make you something *nice*, you trashed my kitchen and threatened me with my own knives," I said. "Bad business that."

She smirked. "So, this was meant to be some kind of punishment? Food that's not someone's leftovers?" She rolled her eyes and said, "Get over yourself."

"Oh, I *am* sorry." I gave her a mocking bow. "I told you how this would work, and you decided to ignore what I said. So, this is what you get. You get basic fare, locked doors and a chemise thin enough that I could use you as a thermostat, do you understand?" I asked.

"I hate your stupid games," she said, looking away from me.

"It is not my game; I didn't set the rules. I am playing by them as well," I said.

"Who's in charge then?" she asked.

"Lach is in charge," I said. "He brought you, he set the terms, and he left."

"I don't know a Lock," she said, frustrated.

"He knew you, he knew your name," I said. "And he said that you were to be brought back to health and your hair returned to its natural color. I have brought your health back, but the hair dye wasn't quite to his liking, said it looked like an amateur did it." Her hand went to her hair, grabbing at it absently.

"It doesn't look bad, actually," she said. "It's better than it was. This Lock sounds like a real jerk."

"Thank you," I said. "At least *someone* now appreciates the work I've had to put into this."

"The chicken the other day was good," she said. "It really was. I haven't had anything like that before, definitely haven't had anything this nice in years." She nudged the tray with her toe. I grimaced inwardly at that. A bologna sandwich was nice?

"The chicken is a comfort food I like to make," I said. "There are many other things like that that I know how to do."

"Like what?" she asked. "I don't always get to eat that well. This is usually my level of gourmet." She nudged the tray with her toe again, sitting on her bed, hugging her knees to her chest, huddling in on herself.

"I'll make you a proposition," I said. "I'll answer your question, if you'll answer a question for me, one for one."

"Like truth or dare, just no dares?" she asked, looking skeptical. I nodded in agreement. "Fine, what else can you cook?"

I spread my hands in a humble bow. "My culinary experience involves the foods of France and my home, England. I have an interest in the dishes of vintage Americana. The spatchcock was a French technique. I can make fish and chips but find it overly sentimental."

"Vintage Americana?"

"Oh yes, the foods of the '50s through the '70s. Tuna casserole, Midwestern style meatloaf, deviled eggs, all those strange salads presented in aspic." She made a face.

"What's aspic? It sounds disgusting."

"I believe you call it Jell-O."

"Gross," she muttered and my smirk escaped its careful prison.

"My turn to ask a question." She nodded in agreement. "All Lach told me was what your name was, and he was out the door again. I've tried my different methods of doing background searches and you're an enigma."

"What, do you want my social security number or something, a driver's license?" she asked and snorted a laugh.

"Well, that would go a really long way," I admitted.

"You're out of luck on that. I couldn't tell you my social if I wanted to, I don't know what it is. I've never had a driver's license but if I had to, I could drive. I have driven, some. Wasn't fun."

"When is your birthday?" I asked. "I'll make you a cake."

"My birthday I actually do know." She rolled her eyes. "It's April 5th."

"Year?" I asked.

"Uh-uh, that's two questions. Now it's my turn. You don't play this game very well. How did you lose your leg?" she asked.

"That's a short and ugly story, and not at all an original one," I said. "I was serving with the Royal Marines in Afghanistan and we were doing a routine patrol, going village to village, making sure the Taliban hadn't moved back in after the Yanks had gone through. The Afghani knew that they could dust up with the American Army, shoot at them, and they would duck and take off. Those guys were, reservists, I think. Weekend warriors who signed up for one weekend a month and two weeks a year and ended up in convoys and patrols for six months to two years. The American Marines, now those blokes were right mad. Some Talibani pops a few rounds off at one of them and they would come out of their vehicles, go charging into the hills and a few minutes later their great ugly jets would come shrieking over." Her eyes were large.

"But anyway, those lads would go ahead, and we would come along behind them. If there were baddies, they would come out after the American Marines had left and we took care of them. My patrol ran over a roadside bomb. Tore the Humvee in half, killed two of my mates, took my leg, and most of the hearing in this ear," I tapped at it absentmindedly. "Almost died. Would have bled out if it wasn't for the commander putting a tourniquet on me before returning fire with the baddies who were coming down on top of us.

"There was a firefight incident, on report. Fancy name for a bunch of Marines, Royal and American showing up like the cavalry in a western, and I remember laying on the ground, medic sticking needles in me, and shouting, and I could see this skinny American kid, on the radio. He goes to shouting over and over, danger close, danger close!"

"What does that mean?" she asked. I smiled and thought about taking her to task over an errant question of her own.

"Meant that whatever the cavalry was calling in, they were calling it in right on top of our heads. About thirty seconds, or three years, my concept of time wasn't great, everything just exploded everywhere. There was just this awful booming roar like every concert I've ever been to but the volume turned up to one hundred. I passed out. Came too later on an evac helo and then it was to a mobile hospital, a quick debriefing, and then I was flown to a hospital in the US," I said. "The rest was rehab, discharge with honors, and fast track to US citizenship."

"That's awful," she said. "Do you know why everything blew up?"

"The official word is that we were shelled by Taliban artillery and an air force strike package eliminated the battery. Truth was that the cavalry commander was green as a goose shite, and called in the air strike on top of us. A big bomber a couple of miles up dropped a bunch of smart bombs and blew up the baddies and half of us in the process. The rest was the brass covering their collective arses. Passed out a bunch of medals, posthumous promotions, and all that. My turn, what is your given name – first, last, and middle, no nicknames and I'd like to have that year as well, please." I raised an eyebrow and won a smile from her.

"This is to find out who I am with your background search?" she asked. I nodded. "You're going to be disappointed. I'm really no one, from nowhere, and I've never done anything," she said, her voice thin and a little sad. She told me her name as I'd requested it, then spelled it, then gave me the year I was looking for. "How does Lock know me?"

"That I don't know, love," I confessed. "He only told me he knew you and to take care of you until you were ready."

"Ready for what?" she asked, apprehension on her fair face.

"Again, I don't know what his motivation is, or how he knows you. I assume you know each other from your respective childhoods, perhaps. You're both near the same age," I said. "You said that you are no one, from nowhere, but that's not true. Everyone is someone from somewhere."

"It doesn't matter where I was born," she said. "I'm from Indigo

City, lived there for a long time, or it seemed like a long time. It wasn't like a sitcom family; we just sort of existed. Both my parents worked, I was an only child, and it was stuff like just making ends meet. We didn't have a lot, you know? But we were happy." She looked up and I could see in her eyes what she was talking about. I nodded. "Then boom, it was all gone. I don't even remember where we were going, but we were in a car accident. They were taken away from me in the blink of an eye. I was fighting with my mother, and my dad shouted something, and then I can't describe what it was like, but when the car stopped moving..." She wiped at her eyes. "When the car stopped moving, I was hanging upside down, and I could smell this weird smell, it was bad."

"Petrol, maybe blood," I guessed. She nodded.

"There was something else in it," she said. "The front of the car was completely destroyed, and my mom and dad..." She choked up and gave a halfhearted shrug. I sat next to her and offered her a shoulder. To my surprise, she accepted it and I put my arms around her while she cried. I was keenly aware of how small she felt, and the heat that came from her. I spoke again once the outburst of tears seemed to slow.

"I apologize for the bologna sandwich," I said. "I'll bring you something proper."

"You don't have to do that," she said. "It's really fine."

But it wasn't. I felt like a right heel now.

CHAPTER NINE

*S*adie...

We declared a truce, Roan and I. Sort of. I mean, I was still scared of him and I was definitely afraid of who this Lock might be.

How did he know me? Did he really know me at all, or was he some creeper that had seen me on the streets and decided I was easy pickings?

Whoever this Lock was, *and Roan too*, they were rich, and I had about as much trust for the super-rich as I could throw one of them. To the rich, I was invisible, until I wasn't and then I was just supposed to magically, somehow, just go away... my existence an affront to their fine sensibilities until one of them somehow managed to see through the dirt and rough living to realize I was somehow pretty.

Then it was a whole different sort of disaster. I don't know. I never really saw myself as conventionally pretty. Too skinny, not tall enough, bony, flat chested, *crazy...* I closed my eyes, the rain pattering against the window pane in front of me, and I hugged myself.

Roan had left, mercifully leaving the bologna sandwich behind, saying he would fix something proper forthwith. I'd smiled, told him again it wasn't necessary, and I was hoping that if I tried to be polite, gracious, and obedient, I might figure out how to get away.

I may be a prisoner here, but I may have been looking at it all wrong… there was no reason to bring even more trouble on my head. I needed to work smarter, not harder at this.

"Sadie." I jumped, rubbing my arms and turned from the window, digging my toes into the plush carpet.

Roan frowned slightly and brought the tray he carried to the little round table with its two chairs perched near the window.

"Are you cold?" he asked, and I nodded. "I see," he murmured and took off his dark gray cardigan. He came nearer, and I shrank out of habit. He stilled and held it out to me.

"Thanks," I murmured and took it, shrugging into it, pushing the long sleeves back over my hands to the elbows. He was so big, and I was so rail thin, I could have wrapped the sweater around me twice.

He smiled and it made him almost… no, not almost. It made him handsome.

Still, he was my jailer, and I wasn't about to buy into this whole Stockholm syndrome shit people were forever on about. I wasn't like that.

"Come, have your tea," he murmured, and he picked up a pot from the end of the tray and poured a measure of fragrant tea into a matching cup.

"Thank you," I murmured, adding a bit of honey and cradling the cup between my hands for warmth.

"Sit," he urged, and I did. He removed the silver dome from over the plate and said, "To start, a lovely potato and leek soup with fennel accents."

"It's the perfect day for soup," I said and my gaze was drawn back to the windows.

"Bless," he said. "Happy to have you in out of that."

"I would be lying if I said it wasn't nice to be warm and dry," I replied. "But at the same time, out there, I'm free."

"Oh, undoubtedly," he said in his crisp and proper sounding accent, standing almost at ease, feet shoulder width apart, hand grasping opposite wrist, over his watch. "Free, yes… but are you really?" he asked.

"What do you mean?" I returned, tasting the soup. It was rich and flavorful, surprisingly so. It was really *good*. I had no idea what a leek or fennel was, but I was on board.

Roan smiled appreciatively at my expression, his chest puffing out in pride and something else. Something that looked a lot like vindication, but I couldn't be sure.

"I mean, out there you lived in a different sort of bondage, did you not? The bonds of finding a warm, dry place to sleep, of scraping by for your next meal… here you have not a care, not a worry."

"I have plenty to worry about," I countered. He cocked his head, and I said, "Will you sit down? I'll get a crick in my neck looking up at you – plus you're creeping me out standing there looming like that."

He pulled out the chair across from mine and seemed to have a little trouble lowering himself into it, his hand going to the thigh above the knee of his bad leg, wincing at a certain point before he became seated, and the discomfort faded from his strong features.

"Does it still hurt?" I murmured, then blushed. "You don't have to answer that. It was rude of me to even ask. I'm sorry."

"Don't be," he said, shrugging it off. "It's a natural curiosity, I imagine."

"Still rude," I mumbled, and he chuckled.

"Afraid of what will happen if you're rude to me now? I'd say we're past that, aren't we, Miss Brooks?" I blushed again and wouldn't look at him, nudging my spoon through the soup in the shallow dish in front of me.

"Just one of the many things I have to worry about," I said miserably.

"Ah," he said, and I glanced up seeing understanding in his lightly colored eyes. "Afraid I'll hurt you?"

"Or this Lock guy. I don't know what either of you want…"

"I see," he said, giving a sage and surprisingly elegant nod for a man of his size. "You're afraid I'll rape you? Or that I am saving you for Lach to do so?"

"Aren't you?" I asked.

He snorted indelicately and shook his head, staring at the ceiling as though praying for patience. "I've no interest in hurting you, Sadie, and if he wants to harm you, it will be over my dead body."

I bit my lips together and regarded him, looking for any trace of untruth. His face was inscrutable, unreadable, and it did nothing to reassure me. Nothing whatsoever.

He leaned forward slightly, the sound of rustling fabric making me jump, my hand tightening on my spoon. I was staring down into my soup again. I didn't want to look; I didn't want him to see me cry again. His hand appeared in front of me and I jerked my head up. He smiled a half-smile that made him even more handsome in a way, although to be honest, I think I liked him better with a little scruff versus the clean-shaven version in front of me.

"Don't cry, Love," he said gently, dragging a thumb along my lower lash line, wiping it absently on his pants. "The soup is perfectly salted as it is."

I couldn't help it, I cracked; a smile dragging at the corners of my lips.

"Ah, see, there you go, now. The chap's not so bad after all, now is he?" he asked.

"I don't know," I said evenly and truthfully.

He leaned back and sucked in a breath saying, "I would like to propose a new beginning."

"A what?" I asked.

"I would like to propose a do-over," he declared. "Allow me, when you're ready, to take you on a tour of the house. You may not be free to leave by Lach's orders, but I would much rather you feel like a guest than a prisoner here."

"Okay," I murmured.

"Okay?" he asked, looking at me quite pleased but still needing... I don't know, validation?"

I swallowed hard and nodded, slowly at first, then picking up speed. "Okay."

His smile was genuine, and a bit victorious, but I couldn't tell why.

"Finish your soup, Love. I'll return with the main dish."

He rose with a subdued grunt and limped out of the room.

I didn't hear the lock click, but I didn't trust that it wasn't some sort of trap. It was raining, and I still didn't have any shoes, and even wearing his sweater the dress being silk? There was no protection from the elements.

Plus, the soup was warm and really good, and it *was* nice not having to fight for my next meal.

Still, I was scared. I didn't know who Lock was, but he sounded like a real asshole. I couldn't trust Roan to know what this Lock's intentions were, but I knew that Roan somehow worked for him so there was no way to win him over. I mean, his loyalty was bought and paid for, right?

I sighed and stared at the rain trickling down the windowpane, at the glimmer of light over the waters out there, white capping in places, turbulent but still beautiful.

I felt that way sort of.

I mean, the clothes… they were soft against my skin and fit me perfectly and were in colors that I liked. You could dress a pig in these clothes and it would most definitely be made beautiful by them. That was partially alarming, though. The material so thin, so scant, it was hard not to feel sexy and pleasing in them but what did I need to be sexy for? *Who* was I meant to please? And why?

I finished the soup, finished my cup of tea, too, and poured another one, using the little accompanying pot of honey to sweeten it.

It was nice. A book in my lap would make it perfect. It was, honestly, something I dreamed about when I fell asleep on the hard, concrete floor of the abandoned warehouse I'd been sheltering in.

A warm place, a comfortable chair in comfortable soft clean clothes, a book in my lap, warm and no pain, the elements shut on the outside of the glass… *and somebody to love me…*

That last part would never be true, I didn't think. I mean, I'd had boyfriends who said they loved me, but none of them ever chose me. None stayed with me over the drugs, or other women. Some got work, got a job and found a place to live but couldn't fathom taking me with them. They wanted to get on their feet first, they would come or send for me later, but of course, they never did.

I was a stepping stone, nothing more.

I sighed and shook my head. I was scared. I was trapped. I didn't know who these guys were. I didn't know what they wanted, but I wasn't dead yet. I supposed I ought to be grateful for that. I mean, I don't know how I got here or anything. The last thing I remembered was standing in Sister Agnes' soup line. Then nothing about the walk back to the warehouse, certainly nothing about a car.

No lights, no sounds, just feeling so hot and then so cold. Just putting one foot in front of the other, marsh grass and the slight whisper of it against my crusty jeans.

Then I woke up here.

Warm.

Not dead.

Clean for the first time in I can't really remember… but a prisoner.

I was having some serious cognitive dissonance with that. I was so much better off right now with the exception of not knowing why, or who, or where? It was enough to make me crazy, and Roan's insistence that he was in the same boat…

The door handle twisted, and I jumped. Roan backed into the room laden with another silver serving tray and I nudged the first one to his side of the table.

"Beef Wellington," he said, whisking the cover off the tray and revealing yet more fancy food – a beef that was layered around the edges and had seemingly been wrapped in like a pie crust or pastry or something.

"Isn't that very English?" I asked, curiously. "Like the only time you see it is at some fancy catered party like a wedding or something?"

He chuckled and cleaned up the other tray, moving my teacup to the new one and standing ready to leave.

"Let me know what you think," he said, and I smiled weakly and nodded.

"It looks good," I said, sounding as brittle as I felt.

"Must get your strength back," he said with a smile.

"Why?" I asked, seized with anxiety at the offhanded remark.

"Easy there, Love. I didn't mean anything by it. You've had a rather bad bout of pneumonia. You still aren't well. In fact, I'll be right back with your next dose of antibiotics."

He frowned slightly and looked at me as though trying to solve a particularly tricky puzzle. I nodded, and he left with the tray. I looked down at the silverware next to my plate and it was no trouble solving the mystery of why; there was a steak knife sitting beside my plate. He'd disarmed me so smoothly and effortlessly in the kitchen, I knew better than to try that trick again.

He returned with a glass of water and a bottle of pills. I took them. I never felt drowsy or weird after them, so I had to believe they were what he said they were.

"How is it?" he asked.

"Really good," I said, and he nodded.

"I'll leave you to eat," he told me and I nodded. At the door, he turned and said, "You're safe here, Sadie Brooks. The safest you've probably ever been." He searched my face and there was something in his eyes like worry or concern.

"Thank you for saying so, Conan," I said sadly, but didn't add that I couldn't quite believe him. At least, not yet.

Nothing about this felt safe.

"Come find me when you're ready for that tour," he said gently. "A proper one."

He left, and I turned my attention back to the windows as a fresh gust of wind sent the rain railing against the smooth glass.

I was warm, I was fed, and I had a good place to sleep… what more could I ask for?

It was a puzzle that I had no solution for. At least, not right now.

I would find Roan for that tour probably in the morning.

I turned back to look at the door to the room I resided in and realized, he hadn't even shut it this time.

CHAPTER TEN

*L*achlan...

Le Jefferson was an old restaurant in DC. One of those places that had lasted longer than some political parties. The walls were whitewashed brick, and the bar running the length of the rear of the dining room was supposedly made from wood slated for ships for the Continental Navy. The dining room was buzzing with a half a hundred conversations, and there were several suits posted outside of the private Lafayette Room. That meant that there were some snollygosters inside. That was one of Roan's phrases; snollygosters were politicians who were politicians for the sake of their own importance and wealth. In fewer words, they were the worst sort.

The restaurant had been catering to those back-room vipers. Half the regulars there were the subject of deranged internet conspiracies. More than one was accused of being a reptile or something. Not cold like a reptile, but an actual lizard person wearing a human suit. I couldn't vouch for any of them being lizards, but they were all cold sons of bitches. They kept *Le Jefferson* in business, shilling bottles of wine that cost as much as cars, imported wagyu and Kobe beef steaks, and a fun little game where nothing on the menu had a price next to it. The lobbyists had rules they had to abide by and the restaurant knew how to dance around them.

It was fitting to be meeting *le Generale's* lieutenants in the regular dining room. They thought they had arrived before me, arriving almost half an hour before our scheduled meeting time. The joke was on them. I had been in DC a day early, and at the restaurant before it technically opened. What sort of hitman could I be if I couldn't even talk my way past busboys and sous chefs?

There were three of them sitting at the table, sharing an appetizer of raw shucked oysters. The tallest was Ajahi Jaarsveld, a black South African ex-pat. To his left sat a blue-eyed blond man who looked like he should be throwing a football or wearing a Nazi uniform. That was Gustaf Malmaison. They had been working for the general for some time. Jaarsveld had been part of some militia group before leaving Johannesburg, something involving AKs, hyenas on leashes, and some pretty unsavory rumors. Malmaison, with his Hitler youth haircut, was a German ex-pat with a file as thick as a dictionary.

They did manage a surprise; I didn't recognize their third. She had blond hair, highly precise makeup, and my first instinct was that she was Japanese. It would fit the general's international composition; he certainly liked his people to come from every corner of the world. I approached, one of *Le Jefferson's* bleeding edge Aviator cocktails in hand.

"I see you are a man of culture," Malmaison said.

I offered a curt western bow at the table.

"Your reputations precede you," I replied and took the fourth seat. "Or at least two of you do. My apologies," I offered. "Perhaps an introduction is in order?"

"Our companion is Gwendolyn Kaijin, formerly of Japan," Malmaison said. "She knows who you are."

"A pleasure to meet you," I said.

"Enough," Ajahi said. "This is not a social club."

"Fair enough. Did you already order, I know you were here early?" I asked.

"Only drinks, and these," Kaijin said, offering me one of the remaining oysters. "How did you know we were early?"

"I was earlier than you," I said.

"He *is* good," Kaijin said, approvingly.

"He is arrogant," Ajahi said.

"Arrogance has to be earned," I said. "And I have earned it. Otherwise we wouldn't be here talking."

"Your rate—" Malmaison started.

"Is non-negotiable," I finished for him. "I have a one hundred percent completion record. There is not a single person who has escaped me, and I have fulfilled every contract above and beyond. If you're looking to save a buck, you should probably get up and leave now." I took a sip of my Aviator. The cool violet flavor was exquisite.

"If you deliver as well as you dress, I don't think we will have any problems. What I *am* concerned about is your conscience." Kaijin was undressing me with her eyes, a twist of a smile on her face.

"I've never been accused of having one," I said.

"That is precisely what we are counting on," she said.

"Since you know who we are, do you know who *le Generale* is, what business he is in?" Ajahi asked.

"International business," I said. "And that's all that matters. So, how about we talk about the job, and not what you and your boss do?"

"You understand our concern," Ajahi said, fixing me with his glare. "There are many men who claim they are killers, but when it is time to spill blood, they become like children."

"You tell me who you want taken care of, and they'll be taken care of," I said. The waiter came by and nodded as I gestured for a second aviator.

"Is this really the safest place for this discussion?" Kaijin asked. "This is… *serious.*"

"Do you see the people around us?" I asked. "These men, and the handful of women in here, they're lobbyists. They're senior staffers. They sit on committees, and that room over there? The Lafayette Room, it's reserved not for people in Congress, it's for the *important* people in Congress. Nothing said inside these walls leave these walls.

Deals worse than you're offering me are going down, right now, in that room."

"Or they are having the crab cakes and the sauvignon blanc," Malmaison said. "I find it hard to imagine that your leaders would be so brazen in their actions." The only thing I could offer him was a polite smile and small shrug. This was the sort of conversation that Roan could wade into easily, but the sort that I had no interest in.

"We have a persistent problem with a rival cartel," Ajahi said. "And not the sort of problem we can sort out easily, ourselves."

"Our rival has contacts, contacts that allow them to harass our… employees… without fear from government reprisals," Malmaison said. "We need several of these key people eliminated from their positions. Once they are gone, we can move forward with our own house-cleaning."

"Cleanliness is next to godliness," I said. "Do you have a dossier?" Kaijin offered me a flash drive, and a manila mailing envelope. I took both.

"How long can we expect this to take?" Ajahi asked. "I am not a patient man."

"Neither am I," I said. "I like to be paid quickly, so I work quickly."

"You men, always rushing," Kaijin said.

"Madame, I only *work* quickly. I take my time when I… play." I gave her a quarter of my smirk and saw the corners of her lips turn up, and a hint of color in her cheeks. She could be fun to play with. Maybe later.

I RETURNED TO THE HOTEL ROOM AND PLUGGED THE FLASH DRIVE INTO the external port that Roan had given me. He would lecture me on how all sorts of dangerous viruses and whatnot could be fit into a flash drive, or even an email. Some didn't even have to be opened, you just had to receive it and it would wreck your system. Roan's external port was protection wrapped in protection with tons of cybersecurity and the rest. I watched as lights flickered on it, and when the flicker turned green, it was clear.

The files were extensive.

It seemed that being in the international heroin trade involved a ton of rivals and complications. *Escadron de Mort*, the Death Squad, original name that, was a group of former associates of *le Generale*. Seemed they had a falling out and the four members decided to try and fight the general for his portion of the drug trade.

I scanned through their faces, the scarred and hardened portraits of career criminals and mercenaries. These would-be hard targets. The sort that didn't blubber and cry. The dangerous sort who might take a mortal wound and instead of bowing out to hold their bloody guts would make their last few moments count. No wonder the pay was good. They were also liaising with at least one agent from the office of the US Drug Enforcement Agency, and more contacts with international organizations. Seemed straightforward to me, if they couldn't take over the operation, they would see it destroyed, burned to the ground.

I forwarded Roan the files that were relevant, so we could start our mission plan.

Less than an hour later, his threat matrix was complete. Both he and his machine with its algorithms worked quickly. The plan could turn into a nightmare just as fast. These Death Squad counter-counter-insurgents had decided to make their base of operations in Texas. *Fucking Texas.* Yee-*fucking*-haw *Texas.*

Damnit.

I made a call down to room service – a bottle of gin, crab cakes, and I let the front desk go over the dessert menu before passing. I was working through the itinerary, figuring how we were going to go in and take down these heroin-smuggling turkeys.

Flying in would be tricky. They were smart and would have something in place to watch the airports and airfields, especially the ones close to them. The answer was an easy one – *drive*. I pinged Roan a note that this sort of long road trip would be a good way to break in a new car, or an excuse to buy one, even if it was a one-shot throwaway car. Those, drive 'em hard and leave 'em abandoned in an airport parking lot kind. A car could sit in economy parking for months without being noticed.

Roan suggested thrashing across the south in a sport truck, and the notion was as intriguing as it was ridiculous. I accepted his proposition, though. It was easy to cruise through a major city in a Maserati or Ferrari, but that drew the wrong sort of attention when you were out in the country, or doing work in the southwest. A big truck could cost almost as much as any of the cars I'd been thinking about except with the added benefit that no one would look twice, other than in cap-tipping approval. Roan told me he'd have a truck lined up for me by morning, and that made travel plans easy – no security checks, no flight plans, no scheduling. The rest would be swinging by the house, picking up what supplies I needed from the arsenal, and then I would be off, tearing across the heart of Dixie.

I considered calling an escort, killing some time, maybe share a bit of the gin. I sighed, my heart wouldn't be in it, I was still in work mode. Work now, play later. A few more texts and my inventory was complete, Roan confirming that when I picked up the new truck, it would have all of my gear already in it. He was efficient like that.

Sixteen hundred miles. I had sixteen hundred miles to settle into the driver's seat of the overbuilt and overpowered full-sized truck. The auto concierge boasted of luxury and comfort, as well as the massive turbos and the amount of movement in the suspension. If he was to be believed, this beast could do eighty miles an hour over sand and rough terrain with minimal vibration to the occupants.

Ridiculous. Overpriced too, but it would serve for this job. If it survived, Roan could flip it. The concierge mentioned how long the backorder was to get into one of these which explained part of the price tag. I did like the overall white paint job with black trim. I told the concierge that the color reminded me of how the Vipers had looked back in 2010; how much I appreciated that.

I hit the interstate and hated the truck as it lugged through DC traffic. I could see the ire in the other drivers, especially the condescending glares from the Tesla and Prius drivers. Once the DC traffic cleared, the truck apologized as we shortened 81, and turned Virginia into rearview-mirror real estate. 81 merged into 40, and I put the hammer down and sped across Tennessee like a white rocket. There were more vehicles like mine, and there became something of a game. For a while I tried to not let myself be drawn into it, but the truck with its massive fire breathing V8 begged to be turned loose.

I crossed the Cumberland Plateau doing 125 mph with two other trucks and a single Corvette playing chase.

Between the spells where I had fast cars that wanted to race the monstrous truck, or other beast machines wanting to see who's big truck was the biggest and fastest, the drive was dull. Normally this wasn't a problem, normally I flew, or where it was possible, I took trains. Pragmatic, and they didn't require my full attention or my sobriety. That left my mind unoccupied, and undistracted. I thought about Sadie Brooks.

How many years had it been? The last time I could remember her, she was just a stick, all skinny legs and huge eyes. She still had those large eyes, and like pools I wanted to swim in them. The stick was gone, she had filled out, not just tits though. Those were certainly something I was keen to see, but she had hips now, and those teenage lips I had kissed had certainly filled out, too. Gone was the sixteen or seventeen-year-old girl; in her place was a woman, and I wanted to kiss *her*.

There were so many questions. What had happened to her after the foster house, after the ongoing disaster that had been our life when we were trapped with the Daughton's? How had she gone completely from the system without making so much as a ripple?

When things were right, I would talk to her about these things.

I had this burning feeling I needed to apologize to her, for dropping her.

Did she think I had forgotten about her?

How mad at me would she be for losing her?

A handful of yellowjackets outside of Nashville let me put a few more hours on the road before I surrendered to exhaustion and checked into a shitstain of an interstate-side motel. I saw hookers before I checked into the room, but I wouldn't have fucked them with a dead man's dick. The escorts that I would spend my money on were almost a form of royalty, not desperate creatures turning tricks for… I shuddered and tried not to think about it. About Sadie and the state that I'd found her in… *had she?* No. She wouldn't have. Not the Sadie I knew.

I slept for a few hours, shoes still on my feet and a Desert Eagle pistol within easy reach.

I saw Memphis while the sun was rising, crossed the Mississippi River before deciding that the local country ham was wasted on a biscuit and discarded both out the window. No wonder diabetes and high blood pressure were a national crisis. Arkansas was overcome with only one stop for fuel. Lunch was a nameless BBQ stand outside Texarkana. It was good, good enough that I felt a moment of sadness that this would probably be the only time in my life that I would ever see this place. It went against most of my own instincts but when I went back to get a few brisket sandwiches for the road, I gave the old man behind the counter a hundred-dollar tip.

I drove toward what I considered the puckered butthole of Texas, the Dallas-Fort Worth metroplex. I deviated from what would have been a straight shot through the city, but all the Chinese owned toll roads and the thirty some odd dollars I would have to pay to use those roads angered me on a fundamental level. The detour was validated by my own sense of victory over those assholes.

It was near sundown when I pulled the truck into the parking lot of the rundown hotel across the highway from the truck stop in Oasis. It was a small town in the middle of nowhere, existing outside of the triangle of Dallas, Houston, and San Antonio. It was dreadfully flat, and everything seemed burned by the fury of the sun. I felt like I had driven two hundred years into the past, looking at sun-bleached buildings, cracked asphalt, and businesses that only survived because of the lack of competition. The surroundings were bleak, a few cracked plastic fast-food joints, an olive drab army surplus store, and the machinery that was constantly in motion, pulling oil up out of the ground.

This place was so small and miserable that there wasn't a single big box store to be seen. It seemed like the largest buildings around were either oil tanks or churches.

I felt a strong desire to return to the mansion on Bootlegger Head. It was green and wet; the sun wasn't a hateful thing beating down on us there. Again, my thoughts wanted to wander to Sadie. I couldn't afford to be distracted, thinking about being on top of her, inside of her, not when there was wet work to do. I had to close my eyes and concentrate on clearing my mind.

Focus.

The nearest airport was in San Antonio, and if the Death Squad had eyes on any airport for incoming trouble, that would be the one. I mean, that would certainly be the one that I would watch.

Roan was planning on some sort of technological wizardry where it would look like the potential assassins and heat would be coming into the Dallas airport and heading toward them, starting in a day and a half, or two. That would set the Death Squad looking over the horizon for their foes. They had to know their reckoning was coming. Why else would they have retreated to a fortress in the middle of Texas?

I drove past the road loading north from Oasis to where the Final Prophecy Center was.

The compound was somewhere between laughable and frightening. There was one hill, probably the only hill in the thousands of square miles of central Texas, and right on top of it, there it was. Squat corrugated steel, a pointed steeple, it absolutely had to be religious nuts, like the Branch Davidians in Mt Carmel.

One of the things that those wanna-be cultists forgot about or didn't plan for was utilities, or the property upkeep. I doubted that these fuckers would make the same mistakes.

There was a single motel near the compound, and as I drove through its parking lot, I saw one of the Death Squad members. A rangy young man with a patchy black beard, shaggy hair, and a sleeve of peanut butter cups on the hood of his truck, harassing a few women with his attentions as they walked by. Part of me knew that taking care of him would feel like a public service.

How many creatures like him had harassed Sadie?

While the Death Squad seemed to have eyes on the seedy motel, they didn't seem to be minding any of the rental houses or apartments, or the easily overlooked Manzana bed-and-breakfast.

There was nothing of interest in Oasis, just oilfields and scrub. The place could just as easily have been northern Iraq, or Afghanistan, or even Egypt where there weren't any pyramids or giant stone tombs. Roan and I definitely wouldn't have made such an egregious error in overlooking the place, but these guys were scrubs by comparison.

The couple that owned the B&B were friendly and gracious, glad for a customer paying cash. I picked the room on the second floor, facing the hill and compound in the distance. There was a little bit of small talk. They mentioned that the compound had changed hands a few times, and they were glad that the old occupants were gone. The new tenants seemed okay, kept to themselves, and the only noise they made was that helicopter that came and went.

Interesting.

The room was perfect, as was the small veranda attached to it. I carried my bags up and unpacked. Two bags were my usual travel companions, low profile and made for aircraft luggage compartments —my clothing, toiletries, the normal things everyone needed when traveling. The other two were the interesting ones. The attaché case with its handsome red leather contained a quadrotor drone, control handset, and a wireless repeater.

I could fly the drone, or Roan could. I pulled it out and checked it for damage, wiping the lenses of its robotic eyes, and making sure everything connected properly. The batteries were green, and in less than ten minutes, all the internet connections were made and the screen on the control console was showing me the inside of my room. I clicked a few buttons and cycled through the visual modes. Low light was blinded by the daylight, thermal looked fine, and the digital and optical zoom worked fine. After a few seconds, Roan pinged in that the drone looked fine and was online. He couldn't take control of it until I released the rotors, a clever little red clip that kept the machine from wrecking itself if he tried to launch it too soon. He would be my eyes in the sky.

The second case was much heavier than it looked and it contained no fewer than six firearms. It was lockable, fireproof, impact resistant and I could attach it to the undercarriage of almost any vehicle I cared to drive. It could roll through anything short of a complete vehicle disassembly inspection, or an x-ray backscatter scanner. I opened it up and ran my hand lovingly over what was inside.

A .45 Longslide pistol with red laser dot. T-800 approved.

A 9mm Beretta 92FS with compensator. Good for killing vampires, werewolves, and whatever else got in my way. Just kidding. It would be nice, but all I had for target practice these days were scum, soldiers of fortune and various other sundry mercenary types.

Also in the case, was a 7.62mm Heckler & Koch SR9. It was an import and gift, a splendid jackal sniping rifle.

Next up, a .50 caliber Desert Eagle, because sometimes you need a really big bullet.

Second to last was a .223 AR-15. I had no love for the weapon, but it was so readily available that I could leave them like empty beer cans behind me, and even if law enforcement got their hands on it, it wouldn't matter.

And finally, the last gun in the case was Roan's addition to my arsenal, his personal touch – a Colt Python .357 magnum. It was a stunning weapon, gorgeous, heavy, expensive, and as far as pistols went, it was a revolver, so after the cylinder was empty, it pretty much became a very pricey bludgeon, but Roan loved his large-frame American revolvers.

ONCE NIGHT CAME, I TOOK THE DRONE OUT TO THE VERANDA AND Roan grabbed it and flew off with it. I watched the screen while he zoomed toward the compound. He had a full setup in the Bat Cave – three monitors, a console, hell even a control column like a flight simulator. He flew the black drone around the Final Prophecy Center, sweeping it with cameras, thermal and low light. As he did his thing, his program was stitching together a picture of the place, like a massive panoramic shot. The thermal showed where people were, or had been, and how long it had been since their civvy helicopter had been in the air. The turbine was cold, so it had been days since it flew.

There was a main approach, the road leading from the highway up the hill toward the compound. It was covered from two different towers, and there was a guard shack and road barricade that made that easily covered. Basic prepper nonsense.

There was a barely noticeable service road leading to the back of the compound, only visible in its temperature difference in the infrared. There was a large truck, likely a military-style vehicle, the heat from its tires and engine glowing like cherries on the screen. If we had some of this back when I was running across the scrub along the Pakistan border, the damage we could have done.

As the drone made its sweep, I found what I wanted; a covered approach to the compound. The eastern side of the compound was a broad downslope that had been planted with an orchard, maybe a vineyard. It mostly looked dead, but there was enough that it would provide the cover I needed.

There was a certain pleasure that came from prep – the zip and song of nylon straps, the crackle of Velcro, the soft metallic sounds the guns made as I checked them. The almost sensual insertion of the tactical knife into its sheath gave me a little thrill. My hostess gave me a smile and a nod as I departed for the evening, but I looked nothing but debonair and handsome in my custom-fit leather coat and sport gloves. The ensemble looked better with an Aston Martin or a McLaren. It seemed strange with a Ford truck, but I wasn't going to drive up to the center. I was going to walk.

A block from the bed-and-breakfast the main strip of Oasis, Texas opened up running more or less east to west. It was a small town so the attractions were limited to a few fast-food establishments, a weathered gentleman's club, and small-town Main Street businesses that were only around because Oasis wasn't large enough to attract a big box store. I slipped between a gold and jewelry store and a hardware store, into a narrow alley that opened out into a dusty courtyard littered with cigarette butts and discarded food and drink containers. *Must be where the employees came for their breaks.*

I kept walking, circling counterclockwise around the perimeter of the hill. I kept different buildings and fences between me and the compound. The only problems I had involved dogs barking when they noticed me. Dogs were the worst, they couldn't be spoofed, bribed, or intimidated. They had to be avoided or killed and I hated hurting animals. Guard and attack dogs were easier to rationalize, but people's pets? No. That wasn't okay. I cleared a few fences, Roan whispering through my earpiece about what was ahead of me.

He guided me to a low spot in the fence where a derelict vehicle was decaying into the desert hardpan. I mounted the hood, then the top, and then hauled myself up over the chain-link. I hit the ground on the other side and took a knee. It was time to get serious. I had the shadow of the failed orchard covering me while I took the pieces of the rifle out of the lining of my coat and fitted them all together, slipping the magazine into place.

"Now, forward fifteen meters, then down," Roan said. I advanced and found where some tractor had been parked and left, taking shelter behind it. "Thirty seconds, one target."

The man stopped, pulled out a pack of cigarettes and lipped one. He flicked his lighter, but when he went to draw on the smoke, his breath bubbled and he managed a gasp. The blade slipped between his ribs and found the sweet spot. I eased him to the ground and took his rifle from his shoulder. He looked up at me, shaking as his life pulsed from the knife wound in his back. I had nicked the aorta to get a flow like that. "Just business," I whispered as I disassembled his weapon and tossed the pieces in different directions. No one would be able to pick up his AR-15 and use it against me. I put the lone magazine he had in my back pocket, that might be useful.

"Thirty-five meters to the base of the wall, three... two... one," Roan said. When he said one, I was gone, covering the distance as quickly as I could. The rifle bumped against my hip as I slid to the wall. I held my breath while a man in the tower waved a flashlight across the night-darkened landscape.

"What was that?" the tower guard asked insistently.

"Nothing, you gotta calm down," his partner for the evening said dismissively.

"I swear to *God* man..." The first man sounded like he was wound tighter than a Timex.

There were at least two in the tower, one of them obviously the nervous type. They were talking, and I could see part of the tower light up inside with a soft blue-white glow. They were amateurs. No professional would do something as dumb as using a smartphone while on guard. It ruined night vision, gave away your position, and took your attention off of what you were supposed to be watching. For a moment, I wished silencers worked like they did in the movies, *fwip fwip*, and these two idiots would be taking dirt naps. But that was Hollywood, and this was real life, so the quietest way to deal with patrols was by blade or submission holds and broken necks.

At the base of their wall, the men in the tower couldn't see me, so I started back toward the front of the compound. Roan whispered in my ear where the door was, and what the guards were doing. I moved like a ghost between them. I paused next to a small door in the wall, banded and reinforced metal, likely a concrete core. I would need explosives to get through it, or some good luck.

Or a bit of good luck by way of some sloppy security.

When I kneeled near the door, there was a small pebble wedged at the base, keeping the latch from engaging. *Super sloppy.* The men on foot probably used this as an access door, which meant that either a bathroom or break area was close to it. I opened it and slipped in, dislodging the pebble. The rest of the men outside wouldn't be using this door. I smiled as I lowered a locking bar into place. Even if one of them had a key, it wouldn't move the iron bar.

Total OSHA violation having a lock like that, I thought smugly.

Bathroom on the right, breakroom past that, both were empty for now.

"You still with me?" I whispered.

"Still here, signal is good," Roan said. "I'm bringing up the building's blueprints. You're in the east access corridor. According to this, you should have bathrooms and a photography lab on your right."

"Bathrooms, yes, photo lab is now a breakroom," I said.

"There will probably be some changes. End of the corridor there is a flight of stairs to your left, sports center double doors to your right, and if you go straight ahead, it should be some sort of central reception area."

"Looks like a mess area," I said.

"The offices and private quarters are upstairs," Roan said.

"What does it look like outside?"

"Dark mostly, no one has noticed the missing guard. There is some action down at the guardhouse. Looks like a call girl brought them some pizza, or the pizza delivery girl was coerced into hands-on customer service."

"They'll be occupied for a while, but not all that useful to me," I said.

"One of the marks is in the guard shack," Roan said.

"Good to know. I can take him out when I'm leaving," I said.

"Just as long as you kill him *after* the date." He laughed.

I took the stairs, staying pressed to the wall side of the stairwell. The office door was open and there were several people inside talking a mix of French and English, a few words of Spanish. Three people, two men, one woman. The woman was younger, and she was the one mixing Spanish into her English. Her accent had a musical quality to it. She couldn't be Death Squad, none of them were women. A phone rang, one of the men answered it, speaking in French. I caught the short version, complaints about a hooker in the guard shack and one of the guards missing. Then something about shit, and bathrooms. I ghosted into the room, drawing the Beretta as the man put the phone down on the desk. He looked up at me, surprise on his face. He should be surprised. Black jacket, black mask, and drawn black pistol.

POP! POP!

He crumpled as the two shots removed the back of his head and the side of his neck, painting the austere white drapes behind him in gore. I pivoted, bringing the gun to bear on the second man. He wasn't one of the Squad marks, but his green tactical vest and the pistol on his hip told me he was security.

POP! POP!

He grunted and collapsed sideways, while his lung collapsed and blood filled his torso. He reached for his pistol; eyes wide with the whites showing.

POP!

His head jerked back and blood sprayed the couch and floor. The woman covered a scream, blood flecked her face and hair. I put a finger to my lips, and whispered, "Hush." She nodded vigorously, hand still over her mouth. I went back to the door and heard the soft sound of metal on fabric, the sound of a weapon being drawn. I turned to face the woman again and saw she had a snub-nosed revolver half drawn and was rising from her seated position.

I put the sights between her breasts while she was still drawing and she froze. I hated shooting women; it always left a sour taste in my mouth.

POP! POP!

She heaved back into the seat and then slumped forward. Her white blouse stained red.

I stepped out into the hallway; the element of surprise was done. The old man who had been on the phone was mark one, the leader of the Death Squad, Phillipe le Clerc d'Chauvignon. Ole le Clerc had opposed *le Generale* for being too young and not having the same amount of military experience. He was dead now.

Two men came out of the doors of their rooms, one dressed, one in just underwear.

POP! POP! POP!

They were down.

I backpedaled into the room the almost-naked man came out of just as the general alarm was sounded. "Trigger the fire alarm," I said. A moment later, a loud ringing filled the building when Roan activated the system. I heard a creak and groan and then the water sprinklers kicked on. There was shouting, chaos. Several men went down the hall, and I heard one shouting orders to the others in French. He shouted Phillipe's name. I stepped into the hallway and saw my second mark and one of his bodyguards. The man was drawing his weapon while the second mark started to take a position behind him.

POP! POP!

The bodyguard went down as I advanced. I saw the man as he tried to escape back into his room. Tan face, curly black hair, Enrico, the Spaniard. He tried to slam the door in my face but I got a boot in the way before the latch could grab. I threw my shoulder into the door, and he did the same, bracing against it to keep me out.

"Fuck you, you are a dead man," Enrico said. "However much they're paying, I'll double it." I put the muzzle of the Beretta against the door.

POP! POP! POP! Click!

The resistance on the door crumpled and Enrico hit the floor, soon to be a corpse. I shoved the door open and looked at him; one round in the shoulder, two in the chest. He was breathing rapidly, and he already had blood seeping out of his mouth. I drew the Colt from my hip and put a round between his eyes. His head exploded like a melon and the sound of the hand cannon going off made my ears ring. *Two down.* I took Enrico's gold plated 1911 as a trophy.

I stepped back into the hallway and reloaded the Beretta while stalking. There was a good deal of shouting and screaming from the room at the end of the corridor. "End of the corridor, east end, second floor," I said.

"Kitchen facilities, water and gas lines, open space," Roan said. "Fire department has replied to the center. I have them delayed, intercepted the call, told them it was a false alarm. Police have not been notified."

"Good to know," I said. I kicked the double door open and there were four women in the room. They all looked like housekeeping, or something along those lines. I waved the pistol in a circular motion. They raised their hands, shaking and some crying, and they took to their knees. I pulled the door shut and jammed it with a broom. They would be able to escape, but it would take them a while to do it.

"Have you got their CCTV yet?" I asked.

"Yes," Roan said. "You've got between eight and twelve security people inbound; they're keeping four at the gate. Looks like twenty potential civilians, mostly women."

"Location?"

"They seem to be gathering in the front lobby, west lower floor, and the vestibule to the chapel, south lower floor," Roan said.

"Conan?" I heard someone speak, a light feminine lilting voice coming through my earpiece. *Sadie...* The knowledge sent a frisson of energy through my chest.

"Give me a few moments, I'm working," Roan said gently, his voice muffled as he likely put his hand over the mic. He took it away and I heard her again...

"Oh, sorry," she said and she sounded... I don't know... Lonely? *Fuck.*

"Alfred, what's Sadie doing in the Bat Cave?" I demanded.

"Keep your mind on the mission, Bruce. Looks like the Prince of Persia is leading the counterattack, he's in the vestibule. They have rifles," Roan said.

"Kill the lights and keep me appraised," I said. Rather than taking the stairs at the end of the corridor, I opted for the express and grabbed the rail and hopped over the edge. It took two lurching seconds before I hit the lower floor and rolled to a concealed position behind a planter. The lights went out, and then I heard the shouting and the cussing explode from the direction of the front lobby. I felt like a walking gun store sometimes, but cases like this justified the weight. I unslung the AR-15 and checked the magazine and walked toward the front lobby. My target wasn't in there, the Iranian, the

Prince of Persia, was a take-chard and lead-from-the-front sort of asshole. I was counting on that.

"You know that being caught in a pincer is a tactical disaster," Roan said primly in my ear.

"It's not being caught if it's a trap," I muttered back.

"It's not a trap if they *know where you are*. Blast it," Roan countered.

"It's still a trap," I said.

I pulled the Colt and fired several times toward the front lobby. The gun was loud, and its voice distinctive. They would know it wasn't one of theirs, and they would start their action. I drew down into a concealed position behind the large stone planter that had cigarette butts in it instead of some oversized mall palm. I let the alpha types burst into the room like the commandos they thought they were. These weren't the French Foreign Legionnaires that the Death Squad had come from, these were locals; Texans and Mexicans with a wild hair up their ass about being mercenary badasses, and getting paid to strut around with guns.

I let them sweep twenty feet into the common area, moving around the cafeteria-style tables, some bumping into chairs. They all had their rifles up, flashlights in hand; a few carried pistols and were comically using their phone flashlights. Idiots, the only advantage they had was numbers, and that was all.

The AR-15 fired in three-round bursts. Where they had flashlights and phones, I had a night vision scope. Several of the men screamed and fell, clutching at wounds, dropping their weapons. The gunfire was loud in the confined space. Some tried to drop and take cover, others tried to fall back to the lobby, but the men and folding chairs behind them tangled up their feet. They had no line of escape.

Fucking amateurs.

On cue, the Prince shouted and his group came up from the vestibule. Their guns were raised and as soon as they saw the confusion and muzzle flashes in the dark, they started firing too. Part of me wondered what they thought they were shooting at. It wasn't me; I could hear the bullets flying through the air, and the ones that hit walls, or the floor near me. The dark, the confusion, how long would they shoot at each other before realizing it?

One of these Texas cowboys might do my job for me. I still got paid, but there was something that irked the professional in me. I ducked away from the planter, back toward the staircase, toward the Prince's flank. Or it would be his flank if his men had considered such things. As it was, they had just run into the room and started shooting. To their credit, some of them had considered taking cover behind tables they flipped over, or behind doorways. None of these things were reinforced or bulletproof.

One of the reasons I carried the AR-15 as one of my choices was for situations just like this one. They all had AR-style rifles, and it was sheer tornadic noise they were making with the guns. I took a knee and started picking my targets, one at a time, one shot.

"Getting noisy, mate," Roan said in my ear.

"Just a little," I remarked. I picked another target and put a round through the turquoise bolo tie he was wearing. Another man with a horrible mustache earned a .223 through his belt buckle, which I could have seen even without the night vision. I can only assume the bullet deflected upward from the thick metal and decided to tumble through his abdomen. He went down in a terrible mess. That was one of the reasons I hated these rifles, tumbling rounds were sloppy.

The rate of gunfire rapidly dwindled, and the Prince started shouting a mangle of French and Spanish, with a few words that I could only assume were curses in Farsi. It was a beautiful disaster.

He stood and waved his flashlight at the remaining men who had come from the lobby. I switched the AR to full auto and lit the Prince up like a blue-light special.

This set off a second round of blind shooting and I made for my escape, heading back toward the door I had barred behind me. I knew it would still be clear, since it couldn't be opened from the outside. There was a surge of people running down the stairs and I fired a suppressive burst, pelting the walls and ceiling. They screamed and tried to run in a dozen different directions at once. I saw they were the women who had been in other rooms upstairs. I was glad that I hadn't fired into them, it didn't look like any of them were armed.

It was pandemonium.

"Is Lock okay?" I heard Sadie ask, and I scowled.

"He's fine, I told you I'm working right now, Poppet," Roan said. "Go on."

"Poppet?" I asked. "You must be getting annoyed." A burst of gunfire shredded the wall entirely too close to where I was standing. I took a knee and put a three-round burst into the wanna-be killed, and dropped him like a bad habit.

"What is your exit strategy?" Roan asked, ignoring my remark about Sadie.

"East door should be clear," I said.

"Drone says it is clear, but the guys at the guard shack are organized and about to head your way," he said.

"Bring the lights back on," I said. I heard the clatter of a keyboard and a few seconds later, the power was restored and the chaos quieted. The survivors came together and closed what numbers they had. Leaderless, they weren't going to come after anyone, not when more than half of their posse was dead, dying, or lying in a pool of their own blood.

Reaching the door was easy enough, and I slipped through it, and eased it shut.

"Guard shack team is almost to the front door. The kid is calling the shots, but looks like a morale problem. His men don't want to go, and it looks like he is a lead-from-the-rear type."

"That's fine, have the police been notified yet?" I asked.

"Yes, just now, several reports of gunfire and noise complaints," Roan said.

"Good, put in a call and tell them gang violence, and bring SWAT."

"It's done," Roan said. "And it looks like our kid is making a run for it."

"I don't really like you calling him a kid," I said. "Dossier said he was thirty-five."

"Fair," he said. "Reese is getting into a black SUV with two bodyguards and they're leaving the property."

"Not going for the helicopter?" I asked.

"Negative. I'll follow them with the drone, or do you want air support?"

"I'll take the air support. Can I call in an air strike on the front of the compound, or the guard shack?"

"You know what I mean, this isn't Afghanistan. We don't actually own any bloody gunships."

"After this, we could afford one, though."

"Technically, yes; *one*," Roan capitulated.

"Thank you," I said. I shouldered the AR-15 as I came around the side of the building. I could see the taillights of the SUV as it burned rubber turning onto the street. The remaining personnel were in a serious state of disarray, and as long as they didn't see me, were no threat. I doubled back and retraced my steps through the dead orchard. Fifteen minutes later, I was back in my room, sitting on the veranda, watching as police vehicles swarmed up the drive to the gate at the Final Prophecy Center. I listened to the shouts through a bullhorn, some errant gunfire, and then silence as the survivors were rounded up. It looked like every emergency vehicle in a dozen counties had shown up.

I sipped a gin and tonic and watched the police swarm across the hill.

I was cleaning the guns when the first news helicopters flew over.

By morning this place would be a zoo. I tabbed my mic to see if Roan was still online. "Whatcha need, Lach?"

"Has our bird come to roost yet?" I asked.

"The chicken has made for the coop," Roan said. "About thirty miles south of your location. It's a four-way stop on the highway, Silence, Texas."

"Silence?"

"Yeah, I've been running a matrix on it, not much there. Looks like a dirty-spoon diner, a bus stop, trailer park, and the remnants of some roadside attraction – maybe one of those awful home zoos that were a thing a few decades ago."

"Drone actually make it that far?" I asked.

"Easily, I'm still recording and have connection to it. Landed it on top of their SUV and the rear rotor caught under the luggage rack on top."

"Handy, I think I am going to pack up and head that way then."

"I wouldn't. Wait until morning. They're bunkered up in a trailer. Probably tweaked out on something, and definitely on high alert. Get some rest and make sure you've not been shot."

"I think I would know," I said, but did check. I had run on a high of adrenaline for most of the job and in that state, riding that wave, I could probably run on broken bones and not notice something like a flesh wound. Thankfully, I was fine. I looked at myself in the full wall mirror in the bathroom. Yeah. I was *damn fine*. "How's Sadie doing?" I asked. Now that the mission was done for now, I could afford a little distraction.

"She's settling in, better now," Roan said tartly. I ignored him.

"That's good. Settled enough for you to let her in the Bat Cave?" I asked, casually. I thought about the skimpy and fancy lingerie outfits Roan had dressed her in and felt my cock twitch.

"Aye, if I give her a little room, she behaves," he said. I imagined her being naughty; some juvenile fantasy of pouting lips, proud nipples, and her sticking her ass out, begging to be fucked, spanked, or both.

"How is she handling the wardrobe?" I asked, pulling my cock, stretching it. It felt good and I thought about how I had seen her, through the monitors, her small breasts, her nipples obvious under the material. I let go of myself. Not going to chase that fantasy, not here in a bed-and-breakfast in the middle of Jesus-Land. I would save it for her, when I could see her in person.

"She's not a fan of some of the sheerer things, but she's warming up to having plenty to eat, regular hot showers, and no one trying to kill her, rob her, or fuck her." I smiled to myself. *If she only knew...*

There was at least one person that wanted to, but I would get to that later.

TEN AFTER NINE THE NEXT MORNING I WAS ON THE ROAD. I DIDN'T check out until after breakfast service was done. The hostess served me huevos rancheros, hash browns made with diced peppers and onions, and some delightfully spicy chorizo. So, there was one positive thing about my trip to Texas, the food was a delight. I might not feel the same way in a few hours, but I had plenty of time to deal with that later.

The road leading out to what I had decided to call the chicken coop, thanks to Roan, was a wide single-lane hammered-flat dirt path, lined with weeds. The air stank of oil, and I could tell why the orchard had died. No rain, the air smelled like a gas station dumpster, and when the wind picked up, I could feel it trying to turn my skin into sandblasted leather.

I parked in front of the dilapidated collection of buildings and crude cages that had formerly been a roadside zoo, maybe some sort of highly questionable animal breeding operation. *Snakes?* I'm sure there were some sunburned churches around here where some crazy preachers would shake some snakes and speak in tongues. It didn't matter, but the cages gave me some unpleasant ideas.

The black SUV was still parked in front of the third trailer in the gas-punk wasteland that presented itself as a park. It didn't deserve the name, not in the slightest. No grass, nothing green, just sagebrush and sand and that petroleum stink everywhere.

I stepped out of the truck, checked the Longslide pistol and its oversized laser sight, and slipped on my sunglasses. They helped with the glare but not the relentless heat. Everything at the Final Prophecy Center had been under the cover of night, and decidedly cooler. This was what I imagined Hell, if the place were real, to be like. There were no guards on the door, the windows were pulled closed, and I could hear the drone of HVAC units struggling to cope with the heat. The trailer I walked up to had an apron of cigarette butts and Heineken cans scattered in front of it, and there was a spatter of blood on the steps leading up to the door. I knocked.

"Fuck off," someone said after a moment.

"Pay me for this beer and pizza, asshole," I said. I lifted the pistol to just about chest level.

"We didn't order any pizza and who delivers beer?" he asked.

"I deliver it. Someone used the Deliverer app, and ordered a case of Heineken and two large pizzas, one supreme, one double pepper-oni. The door cracked open and I saw a glimpse of one of the chick-en's bodyguards. The .45 blew a hole through the thin door, and then a second hole in his chest. He staggered back and pulled the door open as he fell. I stepped in, spotted the second guard and the first round ensured that he would have a closed casket funeral, the second round was just to ensure that he wouldn't try to shoot me in the back, even with half of his head missing. I heard a woman scream, and Reese shouted something inarticulate. I held the gun ready, expecting Reese to try something.

"Don't fucking shoot me. Jesus fuck, I give!" he shouted. He came forward, a woman in front of him. He had her arm pulled behind her back and was using her like a shield. He was seemingly unarmed, and the woman was almost completely naked. She had blood on her, and her skin was blotchy from abuse. Bruises were blooming on her face and neck. She was shaking as he held her between us.

"The only reason I haven't put a bullet between your worthless eyes is because this young lady has already seen enough torment. Is this the delivery girl from last night?" I asked.

"How do you…? Who the fuck are you?" he demanded.

"Who do you think put your co-conspirators down like dogs?" I asked.

"There was a whole commando squad up on that hill, a total war, man."

"Oh, there was a total war, but it was just me. Let the girl go," I said.

"I give you the girl, and you let me go," he said.

"Sure," I agreed.

"Move away from the door, Terminator," he said. It was all I could do to not smile; it validated my carrying the Longslide with its dated laser sight. I stepped slightly to the side and gave the smallest gesture for him to proceed. "That's right, big man," he growled. He edged around me, dragging the woman with him. Near as I could tell, he was completely unarmed, and was just using leverage on her arm, simple pain, to control her.

"Are you going to let her go?" I asked.

"No, not happening. I let her go, I've got nothing between you and me."

"That is unwise," I said. I put the bullet into his leg, just above the knee. Reese fell, and the woman bolted like a rabbit, and hid in the corner, all but vanishing behind a worn lounge chair. I grabbed Reese and pulled him to his feet, screaming, bleeding profusely from the crater in his thigh. "What is your name, miss?" I asked.

"Rosalyn," she mumbled.

"Did he hurt you?"

"Y-y-yes, yes," she stammered.

"I'm going to take him outside, and you aren't going to see either of us again, Rosalyn. After I take the trash out, help yourself to any money you find in here. I'm sure there is some stash of cash in here, isn't there, Reese?"

"Fuck you, man!" I ground the barrel of the gun into his leg and he screamed, pissing all over himself. That didn't take long, he was soft. He let out a few sobs before pointing at a black nylon bag by the sofa.

"There, take whatever cash you find in that bag, dress yourself, and the keys for the SUV outside, Reese?" He gobbed out another blubbery noise but pointed toward the bar between the kitchen and the common room. "Thank you," I said. "Why don't you take a shower, give me a little time to talk to our friend here, alone." I dragged Reese out the door and paused a moment to pull the flimsy thing shut. I threw him off the minimalist cracked deck and holstered the pistol while I walked down the steps and collected him again. He tried to crawl a few steps, but the wound in his leg made him scream like a bloody dog. It was amusing so I followed him for a few steps before putting my shoe in his ass and sending him face first into the dirt. He cried and coughed, then made a retching noise.

"How did you get into the Death Squad?" I asked.

"My… my father… my father," he said.

"Was he in the Final Prophecy Center?"

"No, he stayed with Guillame," Reese said.

"Playing both sides?" I asked.

"No, he supports the general, and I didn't."

"That might have been a mistake," I said.

"My father will pay you… ransom me to him," Reese said. "*Please…*"

"Let me ask you something. Did she ever ask you for mercy, did she ever say *please*?" I found a length of chain anchored to the ground, something a person who doesn't deserve a dog keeps a dog on. I unhooked the chain and tied it around Reese's good foot and he screamed. "You really disappoint me," I said as I tossed the other end of the chain over a thing that once, many years ago, might have been a tree. It would do to hold his weight and I dragged him up like a fish.

"Please, man, please don't hurt me anymore," he cried.

"No more?" I scoffed. "*No more*? I haven't even started."

"You shot me. You fucking shot me!"

"That's just because you tried to run," I said. I pulled a small pocketknife and showed it to him. "I'm going to ask you a few questions, and this is going to make sure you answer me, and that you don't lie to me." I drew the blade across his ballsack, lightly, just so he knew where the knife was. I had to step back because he pissed himself again, and started thrashing against the chain, and his own weight. Reese sang like a bird. He vomited too. I'm sure if he hadn't pissed out of fear twice already, he would have done it again. He told me everything he knew about the Death Squad, about why they had their schism with *le Generale,* what he knew about the finances, and then what I was expecting.

Reese confessed to a laundry list of sins, crimes, and things that I considered unforgivable, even as a professional. I thought about Sadie again, about what might have happened to her between the foster home we'd been in and the road when I almost hit her, and I imagined him… putting his hands on her, her face and body bruised and bloody like the pizza delivery girl; like Rosalyn…

I cut his balls off, then put them in his hand. He started weeping once he realized what he was holding.

The rest of what I did to him was cruel, but if his confessions were true, it was not unwarranted or undeserved. Rosalyn had gone, driving the SUV through part of a fence in her escape. I put what was left of Reese inside the trailer, with his goons next to him. The trailer caught fire easily and went up like well-seasoned tinder.

The drive back home would feel very long. I had Sadie in my thoughts making it even longer. The only way to get back in my right mind would be taking her. I didn't think an escort would do it this time.

I needed it after such a swath of killing.

I needed her.

CHAPTER ELEVEN

*S*adie...

I didn't know why I cared about this mythical figure... this Lock. I didn't know what had prompted me to even ask.

I swallowed hard, sitting on the end of the sofa, staring out over the windswept Chesapeake Bay, hugging my knees. What felt like a tennis ball was in my throat as I replayed the images from Roan's screens over in my mind.

I thought he'd been playing a video game. The rainbow figures in the thermal imaging collapsing, jerking backwards... falling...

"Sadie?" I jumped slightly and felt tears roll down my cheeks.

"Come now, Poppet... talk to me." Conan's voice was gentle. I sniffed and fixated my gaze on his reflection in the night-darkened glass in front of me.

"Th-that wasn't a video game, was it?" I asked.

He sighed, his broad shoulders dropping slightly. He was impeccably dressed, as always. Gray slacks and a matching gray vest, crisp white dress shirt... although no tie. Not now. Instead, his collar was open at the throat, his sleeves rolled back over his muscular forearms, his big hands gripping the silver head of his cane, folded neatly on its top, the rubber foot sinking into the plush cream carpet between his expensive shoes.

"No. No, it wasn't a video game, Love."

I closed my eyes, the ball in my throat expanding, the tears pressing at my nose and the insides of my eyelids, my face growing hot.

Not a game... but you knew that didn't you?

"I have never lied to you," he said and I jumped, his voice much closer than it had been the moment before. "I will never lie to you," he promised.

I sniffed and opened my eyes, dragging them up the length of the glass. He stood beside me, where I sat balled on the couch. His expression said it all. He was pained for me, for the way I was feeling, but he wasn't entirely apologetic at the same time.

"What's going to happen to me?" I whispered and he sighed deeply, shifting uncomfortably.

"Nothing bad, I can promise you that," he said.

"Who *are* you people?" I demanded, rising, but he didn't answer me. We stared at each other, barely a foot between us, and he didn't move, didn't budge. He simply searched my face with his worried bright green eyes and let me go when I walked away from him with a noise of disgust.

That had been two or three days ago.

I felt as though I had been wandering the big, empty mansion with its locked doors and hollow vibe ever since. A living ghost, waiting to become one for real.

I'd refused to speak to Conan, to even look at him. I couldn't.

Those had been *people* falling to their deaths on his screen – riddled with bullets, bleeding, hurting... sons and maybe daughters. Brothers and maybe sisters with families that would miss them, no matter what bad things they did. I mean, maybe some of those men had wives or God forbid, *children,* waiting for Daddy to come home that night – and he never would. The question rattling in my skull that I was too afraid to ask was *why?* For *money?*

I had survived without money *every day* since I'd aged out of the foster care system. I mean, I had been poor, sure, and my good grades in high school hadn't been enough to buy me anything. I had worked, had scraped by for the longest time, but eventually... eventually the jobs and the money had run out but I had *still* made it.

Hadn't I?

I went down a hall I hadn't remembered seeing before, trailing fingers along the wall, bare feet padding softly over carpet until I came to another set of stairs that I surely didn't recognize.

Curious, I followed them down, a gentle half-spiral ending in a tile floor, the tiles broad, square, and a rusty brown color. No doubt something expensive that had a fancy name, but I certainly didn't have one for it.

I peeked left, the hall stopping short, a door on the left, and a door on the right. I didn't go that way. There were so many locked doors in this place, I just assumed they were locked, too.

To the right looked interesting. I turned that way and stood, listening, I always listened. I didn't want to encounter anyone on these snoops. I mean, I knew Conan was probably watching, tracking my every movement, I just didn't want to see anyone in *person*.

The hall went down a way and ended, but on the left, there was a bank of windows, and to the right? Just more wall, some framed something-or-other on it. It was what was coming through the window that interested me.

Wavering patterns of light.

I stepped carefully, my bare feet silent against the tile floor as I walked gently, toes down first. The dress I wore today was a deep lavender silk, fitted toga style on one shoulder, the hem asymmetrical cutting a dramatic line to a point opposite the one shoulder that very nearly touched the floor. Or it would, if the material weren't so light it floated when I walked.

It felt good against the skin which was part of the problem I had with the wardrobe that had been chosen for me... nothing about this captivity should feel *good*. Not the accommodations, not the clothing, not the warm food in my belly with flavors meant to tantalize the tongue.

Nothing about being a prisoner should be comfortable. It made it hard to remember that I *was* a prisoner... that I *wasn't* free to leave.

Still, when I laid eyes on the swimming pool, which was gently steaming beyond the glass, I was *weak*. I took a deep breath and laid my hands on the door letting out a shuddering breath. I pushed.

The door swung open freely and I gasped. I had fully expected it to remain locked.

The smell of chlorine and pool chemicals assaulted my nose and I closed my eyes as memories flooded in.

Memories of my mother and father, them teaching me to swim at the community pool, the sun shining high in the sky. I didn't even have *pictures of them* anymore. My meager belongings left behind in the warehouse I'd been sheltering in. The warehouse I wasn't *allowed* to go back to.

I padded to the stairs and gathered the skirt of my dress in my hands, stepping down onto the first step into about three inches of bright blue water.

It was warm...

I closed my eyes and breathed in, listening to the quiet hum of the pool's filtration system, the rhythmic hush of the HVAC system just beyond that. I turned and looked around. If there were cameras in here, I couldn't see them. I could never see them, but they were always there. I swore Roan was always watching, his voice quick to come over the house's intercom system if I strayed somewhere that I wasn't supposed to be.

The pool was encased in a glass and steel structure, old-fashioned, like a pagoda, the glass crystal clear with a view of a surrounding patio. A low rock retaining wall was beyond it and beyond that? The trim mansion lawn and gardens sweeping to a terraced bluff that had paths that wound down to the beach along the bay. The doors leading outside to that patio were predictably chained shut but so far? Of all the places in the house I had explored to date? This was the closest to tasting freedom.

I stared out of those windows, the glass dark, and felt my fingers unfurl. I took the next step down into the water, and it climbed almost to my knees.

Warm, so warm...

I remembered the weightlessness the water brought me as a child, as I lay back, breathing deep and even and I wanted that. I *missed* that. That feeling of being lighter than air, of being supported, of my mother and father at hand to catch me and raise me up should I sink.

I wanted to capture that feeling again. I wanted to drift away from my nightmares, away from this *waking* nightmare...

I took the last step into the water and took a sharp breath. The water was as warm as a bath. I waded out; my hands raised until I felt the bottom slope from beneath my feet. I turned around and tipped back, my hands slipping to my sides, my eyes closing and I caught that weightless feeling.

I lay back, the light silk of my dress clinging to me, a second skin, and I put my arms out, imagining I was flying. Flying far, far, away from this gilded cage with all its wickedness and death.

The sensation of free floating took my breath away at first, and then that was all I could hear as the water rushed into my ears and muted everything. Just silence, the sound of my own breath, and if I happened to raise my hand from the pool, the light tinkling of the water streaming from my fingertips to drip back into the body of water.

I lay in that water's embrace and let go of the here and now and went to live some other place in memory and imagination.

I don't know what it was that finally had me open my eyes, but when I did, the light of the pool was cast against an angelic face. One I recognized from the not so distant past. I sucked in a sharp breath and cried out, wavering, nearly going under, but then there was a strong arm beneath my shoulders to catch me, his other hand pressing me to stillness against my chest, between my breasts.

"Relax, Shady... it's just me. Shhh..." His voice was muffled, but it was *his*, just deeper, more masculine. *We weren't teenagers anymore.*

What had he called me? *Shady?* Ugh... I hadn't heard that name in *years* and I would have been perfectly happy to let it die.

"Relax," he ordered. "I've got you, Shady."

I stared up into Kyle's face, older, wiser, that same scar in his left eyebrow, those same lush lips curving into a wicked, devil-may-care smile, and I forgot to breathe.

"That's it," he said with a dark chuckle, then his equally dark eyes swept over me from head to foot.

"Look at you," he said, his voice muffled, very nearly indiscernible were I not adept at reading lips. A habit you learned when you lived on the streets among mentally ill men who whispered and muttered to themselves, or rather to the voices in their heads. Any advanced warning was better than nothing when they thought you were some sort of government plant or dark angel sent to harm them.

I searched his face, looking for answers to *so many questions* when it clicked.

Not Lock... Lach.

Kyle Lachlan was *Lach...* the man on the screen shooting all those people.

I scrambled out of his embrace and backed off, chest heaving, feeling as though I couldn't get a breath.

"Oh, I see, figured it out, have you?" he asked and he bowed his head, smiling almost ruefully but with this edge of such... *I don't know...* but the look made my stomach flip.

"*Kyle?*" I asked, aghast.

"Hello, Sadie."

I put my hands to my churning stomach and swallowed back bile.

"*Why?*" I demanded.

He lowered his hands to his sides. He was dressed too. White dress shirt, open at the collar, clinging to his body, which was obviously muscular. I believe the term was *shredded*. Black business-like belt and black slacks, same dark hair and smoldering eyes just set in a slightly older face... like mine... *not kids anymore...*

"Why not?" he asked. "You're warm, you're safe, you're fed..."

I shook my head, eyes brimming with tears and I couldn't get any other words out. All I could do was let the same one fall.

"*Why?*"

He smiled then and it was a thing of pure evil, I swear. He moved toward me and I stumbled back, turning to the side. He didn't approach me, though. He was headed for the stairs.

"I told you, Shady Brooks, I'm not one of the good guys. I never was, and I never will be." The water sloshed as he took the steps up out of the pool and I stared at him in open-mouthed horror.

"The next time you want to take a swim," he said casually over his shoulder, "do it in the nude. I'd like that, and it won't ruin any more of your wardrobe." He pulled open the door to the hallway that I'd come through and turned back to look at me with cold, dead eyes and said without emotion, "That was a four-thousand-dollar dress."

The door swung shut behind him and my eyes followed him down the hallway until he went out of sight.

I drew breath, not realizing I'd been holding it very nearly the entire time I had been in his presence. Gasping, I tried to breathe around the four-thousand-pound boulder on the center of my chest, where his hand had been, where my hands covered even now.

No, no, no, no, no...

My mind turned the word over and over in my head.

No, no, no, no, no...

Fury welled up in the center of my chest and I thrashed to the edge of the pool, taking the stairs that Kyle had just taken. Only one thing on my mind now...

Conan.

I stormed through the mansion and found him, predictably, in his stupid fucking *Bat Cave.*

"What ever happened to never lying to me?" I snapped. and he tipped up from where he was leaned back in his seat, spinning around to face me. "A lie by omission is still a lie!" I spat at him.

He took me in, his ginger eyebrows crushing down into a frown.

"Where the bloody hell have you been?" he demanded, rising out of his seat. I took a step back and put up a hand.

"No! You stay right there!"

He froze after crossing his arms.

"Were you ever going to come clean?" I demanded.

He raked a hand through his hair and demanded, "About what?"

"Kyle!" I shot back. "Lach! Kyle *fucking* Lachlan!" I screamed.

"Bloody hell," he muttered and turned back to his console, bringing up the swimming pool. Rolling back a dial, Lach and I appeared on the screen. "That cheeky bastard," he muttered and when he turned back to me, I was shaking my head.

"You just stay away from me," I said coldly. "Both of you. Just stay the fuck away from me!"

I turned on my heel and fled.

And to think… I was beginning to believe Roan, to trust him that he had my best interests at heart.

What a fucking joke.

CHAPTER TWELVE

*R*oan...

I echoed Sadie's sentiment, *Kyle* fucking *Lachlan*. I hadn't known he was back; he hadn't given me his itinerary and I hadn't pushed. Considering the long drive back from Texas, the number of people he had killed, and the intensity of the mission, I had automatically assumed that he would lair up in some large city soaking up his precious gin and indulging himself with high-end trollops until he was ready to come back to the house. He must have driven straight through, only stopping for gas and God knows what sort of tweaker truck-stop pills to keep his eyes open. If Sadie had come to scream at me about being a liar and the rest, he could stay awake for a little while longer, I had a few choice words for him.

I stalked the house; he wasn't in the bar, or the den, or even the pool. He was in the arsenal, shirtless, in a fresh dry pair of sweatpants, his mouth tight and hands moving quickly. He must have been in a foul mood to be cleaning his guns again and putting them back in their places along the wall himself. Usually, he left that to me. He gave me a side glance when I walked in.

"I heard you coming," he said.

"I'm a terrible ninja," I said. "I hadn't expected you to be back."

"I didn't feel like staying in another roadside motel," he said. "I am pleased that Miss Brooks looks to be much healthier. I am *not* pleased that she decided to go swimming in a four-thousand-dollar silk dress. If it comes down to it, I would rather have the grotto drained rather than waste money on expensive drowned dresses."

"She's bloody furious, mate," I said, trying to not clench my jaw.

"I didn't hurt her, I just told her to not ruin any more of the dresses," he said.

"I'm getting right tired of this game," I said. "You bring this scrap of a girl here, and you tell me what you want done with her, and you vanish. Yes, I know some of that was work, but I also know a good bit of that was you swilling gin and choking prostitutes, so don't try to put me on."

"Does that suddenly bother you now?" he asked, his voice was cool.

"Oh, that's not what has my bollocks in a twist. I've been trying to make friends with this wee chippie of yours, not knowing who she is to you. She didn't know who you were, and fuck *me* if I'm going to throw that into the mess! It's like making friends with a feral cat. She doesn't trust anyone, everything is suspicious, she's constantly on bloody edge and it's enough to make my hands shake because I'll be fucked if I break my sobriety because of some wee piece you've trotted into *our* house."

"All you had to do was make sure she didn't die and get that awful blue out of her hair; you did everything I asked," he said. "I didn't ask you to *befriend* her, just *take care of her* like you would take care of anything else for me."

"Oh, for *fuck's sake*," I swore. "She's a *human being*, Lach! A scared one, and you want me to treat her like one of the *cars,* or one of our bloody *guns*?"

"Yes. Precisely," Lach said. "She's one of my things and should be treated accordingly."

"She's not a *thing*," I said. He raised an eyebrow. "She's not, she's a human being."

"So were all of the people I killed three days ago, though one was more an animal than a human. Killing him was a service to the gene pool," he said.

"What happened to the line where we justified this by only killing bad guys for other bad guys. Where are our morals?" I snapped.

"I tortured a man, cut his balls off, and watched him hang from a dead tree until he died. I killed over a dozen men in a series of fire-fights and executed several at close range. A woman with some of the nicest tits you've ever seen tried to pull steel on me and I blew bloody holes in her cleavage. The mission went almost perfect, and after all that killing, all that death, all those bodies, you're upset because of *what?*" he demanded.

"Because you've lost your bloody humanity, and have me playing jailor to a kidnapping victim, one that is particularly upset right now," I snarled.

"Come down off your high horse, Conan," Lach snarled. "She's homeless and has no family; she can't *be* kidnapped, because there was nothing to steal her *from*. Everything is going to be better for her now, she just has to adjust to the new environment."

"And her new environment is as your property?"

"Functionally, yes." I wanted to hit him. "She belongs to *me* now."

"Who is she to you?" I felt my anger close to boiling. He picked up the Beretta he had carried on the last mission, turning the pistol over in his hands.

"Maybe I should ask who you think she is to *you*," he said more than asked.

"She's a scared girl being held against her will," I blustered, hating how he was trying – and *succeeding* – to put me on the defensive.

"Would she even be alive if I hadn't brought her here?" he asked pointedly.

"Well, likely..." I considered the severity of the pneumonia, the anemia, and the other issues she had when the doctor diagnosed her. If she had gone to a clinic, they might have taken care of her, but she was homeless, undocumented, *no one*. I knew the point he was getting at, and I hated that he was right. "No," I admitted.

"Correct; if I hadn't almost hit her with the car, she would have continued on for a few days, maybe a week, and then what? She would have died. From one medical thing or another, doesn't matter which. She'd still be dead." He dropped his gaze back to the Beretta in his hand and almost softened a bit. "But now she's safe and in much improved health, and for that, for the cost of the medical care, and the car, and the fucking dress, she's *mine*." he said, the hardness and his resolve redoubled by the time he finished his sentence. He began to take the Beretta apart.

"You are unbelievable," I said.

"Lima," he shot back.

"Lima? What's Peru got to do with any-bloody-thing," I demanded, scowling even harder.

"Lima Syndrome," he said. I gave him a vaguely aggressive glare. "Oh, *holy fuck*," he said with a feral grin. "Is there something I know that Conan Roan *doesn't*?" He gave a laugh. "It's the opposite of Stockholm Syndrome," he said.

"Stockholm..." I paused.

"Stockholm, where hostages become sympathetic to their captors, you know, *Beauty and the Beast*. Lima Syndrome is the opposite, where the hostage taker, that would be you in this scenario," he pointed at me with the cleaning wand for the gun barrel, "is starting to catch feelings for the woman he's supposed to be watching."

"I know what Stockholm Syndrome bloody is! And I don't have feelings for her," I said, back on the defensive worse than I was before.

"That's very, *very*, good," he said. "Because Sadie is *mine*. I've known her from years ago, same foster home. She was the first girl I kissed... If you and your red eyebrows even think about psychoanalyzing that, I'll put you on your ass faster than you can blink." Part of me wanted to prove him wrong, but wisdom reminded me that there was no telling how jacked up he might be on interstate stimulants, energy drinks, or whatever else he might have been willing to pick up. Lach was a bit cavalier about stimulant and drug use, though his self-control and resolve were next to none... including myself. It made him a certain sort of unpredictable in his predictability.

"You know what, *fine*," I said, knowing there would be no further reasoning with him when he was like this. I slammed the door as best I could, but the whisper hinges reduced my desired stab of violent sound into a hiss and a soft click.

I half stalked, half stomped my way to the kitchen and put my hands on the slab of marble cutting board. I had to do something; I couldn't let all of this anger settle in. I had to *make* something. There was a block of gourmet chocolate in the cupboard, Oaxaca dark, and a jar of Ceylon cinnamon sticks.

The meteoric steel santoku knife made easy work of the block, reducing a corner of it down to fine shavings. This went in a steel bowl, over a pot of water. The induction stove would make quick work of this, rendering the shaved chocolate down to a smooth liquid. I micro-planned the cinnamon into it while it did its thing, and then whisked milk into it all to make a smooth, gourmet drinking choco-late. This felt ridiculous, but I could think of nothing else that I could do that wasn't pointless or destructive. I topped the mug with a dollop of whipped cream. There was something about the stuff from the can that was unique, and though I preferred whipping up my own, I much rather preferred speed in checking on Sadie.

I carried two cups of the finished cocoa into Sadie's bedroom and found it empty. I knew she had come this way – there was a trail of wet footprints on the hardwood floors of the hallway. I left the cups on their platter sitting on her dresser and followed the tracks in her bedroom carpet. She was sitting in the walk-in shower, the rainfall head turned up to high. The water had hidden her tears, but she seemed so small, so vulnerable and weak, huddled as she was, clutching her knees to her chest.

I sighed in utter defeat, and went to the shower door, opening it with a clack that made her jump like a spooked horse. I went in with her, and changed my mind from hauling her to her feet, instead, easing myself down next to her. The water was cold, which was absurd, as our water heaters were the best that money could buy and would never run out of hot. I reached up and turned the knob to get it warmer, the falling water instantly plastering my shirt to my skin.

I settled beside her and raised my arm closest to her passively, in invitation. She sniffed and wouldn't look at me but moved closer. I put an arm around her, and I expected her to change her mind; to pull away or recoil from me, but she didn't. She leaned into me, and I could feel her tiny frame shuddering next to me and though I wished to convince myself that it was only shivering, I knew it for what it was – weeping. I just held her; I knew none of the things that came to mind to say would help her. She had seen the screens, the men being killed, and realized that Lach, however and in whatever context she had known him before, was a professional killer. A lot of people weren't equipped to deal with that sort of thing.

I reached over and took her hand in mind, lacing my fingers through hers. God, she seemed so *small*, so delicate. I knew she was made of sterner stuff, but she was such a wee thing.

She had a good cry. There was no telling how long that she had been holding it in, and how much of that was just because of Lach and me, and how much were older things. How much was emotional debris from her life before she crashed into ours.

After what felt like hours, I reached up and turned the water off. Despite its warmth, I was chilled, and she had to be freezing having been wet for far longer. I pulled her hand to my lips and gave the back of it a slow kiss. She seemed more composed and sniffed loudly. I stood, nowhere near as smoothly as I would like. I groaned, though I didn't intend to, damn stiffness.

"Are you okay?" she asked softly.

"Aye, I'm alright," I said. "Just wet. Let's get you dried off and warmed up." Her nipples were completely exposed, the material soaked and clinging to them like a second skin. I tried valiantly to ignore them as I wrapped a towel around her, rubbing her down briskly through the rougher material, attempting to dry her off. She gave me a small laugh.

"I don't think you can dry silk with a towel, no matter how many threads or where the cotton came from," she gently chided. I gave her a small chuckle in return.

"Egyptian," I said softly.

"Of course, it is," she murmured and there was a sadness to it. I offered her a second towel. She took it and I stepped out of the bathroom and let her strip out of the clinging silk. I took a few deep breaths and pushed my desire down. I prided myself in being stoic but I was not made of stone. When she emerged from the bathroom, it was with just the towel wrapped around her. Eyes red, a little puffy, and with her drawn-in posture, she seemed so vulnerable.

I felt something in my chest, and then, less honorably, something between my legs.

I offered her the mug of Oaxaca chocolate, and she took it, hesitantly. The mug seemed large in her hands, as she cradled it with both of them. "What's this?" she asked, curiously, and it was a habit of hers. She always asked, no matter what I offered her, and I had to wonder if there was something there other than idle curiosity.

"Hot chocolate," I said.

"Just hot chocolate?" *Ah... there it is.* I sidestepped the inquiry designed to elicit a guilty response, to clue her in if I had perhaps slipped tranquilizers or some other type of drug into her drink.

"No, it's fair-trade dark chocolate from Oaxaca, Mexico. A dash of ground cinnamon from Ceylon. Some turbinado sugar, from Natural Foods Grocery, and the whipped cream came from a can."

"A can?" she asked, amused. "And here I was going to say that nothing is ever simple with you, is it?" she said softly.

"I've had a belly full of simple and low, and poor, and I don't ever want to go back to that," I said quietly. She watched me over the rim of the mug as she brought it to her lips and sipped, her eyes slipping closed as she made a blissful face. She looked like she had been plucked from a shipwreck or a warzone, with a bit of shock, and that distant gaze. Lord knows, I'd seen it often enough in men's eyes. There was something particularly poignant seeing it in hers.

"It's good," she said.

"I wouldn't have anything in this house that wasn't the best that could be had," I returned.

"I wish you had told me," she murmured, and though the change in topic was abrupt, I knew precisely what she meant.

"Yes, well... I do enjoy my puzzles," I said. "Though, I suppose, I was going to tell you, when the time was right... if he hadn't bloody beat me to it," I said. Truthfully, I felt a fool to not have asked her if she'd known a Kyle *fucking* Lachlan... though on another note of truth... "I was more concerned with your health," I said.

Part of me also knew that Lach had some things right to his observation – I did like her and wanted her to be a friend. My eyes glanced across the expanse of her chest and the hint of cleavage above the towel, and I knew that if I didn't do a better job guarding my emotions, they could get me into some serious trouble. "And considering what we do for a living, we don't talk about the details of it often." *Especially with mysterious kidnapped girls...*

"What do the neighbors think you do?" she asked, her gaze drawn to the night-darkened windows.

"Officially, I am retired on disability and a military pension," I said. "Which is technically true." I reached down and gave a knuckle rap on my prosthetic leg. She gave me and my leg a look. "As for Kyle, on paper he's a consultant, in the vaguest terms I could manage."

"Are you sure you two aren't..." She let the question linger, unasked, and yet I perfectly knew her meaning.

"We're more like brothers than anything, and I assure you, we're both straight; if that was what you were asking," I replied. "I don't know who Lach is to you, and who you are to him, he didn't tell me. I couldn't bring up who we are and what we do without knowing that. Your records are almost non-existent. You are as close to being a ghost in the machine as anyone I've met." She gave me a quizzical look.

"No credit cards, no employment records for at least the last six years, no driver's license or even local ID. Your records start with birth, a few vaccination records, and a few years of public education and then an incomplete filling with the Maryland Department of Health and Social Services. They had butterfingers and dropped you through the proverbial cracks. There's simply nothing after your eighteenth birthday. I can only guess what you've been up too since your last known record entry, which was working for a downtown café," I said.

"Surviving," she said softly. "Just surviving. Avoiding the bad people, avoiding the police, avoiding people who look at me the wrong way, and then I wake up here, with literally nothing. I had a bag, just about everything I owned in the world was in it, and a small box, back where I was sleeping. Not much, but some old photos, important photos."

"I think I can arrange for finding your things, if it was stowed somewhere safe and hidden," I said. If Lach wouldn't, I would go look for it, I would. The girl had nothing else.

"Kyle is a murderer," she said softly, her dark and lovely eyes distant, somber, as the reality overtook her.

"No," I said with conviction. "Kyle and I are *mercenaries*; we don't go around killing just anybody. Especially innocent people." She gave me a critical look that I thought bore some further explanation. "Kyle and I were both in the military, and after the military, we kept the same profession, just went from being government employees to being self-employed."

"Who were those people?" she asked. If Lach truly intended to keep this woman, which I knew Lach, and I knew he did, she deserved to know.

"A splinter cell from a heroin-smuggling cartel," I said. No reason to obfuscate things. Not now. "We were contracted by the head of the main cartel to step in and take care of their internal dispute."

"You work for a heroin cartel?"

"One job, this time, yes. We took a *lot* of their money for it, reduced the number of drug dealers and cartel leaders, and later, if we're offered a contract to go deal with the cartel that hired us, we'll do that job, too," I said. All in all, it was a net positive for humanity by my reckoning. No need to delve further into the mathematics of it now.

"We eliminate bad guys and their organizations, and most of the time we work for other bad guys. We don't hurt innocent people, never children, and very rarely women." Sadie's eyes flashed at the last.

"Only rarely?" she asked. *Of course, she's more scared than ever.* I was beginning to worry my honesty was having the opposite of its desired effect.

"Women can be bad guys too, and anyone carrying a gun in a firefight is a valid target. Unarmed people don't get shot," I said. "I like to think that the work we do makes the world, in a small part, a better place."

"That's a nice way to look at it," she said. She took another sip of the cocoa. "It's also hard to argue with you. I meet *nice people* all the time, and they all end up being bastards. You have been one of the nicest people I've met, and you're a mercenary, and Kyle is a what? A... a... hitman?" she asked finally, as she groped for the right word.

"That seems accurate," I said.

"All those nice people out there, they would have taken advantage of me in a heartbeat, and some tried. I showed them," she said. "I had my freedom, and nothing else. I ate out of dumpsters behind restaurants. I showered when there was a chance at the women's shelter, but even they had their *hungry eyes*, wanting me to take their pamphlets, join their church, their organization. Plenty of *nice guys* were more than willing to let me do things for money... you know, *things* for them, and they would be so good to me and give me twenty bucks."

"I'm aware of the type," I said. The cocoa was good, I took a small sip.

"I always said 'no.'" she said defensively.

"Naturally," I agreed readily. What she had done to survive before we found her – there was no judgment.

She sank down onto the edge of the bed, carefully adjusting how she sat so she wouldn't lose her towel, keeping her upper arms pinned to her sides to ensure it as she took a careful sip of her hot chocolate. "You've given me medical care, fed me, entertained me, tied me up a few times, which I did *not* appreciate, mister," she said pointedly.

"You've not been tied up since you tried breaking a window to get out," I said. "It was that, more than anything, that landed you in that sort of trouble."

"Who has bulletproof glass in their living room?" she asked softly, making eye contact, the sorrow clear in her gaze. She didn't expect an answer – she knew the answer now – but I smiled sadly, simply, and gave one to her anyway.

"Professional mercenaries," I said. "The Bat Cave is technically a safe room, and most of the house has a large degree of protection. In case something goes badly, there is also an escape tunnel."

"That seems… weird, but makes sense," she said.

"Aye," I agreed, and told her more. "This place was built during Prohibition. The tunnels date back to when the original owners were brewing bathtub booze in the basement and then smuggling it across the Chesapeake via small boats from the beach just there. If the Feds showed up, the bootleggers used the tunnels to escape to their boats and vanish while the cops would search the house and never even find the door to the basement," I said. "The escape tunnel leads down to a concealed dock, and we have a boat down there. We call her the *Rum Runner*. It seemed apt."

"And now it's full of electronics," she said. "And you look cold in those wet clothes. Maybe you should go warm up yourself and put on something dry."

"Sadie," I said, offering her my hand. "I am sorry I didn't tell you everything, but I hope you understand my reasons. Now that the big secret is out, if you have any questions, I'll answer them."

She laced her fingers through mine when it came to my proffered hand and gave it a squeeze, nodding, though she wouldn't meet my eyes. Instead, she stared down into her nearly empty mug. "After you put on dry clothes," she said, and her concern was rather touching.

CHAPTER THIRTEEN

*S*adie...

The bunk beds at the Daughton's were uncomfortable. The mattress thin, the sheets threadbare, and the blanket even thinner than that. There was no turning on the heat in the bedrooms – that cost too much electricity and Pricilla and Dean Daughton were all about 'saving money' despite the fact they were being paid for six of us kids, and Dean Daughton holding down a lucrative job as an Indigo City longshoreman.

They were the type of foster parents that weren't in it for the good of humanity and for saving kids. They were in it to line their own pockets and they were my first lesson in just how cruel the world could be after the death of my parents.

The only sliver of goodness out of this place was the fact that Dean Daughton wasn't a pedophile... just a mean drunk.

"Ugh, will you just shut up *already!" Tara was seventeen to my fifteen and had the top bunk. I could hear her punch her already flat pillow up into some semblance of a useable shape. Either that, or she was putting it over her head to drown out my sniffing for the umpteenth millionth time.*

"Leave her alone, Tara." Melanie was eleven and had the single bed opposite mine. She was the Daughton's real daughter. They had a son, too. Caleb,

who was fourteen. He was in the room across and down the hall with the two foster boys that lived here – Kyle, and Demetri.

I sniffed slightly and turned on my side, my back to the open doorway and to Melanie. We didn't have a door. Tara had pissed off Mr. Daughton, and he'd taken it off the hinges.

"She's right, though," Melanie said after a moment. "You don't stop crying; you might wake up Daddy and I wouldn't want to be you if you did that."

"I know," I whispered. "I'm trying... I just can't help it."

My second lesson in cruelty was the new school I'd been thrust into midway through the school year. My parents hadn't been rich, I mean, I was used to being poor, but the Daughton's was next-level low.

I tried my best with outdated clothing and making the thrift store finds uniquely mine and fashionable, but kids were freaking mean as shit and as soon as I'd arrived, no one knowing where I came from, I'd earned the new nickname of Shady. Shady Brooks. It would have been almost pretty if the intent behind it weren't so cold.

Rumors started almost immediately, fueled by Tara who was two grades above me, that I'd killed my parents and it was just downhill from there.

I hadn't. It was just a stupid accident... but today had been beyond the pale in humiliation and a lesson in pain, when one of the other girls who was bullying me shoulder checked me into an open locker which had torn the back of my shirt. When I'd come back to the Daughton's, Pricilla Daughton had raged about it. When I had tried to protest feebly that it hadn't been my fault, she'd slapped me and had sent me up here without dinner. I was hungry, and my stomach hurt. We didn't get a lot to begin with, so any missed meal could be torture.

"Psst!" I jumped and Tara sat up above me. "Shady," Kyle whispered from the door to the bedroom.

"Go away," I murmured tiredly. He insisted on calling me Shady, too... but for a different reason. When I'd asked him to stop, he'd said 'no' and that I needed to learn how to be tougher. I just wasn't built like Kyle Lachlan, though... I wasn't confident and I cared what people thought of me. I just couldn't be anyone else.

He chuckled darkly and the bunk dipped behind me. I sucked in a sharp breath and whispered sharply, *"Dean catches you in here with the girls and he's going to kill you!"*

"Like to see the fat bastard try," Kyle said darkly. He laid down behind me and reached over the top of me. "Here," he said, and I swallowed hard.

He had two crescent dinner rolls wrapped in a paper towel.

I took them, and his hand went to the dip of my waist, right before the swell of my hip and I shivered at his closeness even as I stuffed my face.

"You're a good person, Kyle," I murmured, and he snorted.

"Am not. I've never been one of the good guys and I never will be." He sighed out and with a frown in his voice said, "You're cold." He shifted, cuddling up to my back. He was tall, even at seventeen. Like almost six feet tall, and he was warm.

"You better get the fuck out of here," Tara warned. "Or I'm gonna rat your ass out."

"Do it and die, bitch," Kyle whispered harshly into the dark, his breath blushing over the sting of my scraped shoulder.

"Tara, shut up," Melanie whispered and if a whisper could be a shout, she'd done it. "They aren't doing anything!"

"Yeah, you would know, you little pervert." Kyle's voice held judgment. His head turned back in Melanie's direction. "You like watching, don't you?" he teased cruelly.

"You don't have to be so mean when people are trying to help you," Melanie said with a sniff of superiority.

Kyle chuckled again, a rich dark sound, and his fingers fanned out over my ribs. He could be such an asshole to everyone else. I didn't know why he chose to be kind to me.

"You should go," I whispered.

"Not until you're asleep," he countered and his tone brooked no argument. I wriggled to give him a little more room, and he sucked in a breath.

"Stop doing that!" he said sharply. "Just hold still and go to sleep. I've got you, Shady..."

I woke with a start, miles and miles and years and years away from the Daughton's but still, I thought ironically, still in Kyle Lachlan's clutches.

I drew in a deep breath and turned in the oversized and over-stuffed cloud of a bed to look at the clock.

3:07 am

I'd gone to bed around two. I closed my eyes and tried to sleep, but by four, I had to give up. I was too restless, and I was haunted by the ghosts of memories I would much rather forget… the what came *after* the Daughton's.

The dead-end jobs, the renting rooms, the fleeing in the middle of the night from one of those rooms when the house's owner tried to get fresh with me in the middle of the night by coming into my room. God, the thing I'd managed to avoid in foster care, that led to my early exit, only to have to deal with it *again* when I was nineteen and paying for my own space. I'd only gotten away because I'd smashed a water glass in his face.

I was lucky the police had believed me. I held up my hand in the sliver of moonlight coming in behind me through the bedroom window and traced the vertical scar in the middle of the heel of my palm with its slight curve at the bottom from that incident.

Once again, I'd found myself with my belongings in trash bags, and lucky enough that Michelle, one of my coworkers at the time, invited me to stay on her couch just until I could find something else… which I did, but it was just as sketchy. My lease hadn't been renewed because the guy was pissed that I'd drilled holes in his door to put in a dead-bolt on my bedroom. He was illegally subletting anyway and was like this forty-year-old guy renting to a nineteen-year-old. Fuck his security deposit.

The next place I'd moved into was with Nick, my boyfriend.

It went well until the honeymoon phase was over and I realized what a child he still was himself. Twenty-four, spending most of his time unemployed after rage quitting job after job and then finally deciding that I could just do all the work… and I do mean All. The. Work. From my regular waitressing gig, sometimes pulling double shifts, to every bit of housework in our little studio apartment while he played video games and watched movies all day.

I couldn't do it on my own, and I packed up and left while he was passed out one night. Never looked back.

I sighed and sat up on the edge of the bed, mind racing. I didn't want to go through the litany of bad decisions and sheer rotten luck that proceeded to follow in the years after that.

All of it leading to this grand gilded cage... coming full circle... right back to Kyle.

Kyle who had been my first love. Kyle who had promised he would find me and come back for me as soon as he was out of basic training. The first man to have lied to me on that score. Kyle who had changed his number or lost his phone or whatever and who I had never heard from again until now...

Kyle fucking Lachlan, I thought disparagingly.

Kyle *fucking* Lachlan who I had spent countless hours with in that final year of his foster care stint. Kyle *fucking* Lachlan who I had believed in, who I had promised he could be *anything*, who I tried so very hard to be kind to despite his sharp edges and who made *me* feel things I had never felt before... or since, if I was being perfectly honest.

Kyle fucking Lachlan who had become a stone-cold killer...

I got out of bed, bare feet sinking into the plush, cream carpet, and I wriggled my toes down into the shag.

It'd been a few days since I'd seen him, down at the pool, and the mansion was big enough that I hadn't encountered him again even though Conan assured me he was lurking and still here.

I hoped I *wouldn't* encounter him either. I didn't know how to reconcile the Kyle of my youth to the man on those monitors, to the man he was now.

I sighed harshly into the dark and padded across the floor, the dusky light teal satin nightgown I wore fluttering against the tops of my thighs as I made my way across the dark room and peeked into the well-lit hallway outside my bedroom door.

My sleep schedule was all screwed up; though I didn't suppose it really much mattered. I mean, what else was there for me to do? This place was already immaculate. I wasn't really allowed in the kitchen without Conan's supervision – that's to say, he had taken to locking up the knives in one of the kitchen drawers after that first incident, and it wasn't like I really knew how to cook beyond reading the directions on the box… and there certainly weren't any box meals in Conan's kitchen.

Still, I could at least heat up some milk or something and calm this gnawing in my gut which was akin to hunger, but certainly wasn't me starving. No, Conan made certain I was well fed to the point I was starting to notice some changes in the mirror. For the first time in a long time, my ribs were no longer showing quite so prominently and my chest seemed to be filling out some.

I was grateful for that. Better than gaining it all in my ass and thighs.

I did warm a small glass of milk, drank it, and still felt restless, so I did what I always did when I was this sort of way – I slipped from the kitchen, ghosting up the hall, trailing fingertips along the expensive wallpaper and just wandered for lack of anything else to do.

I found myself on the single step to the sunken living room. The mansion, being so close to the Chesapeake, had certain built-in features, Conan had explained, in case of storm surge and flooding.

I stepped down off the hardwood and relished in the feel of my feet sinking into the rich carpet in here, too. Cream, like the rest of the mansion that I could tell. A red Persian area rug, bigger than I had ever seen, really tied the room together with its overstuffed couches and wildly oversized entertainment center.

It was the glittering moonlight over the Chesapeake that brought me down here, however, and up to the windows with their marble ledge about knee height. Another defense against the elements, should it come to it.

Cold radiated off the dark glass in front of me, and the marble before my feet, and I hugged myself tightly, letting my eyes wander over the freedom just beyond the thick, bulletproof glass, over the water, and along the rim of the bay with its glittering city lights.

I felt such a mixture, such a jumble of feelings about things. Like I should be grateful… and I mean, I guess I should be for some things.

Roan had gentled and was kind enough to me and though Kyle was a stranger to me now, he still held such a familiarity – a tenuous link to my past for as awful as it was after my parents had died, leaving me with nothing and no one, no family to take me in.

A flicker of movement in the glass made me refocus, and I sucked in a sharp breath as Kyle's reflection resolved in it. He was behind me by several paces, standing on the lip of the stair down into the living room – hands in the pockets of his black slacks, dressed identically to how he had been in the pool.

His eyes fixed on mine in the reflection of the window and slowly, almost predatorily, he stepped down in his socked feet into the living room. His eyes were sharp, cutting like chips of obsidian as he made his way to me, stopping just behind me. I touched a hand to my throat, my other arm around my waist, as I subconsciously tried to hide myself in the scant nightgown from his gaze, which was doing a slow sweep down the reflection of my front.

I felt my pussy clench and very nearly stopped breathing at the visceral reaction my body had to seeing him. He was still just as handsome, just as gorgeous as he had been to me when I was fifteen, only now, neither one of us were teenagers. Though Kyle Lachlan had been my first kiss, though my ribcage very nearly burned with the memory of his hand, slipped beneath the hem of my shirt, that was as far as it had ever really gotten between us.

I pressed my thighs together, subtly, I hoped, and put one foot on top of the other, very nearly shrinking in on myself, wobbling a bit off balance.

Kyle's hands grasped my hips over the thin satin of my nightie and I forgot how to breathe as he stepped so close, up to my back, I could feel his warmth radiating off of his chest. He closed his eyes and breathed me in, a slight smile playing along his lips.

"Hi, Shady," he whispered, fixing my gaze with his in the reflection of the window.

I swallowed hard and whispered back, "Please stop calling me that."

He shook his head, once back, once forth. "Not until you own it," he whispered.

"Kyle," I said, swallowing hard. "We aren't kids anymore, so please... just stop it."

His lips curled into a nasty little smile as he reached up, grasping the weight of my hair at my back and laid it carefully over my shoulder, baring my neck and other shoulder on one side.

"You're right," he said. "We're not."

His lips were gentle against my skin and my breath shuddered out, my eyes slipping shut, my pussy growing damp with need.

Not a good look, Sadie... he kills people for a living. Get it together.

But I couldn't, because it was *Kyle*, at my back once again, keeping me warm in the night, just like that long-ago distant memory...

"Please, don't... stop..." I whispered.

He chuckled darkly. "I have no intention of stopping," he murmured. "I've waited too long for this."

I gasped as his mouth found the sweet spot in the side of my neck, below my ear, that sent shivers cascading over my shoulder, down my arm and down my back.

"Mm," he grunted in satisfaction at my reaction, his arms going about me, body pressing closer to my back as he pressed light kisses to my skin, running the tip of his nose behind my ear and whispering in it...

"I've waited a long time for this... too long."

"Don't," I murmured feebly, my resolve weakening as he cuddled me close.

"Put your foot up on the ledge," he ordered, and I swallowed hard, my leg moving of its own accord, my mind screaming to stop.

Stop, stop, stop, stop, stop!

But part of me didn't want to. My heart overruled my head, as emotions crashed into one another in confusion in my breast, making my heartbeat erratic, stealing my breath, and twisting to the point of pain as he rubbed his erection against my ass.

He chuckled, that same, rich, dark sound from when we were teens when he got his way despite my feeble protestations. Like sable soft fur against my body, if sound could have such a feeling. I whimpered as his hands traveled to mine, fingers interlocking, his palms to the backs of my hands.

"Good girl," he whispered in my ear. "That's my good girl." He pecked a kiss to the shell of my ear and I felt the tears start, the emotions building, overwhelming, so many mixed feelings raging to the fore, the dam broken, years of built-up emotional scar tissue being excised away with his precision touch and slick words.

"Keep your leg right where it is," he ordered firmly when I went to put it down. Hating myself, I moved swiftly to obey.

"God, you're even more beautiful as a woman than you were as that skinny teen girl," he said, his hands deftly sweeping mine down my body and up my thighs, easing the nightgown off my shoulders, letting it drop in a whisper against my skin before pressing my hands to the cold, hard glass.

"Keep them there," he ordered firmly, pressing them against the glass hard, pressing his body against mine, the heat of him nice as the chill seeped through my front.

"Think anybody's out there, watching?" he asked. "Hm?"

I swallowed hard and felt another tear slip down my cheek, angry at my body's betrayal as my pussy gave another low, aching throb of need.

"Hm?" He pressed me and my mouth worked, though no sound came out at first.

"I don't know," I croaked.

"Well, if they are," he said, reaching down in front of me, slipping his hand up the side of my leg to the front of the lace scrap of panties I wore underneath, my breath barely moving in and out of my lungs. "They're going to get one hell of a show," he promised.

His fingertips grazed my clit, parting my folds and I jerked my hips back away from his touch. He thrust his hips forward, pinning me to the glass in front of me and growled, "This is happening." Then, his voice gentling, he softly said "I've got you, Shady... and I'm never letting you go."

I closed my eyes, my resolve in tatters as he slid that hand away from my pussy, back over my hip and bunching my panties in his palm, jerked them roughly at the seam, popping the stitches, tearing them off.

He let them fall away, and they sagged, but didn't come down completely. He took that hand and put it over one of mine against the glass, his other drifting down from my shoulder to find the hip of the other side of the scrap of cloth and repeating his efforts. It took two jerks for the material to finally come away. I fought down a bubble of a sob as again, I had a surge of desire at odds with my moral standing.

I wanted this, I wanted Kyle, I just couldn't reconcile the man behind me, working at his belt, at his fly, with the roughly sweet Kyle I had known at the Daughton's house.

This man was meaner, stronger, more terrifying, but underneath, there was *still* that tenderness of long ago and it was all so confusing.

I took in a sharp breath when he went questing for my opening with his cock.

"Kyle, please!" I didn't know what I was begging for as I writhed slightly against the window glass. For him to stop, or for him to hurry.

"Easy, baby. I got you," he said and with a grunt of triumph, the velvet head of his cock found my entrance and he pushed his way inside.

I cried out, legs trembling as he pressed his body against me and in me, his arms around me as he filled me up and out. I gasped, breath sawing in and out of my lungs as he pressed one hand between my breasts and the other to the top of my sex and thrust into me even further, despite being all the way in.

I cried out again, voice trembling as he set one hell of a rhythm, a punishing pace, his breath hot against my ear and neck as he took me, his fingers causing a delicious friction against my clit, my pussy feeling as though it was heavy with the gravity of its need to be satisfied.

God, it felt good... it felt so good, and I didn't know what scared me more – the fact that I should have hated it or the fact of how much I *liked it.*

I gasped in a sharp breath as the sensations rose an octave inside of me and Kyle grunted, a satisfied noise, and said encouragingly, "That's it."

I felt myself tighten around him as he fucked me mercilessly against the glass, one hand on my shoulder pulling me down onto his cock even as he thrust up inside me, the other one still at the front of my sex, torturously sweet, and I felt like I should hold off. I didn't want to, but it was the right thing to do and all I could think when I came, throbbing and strobing around his shaft, sensation bursting in a warm shower of sparks up through my body to cascade back down in a second sweeping pass which became a third, and a fourth, the pleasure sweeping through me and crashing against my edges to wash back in, was *you should not enjoy this...*

But I did. *I so did.*

He thrust up hard inside me, harder than any before and let out a strangled grunt as he finished himself, both of us leaning forward heavily on the impervious glass, panting, heavily burdened with the battle to slake our lust. The only sounds filling the cavernous space of the living room, our breath mutually sawing in and out of our chests until it was interrupted by Kyle's groan as he pulled out of me, his hand leaving my pussy, falling on my other shoulder, thumbs digging and sweeping up in a short, intense massaging pass through the knotted and corded muscles of my back.

I let out a shaky, stuttering breath, closing my eyes, fresh tears of confusion tinged with regret slipping from my eyes as Kyle let out a sigh of satisfaction and hands sliding from me and taking a step back, he asked coolly, "Did you enjoy the show?"

I sucked in a sharp breath and looked up into the reflection of the room in the glass, and to Roan's light-colored eyes, dark with some internal, unnamed pain, met mine.

I felt the color drain from my face the same time a flush of embarrassment crept up. Swallowing hard, I tried valiantly not to faint then and there.

Conan turned, his expensive shoes clacking against the hardwood floor in his familiar uneven gait as he strode away from us.

"Clean yourself up," Kyle said coldly, the threat of anger in his tone, and tucking himself back into his pants, he left me there, too.

I slipped first to my knees and then onto my ass on the plush carpet of the posh living room and completely shattered.

What had I done?

CHAPTER FOURTEEN

---

*L*achlan...

One of the delights about the Bat Cave was all of Roan's spy stuff. I could take a bottle of Botanist gin, sit in that fancy gamer chair he bought, and watch almost every room in the house and across the grounds with the wall of monitors he had in it.

I clicked and found Roan in the garage. He had the hood of his Aston Martin DB5 up, some crusty old, but *expensive*, British car.

Boring.

If I were going to blow a wad of cash on a British car, it would be a McLaren.

The grounds were clear, and again – *Boring.*

Then I found what I wanted, the guest room Sadie was in. I watched her exit the bathroom in silence. She was gorgeous – thin, and her hair, longer now than it had been, looked good when it was the right color. I gave a sigh as she sat on the bed and picked up a pair of paper-thin panties. She regarded them and then slipped them up her legs. There was a flash of dark bush from beneath the hem of her nightgown, neat, trim, and then it was barely covered by the purple silk.

The nightie itself was almost as sheer as the panties – *delicious.*

Roan was showing a bit of taste that even I could appreciate. I had imagined that he would have done something ridiculous and overblown, like he did everything. Maybe something lacy, frilly, or, *gag,* with bows. Maybe a Victorian baby-doll, a corset, some piece of fancy pants that I wouldn't know the name of… but this, this was tasteful. Even in the monitor I could see the shadow of her nipples through the fabric. God, she had grown up, and filled out.

Oh Shady, my Shady. When we were teens in the foster home, I remembered touching her, hands resting on her hips, laying behind her, sliding my hand into that sultry dip in her side, feeling her shoulders and ribs. The way she had smelled then, how hard my cock would get when I didn't have enough real confidence to fill a thimble; it was all bravado and faking it back then. Not anymore.

I remember that first kiss, how my nerves had wadded up in my stomach, and how close I had come to touching side boob and I laughed at myself now. Oh, how young me couldn't have imagined how I would turn out. The places I had gone, the sights I had seen, and the women I'd fucked. And how, fuck all, I kept coming back to that skinny stubborn girl with that gorgeous neck and at that point, her all but non-existent tits. Those had *certainly* grown in and I couldn't get my mind off them.

Fuck, Shady, where have you been? I thought about how long I had searched for her, wondering where she went. I gave a sigh and poured another round of Botanical, gave it a swirl and a thoughtful sip. Then she got up and left the guest room.

Where are you going? I wondered, watching as she walked through several different camera fields and stopped in the living room. She wandered up to the dark window glass overlooking the bay, and I got up from the chair. I finished my gin in a final rushed gulp, which was a shameful way to treat such a finely crafted liquor, but the call of my Shady girl was too much to ignore, especially when she was so close. I walked to the front room, making silent strides, stopping short in the archway.

Her ass was amazing, the way the satin clung to it.

What had come after the Daughtons for her? I wondered, not for the first time. *After Prissy and her perpetually drunk asshole husband, Dean?*

I leaned against the arch frame and watched. This was better than watching her while she was asleep through the impersonal camera. *Mm*, this was so much better. I felt my cock twitch, tighten. I stepped closer, silently, until I could see my own reflection in the glass along with hers. I stood a few feet behind her on the lip of the stair at the edge of the living room, close enough to smell her – the shampoo Roan had provided her, the bodywash, and underneath it all? That scent that was all her.

"Hi, Shady," I said, using the name I hadn't thought of seriously in a long time. She jumped, her dark eyes fixing on mine in the glass.

I stepped down into the room and walked up behind her, the plush carpet absorbing the sound of my footsteps.

"Please stop calling me that," she murmured.

"Not until you own it," I said. Owning a name took the power away from it. The girls and other kids had used it as an insult, but I adored it. *Shady Brooks.* It reminded me of a peaceful, idyllic scene… capturing my imagination.

"Kyle," she said. "We aren't kids anymore. So, please, *stop it.*"

"You're right, we're not," I said, pulling her dark hair away from her shoulder, exposing the magic spot on her neck. I hadn't met a woman yet who didn't melt at a touch or a kiss there. She was no different, and I felt my heart as it jumped in my chest. *This was really going to happen.* I brushed my lips against her skin and felt her shudder and tense. I knew where that tension was going – right between her legs – and the thought aroused me. In our reflection, I could see her nipples stiffening under the sheer satin.

Fuck, Shady.

I could feel the flush from the alcohol in my face.

"Please, don't stop," she whispered, her voice husky with repressed need.

"I have no intention of stopping," I said. "I've waited too long for this." My cock was completely hard and starting to ache. I kissed her neck, below her ear and down toward the point of her shoulder. "I've waited a long time for this, too long." *Shady, if you only knew how many times that I beat myself off thinking of you.* She murmured something soft. It might have been don't, but I could feel her starting to melt into me.

"Put your foot up on the ledge," I said, gliding my hand down her back, cupping her buttock and then putting pressure on her thigh. She smelled delightful. She trembled with a moment of resistance and then lifted her leg.

Mmmm...

"Good girl, that's my good girl," I whispered, kissing her ear. I felt her shudder, and I saw a confused look in her reflection. Her cheeks were pink, and I could smell her sex, and when I rubbed my cock against her, she ground back just a little bit. *My Shady, you were always shy.* "Keep your leg right where it is." I let my hands explore her, caressing her small breasts, feeling the slope of her chest, her hips. I eased the nightie straps off of her shoulders, exposing her breasts. I felt my breath draw in. "God," I struggled to keep my composure, "you're even more beautiful as a woman than you were as that skinny teen girl."

I knew that I was nothing like the equally skinny shit that I'd been at that age. The nightgown slid down her body and pooled at her feet, forgotten on the ground. I traced my hands from her shoulders down to her hands, and wrapped mine over hers, fingers interlaced. The glass was cool when I put her hands against it. "Keep them there," I whispered in her ear.

I saw another pale face reflected in the window, one with bushy eyebrows and a big nosy nose. I smirked.

"Think anybody's out there, watching?" I asked. There was zero chance there would be anyone between this window and something like the five hundred yards to the coastline at the end of Bootlegger Head. I didn't meet Roan's eyes in the reflection; I could have, but not yet. That look on his face, though...

I felt a stab of resentment. *Shady was mine.* I realized in that moment, the fancy food, the quality of the lingerie, he was actually catching *feelings* for her.

"I don't know," she said in a voice that cracked.

"Well if they are," I said, meeting Roan's cold glower defiantly, "they're going to get one hell of a show." I slid my hand inside her sheer panties, feeling the heat between her legs and suppressing a groan of satisfaction. I teased her pussy, fingers between the lips, stroking her button. She was so wet, and I leaned into her bodily, trapping her between me and against the glass, feeling the friction as I ground my cock against her.

"This is happening," I said, almost in disbelief, trying to convince myself. "I've got you Shady. And I'm never letting you go," I promised. I clenched her panties and tugged hard on them, and I heard stitches pop, the fabric tearing. They didn't come completely free like I really wanted them too, but they were normal panties, not any sort of tear-away garment. I switched sides and several tugs later, the material surrendered and she made a guttural noise. I held one of her hands against the glass as I undid my belt and let my slacks drop to the carpet. Roan was still glaring, his face chiseled out of stone, like some ancient British statue.

I was so ready for her, my cock aching and hard. I sought out the silky entrance between her legs. *How many times had I jerked off thinking of this exact moment?* How many escorts and rich married women had I closed my eyes with and imagined my awkward Shady taking my thrusts? I could feel her, her pussy wet, my cock dripping with desire. I rubbed against her a few times, savoring the moment, knowing that I would only get to have one first time with her.

I'm rushing this, fuck me, I'm rushing this.

"Kyle," she rattled. *"Please."*

"Easy baby, I got you," I murmured. I parted her pussy lips with the head of my dick and pushed forward, and then the fantasy was made real; I was inside her.

Her pussy was heaven, and I had to go slowly. I could already feel that ember glowing in the base of my cock. It was almost too good to be true. I was finally there, balls deep inside her, inside my Shady. A younger me, a less experienced, less disciplined me, would have shamed himself – two strokes in and then popping my load. I wasn't that kid anymore, just like she wasn't that girl. I wondered for a moment, *if I was her first?*

The tension passed, like a challenge accomplished, and I felt free to move. I looked up into Roan's unsmiling mug. His face was an unhappy mask, and I wondered *what the fuck was his problem?* He could have left. He could have said something and ruined it all. Instead, he only stared… Stared as I caressed her tits and teased her pussy with my hand, her soft voice lilting in a pleasure-filled moan.

I used her body to grind her hips against mine. I wanted to give her everything I had, all the cock I had, every inch, I wanted it inside her. I wanted to fill her like a hurricane's storm surge. More, I wanted all of her. I picked up my tempo; she gasped and pushed back against me as I moved to a faster paced pounding. I felt myself hammering her, and her pussy clenched and squeezed me. Oh, *I knew what that was*, oh *yes*, I knew what that was.

"That's it," I said, encouraging her. I didn't want her to hold back. I wanted her orgasm to break on my cock like that storm.

She came, and she came again. I was relentless, never letting up. I wouldn't let up until I felt that last orgasm come out of her, when instead of gripping my cock, her pussy fluttered and her knees turned to jelly, *then* it would be my turn. Young me fantasized about this countless times; about pounding this pussy. Not even the unwanted audience would take this from me.

She gasped and shuddered. My breathing labored; I could feel the sweat that was dripping down my back. I started to relax, letting the iron discipline go. I let my imagination loose, closed my eyes and let myself be in just that perfect moment. She was spent, her pussy sopping wet and her breathing sharp and ragged. *My Shady, my Shady had come all over my cock.* I could feel her juices running down my balls, my thighs starting to fatigue with my thrusting up inside her.

I exploded. Years of fantasies, years of masturbation, and I was finally *here*, balls deep inside my one true desire. It felt like something more than cum was shooting out of me. Was it my soul? Was it something deeper, something else? I didn't come like this very often. My God, I didn't come like this at all!

I gave her neck and shoulders a squeeze, and ran my hands down her sides, releasing her tits, and letting her clit rest. Her chest was heaving; I could feel her ribs beneath my fingers.

"You enjoy the show?" I asked Roan's reflection in the glass. I pulled out of her, knowing that all my jizz was going to gush out onto the cream carpet he picked out and was fastidious about. Sadie gasped. I wanted to be tender with her, to cuddle her, kiss her, but he was glaring at me like some fucking cuckold.

"Clean yourself up," I said, colder than I intended.

The show was fucking over.

I held a grim satisfaction that he would be cleaning that carpet later.

I LEFT THE ROOM, HIT THE CAN AND TOOK A PISS. I'D WANTED TO enjoy our first time more than I actually got to, my Shady. Still, smelling her scent on me right now was nice. Roan's staring hadn't been so awesome, but there had been a certain thrill to having an audience.

I wanted to pour myself a fresh gin, but fuck all if that bottle of Botanical was still sitting in the Bat Cave. I bet if Roan wasn't on his knees cleaning my spunk out of his carpet, he would be in the lair. I wanted my drink. I'd wanted to enjoy my first time with Shady completely differently. I had wanted to draw it out. I wanted to play her like a concert violinist, finessing orgasm after orgasm out of her, until she gazed into my eyes, breasts sweaty and heaving, arms reaching, drawing me down to kiss me.

But no, the fucking limey, he had to start getting feelings for my Shady. *My* fucking Shady. Jealousy burned like cold fire in my brain as I stalked to the Bat Cave, ready to confront the bastard, to yell at him for being a beady-eyed voyeur, for having feelings for my girl.

Surprise, surprise… the Bat Cave was empty. The only thing I found was my bottle of gin and thank fucking God for that! I took a drink directly from the bottle. This shit was fucking *good*.

I should feel like a god. I'd finally fucked the girl I had dreamed about for years. For fucking *years*.

I sat down in his chair and started flicking through the screens.

Where was his limp-dicked ass?

He wasn't in the front room, or his room. I clicked the feed over to the guest room, and the motion detector indicated someone was in its bathroom. *What sort of voyeur doesn't install cameras in the shower when there are cameras everywhere else? An asshole, that's what sort of voyeur does that.*

I took another drink from the bottle. Maybe he did something completely unexpected. Maybe he got in one of the cars we owned and actually went somewhere.

My bottle was empty, and that was just annoying as fuck. I tossed the bottle in his trash. He hated that – finding my booze bottles always made his eye twitch. I wanted to make more than his eye twitch. I wanted to sock him in his stupid eye!

I spun his chair and watched it smack into the side of the desk and almost fall. *Stupid fucking chair.* There was more gin in the house bar, and I decided that the best course of action was to go there and get another bottle – maybe not Botanical, maybe something basic top shelf. No need to waste the good stuff when I just wanted to get truly and completely hammered.

The last fucking thing I expected to find in the bar was Roan. He was leaning against the whatever vintage some kind of wooden bar he had bought, holding a highball glass of whiskey.

"You've got some absolute bloody stones, you pillock," he slurred.

"Those sounds coming out of your mouth, do you think they're words?" I asked.

"I forget you're an American. I'll try to use smaller ones, try and keep my sentences short." I pointed a finger at him and gave him half a laugh.

"Look at you, you big moosey bitch." I reached across the bar and grabbed one of the bottles of gin from the glass shelf. "One little brown-eyed girl, and boo fucking hoo, you have to drown your stoicism in whiskey."

"You better consider what you bloody say right now, *mate*." Roan glared at me.

"Or what, you'll have another drink?" I snorted. "You really showed me." I mocked him without mercy.

"What's wrong with you, you absolute... *donkey*?" He sputtered, setting his now empty glass down on the bar. "How could you do that to her?"

"What, mad I got there before you got the nerve up to try and hold her hand first?" I shot back. He lunged forward, grabbing the front of my shirt and powering me across the room, slamming me against the wall. The art rattled on its hangers, and I laughed at him. "I'm sorry," I said, still laughing. He relaxed and stepped back. "Is hand holding third base for you limeys?"

I ducked as he punched a framed glass picture of a sailing ship. His meaty fist shattered the glass, and I could feel the air displaced by the swing.

That was close.

"Look what you made me do," I said, looking down at the gin spilling out on the floor from the neck of my dropped bottle. Before I could pick the bottle up, he slammed me into the wall again. "You keep this up, you're going to piss me off," I grated.

"Piss *you* off? You think I care about making a spoiled wanker like you angry?" he demanded.

"You *should* care, I could kick your ass from here to Kandahar and back," I threatened, politely.

"Oh, you wish you could," he said.

"I just want to pick my bottle of gin up off the floor and go back to somewhere comfortable," I said. "If you insist on being a pussy about this, what happens, happens," I warned.

"Oh, I know what happens around you, you insensitive prick," Roan growled.

"I am hardly insensitive," I said.

"You've not seen this dolly of yours in years, maybe a decade, and the first real time you spend with her is dogging her against the living room window. She was *crying*, you great arse!"

"She wasn't crying, you fool," I said, but I felt a tug of doubt.

"She had literal tears running down her face, had you bothered to look," he said. "You might have noticed if you knew women had things besides a cunt to stick it and a pair of tits for handles."

"Is that what you were staring at, watching her cry while I fucked her?" I asked sharply. She was *mine*, mine to do with as I wished. "Is that why you were rooted like a tree?" He slammed me into the wall again. "You really need to stop doing that," I growled, losing my patience. I really didn't want to kick his crippled ass, but I would.

"I'm not rooted like a tree now," he grated.

"You're drunk," I spat.

"You treated her like one of your whores and she isn't that, mate. She will *never* be that," he said coldly.

She hadn't pulled away, but she *had* whispered no. Lots of women said no, though! That was part of the game. If they said no, and they enjoyed some deviant thing you did to them, they could moralize about it – even when they loved it, when they came like animals. *I'm not a dirty whore who likes my asshole pounded. I told him no.*

Fucking female games, I told myself but I couldn't make that line up with Sadie in my mind. She wasn't like the escorts I paid; she was something much purer than that.

"No, I didn't," I said, but the seed of doubt was planted, and the vines were starting to creep.

He slammed me into the wall again. I looked down and could see the last glug of gin slop out of the bottle onto the hardwood floor. I was fucking over this. A perfectly good bottle of gin was destined for a mop bucket, my balls were drained, and now this doubt was chewing on my mind.

"You just use women, Lach. You use them like tissue paper. They're just something for you to seduce and then dump your spunk into. How could you *do that* to her? She's been a victim her entire life and you're just the last predator in a long line of 'em to lust after her." He slammed me into the wall again, like it was punctuation.

I put my knee in the middle of his gut and returned the favor. He stumbled back and hit the bar harder than I had hit the wall. He grabbed at the edge of the bar, and for the stool next to it but missed both. Before he could get to his feet, I kicked him sharply in the lower leg. His prosthetic came loose from its normal position, making getting back up on his feet all but impossible now.

He really is a one-legged man in this ass kicking contest... I choked and sputtered on a laugh.

"Shady belongs to me," I said. "I know you like her, but that's just not going to work for me, dawg. She's not a timeshare where I get her so many days a week and you get her the rest." I picked up the bottle of whiskey and poured it out on the ground. "Doesn't feel nice, does it, seeing this expensive shit wasted?" He looked up at me, his features dark with anger.

"You certainly like spilling other people's things, like her tears," he said.

His head smacked against the bar when I punched him in the jaw. "That, that was for wasting my goddamn gin."

I stood, brushed the front of my shirt off, and walked out of the bar.

I heard a glass break behind me.

<hr>

CHAPTER FIFTEEN

<hr>

*R*oan...

My hands were shaking, and I could keep my cool in any situation, from the moment when the IED had almost torn our loaned Humvee in half, to when in an online game raid that we had spent weeks building up to was nearly ruined when 733tID10T jumped the gun and charged the Temple of the Shattered God. My hands didn't shake when I had applied a tourniquet to my own leg. They didn't shake when I was filleting a Spanish mackerel, and they didn't shake when I was the keyboard warrior in one of the games I played when I couldn't find sleep.

They shook now. My head was overly full, my imagination and memory playing in a violent dance with one another. I could see her tears reflected in the glass, but I could also remember the wet sound as he shagged her. All the macaroni and cheese jokes on the internet suddenly made sense, and instead of laughing, or having that moment of enlightenment, I trembled with fury, the sound taunting me.

I wanted to tell myself it wouldn't have been so bad. Instead of struggling to find a single reason that made it worse, almost *every* reason made it worse. How long had it been since I was with a woman? I had, since the accident and therapy, but it had been awkward, and strained. The handful of women had been circumspect, mostly, about my missing leg, my scars, my lack of frothing over machismo and bravado. Mostly.

Lach had never picked any of those women up and certainly had never shagged any of them in front of me.

The part that really hurt was that I hadn't been able to do anything. I wanted to grab him, stop him, pull his hands off of her. But no, all I could do was stand there, staring, my cock hard, my heart racing, pounding in my temples. There had been an almost hypnotic motion to the way Lach's lower back and ass had flexed as he'd shagged her.

Was this what it was normally like for him, for the women who were with him?

Fuck.

My balls still hurt like a bloody stupid teenager.

Idle hands are the devil's plaything, so I made my hands busy.

My old coping mechanism had been the bottle, and last night, the bottle had gotten me a blackened eye and a bloody lip. My new coping mechanism had been learning to cook and though I'd mastered it, it was still as good a coping mechanism as any. I needed to make something, and I wanted to do something for Sadie. I needed my hands to stop shaking. It might be cliché, but I decided to make one of the oldest comfort foods I could think of, chocolate brownies.

The important thing was that the recipe was simple and didn't require a high degree of precision or knife skills. The other thing was that there were two paths to making the best brownies – simple perfection, or over-the-top decadent. As much as I wanted to do the latter, with tiny marshmallows, fudge ripples, maybe sprinkles, simple was best. I had already picked up on the fact that Sadie preferred more simple fare.

The stand mixer handled the batter like a champ. I was pouring the second pan of batter when Sadie wandered into the kitchen. She had that quiet church mouse thing going, those big brown eyes, those pouty lips. Her eyes were quick, taking in everything I was doing while taking up the least amount of space possible.

My breath caught in my chest. She was wearing the lilac satin baby-doll that had been a recent addition to the collection, and she was achingly gorgeous in it. I felt a little ashamed for having picked out something like that for her. There was no modesty to it, and she might as well have been nude for as much of her that it concealed. My eyes flitted from her lips, to her nipples almost visible through the cups, to the shadow of pubic hair under the fringe of lace and thin panties.

"Hey," she said softly.

"Hey," I managed to croak back.

"What are you making?"

I cleared my throat. "Brownies." I gestured to the square pan. The oven beeped that it had heated and was ready. I put both trays in and set the timer.

"Oh, nice," she said. "Did you make them all fancy?"

"I didn't," I said. "They're plain, or as plain as I could make."

"There's nothing wrong with plain brownies," she said.

"I was making them for you." She smiled and stepped closer to me.

"I don't know what you could possibly think of me after last night." Her eyes were wet, and she wasn't able to meet my gaze. "But I'm not a whore. I-I don't know why I let him…"

"I know," I said quickly. "I know how he is, how he does." I gave the smallest of shrugs. I felt the urge to make myself small. In the back of my mind, I could hear the noises she made, the moaning and whimpering, his cold stare. "And I could never think that about you," I confessed. She put her hand on mine, her touch was light as a butterfly's.

"So, I'm going to guess these brownies aren't from a dollar mix," she said.

"No, no," I said, looking at where her hand laid on mine. "The cacao powder is fair trade, from somewhere, I don't remember. Used some of the same dark chocolate I used to make the hot cacao. The rest? Well, it's hard to get fancy with flour and eggs."

"What happened to your face?" she gasped. Her eyes flicked from my blackened eye, to my busted lip. I could see concern darken her features.

"I told Lach that I didn't care for the way he treated you, but I think you probably guessed that." I gave her a shadow of a smile.

"You got in a fight with him, over me?" Her voice was thick with disbelief.

"Aye, I'm not proud of it. I let my temper get the best of me," I said.

"It's been a long time since anyone's really stood up for me," she whispered softly and I could drown in her eyes.

"That's terrible that no one has stood up for you," I said, close to stammering.

"I think the last person who really did was Kyle. He was always getting into fights; I mean all the time... At school, at home... He even punched Dean in the face over me, once." I recognized the name from her background check, Dean Daughton, her last foster father.

"You deserved better than all of that," I said.

"You're too sweet."

She gave me the first real smile I had seen on her face, and I could feel my cheeks redden. She pulled herself up and kissed me. Her lips were so soft, softer than I had expected, and for a moment, I could only close my eyes and linger in that moment. And all too soon it was over and she was leaning back. It felt like my face was tingling where her lips had been.

"I was thinking about where Lach said he found you, over by the highway," I said. "He said you didn't have anything on you, but maybe you were staying around there somewhere, maybe had a place or something," I said, looking up to meet her gaze.

"I had a stash, not much in it, but it is everything in the world that I own."

"I've been thinking about going; help you find it," I said. "Or really, finding whatever you had."

"That would be hard. You couldn't find it, even if I told you where it was. Mostly because if any of those old warehouses have names or numbers, I don't know any of them. And, I don't think that satin slips and a negligee are suitable for visiting the warehouse district."

"I have regular clothing you could wear," I said. "I'm not sure on the fit of the shoes, but the rest should be fine."

"But you can't let me out, because he says so." Her lips drew thin.

"I would give you normal clothes, drive you out to the warehouses, and help you get your things back." I felt my will stiffen. "If you wanted to leave after that, I wouldn't stop you. You'd be free to do as you wish."

"Won't he be mad if you let me go? I remember how Kyle used to be, and I can still see that side of him." She sounded concerned.

We talked a bit more, nothing of importance or note, because we'd already made our decisions. In the morning, I was going to take her back to where he found her and release her. She would look at me with those doe eyes, and then would go bounding back into the sprawl of Indigo City like some wild deer.

"Come with me," I said when the brownies were finally out of the oven, gesturing for her for her to follow me, which she did. When we arrived, I opened the door to my bedroom, and let her step in first. After I shut the door, I disabled the camera feed from my phone. There was a certain irony that even I could appreciate, having set up the security system with backdoors and loopholes that only I could exploit. If for some reason that drunk asshole ended up back in the Bat Cave, he'd be left sitting watching a closed loop of a recording. *Thank you, Speed, and thank you, Keanu Reeves.*

She walked slowly around the room looking at the wall and the pictures hanging there. "This was you, before?"

"It was, Her Majesty's Royal Marines." I gestured to the nearest picture. "I was going to be career military, planned on serving until retirement or death, and then, lost a leg. They don't like handing out desk jobs when the crown is looking at drawing down forces. One honorable discharge and rehab stay in California." I pointed at a picture; one I had no recollection of – myself being rolled into surgery. "A few months later, I was looking for a new job with my new nationality, and there Lach was."

"He shows up, just like that?" she asked.

"Yeah, he did," I said. "But this is what I have for you." I went into my closet and returned to her, handing her a small leather bag. She opened it and pulled out the Converse shoes first.

"Are these new?"

"Like I am going to buy used shoes?" I raised an eyebrow.

"Nicest shoes I've probably ever owned, if I can keep them."

"Of course, you can." She looked pleased.

"The rest is more modest fair, off-the-shelf denim, that sort of thing," I said. I was painfully aware of every inch of her, here in my room. "Tomorrow we can see about checking things out and see if your things are still where you left them."

"I'll need to check my schedule," she said.

"Are you available around seven AM?"

"I mean, I'll have to reschedule my meeting with the Prime Minister, but I think we can make it work." She smiled.

WHEN I OPENED THE DOOR INTO THE GARAGE, SADIE'S EYES BULGED.

"Lamborghini, McLaren, Koenigsegg, Audi." I gestured to the small fleet of exotic cars. "But we're taking this one." I gestured to the diminutive and rounded form of the antique Aston Martin DB5. She looked at the choice of cars and then back to the satin silver and chrome DB5.

"Why this one?" she asked.

"Because it is mine, and if it's not in the garage, Lach won't care. He'll know I went somewhere," I said. "Plus, these other cars, too loud, too flashy, too chavvy for my tastes. Even the McLaren, it's just too much."

"Chavvy?" she asked.

"Chavs are people who have no taste and are loud and obnoxious. Like this." I gestured to the Koenigsegg. "It's loud, and obnoxious. It's dreadful to ride in, and aside from being fast and expensive, it has no redeeming features."

"Your car seems familiar," Sadie said, a hint of a smile on her lips.

"I don't know how many movies you've seen, but her Majesty's finest spy, James Bond, used to drive a car like this," I said, opening the door for her. She slipped into the car and gave a laugh.

"Your steering wheel is on the wrong side!"

"Oh, that is where you are wrong. My steering wheel is the only one that is on the correct side. All of these American cars have the wheel on the wrong side. It's okay, at least you've not made the mistake the Germans did and put the engine in the back." I shut the door and clicked the button for the garage door to cycle open. I sat in the driver's seat – clutch, break, ignition, and the car purred to life.

It was pleasant driving with Sadie. She didn't have a smartphone and hadn't developed that certain bubble posture where the spine and head are curled down to face the upturned phone in the hand. She was alert, looking at the scenery, and she pointed out things that were of interest to her. I appreciated that more than she would know. I drove until I got to where I thought Lach had found her but picking out the spot was difficult. The guardrails along both sides of the highway had years of abuse beaten into them. She pointed toward the Blue River District – row after row of abandoned and dilapidated warehouses.

I took the next crossover, leaving the highway behind for the neglected service road. There was a single lane of still present but struggling businesses fronting the district, notable only for their omnipresent iron bars over all the windows, and the reinforced doors. Title loans, cash for gold exchangers, a battered laundromat, several hole-in-the-wall pool hall dives, and a food truck lacking wheels, but apparently still shilling some sort of fried sandwich.

"The food there is terrible," Sadie said.

"I don't think I would patron a food truck without wheels," I said.

"It was bad before the wheels were stolen." She laughed. "We can park somewhere around here and walk."

"You think I'm going to let this car out of my sight, in this neighborhood?" I shook my head.

"There are several gates, and some of them are locked. You can't drive through, and I was maybe five lots back. You can see the building from here." She pointed, indicating one of the larger structures, one with a sawtooth skyline and faded tan paint.

"I can open locks." I gave her a wink. When we pulled up at the first gate, a tubular steel gate designed to only stop cars, I laughed. I left her sitting in the car, walked up to the lock, and popped it. Sometimes the police-issued lock popping tools didn't work, especially on the newer cars or higher end locks. On these cheap locks, it worked like a charm. I left the lock hanging from the pole and swung it open.

There was only one other lock that had to be dealt with, a chain-link gate closed around the large building Sadie had indicated as her prior residence. She pointed at where the fence was broken and we could squeeze through on foot. I opted to use the tool again and slid the gate open. It was a hard job, it seemed like it might have been years since someone worked the wheels or rollers. Sadie ended up helping me push it all the way open. I pulled the car up next to the building while she walked up to a side door.

"This is where I've spent the last half a year, or so," she said, dragging the door open. I gave the car a look and then followed her into the perpetual gloom inside. There was no power, but the warehouse had large skylights, high above in the ceiling. Some of them were broken, but the darkness inside was consuming. The stink inside was likewise consuming. "Yeah, that sort of happens from time to time," she said, noticing my expression. "Sometimes something will get inside and can't get out. It dies, then starts to reek. Usually it's a bird, but the worst time was a snapping turtle. No idea how it got in."

"Splendid." I coughed. I followed her across the main floor, and I could see impressions form the past – damage in the concrete floor where heavy machinery had been, factory equipment, the worn paths where decades and millions of footsteps had shaped stone. She didn't seem to notice as she avoided where part of the ceiling had fallen in to the offices. Wooden frames and boarded up, they looked amateurishly built, maybe even by men who had worked here before. She opened a door and vanished inside. I felt a lurch of panic. If she bolted, I wouldn't be able to catch her. *What am I thinking, doing this?*

She was immediately inside. It had been an office, one the size of a large closet. There was an improvised pallet of blankets and card-board, a shelf made from blocks and old scrap wood with a few battered books and tchotchkes accumulated from living in absolute squalor – an unusual rock, a roll of toilet paper, some fragments of makeup, a mangled bar of soap. I could feel my heart breaking. She had *lived* here.

I saw a crumpled box of supersaver cold medication, and wads of discarded tissue. The remnants of her sickness, she had almost *died* here, too.

Sadie picked up a battered nylon backpack and unzipped it. She let out a sigh, and it seemed like she found what she was looking for. The irrational part of my mind surged with a twitch of adrenaline. *Was there a gun in the bag?* But I knew there wasn't, she wasn't the sort who would own a pistol, and given that she had dollar brand over-the-counter drugs, there was no way she could have bought or stolen one off the streets. Instead, she had a handful of film prints. She clutched them to her chest and almost gave a sob of relief.

"This was my family, my parents." She held a picture out for me to see. They looked like almost any other family, which was expected. There were several Polaroids. "This was Kyle, back when he was a teen, and this was me. This one was both of us. You can tell it's him because he wanted to look like he was too cool to have his picture taken."

I laughed.

"This was Sister McDowell, she worked with me when I was still kicking around in the orphanage. I saw her a few times after that. She volunteers at the soup kitchen on Promenade Avenue, or she did." She shuffled through several more picture. "This is Agnes, but she wanted us to call her Razor, because Agnes was an old woman's name." The girl had a bad dye job and cheap tattoos on her shoulder. She might have been pretty once.

"This was Lupe, and Trent. Trent would *ghost ride* cars after he stole them. The police, well, they shot him. He died in the back of a squad car." She wiped at her face with her sleeve.

"Anthony, Mike the Flea, we called him that because of how skinny he was. He overdosed." She showed me others, more names, more faces, some she didn't remember. Some had real names, some only had street names or nicknames.

This was worse than I expected.

I felt a little sick.

It wasn't that I hadn't seen worse, I had. I had seen refugee camps in Afghanistan, and places where the Taliban had kept people prisoner. Those people had been forced to sit in their own excrement, given little or nothing to eat, left to die. It had been deliberate cruelty, deliberate evil, and I knew what to do with that. Most of the world knew what to do with that. It had involved bombers, the smartest explosives ever devised, a sky full of drones, and men like Lach and me on the ground, putting boots and bullets into the asses of the people who did things like this.

Sadie didn't have a bucket for a toilet, but she also didn't have a violent regime standing on her neck with a high-laced boot, waving machine guns at anyone who didn't sing their version of the *My God is the Only God* song. There wasn't a person or even a group of people who could be wiped out with a JDAM strike, or a called-in artillery. I couldn't rescue her with a P90 or Walther PPK.

"I've got something planned for dinner tonight," I said, breaking the silence. "Something that is a compromise between plain and over the top."

"Oh?" She looked up from her pictures.

"Duck." I smiled.

"Like quack-quack duck?"

"Yes, that sort of duck," I agreed. "With a cranberry-orange glaze."

"I was waiting for the other shoe," she said with a smile.

"Are you ready to go back?" I asked.

"I think so, yeah." I was relieved. I had considered giving her a second bag. It was stuffed in the boot of the Aston – few changes of clothes, a bundle of cash, and a burner phone. I was going to offer her freedom, let her go. But I had a different notion of where she had been before. I had expected something more Bohemian, more of a romanticized notion of a free spirit unbound by social expectation. I didn't expect her living in a deathtrap building that was collapsing around her, reeking of dead animals and old chemicals.

Lach had been right without seeing any of this. Taking her into the house, even against her will, had been for the better. I could feel relief running through me like a cold drink on a hot day. My anger at her captivity seemed overwrought, and eventually I would have to talk to her about this.

"Hey, Roan?" Sadie asked as we walked to the car. "Would it be asking too much to get something to eat before going back to the house?"

"Not at all," I said. "Did you have something in mind?"

"Your food is good, but I was thinking about some of the stuff I was eating before, and this is going to sound strange, but I want some of that."

"Okay, it'll be my treat." I nodded and opened the car door for her. She gave me a sweet smile as she dropped into the passenger seat.

"Burger World?"

"Burger World?" I made a face.

"Have you eaten there?" she asked.

"I generally make a point not to," I confessed. "Have you seen the articles about how they make their food?"

"There aren't many food magazines in the dumpster behind Burger World. I want to have one that wasn't thrown away for being too old to sell," she said. "And fries that are hot. And salty."

"As my lady wishes," I agreed.

LACH WAS WAITING IN FRONT OF THE GARAGE WHEN WE PULLED IN. I thought that we might have been able to sneak in without him noticing, but how realistic had that been? Not very. He had the McLaren pulled out front, and he was leaning against it. This was an ambush, and I knew it. That charcoal suit, the emerald green and teal tie, the thick cigar in his hand, no different from a tactical vest, body armor, and sniper rifle. He would have words instead of bullets, and those I might not be as well prepared for.

"Have a nice afternoon out?" he asked.

"Roan took me to go get my stuff from the warehouse. I found my photographs. Do you remember these?" She bounced from the Aston to show him the handful of pictures. A smile cracked his face, a real one, not one of those precision-assault smiles. She went through the names, the faces, and there were some that she had forgotten along the way that he remembered. A skinny boy with a shaved head Lach remembered, Bobby, and the girl he called a sister, Dolores.

"Oh my God, how could I have forgotten Bobby and Dolly?" She smiled, but there was a hint of sadness to it.

"Because Bobby didn't have a personality other than smoking cigarettes and acting like he was hard as iron and Dolly was a wallflower," he said. "Could you give me and Roan a few minutes?"

"Sure," she murmured, looking at him wistfully, and beaming a little bit at the same time. She cast a backward glance in my direction and dutifully drifted inside.

He waited until the door into the mansion was shut firmly behind her before turning his attention toward me. I braced myself. The last confrontation had not gone my way, and I didn't want this to get violent. Not again. "Relax," he finally breathed out. "I don't want to fight."

"Aye, I'm glad," I said.

"I'm not a monster, Roan. I just sometimes lack impulse control," he said. "That's nothing new."

"It's not, you've always been the point of the spear, first man through the door," I admitted.

"And as long as I've known you, as long as we've worked together, I've never worried about my six, never looked over my shoulder. You've always had my back."

"You had mine when we were in rehab," I countered.

"Rehab, I was there because I was half faking a heart arrhythmia, and my old CO was a little concerned that I was a little too good at killing people and not having a moral crisis." He scoffed. "You needed a bannerman, and that wasn't a role I was familiar with. That might have been the only time I was halfway decent about it." He was unusually introspective, and this was far deeper than he usually ever went.

"I did the best I could then, and it got easier, then I think I started slacking off, taking things for granted,"

"What are you talking about?" This was getting into unfamiliar territory with a man whose middle name could have easily been Arrogance.

"Where did you take Sadie today?" he asked.

"Down to the Blue River District, the Stove Plant warehouse, then Burger World," I said.

"And you hid it from me."

"Aye, I thought you would get angry and possessive, start calling her Shady and making fists again." I crossed my arms across my chest. This was where he was most likely to throw off the charade of being calm, cool, and collected.

"How bad was it, where she was staying?"

"Not as bad as outside of Kandahar, ten times worse than the bridge at DC."

"I think that DC was the worst of the two. I like to think that after we rolled out of that hellhole, things started to improve. But the people living under the bridge, seeing that here, here almost on our doorstep…" He sighed. "I'm not surprised. Sadie was always quick witted, and definitely a survivor. That's why I brought her here, to stay."

"What's that got to do with it?" My curiosity had been piqued.

"That is a good question, what does it have to do with it? A lot. You know I care for her. You're the only person who's come close to what she means to me, and you're my brother, Roan." His eyes held an unusual intensity. He put a hand on my shoulder. "You're my brother."

"She cares for you, too," I said.

"She cares for both of us, for you and for me," he said. "I need her to be safe here. This is hard, but I need her here with both of us."

"Both of us?" I winced internally. I was repeating the last words he said, something I had called Sadie out for doing.

"I know you have feelings for her, it's obvious. If you deny it, I might revoke the no fists thing," he said with a smile that was half-joking, and half-serious. "If you didn't, you wouldn't be serenading her with your duck confit and the high thread count sheets."

"Aye, I do care," I admitted, hesitantly.

"I also feel that there's an," he stumbled over the words, "apology, due."

"It doesn't have to be said." I nodded.

"So, what do we do about this? She has nowhere to go, no one but us to miss her. We have to share her. Like, a timeshare…" He squared his shoulders, gripping the cigar tightly.

"Now that's a thought. It's a shite one, but it *is* a thought." I scowled.

"It's not ideal, but we've always been able to share everything in the past. Vehicles, guns, we've even shared blood. Remember when the doctors said you were still anemic, and you needed that transfusion? They hooked us together. For a short amount of time, we technically shared circulatory systems. Circulatory is blood, right?"

"Aye, it is, and aye, we've shared everything including blood." I felt my chest tighten. There had been an ugly go-round over that – him admitted for what they thought was a previously unnoticed heart condition, me dealing with internal bleeding, and we were a match. Watching him convince a VA nurse and a doctor that he could be a donor despite all of his medical *concerns* was proof enough for me that his jokes about going freelance could actually work.

"So, what's the difference if the thing we share between us happens to be a woman?" he asked casually. "I mean as long as she's okay with it, there shouldn't be a problem."

"That is going to be the hard sell, Lach," I said.

"Do you think you can sell that to her? Can you make it an order? I think she respects you more than me. All she really remembers is a younger version of myself. Just a cocky, headstrong boy who was always picking fights and getting his scrawny ass handed to him."

"I find some of that hard to believe." I laughed.

"But I think she really cared for that dumbass I used to be, and maybe I need to find some of that kid I used to be." He looked down at his Italian leather shoes, almost penitent.

"I was going to give her the option to leave, I thought you should know," I said. "There's a bag in the Aston, a few grand in small bills, some clothes… if she wanted to go."

"I take it she didn't want to leave." He smiled.

"She wanted Burger World, to eat from the front of the restaurant instead of from the dumpster." I gave a shudder. "And we're having that duck tonight, assuming you didn't already eat it."

"You know that's how you tame a stray, warm place to sleep, and hot meals." He gave me a nod. "And that's how you'll be able to hook her with the idea of us sharing her, like a timeshare but not like a fucking horrible real estate deal."

"I've never done bad investments. How does your version of this work?"

"Three days a week, she's mine. The next three days, she's yours," he said.

"And on the seventh day?"

"And on the seventh day, Sadie rests. The day is hers to do what she wants."

"Magnanimous of us, giving her a whole day off." I laughed.

"It's not like anything she'll do on those six days with us will qualify as labor. She's not a worker or employee. If I want to do something with her, I set it up for my time, you want to do something, on your time."

"That actually makes sense," I admitted.

"Of course, it does. We've always been able to handle anything that's come our way."

"Aye, that we have," I agreed, although this was still something completely different, wasn't it?

CHAPTER SIXTEEN

*S*adie...

I waited in the kitchen for the men to return and I would be lying if I said I wasn't a little disappointed when the door leading to the garage opened and Roan was the only one to step through. The whining roar of an expensive engine starting outside clinched it that Kyle wouldn't be coming back... at least not anytime soon. I sighed and felt my shoulders drop.

Roan looked at me, a war of emotions on his face, not all of them readily definable.

"You were hoping to speak with him?" he asked in his crisp British accent, and I nodded without saying anything.

He nodded and said crisply, "He'll be back. Perhaps not tonight, but sooner rather than later."

"Is... is he going to kill someone?" I asked softly, and I was still struggling mightily that my Kyle would go that far and so easily.

"No," Roan said with a reassuring smile that was entirely too brittle for my liking. I didn't honestly know how to feel about Roan and how he helped Kyle to kill people – it was all so Hollywood and dramatic. I mean, things like this didn't really happen in real life, did they?

Life imitating art or art imitating life, Sadie... honestly, what do you think?

The voice in my head sounded suspiciously like Kyle's, only from when we were kids. Just another lesson in street smarts, I guess. He'd forever been 'educating' me on how life 'really worked.'

I guess some things really never did change.

"Are you alright, Poppet?" he asked quietly, and I nodded.

"Just... just a lot to think about still, I guess," I murmured.

He came through the kitchen and stopped across the stone countertop from me, hanging his cane off the edge and putting his hands flat upon it, looking down at me, searching my face.

"Why did you choose to stay?" he asked. "You could have gotten away from me out at the warehouse today, but you didn't."

I heaved an even bigger sigh and said, "You know what? It's a good question. I wish I had an answer for you, but I really honestly don't right now." I did, in my heart of hearts... because *Kyle*... and because... I glanced up into Roan's stony green gaze, searching out every microexpression on my face, his eyes roving my face almost lovingly, a gentle quality to his look.

"I had a bug-out bag packed for you in the boot of my car," he confessed.

"You did?" I asked and couldn't parse out the frisson of anxiety that swept up my spine, an almost fight-or-flight reflex making my gut clench. Visceral, a powerful reaction to his words, and oh, so, confusing because it landed firmly on *fight* and that reflexive *fight* reaction was to *stay*.

Interesting.

"Aye. Some warm clothes, a few grand in smaller bills... untraceable."

I frowned.

"Why didn't you give it to me, and more importantly, why are you telling me this?"

He smiled, and it held the ghost of sadness.

"I think you know, lass," he murmured and reached a hand toward me, tracing a tendril of my errant long hair away from my face, behind my ear, his fingertip tracing the edge of the shell.

I fought not to shudder and lean slightly more into that touch, my chest growing tight, my throat closing up with emotion. I honestly wanted to hear him say it.

"Say it," I whispered.

His smile grew and some of that wistful sadness fell away.

"I couldn't after seeing where," he cleared his throat, "*how* you lived."

"So, pity then?" I asked, deflating just a bit, the hope let out of my balloon.

He chuckled. "No. Hardly that," he said.

"Kyle – I mean, Lach, then?" I asked.

His smile grew a little more, and he shook his head, stopped mid-motion and corrected himself verbally with a, "Well, not entirely."

"Then what?" I asked him, fixing his eyes with mine.

"You are a treasure, Poppet… on that, Lach and I can and do agree. I didn't give you the bag because like Lachlan, I have some controlling aspects to my personality. With you living so efficiently off the grid, I was afraid I would never know what became of you and I couldn't do it. I could not fathom turning you loose out there to wind up in some different warehouse in a different place, cold… hungry… eventually ending somewhere worse." He bowed his head and shook it violently as though to banish the image from his mind.

I reached out in sympathy and covered his hand where it rested on the countertop with mine.

"It's alright," I murmured. "I get it. Believe me, I do."

He looked at me then, somber, and I forced a smile when, for whatever bizarre reason, all I wanted to do was cry for him. For worrying about me…

Or maybe I wanted to cry for myself for finally having someone standing in front of me who wanted to worry about me. I hadn't had that in a very long time. So very long, in fact, I couldn't quite pinpoint when it last was anyone would have missed me. Except maybe for Kyle, but even that was… wow… twenty years ago, maybe?

So long…

Roan reached up with the hand that wasn't covered by my own and touched the side of my face, lightly stroking my cheek with his thumb before almost too swiftly withdrawing it.

"Bless," he said and dragged in a deep breath. "I'd best get cooking; the duck will take its time in the oven." His voice was rougher than it had been a moment before, the emotion hanging in the air between us, thick, almost visibly distorting the air.

"Why don't you put your things away, go for a swim or a walk on the grounds?" he asked.

"What, really?" I asked, surprised. Roan smiled and nodded.

"Just stay warm. The cameras have a view to the shore and out as far as the road. I'll check on you… but I won't stop you."

"You really mean that," I said and it very nearly felt as though the earth shifted beneath my feet as the entire axis of my world tilted.

"Aye," he murmured. "You're not a prisoner here, Sadie. Despite Lachlan's rough exterior – despite mine – we really do wish only the best for you. We want to keep you *safe*. Cared for."

I sighed and pulled my hands back and he shifted his weight slightly.

"I think, deep down, I somehow knew that," I murmured and Roan tilted his head considering me.

"That's good," he said. I smiled and nodded slightly.

"What time do you want me back here?" I asked, and he smiled.

"Whenever you'd like."

I smiled, nodded, and shouldered my worn out, old black backpack.

"Thanks," I said and his smile grew.

"You're most welcome," he said and inclined his head. I pursed my lips and turned leaving the kitchen and the heavy emotion of the moment behind. It'd honestly been like that all day. These heavy intense moments followed by feeling lighter than air for a time. A real rollercoaster of a time.

I wanted to talk to Kyle. To try and understand some things, to piece together some of our broken childhood and what came after…

to *understand...* but like always he didn't seem to be interested – making himself busy, too busy to confront the things that needed confrontation.

I don't think I was as patient as I used to be, at least that was how I was feeling now, looking down at the photo of us when we were still just kids.

I sucked in a deep cleansing breath and let it out slow, staring out of the windows of my room over the choppy slate gray bay. It was rainy and chilly out there, so as much as a walk sounded sublime, I honestly had had my field trip for today and just wanted to stay warm. To that end, a swim sounded wonderful.

I opened up the wardrobe against the wall and took off my brand-new shoes, setting them in one of the cubbies meant for them as I opened drawers to check and see if a swimsuit had found its way inside one of them.

Of course, one had; Roan thought of everything.

I was beginning to think his favorite color was purple. Just about every one of the silky, satiny, clingy fairy dresses he supplied to me were some shade of purple, until some blues and greens started to show up.

The swimsuit, though a revealing two piece, was thankfully unrelieved black except for a line of what were likely expensive crystals, but could also be diamonds... with these two, you never did know, in the metal piece between my breasts. The suit fit like a dream, and I felt sexy in it as I stood in front of the full-length mirror in the bathroom. I also felt incredibly exposed and dressed like a doll for the male gaze.

Right now, that bothered me when it came to Kyle. We *really* needed to talk... but I couldn't help but feel a thrill of excitement knowing that it could and would potentially excite Roan – which was also confusing as all get out in its own way. Like, yikes on bikes!

I felt an old nostalgic longing for Kyle. For the long-ago safety he represented, and for the lost, stolen touches and kisses in the dark of the Daughton family foster home. I was still wholly confused about our first sexual encounter of a couple of nights ago... God, how I'd ached for him to touch me; but... but not like that. I'd always wanted my first time with Kyle Lachlan to be the fairytale kind. With deep longing looks and whispered promises of love. Something with low mood lighting and a cloud soft bed.

Not ice-cold window glass and a dirty fuck while standing up, though it'd been hot in its own way... even now, thinking back on the way he'd moved inside me, I could feel myself growing wet.

I flushed with humiliation and embarrassment at those cutting green eyes in that night-darkened glass... watching us, fists clenched at his sides, erection prominently pressed to the front of his slacks.

The image evoked enough shame mixed with heat that I pulled down the thick, white, spa-like terrycloth robe down from the back of the bathroom door and covered myself before stepping back out in front of any cameras.

I grabbed one of the big bath sheet luxurious towels off of the bar by the shower and went padding barefoot through the house to retrace my steps to the beautiful, gilded mosaic swimming pool with its crystal blue waters in the depths of the large house.

I set my towel aside on one of the lounge chairs and took a deep breath. Even knowing Lach wasn't home, knowing that Roan was in the kitchen didn't help... I always felt like eyes were on me and some-how, it was worse being in the skimpy bathing suit than it had been with Lach moving inside of me, my body pressed between his and the window glass.

Did that make me crazy? I don't know... I honestly think it had to do less with them than it did with *me* at this point. Lach had had me, but I was quickly realizing that I wanted Roan. It was confusing, slightly dirty, and left my mind reeling in so many ways.

I dove into the deep end of the warm pool as I thought about it.

I felt things for the both of them, some rooted in the distant past where Kyle was concerned, but those feelings were strong and it was, as yet, undecided if they would survive the cold, brutal nature of the man now in juxtaposition of the strangely warm yet wintry boy that he had been.

Roan, on the other hand, was easy to love. Pragmatic, yes, but warm, caring, loyal, and so beautiful in his perceived brokenness. I wished, in some ways, that he could see himself through my eyes… he was so incredibly gentle and firm despite his infirmities and the more I got to know him, the harder it was becoming to walk away. He cared so deeply and I could see it every time he looked at me.

I swam laps, back and forth, and it was as though each man stood at one end of the pool from the other. Back and forth, back and forth, I went until I was breathing hard and no less confused than when I had first entered the water.

There was a click and a buzz and Roan's voice came over a house intercom system.

"Tea will be served at half past the hour, Poppet."

I stilled, treading water, chest heaving, and when I had half caught it, I made my way to the ladder out of the pool.

I toweled off and wrapped myself in the robe and sighed, arm muscles trembling with fatigue.

I was no less unwrapped from the two men than when I had entered the water, the gordian knot of my emotions and anxiety surrounding my current living situation drawing ever tighter around me. A strange, displaced torture that was at once unusual and familiar, filling me as I made my way back to my room, looking for a clock to tell me precisely what time it was *now* as I made my way.

The torture I was feeling over the two men who had crashed into my life was unusual in that I wasn't so used to being lavished with attention. No, I was the forgotten girl. Just another orphan waif of Indigo City's mean streets. A poor unfortunate soul who was used to going unseen and who, when I did manage to be seen by someone, was keenly aware of how much that person wished I could go back to being out of sight and out of mind. Sometimes, I wished I could go back to being unseen, too… except now.

The familiar part of these strange anxieties I was having was just that… the anxiety itself. I was used to being anxious and on guard for a variety of reasons, just now all of those reasons had been upended and drastically changed.

Before, it was where would my next meal come from? Would I find a dry place to sleep? If I got sick, what would I do? Where would I go? Now… I just felt like I should be doing *something*, anything to continue existing. My lack of having to do everything in my power to basically *survive* was leaving me at loose odds and ends and it was enough to drive me *crazy*.

I didn't know how to just… be.

I found a clock in one of the halls and realized I needed to hurry up. I had just enough time to shower and find something to put on to meet Roan for dinner and now I was looking forward to seeing him.

When I was around Roan, I had something to do… talk, watch whatever he was doing, just *something* to fill that void that simply surviving day to day had filled.

I showered quickly, soaping and rinsing my hair, drying it which still felt like a strange habit to do, luxurious and indulgent, so of course I did it every time I showered. Dressing was another story. I paused at the open wardrobe, eyes roving over the fairy dresses and lingerie. I could always change back into the clothes Roan had taken me out in but…

I swallowed hard, realizing that it *was* Roan.

Roan who chose everything for me… who obviously delighted in dressing me in all these pretty things, which yes, they clung in places yet flowed in others but the one concession I had to give each and every article of clothing that he had chosen? That despite leaving little to the imagination everything in this wardrobe was exceedingly *comfortable* and felt so good against my skin.

My mind made up, I donned one of my secretly favorite night-gowns. Long, creamy satin. Glamourous, beautiful, and clinging in all the right places making me look like a nineteen-fifties bombshell.

I braided my hair over my shoulder and pinched my cheeks in front of the bathroom mirror and with a sigh, pleased with how I looked, I went to find Roan.

I found him in the big, formal dining room, setting a platter of finely sliced meat on the table runner, two places set, one at the head of the table and one beside it.

"Ah, there you are," he said looking me over, a smile curling his generous lips. "Lovely."

I blushed beneath the compliment and he limped my way, holding out a hand to me. I took it and he drew me into the room, the bank of floor to ceiling windows along one side providing a view of the lights of Indigo City glittering along the wavering surface of the Chesapeake. The lights of the bay bridge a steady line in the distance, a pearl necklace on the grand body of water's bosom.

"Have you not seen the view from in here?" he asked.

"Surprisingly, not after dark, no…" I murmured.

"Ah."

He stood with me, soaking up that marvelous view for a time. His touch, when it landed on my shoulder, was light, almost a caress. I looked up at him and he smiled down at me and murmured, "Come sit, before things get cold."

"Sorry, right!" I laughed at myself and lightly shook my head hoping somehow to clear it.

Roan guided me to the seat beside his at the head of the table and pulled the chair out for me, I sat and he helped scoot me closer. I looked up to that fantastical view once more as he took his seat.

We'd never taken a meal like this… together, in the formal dining room, I mean. Usually, I was either served in my room or, once or twice, we had stood at the kitchen counter and eaten. This was a departure from that. Oddly formal, and it felt… different. His effort showing in gleaming silverware, platters, and fine China.

"This is all so beautiful." I made it a point to compliment his efforts. I wanted him to know, I *saw him*, not just his physical self but that he cared. I wanted him to know that I cared, too. His smile was plenty a reward and brought an answering one to my lips as he dished up some of the slices of duck onto my plate and laid an artful arc of cranberry-orange sauce over the neat little fan of slices.

A warm, red beet salad came next, and some lovely roasted fingerling potatoes. He finished the meal by pouring a bit of Pinot Noire into the waiting cut crystal wine glass in front of me.

"I thought you didn't drink," I said softly eyeing the empty wine glass in front of him. "Not a judgment at all," I quickly rushed out. "It just surprises me, that's all."

"Ah." He nodded and smiled a bit ruefully. He set the bottle down and didn't pour any for himself. "Just because I choose not to, does not mean you need to abstain. My troubles with alcohol are mine. I don't make others responsible for my comfort nor my sobriety."

I felt myself turn as red as the wine in my glass.

"I'm really sorry," I murmured. "It really isn't any of my business. You're a grown man and I—"

"Stop," he said gently, and I lifted my eyes to meet his steady gaze above an equally steady and pleased smile.

"You care," he said. "It's not from a place of judgment. I know the difference, Poppet."

"Right," I murmured, nodding. "Sorry."

"What for?" he asked, taking a sip from his water glass.

"I really shouldn't jump to conclusions. You've sort of always done what's best for me since I was brought here and I really don't want to make you feel—"

He chuckled. "I'm sorry," he said. "I'm not laughing at you, love. I'm laughing at… well… 'sort of?'"

"Hey, to be fair there was that one time you hog-tied me on my bed almost naked."

"To be fair," he argued good naturedly, "that was *after* you pulled my best kitchen knife on me."

I blushed and nodded slowly. "Which was rude, and for that I'm sorry."

"Not at all, it was perfectly understandable given the circumstances at the time." He had set down his glass and was rubbing the sweating cylinder up and down between forefinger and thumb, staring into the cool, clear liquid thoughtfully as I tried my duck.

Mm, perfect as always… he was a real talent in the kitchen.

"I'll forgive you if you'll forgive me," I murmured softly and his green gaze flicked from his water to my eyes.

"There's nothing to forgive," he murmured back, the silence stretching between us.

We ate quietly for a while and I complimented the food on its flavor at least once. As we were nearing the end of our meal together, Roan asked me, "Would you like to watch a film with me?"

"What, tonight?" I asked, taken aback. He'd never asked me for anything like this.

"Yes," he said, and I smiled and nodded.

"I'd like that," I said not at all surprised to find it was true. I couldn't remember the last time I'd enjoyed a movie. I'd found the large television in the living room and its entertainment center with all its remotes intimidating, so I hadn't honestly tried to watch anything yet.

"What are we watching?" I asked curiously.

"An old favorite of mine if you don't mind," he said. I cocked my head, and he smiled. *"The Bridge on the River Kwai."*

"Never heard of it," I said, shaking my head slowly. "What's it about?"

"Ah, a true classic. Released in nineteen fifty-seven and starring Alec Guinness."

"I don't… I don't know who that is," I said laughing lightly.

"You would know his much older self as Obi-Wan Kenobi in the original *Star Wars* films starring Carrie Fisher and Harrison Ford."

"Oh, I know who they are."

"Aye." He laughed.

I scooted back and got up with Roan, saying, "Here. You let me get this. You cook and clean all the time… let me do the dishes and you go get comfortable and set up the movie. I'll meet you there."

"Are you certain?" he asked, skeptically.

I nodded. "Please. It's honestly driving me more than a little crazy not having anything to do." I smoothed my slightly sweaty palms along the satin over my outer thighs with the admission. "You spend all day every day in survival mode and suddenly you don't have to… it's sort of an abrupt change, you know? Don't get me wrong! It's not unpleasant by any means, it's just a wild period of adjustment, I think. I'd just really like to help. Do something useful and keep my hands busy, if that's alright."

"Of course," he said, inclining his head. "Just no sharp knives in the dishwasher and the same with the real silver. Just stack them beside the sink and I'll contend with those tomorrow.

"Okay," I said with a smile.

He unhooked his cane from the back of his chair and came toward me, stopping beside me with a gentle hand on my waist to lean down and kiss my forehead. I closed my eyes under that comforting touch and melted a little from it.

"I shall see you in the lounge," he murmured.

"Is that Brit for living room?" I asked softly.

"It is, very good, Poppet."

I glowed a little from the praise and watched his suited back leave out through the doorway into the rest of the mansion. With a settling sigh, I gathered some things and backed through the door into the kitchen, half expecting to find Kyle eavesdropping but there was no one. I wondered, idly, as I rinsed things and cleaned up if he would be coming back tonight.

I still wanted to talk to him, but the Kyle of then matched the Kyle of now in one regard – he was going to do whatever he wanted to do whenever he wanted to do it.

"The more things change, the more they stay the same," I murmured to myself.

I finished up the nominal number of dishes, grateful that Roan was good about cleaning as he went, and washed my hands at the sink, drying them on one of the nearby kitchen towels. I smiled at how much of this house I considered Roan's domain and felt that smile slip when I wondered just where Lach tended to lurk when he was home.

Sighing, I pushed Kyle Lachlan from my mind and went out into the living room, decidedly *not* looking at the window where Kyle and I had been and instead focusing on Roan who was closing one of the cabinet doors on the entertainment center before turning. I let my eyes rove over him curiously.

"What? What is it?" he asked looking down at himself.

"Nothing!" I cried, laughing. "I've just never seen you in anything other than a suit."

Which was true. Now, he wore a crisp, white cotton tee-shirt over a pair of loose-fitting blue plaid pajama bottoms, his feet in a pair of sheepskin slippers.

"You look… cozy."

He chuckled and waved me in the direction of the couch, limping around the coffee table to take one end. I stepped down into the living room and came around the couch, settling myself nearby him.

The giant, and I do mean *giant* television screen lit up as he manipulated buttons on the remote that he held.

I took the time that he was otherwise focused to study his profile… he was painfully handsome. Not even close to Kyle who had always been painfully beautiful to me. No, Roan was ruggedly handsome. Strong jaw shadowed with copper stubble, an equally strong nose but not out of place on his face. His shoulders were broad beneath the thin cover of his soft looking tee and they tapered down to a trim waist despite all the rich and decadent food we seemed to eat. I mean, I was filling out already, and I'd only been here a matter of a few weeks… a month or more? Really, time was beginning to blur together. One day bleeding into the next and onto the next…

"You alright, love?" I shook myself as though coming awake.

"What? Yeah!"

He stopped what he was doing and eyed me critically as I felt myself blush.

"I'm fine, I swear," I said breathlessly. It was hard to be anything else when he looked at me like that. He was breathtaking when he turned the full force of his green eyes onto me.

Maybe it was a trick he learned from Kyle… and maybe it was. Kyle had the same effect when he turned his dark, almost black, gaze on me.

"He thinks we should share you," he said abruptly, and I gave one long, slow blink as I tried to comprehend what had just come out of his mouth.

"I'm sorry, what?" I asked, completely taken aback.

"Bollocks," he muttered and sighed, closing his eyes.

"No, go back, I need you to repeat what you said." I needed to be sure I'd heard him correctly.

"No, forget I said anything," he said, and I shook my head.

"You're not getting this genie back into the bottle," I told him gently. "Please, just tell me what he said."

He took a deep breath and let it out in an explosive rush and repeated himself, "Lach thinks he and I should share you. Told me I should recruit you to come around to the idea of it."

I was shook.

I stared at Roan for several silent moments that felt like minutes but was likely barely two seconds…

"What like a timeshare?" I asked sarcastically.

"That phrase was mentioned," he said unhappily. "Three days with me, three days with him and one to yourself if you'd like."

I swallowed hard and stared at Conan Roan for what felt like forever as something like *relief* flooded me…

You don't have to choose… you could have your cake and eat it, too.

"How long do I have to decide?" I asked, turning the thought over and over in my mind. "I mean…" I shook my head as though to clear it, and asked, "Is that what *you* want?"

"It doesn't matter what I want, love. It matters what's best for you." I tore my gaze from where it'd fixed itself to my knee and swept it back to the utter, solemn sincerity in his eyes and whatever misgivings I had started to crumble and break.

"If you had to choose, though?" I asked.

"If I had a choice? I'm a selfish bastard Sadie Brooks… I would have you any way I could get you," he confessed. He swallowed hard and looked like he was vaguely ill as he said, "But it's not my choice, and you're not to be passed around like some… some…"

"Joint?" I suggested. "Or bottle?"

He pursed his lips, and I closed my eyes and shook my head slightly.

"Shut up, just stop being so… so… *noble* for one god damned minute and be honest with me." He looked at me, and I swear he was holding his breath. "Do you think it could work?"

"Aye," he murmured, barely above a whisper. "Aye, I think it could work." His voice held caution as though he dared to dream.

I nodded slowly and scooted closer and he twisted, putting his good leg up onto the couch and opening his arms to me. I laid down against him gingerly, and put my ear over his heart, tucking one arm between him and the back of the couch, laying the other along his chest.

"Play the movie," I murmured quietly, and he hit the button on the remote to play the film, turning up the volume that he'd had all the way down while we'd talked. His hand fell lightly against my back and I closed my eyes for a moment, relishing the comforting touch.

He didn't say anything, and I didn't either; instead, we watched his old film and cuddled on the couch, each of us lost in our own thoughts. Mine, particularly bizarre and whirling in circles over what Roan had told me. I had no reason to doubt him, I mean he was loyal and honest… and it was so something Kyle with his pragmatic ways would say.

"You alright, love?" he asked midway through the film, pausing the screen.

"Yeah, why? You need to get up?"

"Aye."

"Oh, sorry!" I went to push my way off of him and sank into the couch awkwardly. He chuckled, and I sputtered a laugh and I put my hand on his chest to try again and froze, catching the look in his eyes. We stared at one another from inches away and his hand swept along my cheek in a light caress. I leaned forward slowly, cautiously, and he met me halfway, our lips touching and all the tension and worry I carried about this attraction and whether it was mutual simply drained away.

Roan made a strangled noise, as though her were a man who had been dying inside only to receive the breath of life. The kiss was sweet, and merciful to me, too… and all too damnably short.

"I'll return shortly," he murmured and with his help, I levered myself up. He got to his feet and limped in the direction of the first-floor bathroom, adjusting himself carefully once his back was to me. I blushed furiously and covered my face with my hands as I flopped back down onto the couch with an explosion of breath.

Holy cow! That just happened!

Everything was moving at the speed of *light* in this new life and it was both exhilarating as it was terrifying.

So many 'what-ifs' played out in my brain.

What if Kyle couldn't adhere to the deal? What if Roan couldn't? What if I couldn't keep them happy? Would I be alright with letting one or both of them go? Was I strong enough for this?

I took my hands away from my face when I heard Roan's uneven, shuffling gait returning across the hardwood. I sat up and looked at him from over the back of the couch. He smiled at me and I couldn't help but smile back. He looked equal parts pleased and nervous and that surprisingly, somehow, helped allay some of my fears.

"Welcome back," I whispered, and he leaned down carefully, brushing his lips against mine. I welcomed the light kiss and again, it was too short.

"Thank you," he whispered back softly, and we re-situated ourselves. He pulled the throw off of the back of the couch and wrapped it around my shoulders, his hand smoothing against the skin of my exposed back beneath it, warm and heavy, a comforting weight.

The *Bridge on the River Kwai* was a *long* movie, but it was a good one. By the end, I was awash in comfort and warmth and was drowsing mightily as the credits rolled. Roan shook me gently awake.

"Mm," I murmured in protest.

"I think it's bedtime for you, Poppet."

"Mm-hm," I agreed sleepily. "Your bed or mine?"

He hesitated, and I looked up at him, "Doesn't have to be for sex," I said hastily, in case he totally didn't want me that way. Also, I didn't want him to feel like I was throwing myself at him. I mean, yikes! Had I just screwed everything up? I swallowed hard, looking at him and murmured, "I just like cuddling with you."

His smile was pleased when I said the last and I felt a tightness borne of anxiety ease in my chest. He said gently, "Mine if you don't mind."

I smiled back and said, "That's why I asked."

CHAPTER SEVENTEEN

*R*oan...

As much as it would have pleased me, I couldn't carry Sadie from the lounge to my bedroom. In fact, it rather pained me. The blow Lach had dealt to my leg in our fight had left more than just wounded pride.

She was going to be the death of me. I almost felt the fool as the two of us walked the short distance from where we had sat, cuddled, to where my bed was. *Had she really kissed me?*

She had. My lips tingled with the memory of it.

I was indeed a great giant fool, feeling like I was being tormented.

She kissed me. She kissed me and wanted to cuddle in my bed.

I took a deep breath and opened the door. This wasn't the first time she had been there, but it was the first time she was going to my bed. She was there for me. My heart trembled, and my hands were filled with nervous energy. I drew the covers back, and she slipped underneath them at my urging. Her hair now loosed from its braid formed a glorious mane around her head, like a halo of beauty. I reached to turn off the bedside lamp, as she was pulling herself close to me.

"Leave it on, it's not so bright," Sadie murmured. She was warm and soft, pressed against me. I felt painfully aware of two things, the dead weight of the prosthetic, and how I was modestly erect. My cock wasn't throbbing or fully hard yet, but it would be soon enough.

I removed the prosthetic and quietly let it slide to the floor. With that released from me, it was easier to move under the covers, and to return her embrace. I rested my face against the top of her head and softly inhaled her scent.

I let my hand trace the slope of her neck out to the point of her shoulder, a flawless line. I could feel her warm breath against my chest through the thin cotton of my tee, and the brush of her lips against my own shoulder. I eased my caress down her shoulder blade to run a course down her ribs, not so prominent as they had been when she'd first arrived, and down to her hip. There, my palm rested flat against her raised hip, and I contemplated following the natural line down her thigh to the knee, or a different direction. The other direction, my hand went there, caressing and cupping her bottom.

I felt the first aching throb between my legs. I wanted her.

I was no better than Lach with her, this vulnerable beautiful creature… I was quite simply not at all good enough, but was anyone? I felt her lips against my neck, and her small hands caressing against my own chest. She was exploring me just as I was touching her.

Did she actually desire me?

That was impossible, not with my scars, not with my old injuries.

She leaned her head back, and I felt drawn to her. Our lips met again, and there was another pulse of electricity through me. Her kiss was so soft, so warm. I could get deliriously lost in her kisses.

"What is that?" she whispered, and I jerked back, turning my hips slightly away from her. She pulled my shirt up, and rather than mocking modesty I let her help me pull it off.

"It's nothing," I said, and gave her another kiss.

"It felt like an awful lot to be nothing." Her voice held an edge of a teasing smile as she caught my lower lip gently between her teeth for a second. I groaned, caught by her words, and still cupping her bottom in the palm of my hand.

"That's more than cuddling," I said softly.

"I really don't mind," she whispered, and her tone lost all of its levity of a moment before. I relaxed, slightly. I felt her lips on mine again, and it was bloody joyous. Her hands found themselves against my skin traveling over my abdominals and chest; intrepid little hands they were, sliding over slick scar tissue and whole flesh as though they were one and the same. I don't know if it was her touch, or my own need but I let myself give in to desire, to touch something more than her bottom. I trailed my fingers from her hip upwards to find the glorious yielding softness of her breast.

It was touching heaven, her nipple firm under the sheer slick fabric. It was easy to liberate her shoulder and then she was bare to me. I cupped her breast and traded her lips for a taste of neck, and a brush of my lips across her collar bone. I took her nipple in my mouth and kissed it. Her hand was in my hair, the other still against my body, trapped between us.

Her moan was silk against my ear. "Conan, yes."

"I should tell you—" I started to speak, but she pulled my face into her chest, silencing me. I wanted to tell her that it had been quite a while, and that I didn't know how well I might do. All the worries and insecurities were close to the surface, only held in check by how much I desired her. Those unwelcome thoughts faded from my mind as I succumbed to her scent, and my own want.

Did I dare?

I thought of how quick Lach had been, how inconsiderate.

I *did* dare.

The movement was nowhere near as smooth as I wanted it to be. I moved down her torso, my lips going to places my hand had been moments earlier. I kissed the dip of her hip and then lower. She turned, and it was to make herself more available to my attentions. I pulled the hem of her gown up, sliding it across her thighs. The material made a nearly silent whisper against her skin, and it was the only thing I was aware of.

My heart was pulsing in my fingers and my face, I felt the skin of her thigh against my lip and I kissed it. Had I been this excited my first time? *No.* The first time I had been an arrogant cocky bastard, convinced I was the dog's bollocks, and spent entirely too long thinking that those first few minutes of urgent thrusting and a panicked attempt at pulling out in time ranked me in the same bracket as Casanova, Romeo Montague, and a VHS porn star. More experience taught me my flaws and conceits, and that was well before the roadside bomb removed half my leg.

My breath caught in my throat, I had expected to find lace or frills, at least one pair of her panties had a bow on them... There was nothing beneath my lips, no satin, no silk, no lace, just smooth skin and a brush of hair. She had nothing on under the nightgown. I shuddered.

I kissed, my lips slowly, patiently, seeking her secret pleasure.

I found smooth skin and then the sacred cleft, and then I tasted her.

Which was sweeter, her pussy or the moan she released, I couldn't guess.

I went down on her with a passion, seeking both the parts of her that made her cry out, and the parts that I was sure that weren't shown the attention they deserved. Her fingers gripped my hair, and it didn't take much attentiveness for her to have her hips moving to put my tongue, my face, where she wanted it.

I ached for her.

Her pussy clenched and released, she sang out a one note song, and then she came. I looked up to see her breasts heaving and a dreamy look in her eyes. My cock strained against the front of my lounge pants and she looked from me down to it and then back. She nodded so slightly that if I had blinked, I would have missed it. I yanked the drawstring loose and pulled the waist of my pants down, finally freeing my aching cock.

If her previous gestures had been minimalist, this one was a surprise. I was fully erect and as I was released from the confines of underwear and pants, I could see a streamer flowing from the head of my raging hard-on. There was a curious look in her eyes, a touch of fear, a measure of awe, and no small amount of desire.

"Wait, let me first," she gasped softly. I felt a moment of confusion until she reached down and wrapped her hand around the base of my cock. "My God, look at this thing," she said almost to herself.

"You don't have to," I stammered. I had intended to mount her, gently, slowly. Now I was giving up ground, and she was rising, still gripping my pride firmly. I felt a churn of emotion in my guts, she didn't have to go down on me. Part of me didn't want her to. Some of that was my own baggage, and some of it was simple vanity. I didn't want her to see the scars, the ghosts of stitches, or the stump.

She stroked me slowly several times, and I tried not to groan, but I couldn't help it. She made a soft sound I couldn't describe and then I felt her tongue on the head of my cock. I groaned again, and this seemed to amuse her.

"This is certainly impressive," she said before going down on me. I had to stop her after what felt like an embarrassingly short amount of time. I felt like I could be seconds away from climax and the last thing I wanted to do was give her a rude blast in the face. My bollocks tightened, and I begged her to stop.

She came off my shaft and rested her head against my truncated leg. Her face inches from the ugly stump where flesh ended and only phantom sensation remained. She slowly stroked me, and I could almost feel her gaze on my cock, she had barely managed to get half of it in her mouth, maybe less. Her hair moved against my thigh and I knew that she was looking at the scars, the things I had worked so hard to hide. I hadn't let any lover previous see what she was looking at. I felt a knot of tension draw tight below my breastbone, and then there was the softest touch above my knee.

She was kissing my ugly scars, her beautiful lips against my ruined roughly healed flesh. I couldn't do anything, her hand around my shaft had me all but paralyzed. "Sadie," was all I could manage. My eyes stung and I could feel tears starting to well up at the corners, then run hot down the sides of my face.

I felt like an emotional train wreck. I couldn't have been any further from my normal stoic self that I was at that moment. She took me in her mouth again, and I felt a hot streak of tear run down my temple. I was glad she couldn't see that, what would she think? I wiped the tear away.

"I can't go all the way down on it," she said. "There's more there than I've ever seen." Her statement ended in a bravely nervous laugh.

"You don't," I said, my voice raw. "You don't have to, what you're doing…" She went back down on me again, and gave my balls a firm massaging grip. "Oh God," I groaned. She bobbed a few more times, trying again to take all of me into her mouth.

"I can't!" she gasped, releasing my cock with a loud wet noise. I shuddered. She looked up at me, and gave it a few strokes, squeezing on the upstroke. "Maybe with a little practice." She smiled and giggled sweetly.

"Maybe." I gave her a weak laugh, but it was damned hard to think with her tugging on me like she was. "Why don't you roll over on your side, and we can do something a little more like cuddling?" She smiled at me, gave my cock one last, extra firm squeeze, and then she did as I asked.

"Like this?" she asked, turning her bottom toward me.

"Aye, just like that." I put one arm under her neck, and with the other took a hold of my cock, it was slippery wet with her attention and my need. I rubbed my head between her legs, feeling how slick and hot she was, she was so very ready. She lifted her leg slightly and kissed my arm where her face rested against it.

I eased the tip inside her. She groaned into the flesh of my arm.

A bit more, slowly.

"Oh my God," she rasped. I hesitated; it was important to not rush here.

"Is this okay?" I whispered. I felt her nod her head.

"Yeah, yeah, I'm *very* okay," she gasped softly. I pushed a bit more. She shifted her hips, and arched her back more, making more room to accommodate my size. The tension eased, and I sank the rest of my length into her. I could feel her tremble, and her breath fanned hot against my arm. She shuddered and moaned when I started to pull out again.

"That was almost all of it," I said.

"Almost?" She was breathless.

"Almost," I agreed.

"I want all of it." She pushed back against me, and I obliged. I gave her the full length, gently, and slowly. There were too many instances in the past where I had not gauged such things correctly, and thinking size was everything I had rushed, become a battering ram or a jackhammer. Those women didn't orgasm, they didn't enjoy it, and eventually I realized that was what had been wrong.

I found my own pleasure not just from them, from the use of their lips and pussies and tits, but from *pleasing them.* Making them coo and come, that was far better and far more enjoyable. I learned I was capable of that. I kept my pace steady and slow. I would be able to go faster, but not yet. She still hadn't fully relaxed enough to take me at anything more than gentle.

Lach didn't have this problem, he didn't have to be this cautious or considerate. He wasn't small, and if the women had complaints, they were never about his equipment. He was, well, normal sized. Why in the bloody hell was I thinking about him at a time like this? I finally let the fullness of my cock fill Sadie, pushing until my hips were firm against hers.

"There is so much," Sadie whispered. "It almost hurts."

"I'm sorry, Poppet," I said and eased my cock completely out of her.

"That didn't mean *stop*, Conan." She reached down between her legs to grasp my cock. "Put it back in, please."

I entered her again, slowly as I had before. It seemed like a blissful eternity, giving her gentle slow half strokes, and listening to her make those delicate small sounds. I felt a certain tension start growing in the base of my cock, a tightening in my bollocks. I let myself flow into a meditative mindspace, focusing on my breathing, the steady movement of my body, and her body against mine.

"Oh shit," I groaned as the spasm pulsed through me and I felt the first jet of cum. I hadn't even thought of one of the condoms in the nightstand, and I knew she wasn't on any sort of birth control; at least not to my knowledge anyway. I tried to pull out but I could only shudder as my orgasm wasn't going to be denied or interrupted. I finally managed to get free of her pussy so that the last few squirts of cum decorated the inside of her thigh.

"Put it back, put it back in." She sighed.

I was never one to disobey a lady, so I did. I quivered, my cock was powerfully sensitive, and she ground against me a few times, and I could feel our mess running out of her. She started clenching around me, and then she gave a shriek and all but collapsed against me.

"That was incredible," she whispered and kissed my arm.

"It was," I agreed, my own breath spent and my cock finally growing soft inside her.

"I am going to be hella sore." She snuggled against me. "But totally worth it."

I put my arms around her and smiled. There were things that wanted my attention, but they would have to wait. I wanted to stay in this moment, content, and spent.

Could this work? I certainly hoped it could.

CHAPTER EIGHTEEN

*L*ach...

The Meerschaum Tobacconist was the sort of place that Roan would have adored, with its dark wood-paneled walls, antique brass light fixtures, and all that stately pompousness. It was expensive, hard to get into, and highly desired as a meeting place for self-important wheelers and dealers. The place was saturated with tobacco musk, from the boxes of cigars, to the drying room where there was some artisanal heirloom tobacco being dried and cured under highly controlled conditions. If I smoked, I might appreciate the amount of effort that was going into creating tubes of flammable leaves.

For me, the great appeal of the Meerschaum Tobacconist was their house bar. Getting a seat at that teak plank bar was a seat at the table of Odin. The wood had once been the deck of the battleship USS Maryland, recovered from Pearl Harbor, where she survived the battle. It was a neat piece of history. The thing I was waiting for was the neat glass of the house barrel aged gin. It was as dark as a nice scotch, and the herbal elements wedded to the time it spent in the barrel, perfection.

The person I was here to meet was likewise perfection.

Kaijin had beaten me to the Tobacconist, and she was a piece of art. She could have stepped out of a 1930s pulp art review, in a metallic green silk cocktail dress, trimmed with gold and geometric patterns at the neck and down the seam. Her makeup had the same elegant precision and accented her eyes.

There were tiger women and dragon women, and all the rest of the racist sexist commentary, but seeing her look at me with those almost black eyes, I saw the truth. Kaijin was a serpent – cold, calculating, and without weakness. "I am most glad to see you, Mister Lachlan," she said with a modest accent

"Always a delight, madam," I offered her a polite bow. I gave her a smile, fairly high power. This was a new game, a new dance. And I knew more of the truth about her, the truth behind all the makeup and performance. Her name really wasn't Kaijin, she wasn't any form of Asian. She was American by birth, raised and educated in France, with a degree in theater, and then a strange jag off into the French Foreign Legion. I considered blowing the ruse open with a few lines of Mandarin, or Vietnamese, just for laughs.

This was not the time.

Plus, her cleavage was flawless, and I found it hard to be nasty to a woman so artfully assembled.

"Le Generale is most pleased with your quality of work. Very thorough. Very effective," she nodded. I gestured, and the bartender brought me a second glass of the battleship gin, and one for her. She picked up the glass, swirled it, and delicately sniffed it. She smiled.

"It is very good, especially if you like gin," I offered her a toast. She clinked her glass against mine. "To missions done and cheques cleared."

"Very much yes," she said.

"I will admit that we rarely ever do follow-up consultations." I gave her a small nod.

"I imagine that your employers seldom ever have anything to complain about," she said, taking the first sip. She pursed her lips and made a pleased sound.

"I certainly hope there are no complaints," I said, giving her another one of my high-wattage smiles.

"You are correct, there are no complaints," she said. "Rather, *le Generale* is so pleased with the quality of your work he wants to offer you more."

"My associate and I are open to new opportunities." I took another sip.

"That is most excellent." She smiled. "*Le Generale* would like to bring you and your associate into the fold. You are brisk, efficient, thorough, and by his tastes, accordingly cruel when the case calls for it."

"Cruel?" I asked.

"He quite enjoyed what you did to Reese, with the wire and how he was left to hang until death. He never liked that one and was actually pleased when the younger split from the elder. He was given a free hand to dispose of the prodigal son while keeping the faithful father."

One of the other attractions of the Tobacconist were the match girls. These waitresses strolled through the business carrying a tray loaded with matches, lighters, and samples of some of the house goods, and other small things that the dapper visitor might require. I knew from past experience that there was a compartment on the bottom of the tray that had condoms.

She smiled at the two of us, her hat jauntily askew, and her uniform vintage burlesque inspired. Roan would be in fucking love with this place, it was so much his vibe. Kaijin picked one of the sample Cubans from the tray. She gave me a dragon's smoldering eye, so I picked up one of the silver case lighters and flicked it to life.

She let me light her short cigar and the way she looked up at me, her cheeks pulling in and her lips on the tip could not have been less subtle. What was she willing to do to get me to give her a yes? Given the look on her face I was fairly certain that if I said yes to whatever her offer was, I could probably have every inch of her.

And that she would very precisely remember everything and when the time was right, she would extract her pound of flesh in retribution. It might be worth it, if she was as skilled at what she was insinuating with the cigar.

"Are you offering us a retainer?" I asked, picked up one of my own samples from the tray. I knew this would be expensive, but we had been very well paid. I lit my own and gave it a few puffs. It was sharp and acrid, and it took most of my self-control to not immediately start coughing it back out.

Tear gas training made suppressing cigar smoke easy.

"More than a retainer," she said, smoke forming a halo around her head. "An invitation to join the Cartel Escadrille."

"To join?" I asked.

"Yes, following the elimination of the disloyal members of the Cartel we have openings, and an idea to reorganize. Considering how much we paid you, you can correctly assume that you stand to make drastically more money."

"My partner and I are freelancers; we don't join anyone's personal crusades or factions." I gave her a slight bow.

"This is not an offer you want to reject," she said, her eyes narrowed.

"I find it deeply difficult to a beautiful woman no," I said.

"Then don't. Mister Lachlan, don't," she said. Her tone was half sex and half menace.

"Gwendolyn," I said. "I can talk this over with my partner, but I already know the answer. We are independent contractors. We have done short-term retainers, but that's all."

"You should talk this over with your partner. I can offer you many different incentives, beyond financial opportunities." Her fingernails were long, exquisitely lacquered, and there were animals on them, but her fingers moved too fast and I couldn't make them out. The craftsmanship was as flawless as the rest of her.

I prayed that she had some elaborate Yakuza style tattoos across her body, that would make it perfect.

"We appreciate the offer, but very politely decline," I said. "Can I get you another drink?"

"You can, and you can tell me what I could offer you to... reconsider, your answer."

"My partner," and for some reason I found myself thinking of

Sadie, "and I are happy with our current setup. We work when we want to, and when we want to take time off, we are free to do so."

"But what about the money," she said.

"We don't work because we have bills to pay, I could retire today and not have to worry about bringing in another dollar." I accepted what would be my third glass of gin. I tried not to think about how much this bill was going to be. I could afford it, but that wasn't the point.

"Retirement might be another option," she said.

"We work because we want to," I said. "On our own terms, our independence means quite a bit to us."

"*Le Generale* considers you such a fine assassin, he would dread to think if someone were to hire you to eliminate him, or damage his operation." She ran her hand down the front of her dress, drawing attention to her cleavage, and I could see that each fingernail had its own, different animal on it. I saw a panda, a dragon, and a koi fish.

"I think it is very unlikely," I said, "In the years that we've been doing this there has never been an instance where a new employer has contracted us to deal with a previous employer."

"So, you have a guarantee that if such an event occurred, that you would refuse the offer. Would you even be obligated to let a - former employer - know about such activities?" Her eyes were hard.

"I can talk to my partner about that, it's never come up before," I said. My gut had turned cold.

"*Le Generale* would also be interested in meeting you, and your partner, in person," she said.

"We appreciate the offer, but unless you have a contract to carry out, I think we're done here." Her expression was carved from ice.

"I think you should talk to your partner, Mister Lachlan, and consider the consequences of your potential answer. Your partner might have some insight that you might be overlooking."

"I'll take that under consideration," I said. She kissed me on the cheek, and I could smell her perfume, lilacs and something fruity.

She turned and walked away from me. Her dress was so tight

across her ass that I half wondered how she got into it, and how she walked without it splitting like a banana peel.

I finished my third round in a gulp and gestured for the bill.

I needed another drink after handing over my charge card.

I HELD THE KEYS TO THE NEW AUDI IN MY HAND, NORMALLY A DRINK OR two and I was still fine to drive, but three in so short a span? That was too much. I pulled out my phone, toggled the ride share app and called for a top end car to come pick me up and take me back to the house. It was a little pricey going that far, but it was cheaper than tearing out the side of the car or ending up crossways with the local police for riding over the line more than once.

I didn't have to wait long, and a Mercedes driver was exactly as his five-star rating claimed. In the fairly long drive back to Bootlegger Head, the only time he spoke to me was to ask if I had a music preference, which I did not, and if I wanted conversation, which I did not. He dropped me at the head of the driveway and I walked the last few hundred feet from the gate to the house in silence. I did give him a five-star rating, and a large tip. Still only a fraction of how much I had spent at the Tobacconist just to tell a smoking hot woman no.

I felt like there might be something wrong with me. It wasn't so long ago that I would have taken her up on her offer just to see how far she would go, what she was willing to do to get the answer she wanted. I would have taken so much advantage of that.

Oh, and yes, I would have taken so much advantage of *her*. I keyed the combination and unlocked the door, and let myself in. When the door shut, I heard the electronic lock engage again and the deadbolt turn with its magnetic whatever that made it work. Roan's wizardry, that. I walked to the Black-Eyed Susan, and it seemed like a sad little hobby bar compared to the decadence and heaviness that had been the Tobacconist. I would have bought some of their barrel aged gin, even an entire barrel of it, but that was a hard no. They only sold it by the glass.

My loss.

Praise God and one-legged Brits, I had a new bottle of that crazy botanical infused gin, and a few others. Was that a sprig of rosemary in the bottle? I poured a measure of the gin, and by God it had a slightly green tint to it.

It was the nectar of some fertility and harvest goddess.

Splendid.

I was in Roan's bar, when I could have been balls deep in Gwendolyn Kaijin's asshole, listening to her make the high-pitch sounds and animal noises that women made when they discovered that they liked it like that. I took a drink directly from the bottle.

I was too restless to go to bed, and there was a bit too much alcohol in me for that to be a good idea. I wandered through the house and into the living room, the big television was still on, holding at the end credits for one of Roan's old long ass movies. I picked up the remote to see what he had inflicted on Sadie. Spaghetti western? Some classic where the last surviving actor was a crusty old 118-year-old woman the size of a Pomeranian?

The Kwai movie, God, that was a long one. I still had avoided sitting through the entirety of it.

I went to the Bat Cave next and dropped down into his captain's seat. The only thing missing were controls on the arms of the chair. I pulled up his keyboard and started scrolling through the last few hours of house feeds.

They literally sat and watched the entire movie all snuggled up on the couch.

The thirty seconds it took to speed through that still felt like an eternity. Oh, they're getting up.

I clicked through the feeds, central hallway. Oh, her nightdress was backless. That was nice.

They were going to his bedroom.

I hit the pause button.

Shit.

Could I watch this?

There was nothing I could do, the timestamp at the bottom of the screen had this starting hours ago. I had still been at the Tobacconist when this went down. Whatever they were going to do, it was already over.

The live feed showed lights off, they were asleep. I was the only person awake in the house. I could feel my heart quicken with a stab of anticipation, a little anxiety.

I settled myself and hit play.

They kissed for a really long time, but there was plenty I could see, Sadie's gown was thin, and fell off of her easily. I saw the shadow of her breast and it was glorious.

I was almost going to start fast forwarding through this, when they started actually doing something interesting, and then Roan was going down on her. I had never gone down on her. I had kissed her a few times, made it to second base a few times, and finally having her, but I didn't know how she tasted. My cock twitched, and I felt myself starting to get hard.

Apparently, I had not had enough alcohol to hamper that response.

This seemed to occupy them for some time. They moved, and then I saw Roan. I knew he was well endowed; I had seen him naked more than once, but that wasn't the same as seeing him fully hard, and then Sadie going down on him.

She was obviously intimidated by him, but she was not a coward and she rarely, if ever, backed down, and she wasn't going to be put off by this challenge. She worked him, and I could see when she was just sucking him off, and when she put what she had into trying to take all of him. There was no way, but she tried. I unzipped my trousers and started stroking myself.

I wasn't going to be fucking Kaijin tonight, and likely never after how she had all but threatened me, so there was a knot of frustration growing in my gut. I wanted Sadie at that moment, I wanted to grab her hips and slide my cock into her, fuck her, while she choked herself on his meat. She managed to get a lot of him into her mouth, and I wanted that too. She could probably deep throat everything I had if she could get that much of him. I groaned at the thought.

They talked, then she would suck him some more, then more

words. There was no audio track, and I wanted to know what they were talking about. What did he have to say, discussing dinner plans, the thematic points of Kwai, the cost of tea in China? Then they changed their position, he rolled her onto her side and her pussy seemed tiny compared to him.

I felt my pulse throb.

They were slow, and I couldn't not watch him vanish into her, less than an inch at a time.

My eyes were glued to the screen, watching his fat cock plow in and out of her at a pace that was almost excruciatingly slow. I can see how wet she was even through the limited field of the camera. By the time he was finally fucking her at a good pace I was jerking off.

I felt a curious feeling. I wasn't jealous, I didn't have those stabbing possessive or aggressive urges. No. I wanted her, and I wanted him with her too. I didn't want his cock out of her pussy, I wanted her to be sucking on my cock while he fucked her. I wanted her asshole wrapped around my dick, him still inside her, my Sadie skewered between us.

I wanted my cum on her; I wanted to see it run out of her holes, down her chin, all over her tits. I jerked quicker, and I saw their pace quicken and then Roan started bucking and trying to grab his cock. He finally got it pulled out, and I realized that he had come himself. He managed a few little dribbles down her thigh, I could imagine his methodical and cautious panic.

He didn't know she had an IUD; I'd gone to the clinic with her when we were kids. Had been prepared to lie my ass off and convince them I was her guardian so she could get one. Turned out, we didn't need to. Maryland was a blue state and all she'd needed to do was go in, prove she was over the age of sixteen and they gave her one. I knew Sadie. She would still have it. No way she would give that up. I knew what she'd feared, and I'd been her black knight back then. I was her dark knight now… I guess that made Roan her white one.

She grabbed him, and I saw him quiver in her grip and he she put him back inside her, I watched her grind her hips against him until she shuddered out her own orgasm… and then *I* came.

"Fuck, fuck!" My goddamn shirt, and the tie was fucking silk.

I shook, and felt my hot mess running all over my hand like I was a stupid fucking teenager again, still jerking off thinking about Sadie. Fucking fuck fuck… *fuck.* I stood up and heard a glob hit the floor with a wet splat. There were no napkins or tissue. Roan never ate or did anything like that in his lair, so I shoved my cock back in my pants, and wiped my hand on my coat. There were already several globs of nut sprayed up almost to the lapel.

I took off the coat and tie and rolled them up. The cleaners would have to handle that, it was what they were paid to do.

I really liked that tie, and if they couldn't get that out, I would find different dry cleaners, better ones.

I sat back down and glowered at the screen. They were laying together, whispering, kissing again, and his cock was going soft, rubbing against her wet as fuck pussy. There was the familiar stab. Jealousy, I was jealous. Jealous that I wasn't in there with them.

I rewound to a few different scenes and did some screen grabs. There was a specific moment when she was going down on him, forcing herself, and I could see her hit her own gag reflex, the cords in her neck standing up. Grabbed, set as a wallpaper, random rotation, pattern one.

Then to where he was grasping his cock, trying to choke up on it like a shotgun, as he nutted on her thigh. Grabbed, set as wallpaper, random rotation, pattern one. Two pictures to populate the cluster of screens.

Another, her rising from the bed, naked. Repeat process.

His cock rubbing against her, going soft. Repeat process.

I sat back and watched the four pictures populate through his screens. After maybe five minutes, the screens traded wallpapers. His macros were as well made as the French chicken stuff he made.

I picked up my gin, rolled up the bundle of jizz-stained clothing, and went to my room. My work for the day was done, as much as it was going to be done.

CHAPTER NINETEEN

*S*adie...

I sucked in a breath and shuddered slightly with my luxurious stretch the next morning, weak daylight streaming through the windows. Conan Roan chuckled deeply, the sound a satisfied purr as my stretch tucked me closer into his bigger body.

"Mm, good morning," I said with a happy, sated smile. I was deliciously sore between my legs and I was glad for it, but a touch guilty at the same time. I'd wanted Roan the night before, badly... but also, partially to erase the dirt and the grit from my encounter with Lach from my soul.

"Good morning, love," he murmured and his big arms went around me, tucking me back into the curve of his body my nightgown gone where it had been trapped around my waist the night before.

"Where did my clothes go?" I asked with a laugh.

"Floor by the bed, it wears it quite well, I'm afraid."

"Oh, better than I did?" I asked and turned, looking over my shoulder into smiling green eyes.

"Quite," he said deadpan, and I laughed.

"Mm, I think I'd feel better in one of your shirts anyway," I confessed and it was true. All the satin and silk were so flashy, too pretty, and just… just not meant for the likes of me.

"Agree to disagree, Poppet," he murmured, pressing a kiss to my bare shoulder. "Though the thought of you in one of my shirts is quite appealing."

I smiled and giggled slightly, changing the subject.

"So, what's the big plan for today?"

"Mm," he groaned as though the mere thought of the rest of the day held too many unpleasant realities to think upon right now and I felt myself deflate slightly. I mean, I didn't know… maybe it did.

"Let me go down to the Bat Cave and check my calendar, see if there is anything that needs my urgent attention, then I thought I might make you breakfast."

"Pancakes?" I asked slightly hopeful.

"Better than that, love. I was thinking I might try my hand at crepes again. It's been a while."

"Close enough," I said with a smile and sat up carefully.

He chuckled and sat up, swinging his leg and what was left of the other over the edge of the bed, bending at the waist to retrieve his prosthetic.

He stopped at his dresser on the way to the bathroom, opened a drawer and removed a crisply folded shirt. With a backward glance at me, he threw it to me and I caught it out of the air with a smile.

We used the bathroom, one at a time, and held hands as we wandered back out into the main part of the house, and I looked up at him. I couldn't help but smile, he was different somehow. Carried himself lighter, like he had shed some awful tension or weight. I was mid-sentence, asking what he put on crepes if not maple syrup like pancakes when he seized up, just froze in the doorway of the Bat Cave, his shoulders bearing down as that awful weight returned to them. I turned and froze myself.

The devastating cruelty of it…

Photos of us, of me and Roan in his bed flitted from screen to screen slowly fading out on one monitor only to come up on another, always shifting always moving.

"Where is he?" I demanded, voice hollow with my rage.

"Sadie, I'm sorry…" Roan began to stammer.

Cold radiated out from the center of my being and I asked him again, "Where. Is. He?"

He was galvanized into some sort of action, letting go of my hand, striding with his uneven gait to the glass desk and smashing his blunt fingertips into keys. The monitors flickered and I felt my mouth go dry.

Of course he would set them as the monitor's background as well…

Roan muttered something about Lach being a twat and I couldn't agree more.

"Home gym," he said dispassionately, and I whirled, my anger carrying me in long strides.

"Sadie, wait!" Roan called, but this wasn't something he was going to be able to stop me from doing.

Years of pent-up anger and frustration came pouring out to the fore, the closer and closer I got to the home gym. I strode through the door to the sounds of Kyle fucking Lachlan bench pressing or whatever and when he caught me out of the corner of his eye, he let go of the bar and let it glide up into its natural position on the machine.

"You're! Like! A! Little! Boy!" I shrieked at him, slapping at him in punctuation of every word and hitting him in his gross sweaty chest while he laughed and laughed.

It just served to piss me off more and I redoubled my efforts to drive the point home, letting fly and scratching his cheek.

He grabbed my wrists and swept my feet out from under me, and we went crashing to the mats on the floor where he pinned me, as I screamed my savage rage into his face, stopping to pant with the fire of my emotion.

"If you're going to hit me, you might as well learn how to do it right," he said, pecking me on the tip of my nose. He got off of me and leaped lightly to his feet. Limber, like a cat, with a grace I would never possess.

I got to my feet, and he wrapped his hands around my hands balling them into fists and putting them up.

"Put 'em up, yeah, just like that. Thumbs out, like this." He held out his fists, and I mirrored him. He nodded, oblivious to the fact I was still seething.

"Okay, now punch." He made a jab to demonstrate and hit only air.

I used one of the first lessons Kyle Lachlan ever taught me. I made to punch and while his attention was on my hand, I swung my back leg forward and up *right between his legs.*

I was honestly surprised he didn't see it coming. His arms snapped in, hands going to cover his junk as he face-planted into the mats at my feet.

"Rip the wings off some other fly, *Lach*!" I spat at him to Roan's booming laughter from the home gym's doorway.

I felt angry tears prick the corners of my eyes as I swept past my new lover and halfway down the hall where I stopped to hug myself.

"Well done, Poppet! Well done," he praised me, his hand falling on my back. I shivered, and he applied gentle pressure to get me moving.

"Let's just skip breakfast and get out for a bit, yeah?" he asked, and I nodded mutely.

"Yes, out; away from that… that… *mutant.*"

Roan chuckled, and we went to my room. He waited for me as I cleaned up and got dressed and thankfully, we didn't see Lach as we left the house. We climbed into Roan's fancy James Bond car and left the great mansion on the bay behind.

"We're leaving the city?" I asked, perking up as he turned us onto the Bay Bridge.

"Aye," he agreed, nodding sagely. "Some distance from Lach will do us both good, I think."

I gave a dubious laugh and smoothed sweating palms over the tops of the thighs of my jeans. I felt out of place in them, my Converse, and my plain tee-shirt and wool sweater that Roan had provided me. I slid my eyes over my lover in the driver's seat of the luxury car.

My lover.

Wasn't Lach, too?

Shit.

I closed my eyes and Roan took his hand off the gearshift and reached over, folding it around my hand.

"Bless. The look on his face! I'm right proud of you, lovie. You stood up for yourself."

"I did not," I said, turning my head and staring out over the water as it flashed by outside the window.

"Oh?" Roan asked curiously. "Then what was that?"

"Me standing up for *you*," I murmured softly, blushing furiously. "He's going to kill me, isn't he?" I asked.

Roan chuckled and brought my hand to his lips, kissing the back of it as he stared out the windshield, piloting the quick little car through traffic.

"Over my dead body, love. He earned it. He knows it too, the twat."

"I'm surprised he didn't remember," I said and Roan glanced my way.

"Remember what?"

"Lesson one of the orphans in foster care survival guide." Roan arched an eyebrow. "Never ever do what they expect. Remain unpredictable. They won't know how to handle you, what you'll tell the caseworkers when, and they'll take it easier on you as a result."

He raised my hand to his lips again and let them linger this time.

"Interesting," was his only comment, probably almost a full minute later.

The drive gave me some time to think and to remember. Lach had always been this way. The one to set the rules and then to change them midway through whatever little game he played. I sighed inwardly and wondered if he really meant for this to work or not? Only time would tell on that one. I'm sure he was thinking about it.

We were silent the remainder of the forty-five minute to an hour drive to DC and by the time we reached it? I felt as though my heart rate was marginally calmer.

"Where are we going?" I asked finally, curious. I mean, I knew we were going to DC, obviously, but I meant where specifically *in* DC did Conan have in mind?

"I thought you might like to do some shopping, a bit of retail therapy."

"Retail therapy?" I echoed, trying to make sense of it. I'd never heard of it.

"Aye, shopping, my treat."

"Oh, Conan... I don't know. I couldn't."

"Nonsense, I insist."

He whipped us down into a parking garage and I swallowed hard, not really sure what to think so instead I changed the subject, back to the one big thing we had in common.

"He's always been like this, you know?" I asked.

"Lach?" he asked, frowning. I nodded as he whirled the car around and around deeper and deeper into the garage.

"Yeah. A bigger bully than all the other bullies combined. He used to do some really awful shit to the people who tormented me in school. I never understood it."

"He loves you, Poppet." I snorted. "No, no! He does. I've known Lachlan a long time now, have seen him interact with numerous women – not to put too fine a point on it – and you? He loves you. I've never seen him so willing to bend or compromise for anyone else." He pulled into a space and engaged the parking brake. "I've never seen him turn so possessive over anyone like he does you."

"That's not love," I said softly, facing Roan, meeting his eyes in the dark of the car in the depths of the garage. It was close, intimate in the car. I unbuckled my seatbelt and sat up, twisting in my seat to face him.

"Obsession, maybe, but what he does? You don't torment the people you love, you don't..." I shook my head.

"Aye," Roan said softly. "But you need to read between the lines, lass."

I shook my head. "No, I don't," I murmured. "If Kyle wants this to work? He needs to pull his head out of his ass and apologize."

Roan chuckled and his smile was beautiful.

"I don't think we're talking about the same man anymore," he said.

"We are, you just need to know the words 'I'm sorry' or 'I apologize' will never come out of his mouth," I said. No, Kyle's apologies were much more bizarre and out of the ordinary. "That's where you need to read between the lines, I think."

"Ah." Roan nodded. "We *are* still speaking on the same man."

I took in a deep, shuddering breath and let it out slowly.

"Yeah, well, fuck it. Let him stew. We'll deal with it tonight."

Roan drank in my features, that smile never quite diminishing. The way he looked at me felt… cozy. I liked it. I liked him, Lord did I like him. I leaned forward and kissed him and he kissed me back.

"Actually, I thought we might stay in DC tonight. Let him stew until tomorrow night."

"Yeah?" I asked.

"Absolutely," he countered, and he opened his car door.

I smiled to myself, relieved to spend time away from the mansion and its many cameras and out from under Kyle's thumb. Roan opened my door before I could think to reach for the handle, and switching his cane to his other hand, held down his hand for me. I stared at it for half a heartbeat, warmed, and took it, letting him leverage me up out of my seat.

The elevator was unremarkable down here in the garage, I'd slept in one or two just like it before being roused by security guards and kicked out before the worker bees returned to whatever building. When the doors opened up into the marble and baroque lobby of the hotel, I gasped.

"Roan, what are we doing here?" I breathed overwhelmed.

"Staying the night; having a spot of breakfast before we shop. Come on now, you belong here with me… to feel or act any different would be chumming the waters. Look sharp, Poppet."

I stood a little straighter as Roan tucked my hand into the crook of his arm and strode into the lobby full of light and dark marble, filled with golden light. The ceiling was high and made of milky glass, the natural light from out of doors shining through it.

I tried not to gawk but it was hard, as Roan stepped up to the front desk with me and said crisply, "Reservation for Frederick Alexander Brett if you please."

"Why hello, Mr. Brett. Identification, please?" the plucky well-made woman behind the counter asked. She was a tall, beautiful, and leggy blonde without a hair out of place, her uniform tailored to her model and statuesque figure. I felt out of place with my plain street clothes that were very middle class amidst all of this opulence.

I looked to Roan who produced a wallet from the inside of his overcoat and handed the woman his license. She scanned it, looked up at him, and beamed as she cross checked her computer monitor hidden below the counter's wrap.

"Will you be needing any help up to your pearl suite accommodation today? Any bags?"

"Ah, no. That is quite the point of this trip I am afraid," he said as he returned his wallet to his coat. "Shopping."

"I see, and would you like to have a personal shopper sent up today, compliments of the hotel, of course."

"Yes, quite! Perhaps after brunch?"

"Of course, will you be dining in the restaurant or…?"

"Yes, I believe that would be preferable."

"Of course." She smiled and picked up the phone and said something too low for me to hear into it. She looked back up to Roan and smiling said, "They're expecting you."

"Thank you," he murmured and led me away from the desk and across the lobby to the doorways leading to the hotel's restaurant. The Aurora Room emblazoned in gilt letters above the open double doors.

Someone actually rushed out to meet us.

"Mr. Brett?"

"Yes."

"Right this way, please."

We were ushered to a hushed corner of the floor, ensconced in a booth cut off from the rest of the restaurant.

"Would you care for a menu or…?"

"Ah, no, I believe I promised the Mrs. crepes for breakfast, which we haven't gotten to as of yet. A mimosa for my lady and a coffee for me."

"Right and would you prefer the crepes savory or sweet?" the gentleman waiter, in actual tux with tails, asked.

"Sweet, if you please..." Roan murmured. "Oh, and a rasher of bacon."

"Yes, of course." The man scurried away, and I blinked slowly at Roan.

"I will never get used to this," I whispered, and he chuckled.

"You will. Your life has changed for the better Sadie. I promise you."

I threaded my fingers between his and gripped his hand lightly and nodded, slightly overcome.

Breakfast was wonderful, the crepes light, paper thin, and rolled about a sweet cream cheese filling and loaded with strawberries and fluffy hand whipped cream.

"What does a personal shopper do?" I asked, nervous.

"She will come to the room, take your measurements, go through some catalogs with you and get a sense of your style then she will either come with us and take you shopping or at our request, will do the shopping for you and parcels will simply arrive at our room."

I felt my mouth drop open and said, "People actually pay people to go clothes shopping *for them?*" I asked.

"Aye."

"Can't we just go to Target?" I asked meekly.

Roan chuckled.

"That would be a 'no', Poppet. We must keep up appearances."

"Alright," I murmured.

"We can go out to any place you'd like," he said finally. "I shall split the difference with you, so to speak."

"Yeah?" I asked curiously.

"Yes. Personal shopper here, and then you and I shall go for a walk through the boutiques down the street."

"Okay, I think that I can handle that."

He smiled at me. "You still look nervous."

"I guess I'm glad we're in DC and not Indigo City," I said. "I'm still low-key worried about running into someone I know... you know, from the street. I'm afraid they'll think I'm a sell out or something. I don't know…"

"Ah." He nodded succinctly. "Worry not," he murmured. "Character is like a tree and reputation like its shadow. The shadow is what we think of it, but the tree is the real thing."

I sat back and looked at him, plaintively, the crystal chandelier above our heads winking rainbows on the slightly iridescent and totally opulent wallpaper behind Roan's head.

"Who said that?" I asked quietly, and he smiled.

"Your American president, Abraham Lincoln… I thought it both truthful and apropos to the situation as well as fitting for our setting."

I smiled and squeezed his hand one last time before taking it back so I could use it to eat some more. He left me to think about what he said and I decided it was one more thing I loved about him. He knew just what to say to make me feel empowered. He was right. I knew the situation at hand and fuck what anyone else thought. They weren't taking care of me… Roan was.

"Thank you," I murmured, and he smiled at me.

"Of course."

THE PERSONAL SHOPPER THING WAS EXCRUCIATINGLY UNCOMFORTABLE, but I managed to send her off with enough ideas that I didn't find horrible and Roan approved of, straddling the line between my old life and this new one. When she was gone, I finally managed to breathe again without my chest feeling tight.

Roan came to me and hands lightly on my hips, dipped his head. I raised my lips to meet his, and we kissed carefully, slowly, and the tension eased from my shoulders.

"Hmm…" he hummed in appreciation, tongue flicking out to lick my taste from his lips as though I were some sort of fine wine.

I smiled and cuddled into his front and we stood like that, motionless, as he simply held me for as long as I needed him to.

"Come now, Love. Let's go for a walk, eh?" he asked with a light chuckle and I smiled.

"Sounds good."

It was strange, yet wonderful, walking down the sidewalk with Roan in the little boutique filled neighborhood. We'd taken a car, another compliment of the hotel, and with how absolutely fancy the rooms we were staying in, I had to imagine for the amount he was paying for one night I probably could have scraped by in a place of my own for like at least a year.

I shuddered at the thought as we passed by a jewelry shop, Roan pausing at the window to scan the necklaces and rings displayed.

"Are you cold?" he asked, bringing my hand to his lips and kissing the back, fixing me with his green eyes.

"Not really," I said with a smile then thought better of it and with a blush and a slightly awkward giggle, I conceded, "Maybe a little."

"Bless," he murmured and tucked me closer into his side. He stilled immediately when I hesitated, pausing outside an artisan soap shop to breathe in the clean and herbal scents emanating from it.

He turned us and urged me through the door and I stepped through reluctantly, but then decided this? This I could do... no one needed to know how dirty I had been for how long and if it was one thing I loved about this new life? It was the ability to shower and bathe every day and be *clean*.

I stopped at the table stacked with globe upon globe of bath bombs... I had always wanted to try one of these things, but it was a luxury that I so had never been able to afford. I mean, who spent upwards of *twenty dollars* on one of these things that you tossed in the water and could only use once? That was like a week's worth of meals off the dollar menu at Burger World!

I stiffened my spine and turned to Roan who was smiling faintly at me and I whispered to him, "I have always wanted to try one of these things."

He raised his eyebrows as though what I'd just said was interesting, but I think I'd surprised him, maybe? I don't know... Roan could be so very hard to read when anyone else was present. He treated stoicism like he'd found God... like it was his own personal religion.

"Color, scent, or sensation, Love? What is most important?" he asked me quietly, and I turned back to the table in the center of the shop.

"I... I don't know," I murmured.

"Right." He smiled and turned to the shop girl and said, "One of each, please; and some of the bubble bars." He turned back to me and asked, "Lotion? Skincare? Shampoo?"

"I... I don't know what any of this stuff does or how it works," I stammered.

"Oh, well I can help you with that." One of the girls came forward and patted my hand and asked, "Do you normally have dry or oily skin?"

I looked back to Roan who smiled and nodded encouragingly and I swallowed hard and said, "I don't... I mean, I never really paid attention before."

"Aw, well I can see why!" She smiled and complimented me, "You really have flawless skin. Here, come sit with me."

She led me over to a chair and I was expertly drawn into what should have clearly been a trap to sell me literally all of the things. I was introduced to a crazy amount of shit! Scrubs, soaps, polishes, and toners... and I didn't know the first thing about if any of it worked. Roan rescued me by whispering in my ear as he stood by to just go with what felt good to me, and I ended up with a very nice sugar and salt scrub that smelled of the ocean. Added to that was moisturizer for my face and some artisan soap for body and a specialty wash for my face, all of it supposedly all natural and handmade right here, locally, in DC.

Roan wouldn't hear of me carrying the large shopping bag.

～

"Aye, I'll make certain." Roan paused and sighed. "Tomorrow sometime." I felt my heart slightly sink in my chest as I stepped out of the bedroom into the living room area of the suite so the personal shopper could check the fit of yet another outfit. This one a close-fitting, yet off-the-shoulder, warm sweater dress that was soft against my skin.

Roan made eye contact with me and I mouthed the name... *Lach?* He nodded and chuckled into the phone.

"I'll make certain of everything; you don't have to worry about me, mate." His green eyes flicked up to mine and his lips spread into a slow grin.

"That you'll have to figure out on your own," he said. "I'll not help you mend that particular fence." I shook my head violently.

Nope. Kyle needed to apologize to me himself and it was going to need to be a *real* apology before I would relent. He'd always said when we were teens that I needed to learn how to be hard. Well now he could find out for himself just how hard I could be. We weren't fucking kids anymore!

"Aye, by what I'm looking at now, good luck with that, mate."

Roan hung up the phone and I couldn't help but laugh.

"How is he doing in the hot seat for once?" I asked and Roan chuckled. "Give us a moment?" he asked the personal shopper, and she nodded, stepping out. I drifted to him and he smoothed his hands over the sweater that covered me.

"I quite like this," he murmured. I nodded.

"It's warm, I think it might be a keeper."

"Oh, there are several things coming home with us that you've tried to pass on."

"You two can be such bullies," I whispered and Roan smirked.

"All in your best interest, Poppet; but I do think you know that."

I sighed slightly and nodded...

"You know he was diagnosed with Oppositional Defiance Disorder, right? I don't know how he even got into the military. He was... he was so broken inside," I whispered. I felt guilty even saying it out loud... I mean, I had always kept Kyle's secrets. Just as he had always kept mine but this was Roan, and for whatever reason he'd let Roan in when he'd lost me and that? That meant something.

"I believe his borderline sociopathy helped with that," Roan murmured. "Although what you just said does shine a light on a few things."

I took in a shuddering breath and asked him, "He ever really apologize before? To you, I mean?" I hugged myself and Roan smiled.

"I think we both know, Kyle *fucking* Lachlan doesn't apologize with words."

"Actions speak louder than words anyway," I whispered softly.

"Aye, he's said as much more than a few times to me."

I twisted my lips back and forth and settled for biting my bottom one. "What is he asking you to do?" I asked. "I mean, I know he asked you to do something in regard to me and—"

I was shaking, nervous, scared, and I didn't know why. Roan leaned forward and placed his lips against my forehead, breathing out slowly, the warm blush of his breath against my skin sort of short circuited my anxiety response and my body lost some of its tension. I breathed out slowly.

"Easy, I would think by now you would realize I would protect you. Even from him."

"Yes, I know," I whispered.

"He doesn't wish me to spoil the surprise, and honestly, I think it's a good one." He smiled and pulled me close, cuddling me.

"Yeah?" I asked.

"Very much so… you two have yet to talk."

"Yeah, well, *Kyle*…" I said. He was the king of procrastination when it came to talking about the big shit.

"Indeed, Kyle," he chuckled.

"How many more things do I have left to try on?" I asked, I was getting weary and overwhelmed.

"I think that's enough for now, there's always tomorrow. Go put on a robe, yeah? I'll settle things out here."

"Okay," I whispered. I went inside and did as he asked, stripping down and putting on one of the hotel's fluffy robes.

He sent the personal shopper away making an appointment for her to return the following morning for her to finish up with me and then came through to the bedroom as I sat on the end of the bed.

He smiled charmingly at me saying, "I know just what you need," before disappearing into the bathroom. A moment later the rush of water into the tub had me perking up.

"You're a genius!" I called out.

"Oh, I know," he called back. "Choose one of your bath bombs for me, would you, Love?"

I gleefully got down off the bed and went to the bag in the corner of the bedroom. There were a lot of them, thankfully they had been individually wrapped in cellophane so I could see them and I finally settled on one that was black, pink, purple, and blue with silver glitter throughout it like stars. It smelled sweet but slightly musky and looked like a Lisa Frank rendition of what a galaxy should look like. I was excited to try it and went into the bathroom with Roan who stood by the jetted bathtub big enough for four as it filled with steaming water.

"I feel so stupid for being this excited," I confessed.

"Don't be, I find you utterly adorable," he said with a smile that gave me all the confidence I needed to be a kid at heart.

I unwrapped the bomb, took a deep breath and with a stupid squeal of delight dropped it in.

Beautifully mesmerizing, I watched the colors flow, the bomb spin, and the water froth and foam around it. Roan slipped the robe from me and held out a hand to steady me as I stepped into the tub.

The temperature was perfect.

I sank into the water with a happy sigh as Roan sat down onto the edge of the tub, watching me.

"Join me," I murmured and smiled, knowing it was lascivious.

"Ah." He laughed lightly, as though the thought hadn't even occurred to him.

"Come on!" I cried. "I really want you to." He shook his head, and I hated, *hated* how insecure he could be when I was really beginning to love him so much. Partially, because he made loving him so *easy*.

"Okay, fine," I said with a gusty sigh. "You asked for it."

I pulled him back into the water, catching him off balance just enough. Thankfully the tub wasn't overly filled, no bright steamy water sloshed outside of it, but Roan was laughing, on his butt, lower legs up on the edge as I attacked his mouth with mine and covered his handsome face in a flurry of kisses. It didn't take much to get him out of his wet shirts, setting them on the edge of the tub.

"I didn't get your phone, did I?"

"No," he said. "Wallet and phone are in the other room."

"Good," I whispered and touched him like I wanted to. He groaned and released his prosthetic leg and shoved his pants the rest of the way down his good one, untangling himself from the rest of his clothing as I gripped him in my hand and stroked him gently to life.

God, he was so big… the biggest I had certainly ever taken, and I was grateful that the day had allowed my soreness to abate. While I was sure I would likely regret being with him again so soon? I was sure those regrets wouldn't occur until morning, and I wanted him so badly tonight.

I relished this, without Lach here to fuck everything up. Without Kyle's petty ass bullshit to leave us feeling guilty or sad.

Roan cupped my face between his hands and kissed me back, sweeping his tongue against mine, and good Lord my body responded perfectly and accordingly.

"I probably should grab a condom," he said strained, as I straddled him in the colorful glittery water.

"I have an IUD," I whispered, and I took him inside of me, slowly, carefully, the going more than a little rough with the bath washing away my natural lubricant initially. He panted and moaned, his hands on my hips, keeping my descent measured and controlled…

"I love that you're so careful of me," I whispered against his mouth and kissed him, taking his reply away from him. I didn't need it. I didn't want it. I just wanted him to feel, to know, how much I appreciated him. His care.

"Sadie," he whispered, strained as I settled into his lap, his cock deeply seated inside of me, stretching me, filling me, pressing out against my walls.

"Mm?" I moaned softly, and ground my hips slightly, slowly, against him. He sucked in a sharp breath, his thumbs caressing me below the waterline.

I reached out and shut off the tap, the tub filled more than enough, the bomb dissolved, the water tinged a lavender pink, the sparkles in it few and far between, one bomb not enough to the water ratio but I didn't care. Not with Roan inside me, his hands gently caressing my body and his mouth latching around one of my nipples to tease it with lips, teeth, and tongue.

"Oh, God!" I gasped, throwing my head back, rolling my hips slightly.

His big arms around me, clutching me to him, I realized that loving Roan was going to be both one of the easiest and one of the hardest things I ever did and that this little reprieve of ours? This was going to be brutally short, and so I was absolutely determined to enjoy it.

Lach was conspicuously absent when we returned, laden with packages that threatened to overwhelm the limited storage space in Roan's car. In fact, I think technically the amount of purchases Roan had made in my honor *did* overwhelm, because I'd heard him making arrangements to have things delivered to Bootlegger Head, which was where the mansion was situated.

He begged off for a bit, stating arrangements needed to be made and there was work that needed his attention. I'd paused, and he'd kissed me on the top of my head and rephrased, assuring me that the work he needed to do was mundane in nature... stock portfolios and investments that needed his attention. He left me to put my purchases away, and I stared at the wardrobe and sighed turning instead to the walk-in closet of my room that was barren, devoid of anything at all except some empty hangers.

"Well, looks like that's about to change," I murmured and began to unpack and hang things up, one item at a time.

It took a while, and when I was finished, I changed into something more familiar since coming to the mansion, a light, amethyst silk, tank dress with spaghetti straps, the asymmetrical hem edged in actual amethyst beads weighting the material enough to keep it from floating up with the slightest of breezes.

I found Roan in the kitchen where we had a light meal sitting at the counter talking quietly, our mood slightly somber knowing that this was it… tomorrow would either be a day to myself or I belonged to Lach for the next three days.

I was trying not to think about it too much, and desperate for a distraction I asked Roan quietly what movie we were going to watch tonight. He smiled, genuinely pleased and said, "Anything in particular you would like to watch?" I shook my head.

"I liked the bridge movie, what else have you got?"

"Any objections to spaghetti westerns?" he asked, and I smiled and shook my head.

"None at all."

"Alright then."

We cleaned up together, went to the living room, and resumed our comfortable positions on the couch, only this time, Roan laid on his back, tucking me on my back between his legs, adjusting himself so that I could rest against his chest, his arms around me. He cued up *The Good, the Bad, and the Ugly* and hit play.

We lay watching the movie play out when fifteen minutes in, like a freaking ninja, Kyle slipped over the back of the couch, half falling on me, on his back, his dark head resting on *my* stomach as he rolled it on his neck to look up at me.

"Hi," he said simply, and I arched an eyebrow.

"Try again," I said.

He grinned up at me recklessly. "Don't be like that, Shady."

"Strike one."

He huffed out a breath and settled down on me, putting a hand on my knee and giving it a squeeze.

"Perilously close to strike two," I said as Roan paused the movie.

"Fine. I'm sorry. I apologize," he said, and I looked up to Roan who looked down at me, both of our expressions mirroring our surprise. "To *both* of you," he added, and I looked down at him.

I couldn't resist, even though I wanted to, but I was weak… I lifted one of my hands from where it lay over the top of Roan's against my chest and pushed my fingers through Kyle's silky soft hair, raking it back from his forehead. He closed his eyes, and I swear, if he were a cat, he would purr.

"Finish your movie," he said. "I'll be quiet."

I looked up at Roan and with a soft smile, he hit play. I played with Kyle's hair, held Roan's hand, and strangely… I found that I could get used to this.

When the credits rolled, Kyle sighed. I thought he had been asleep, he had been so still, his breathing deep and even.

"You pack her bag, mate?" he asked.

"I shall," Roan said. "Everything will be ready by morning."

"Good deal… sleep tight. It's wheels up at nine am," he said and he sat up and heaved himself up over the back of the couch leaving me open mouthed and wondering out loud…

"What is he talking about? Where are we going?"

Roan simply chuckled and kissed the top of my head.

CHAPTER TWENTY

*L*ach...

There were a few things that Roan was good at, but picking movies was not one of them. The movies he liked were long, and while there was certainly some good action, most of the movies had really long sections where nothing really interesting happened. One of the upsides was finding out that some jingle for a liquor brand, or a pretty common sales campaign had come from something that had actually been pretty violent was amusing.

His spaghetti western was too long. And it was a western. None of the women were good looking, there were no cars, and unless I recognized part of the score, it was mostly just background noise. Words don't mean shit, the only thing that really mattered was what a person did. All the people in the foster care system, they had enough words that they could have pushed that Master and Commander guy's ship around the world in like, eight days, instead of eighty.

I sat with them and watched their movie.

No complaints. No jokes. No questions.

Clint Eastwood was actually pretty badass, even if he was wearing a Navajo tablecloth.

Sadie's lap wasn't such a bad place to be either, especially with how she played with my hair like she used to do as she read her books while we lounged around the Daughton's.

I tried to pay attention to the movie, but there were too many other thoughts going through my mind, like the itinerary for the next day, and getting her documents from Roan for travel. I wondered what sort of false identity she had, what he had found or made up for her.

I would find out soon enough.

After what felt like two or three eternities, the movie ended, I exchanged a few words with Roan, and Sadie looked properly perplexed and that suited me well enough. Oh, the surprises I had in store for her…

By 7:30 AM, the Audi was at the curb in front of the main door to the manse, Sadie and my bag stowed in the trunk. Roan handed me her new ID and passport. "These look really good, new printer?" I asked, flipping through the new documents. My eyes stuck on her alias, Roan Lachlan. Someone was a comedian.

"Aye, new printer, much better quality than the last one." He nodded.

"I'm looking forward to having a new passport myself," I said. "But keep the names that are still secure, I hate having to break in a new identity. The last one, the Mister Brown, ugh, they were paging me over the airport intercom for fifteen minutes before I realized I was the Mister Brown they were looking for."

"That was a poor fit," Roan said.

"Does she have any idea?" I asked.

"None," he admitted.

"Tell me she picked up a bathing suit on your shopping jaunt."

"Two actually. Well, the personal shopper picked her out two."

"Have you seen them?"

"I have; a black one piece with no back, and a royal purple bikini," he answered.

"No pink, no pastel, did the shopper listen to her and not you?" I asked.

"It was actually hard to let her lay out what she wanted," he said. "She's not used to such finery. Or even color." He made a face.

"I can imagine." I gave a laugh.

"You know you said you were sorry, the actual words, last night?" he asked carefully.

"We don't need to talk about that," I said. "I was an asshole… and serves me right, I was sloppy, she should have never been able to tag my balls like that."

"She was quite upset." He nodded. There was a shadow of a grin on his face. I gave him a smirk and nodded back.

"I think we might be even on that." We both looked up as Sadie came out of the front door, looking for all the world like a woman who had fallen into a moviescape and was struggling to make the best of it. Roan stepped up and opened the door for her to slide into the passenger seat of the Audi and bent down to tell her to enjoy her trip. He told her that I had her passport, ID, and a personal charge card. He kissed her goodbye.

He looked up at me over the top of the car. "Thank you, Roan," I said, flipping him the middle finger. He smiled back, and did that British thing with two fingers, that was something to do with archery and meant almost the same thing. The look on his face was jovial, but there was an unspoken ultimatum that she was now in my care, and that I had to look out for her in his stead. He didn't have to worry about that. I lost her once, and I was never going to do that again.

I handed her the passport and other documents, and told her to familiarize herself with the new name, and birthday, and that if they asked questions beyond that, that I don't know, and isn't it on there, were perfectly acceptable answers to any questions she might be asked at the terminal.

"Roan Lachlan, that's too cute!" She stifled a laugh. "Wait, what terminal?"

I chuckled. "We're taking a shuttle flight from the airport down to

Atlanta, will have about an hour and a half layover, and then will be picking up another flight to our destination," I said.

"I've never been on a plane," she said, sounding hesitant.

"Don't worry, it's perfectly safe, and we're flying first class," I said.

"I've *never* been on an airplane," she said again. I put my hand on her knee.

"It'll be okay, I've been on so many airplanes that I don't even think about it. We'll spend a little while in the sky lounge, then have priority seating, the flight down to Atlanta is one drink long."

"One drink?" she asked.

"One drink, that is all they have time to serve, between takeoff and landing," I said.

"That doesn't seem long."

"It isn't," I said. "Certainly not long enough to get you into the mile-high club," I said.

"What, you mean you and Roan couldn't swing that upgrade?" she asked. I barked a laugh and smiled at her.

"Sadie, the mile-high club," I leaned over and whispered in her ear, "you can't claim to be a member until you've fucked on an airplane, midflight." Her eyes grew large, and she goggled at me.

"Certainly not a on a shuttle flight, those are short, and full of unimportant people going boring places," I said.

"What about us?" she asked.

"We are most definitely important people and we are *not* going somewhere boring." I gave her a nod.

"Where are we going?"

"You'll find out in Atlanta. Let me keep this surprise," I said. She relented, and we drove to the Indigo City airport. This wasn't normal protocol, but this also wasn't work. Work flights went through DC, never Indigo. She was nervous as we went through the mundane check-in, walking through the x-ray scanner, and metal detectors, and the rest of the TSA nonsense. I gave the people working the turnstiles a haughty look. They wouldn't deter anyone but the most idiotic terrorist or the most self-absorbed Karen, insisting that her water bottle was exempt from the flight restrictions. We walked through with ease, and the few times I saw the tension at the corners of the TSA mook's eyes, I covered deftly. Her first flight, and that she had never even been on an airplane before. Between her innocence and my charisma, I was fairly certain that I could have smuggled a tactical nuke, or a flamethrower onto the flight.

Instead, I was smuggling an incredibly nervous woman onto a mundane shuttle flight. Thankfully that went off without any enhanced security, no pat downs, and no opened luggage. There was nothing to find, no concealed weapons, no special tools, not even anything conventionally embarrassing other than the normal toiletries and unmentionables. The thought of some minimum-wage government goombah fondling Sadie's panties made my eye twitch.

Less than an hour later we were aboard the flight, and shortly after that, we were winging our way to Atlanta. I skipped the offering drink service, only taking the little biscotti cookies and a swillish coffee, while Sadie giggled at getting a soda and a package of peanuts. She was almost giddy once we got over the apparently terror inducing takeoff. I realized that maybe I was more jaded than I realized, but when I had been in the Marines I hadn't just been on airplanes. I had shot at them, jumped out of them, and in the case of that one time with the POS Blackhawk near Marjah, had survived crashing one.

Fucking Blackhawks.

If I hadn't been in a first-class seat, I would have spat on the ground.

The plateau of the flight was all too short. Not long enough to settle in, or sleep. Certainly not long enough for a movie, a meal, or even really a decent drink. The landing had Sadie gripping her armrests again. Hopefully the shuttle flight would ease her through some of this flight anxiety.

The layover in Atlanta was brief, and she struck me as almost star-like. I could have imagined her being superimposed over Audrey Hepburn in one of the movies Roan liked. When we got back, I might have to ask him about that. *Was it Audrey? Were there other Hepburns?* We were in the second pre-board group, expectant mothers and handicapped still went on first, but that was fine.

Once we were in our first-class seats Sadie was all eyeballs and elbows. The seats were much larger, the stewardesses much better dressed, and we were still boarding when our stewardess came by to take out food and drink order. Sadie looked like a fish when she was given her choices for the lunch service.

I order the chicken Milanese and told the stewardess that I would like something like three to five gin and tonics, depending on how long it took to get in the air, and how long we would spend circling the field.

"I can't believe we're going to St. Henri," she said. "I don't even know where that is."

"It's completely real, I went back and forth several times over this," I said. "And I asked myself if I was Roan and wanted to take you to a totally over-the-top exotic vacation with a three-day limit, where would I take you?"

"What were the other choices?" she asked.

"The Florida Keys, the Bahamas, any of the islands listed in that Beach Boys song," I said.

"We could have gone to Kokomo?" She looked up from the Sky Mall brochure.

"There is no Kokomo," I said. "Well, there's one in Indiana and another in Arkansas, but those aren't exotic destinations."

"Oh," she said.

"Don't worry, St. Henri is better than Kokomo. Everyone speaks English or French. It's all sand and palm trees, and every island photo-spread you've seen in any magazine."

"Are you going to try to get into the mile-high club?" Sadie asked me about an hour into the flight, giving me a raised eyebrow.

"I'm already part of that club," I said.

"Really?" she asked.

"Yes, more than once actually."

"Oh," she said.

"Sadie." I looked over at her, and saw that my words might have been too curt, and not soft enough. This was going to take work. She looked up at me, slightly. "The mile-high club is overrated. If you step into the cabinet that passes for a bathroom on an airplane these days, you'll see. The last time I got Roan on an airplane, it was like watching a bear fighting his way into a clown car."

Thankfully, she gave me the smallest hint of a smile.

I would have to do better. Roan made this look so fucking easy.

The flight was exactly three-and-a-half drinks long, and I even managed to coax Sadie into having a pair of drinks. She politely disliked the first one, and it seemed that she wasn't going to be a run-of-the-mill fruit juice and vodka girl. That actually made me rather happy. The second drink, a rather lowbrow attempt at a Moscow Mule, she actually smiled as she sipped it.

"I like that," she said.

"They're nice," I said, and bumped my plastic cup against hers. She would have had another mule, but the stewardess had to stow her cart because we were already coming into landing procedure. St. Henri wasn't a large island, and it didn't take long for us to touch down and taxi to the terminal. I took Sadie's hand, and we were among the first to leave the plane.

It was easy picking up our single checked bag at the jetway, and minutes later we were whisked away from the airport by what seemed like a century old Citroen 2CV. Roan would likely know all about this quaint old car and its sputtering engine and complete lack of performance. It was passably comfortable, and it delivered us to our destination without incident. I thanked the driver, passed him a small tip, and we were left to walk up to the registration desk. Her eyes were huge, taking in the crystal blue sky and the sapphire blue waters.

Then she burst out laughing when a large blue parrot, or was it a macaw, started talking to her in clipped English. The man handling the birds earned a polite tip, and I shooed him away before he overstayed his welcome.

He came very close, thinking us to be easy tourist marks.

A porter carried our one bag down the beach, to a wooden pier. We followed behind, while the man spewed out the list of services and amenities the hotel offered, and how and when we could find them.

I was glad when he finally wrapped up his sermon, presented his hand for a tip, and clutching a few bills, left.

Fucking, finally.

It was worth it though. Our hotel was a series of huts, sitting on pylons driven into the white sands of the beach. When the tide came in, we were completely out in the water, with only the pier connecting us to land. When it was out, we could use a ladder to pop down to the beach for whatever delights we wanted.

"Bathing suit," I gestured. "The beach and view are why we're here." She looked around and found what passed for a bathroom.

"Is there no running water?" she asked.

"There is a clubhouse up above the waterline, with bathtubs and showers, and all the hotel things. The toilet here is… primitive," I said. "Put on your bathing suit, this isn't the nude section of beach." Her head jerked up from where she was digging in the bag.

"There is a nude beach here?"

"Of course, there is, but we aren't going there," I said.

"Would you want to?" she asked.

"Only if you want to watch rich, mostly older, almost always overweight American and European tourists wander around with their cellulite jiggling for the sun to burn to a crisp," I said. She made a comical face.

"Ew, no thank you," she said.

"We would certainly be the prettiest people there." I made an offering gesture, not wanting a repeat of the mile-high club gaffe.

"I think maybe, maybe next time." She smiled. It was infectious, and I smiled back. While she excused herself to the divided section of the 'room', I took the time to slip out of my casual slacks and shirt and traded my briefs for a simple black speedo. I adjusted myself into the hammock, snapped the waistband, and waited for Sadie to figure out her own bathing suit.

I was not disappointed in her personal shopper; the one piece was very tasteful, and had a spray of some crystal across her side, mimicking the profile of a flower. Her eyes ran down my chest, my abs, and then to the prominent bulge of the speedo and then she turned red. "Oh my God, is that - is that a speedo?" she asked.

"It is." I gave a turn and a little flex. "Too much?"

"Not enough." She coughed a laugh. "Do you have something, uh, less provocative?"

"*Less provocative?*" I asked, feigning innocence. "I work hard to have abs like this."

"It's not your abs," she said.

"Too cocky?" I raised an eyebrow at her. She burst out a laugh and seemed like she wanted to catch it with her hand, clapping it over her mouth.

"Cocky!" She laughed, her face flushed red.

"Oh fine," I said. "I do have a different pair of swim trunks, that are more modest, Miss Sense and Sensibility." I changed, and it was much less entertaining than the conventional speedo. "Is this better?" I asked, modeling the tight-fitting blue swimmer's trunks. I was much less bulgy, but still had my abs on display. This was acceptable, if less amusing.

"Thank you," she said, giving me a peck on the cheek. "We'll have plenty of time for that, later." She looked away, and I saw a hint of a blush on her cheeks. *Was she being forward?* My smile, for a second, was genuine.

The delight of places like St. Henri and the other tiny islands scattered across the ocean was that the outside world was not invited in. There were no skyscrapers, no urban sprawl, and until they had installed towers, there had been no phone service. I liked it better when communications had been limited to a handful of phones on the island, but there was a certain utility to my phone working again. The intrusion had been minimal, there were still no televisions in the rooms, no guest office at the hotel club. If you had to do anything approaching business, you had to leave the beach and the resort and go into 'town'. The term was loose, and it was walking distance to almost any point on the tiny island.

You could spend hours on the beach and they could feel like

minutes. If you did it right, a few hours on those sands, with the world forgotten, like some shit dream? Those hours could feel like *days*.

That was what I wanted. I wanted the two days I would have with Shady to feel like weeks. The sun and the surf made the day slow to a crawl, and it took a little to settle into the doing nothing pace. The only things that had to happen was the rhythm of the waves lapping gently against the beach.

What would Roan do now? I pondered. He would hold her hand, and kiss her, and talk a lot about a lot of nothing. What was the history of the island, pirates who had come here, what countries and crowns had claimed it through its history?

Boring.

Somewhere between a Papa Doble and a few ginger and rum concoctions full of shaved ice, we found the perfect pace. The sun moved at a crawl, and Sadie had a perfect sheen. Glistening with bronzer and sweat, she looked like a delectable treat. I watched her breathing slowly, beads of sweat running down her sides, over her ribs.

I wanted to kiss her.

Is that what he would do? It is, he would. I rolled onto my side and kissed her on the collarbone. She made a soft noise and looked at me through half-closed eyes. I kissed again, and she tasted of salty sweat, the ocean breeze, and the undernote of coconut.

What would Roan do? He didn't have a curt negotiation before swiping a credit card, he kissed, and did the foreplay game. That was the currency he used.

She moaned as I kissed her neck and shoulder and caressed her breast through the sheer fabric of the bathing suit. It didn't take too much effort to get the top of her suit loose and her breasts exposed to the fiery kiss of the sun. Then I gave them my kisses.

This was actually fairly nice.

I pulled the suit lower, pressing my lips against her stomach, and then I felt her hand in my hair. "Are we alone?" she asked, tense beneath me.

"Yes, I made a group deal and the entire beach is ours for the day," I said. "No one will see, and if they do? Fuck 'em."

"You are too much." Her voice was soft on the end of her giggle. "That must have been expensive."

"What's the point of being rich if you can't do things that are over the top? I mean, I didn't buy the entire resort."

"You could do that?" She sounded surprised. She shouldn't have been.

"Well, we could buy an island, but not an island like this one, it's not just expensive, it's an independent country."

"Is it?" she asked.

"I have no idea; I've never priced an island." I tried to hold the sharpness out of my voice. Thankfully, she laughed again. She didn't resist as I worked her out of the black suit, revealing hips and then the dark triangle between her legs. Once I had her peeled and nude, I went down on her.

This was unfamiliar territory. When I had my escorts, this wasn't part of the program. Escorts knew what to do to get themselves ready. There was almost a stigma against going down, or even kissing. I tasted her. There was a savory musky note suddenly in the sweat and coconut. It was enticing and thrilling.

Were these the noises she made when Roan was going down on her?

I wanted to do better than he had.

I wanted her to scream.

That might take some practice, and more patience than I could manage. I pulled the trunks down around my thighs and mounted her. This was much better than the living room against the glass. She sighed as I entered her.

She felt like heaven, even better than before.

I kissed her, and then I felt her hands on my back. She wrapped her legs around me, pulling me in, and it was almost a completely new sensation.

Even after what I had done to her, after she'd had Roan and his attentions, she still wanted me. This wasn't the embrace of an escort with expensive manicured fingernails and top shelf shoes. This was my Sadie, and she was breathing against my cheek, moaning in my ear. This was real.

This was real.

I felt a tightness in my chest.

I looked into her deep brown eyes, eyelids fluttering lazily, and the tight feeling became more intense. Was this…? No. It wasn't that. I didn't deserve that, to feel that from someone else.

"Kiss me, kiss me, Kyle, please?" she whispered and lifted her lips to mine.

I kissed her.

I came.

She moaned into my mouth, and her kiss was hungry. I felt like I was vibrating, like a balloon with a hole poked in it. Instead of air spewing out of me, it was cum and a tension I didn't know I was holding.

"I think I have sand in my ass." She laughed after a few minutes. "And I might need a shower now." I nodded and eased off of her. She pulled her bathing suit back up and dusted herself off. Sadie put her hands on her knees, adjusted her sunglasses, and looked around. "So that was sex on the beach?"

"Sand and all, yes,"

"Better than the mile-high club?"

I laughed. "I would have to say yes," I said. "We can rinse off and head to the dining pavilion. See what the fishermen caught this morning." She nodded, and we slowly surrendered our spot on the sand to wander back to the hut. Sadie stripped out of her bathing suit and took a quick rinse in the mock shower. She complained that the showers at the house were better, but I told her the view here was better. It took her a moment to realize that I could see her and was watching her rinse off.

With a grin on my face.

❧

Roan would have been impressed by the size of the swordfish laid out on the banquet table; the array of fresh fruit around it was artistic. The drinks were flowing generously, lighter fare, mostly wine. Neither of us were especially sophisticated wine drinkers, Sadie preferred the sweeter, and none of it really appealed to me.

"This is beautiful," Sadie murmured, looking at the sun setting, and the stars peeking out. "All of it," she leaned forward and braced her head in her hands and looked a little… off.

"You know, we spent a lot of time outside today, like all day," I said. She smiled and nodded. "If you're feeling a little lightheaded, you might be dehydrated. You doing okay?"

"Feeling a little woozy, I don't know…" she murmured. I nodded.

"There's bottled water in the room. If you want to head back, have some water and a lie down, I'll bring you a couple of Aspirin and I can find us something to pass the evening," I said.

"Oh," she asked. "What do you have in mind?"

"You liked those half-assed Moscow Mules on the plane, I think you might like a drink called a dark and stormy. It's made with some of the same ingredients, but I think you might like it better."

"Sounds good, I'd like to try that." She stood up and stretched, and from where I was sitting her tits were perfectly illuminated by the last light of the dying sun through one of her silky dresses. It was fleeting and oddly profound.

"Thank you," I hesitated. "For everything."

"Are you okay?" she asked, looking over my face worriedly.

"Yeah, I'm more than okay. I'm here with you. Let me go get a few things from the dispensary and I'll be right there." She smiled and slowly turned to walk away. I had to appreciate her ass as she walked. I took a deep breath and let out a sigh. There went my Shady.

The hotel dispensary wasn't far from the pavilion, and there were a few people milling in the area in front of it, mostly locals; a few looked like employees. I picked up a few bottles that would be useful for enjoying the evening, a few basic snacks, and a small bottle of lube. That was always useful, especially considering some of the things I had in mind for later.

"If it isn't Carl Winthrop," a man said, in a surprisingly deep baritone. I turned casually, but my blood had turned to ice. Winthrop was an old alias, almost three years retired, and no one should remember that name.

"Sorry, you have the wrong person," I said. He was huge, a brick wall of a human being, thick muscled arms, broad chest, gold teeth gleaming in his predator grin, and dreadlocks hanging down past his shoulders.

"No, no, I don't know what name your little white ass is going by these days, but when you killed my brother, set his warehouse on fire, and sank his boat, you were Mister Winthrop. I remember that, you left me with a gift." He raised his shirt to show a ragged scar going up the side of his torso. I remembered him now, I had taken him down with a tactical strike and then tossed him into the water where he ended up tangled with a boat propeller.

"Ah, last time I saw you, you looked like chum," I said. This was possible the worst place to run into a hostile. I had no weapons on me, and there was a fair chance that there were literally no guns on the island. I sat the bag of sundry goods on the ground and gestured. "Are we going to do this?"

"Not going to beg?" he asked.

"I kicked your ass once, I should give you a chance to apologize to leave with your dignity and all your teeth." I flexed my hand and popped my neck.

"You cocky piece of shit," he snarled and brandished a fishing spear head. It looked wickedly sharp, and the hooked blade was sure to snag in flesh. If he got that in me, it would leave a nasty hole that would be hard to sew up.

He swung a tight slash, blade a silver blur.

I stepped toward him, evading his steel and getting into the last place he expected, right in his face. Right fist to the solar plexus, right foot inside his instep, he grunted from the hit, left fist to the chin.

His teeth clacked together and his head rocked back. He might have been bigger than me, and stronger, but he was a stereotypical big guy. Strong, but slow. More bluff than actual show.

Right fist to solar plexus again. His feet tangled with mine when he tried to back up, I was too close to slash or stab, inside his arms. If he was smart, he would have done what Roan would do in the sparring matches we had. Grapple, submission hold, choke hold.

He did none of these things, the only weapon he had was the spear point.

Left hand to nose, rocking his head back again.

His feet came out from under him, and then he fell.

Right foot to groin, left foot to face. There was a crunch, and he spewed a ribbon of blood from his mouth and nose, and his head bounced hard against the ground. I stepped forward again and finished by stomping his right wrist, forcing him to yield the spear point.

"You're a dead man." He spat blood.

"You made quite a few mistakes," I said, and stomped my heal into his larynx, crushing cartilage with a horrific wet sound. "First you tried to come after me. Second, you came alone. Third, you only brought an improvised knife. Do you know what the worst mistake you made was, the one that cost you your life?" His eyes were bulging, struggling to breathe through a crushed throat, with a bruised diaphragm, and a shattered nose.

"You took the time to talk to me. Fucking rookie mistake." I picked up his spear point, a precision-made piece of titanium, with a long shank intended to be attached to a graphite or carbon fiber shaft. "This is a nice point, but if you had actually brought the entire thing, the speargun, the spear, and you shot me, you might have survived. Instead, you're choking on your own blood."

He grunted, and I heard his bowels loosen.

I felt my hand tremble, the adrenaline was still boiling under my skin. I grabbed the big man under the arms and dragged him out of sight. Fucking cleanup? Ugh. The last thing I wanted on my mini-vacation with Sadie to be ruined by some island Clouseau Cop to bumble their way through a dead foreigner.

Fuck.

At least the island was low tech, there was no massive surveillance system, no constant electronic observation, no CCTVs, and with the hour growing late, no witnesses. Thank God for that. I left him under a stone quay. They would find him, but it might take a day or two, maybe longer if the current or a scavenger found him.

When I returned to the small plaza near the dispensary, my bag was still sitting where I left it. The spear point fit easily into the bag, and I almost walked right back to the hut where Sadie was. I felt another tremor run through me. I didn't need to go to her right now, I was still sharp, still on the edge of being ready to react, to lash out.

I went the other direction and found the cabana, and more importantly, the bartender hadn't packed up yet. "What time do you close shop?"

"If you need a drink, I don't," the woman said. She was gorgeous ebony, with an electric smile. I smiled back, but it was a façade, practiced and proven to be disarming.

"Thank you, what do you have that's strong?"

"How strong do you need?" she asked.

"Have anything one hundred proof or over?" She did, a 103-proof island rum. It wasn't dark, wasn't aged, and it was harsh. It burned through me and blunted the twitches and knives that were jagging through my body.

The walk back to the hut was uneventful, and I was thankful for that. There were no police, no pedestrians, nothing to indicate that anything had happened, nothing to indicate a very large angry Rastafarian drug dealer had been killed there.

Sadie was asleep when I pulled the curtain of the hut back. I had let my guard down, this place had no defensible points, no cover, and I had no firearms. What had I been thinking? I paced a few times and then hid the spear point in the luggage. She looked so peaceful, sleeping.

I laid down next to her, putting an arm around her shoulders and my face against the back of her neck. She didn't smell like coconuts, just the faintest hint of bodywash and clean water, the scent of the linens she was wrapped in.

I crashed, the low after the adrenaline high.

∾

WHEN I WOKE AGAIN, THE SUN WAS WELL UP, AND I WAS BY MYSELF. Sadie was out on the beach, basking. She was topless, in all her glory. I sighed, brushed my fingers through my hair and made brief use of the hut's mock bathroom. The lack of a true shower was one of the few things I regretted about the location, besides the tactical ones. I needed to talk to Roan, to make sure that this was just a coincidence.

She sat up, saw me watching, and blew me a kiss. I walked down to where she was sitting, the surf rolling up to her toes in the sand. "I'll have to move soon; the water is getting closer."

"The tide does that. Do you want to cruise the island in a bit, see the sights?" I asked.

"I do, but what happened last night?" she asked.

"Nothing, the line at the dispensary was long," I said, remembering the impact of flesh on flesh, the crunch of bone and cartilage. "There are always people who come down here and think every island in the Caribbean is a haven for hashish. They pester the dispensary people for it," I shrugged. "Tourists."

"Aren't we tourists?" she asked.

"Yes and no, we aren't bad tourists. No fanny packs, no shouting loudly and slowly in English, and we're respectful of local customs," I said. "There is a spa up the hill, I understand it's quite popular."

"I've never been to a spa." She giggled.

"Top notch, we'll remedy that. The full Princess package."

"What's in that?" She stretched and then put her top back on.

"No idea, but I am one hundred percent sure that they have something like that." I wasn't wrong. Not quite an hour later, after something not unlike tapas, we were at what was a French fort, or monastery, overlooking the bay, while a troupe of dark-skinned men and women were vigorously doling out decadence and pampering to a small number of wealthy tourists. I used what conversational French I could manage and rounded her up a top-tier package. Manicure, pedicure, stone massage, a facial, and they would do a few other things, stuff that was outside of my expertise.

Yesterday, I would have joined her in the preening but that was before the attack last night. I pulled out my phone and waited for the connection, and then Roan was there. "What's up, mate?" he asked.

"So, I am looking at a princess package at the Mont St. Henri spa, and they're asking about hair, do you have any suggestions?"

"Sadie doesn't know?" he asked.

"She doesn't and you've always had better taste in such things. I'm certainly no cosmetologist."

"You had an opinion when she had blue hair," he said.

"The blue hair was fucking awful, and you know it." I felt a moment of tension as a police officer pedaled up to the gate of the spa on a bicycle, but it was short lived. The conversation was brief, and topical. The man rode away, and the woman who had met him at the gate watched him go. Lovers? Spouse? Everyone had their own intricate and rich lives, that we were oblivious to. Just as they were unaware of mine, or Sadie's.

"Victoria Lake peek-a-boo," Roan said. "It's classy, clean, and Sadie has the mane for it."

"Isn't that a place in Africa?" I asked.

"Lake Victoria, yes. Victoria Lake was a 1940s film star and was a pin-up model for WWII artists."

"Oh, pin-up, that's classy," I said.

"It will keep the hair off of her neck and might keep her a bit cooler. Probably a bit warmer in the islands than it is here on the bay."

"Speaking of heat, I had a King Kong," I said.

"Is Sadie okay, are you okay?" His tone changed. King Kong was a code phrase, Kong was a gorilla, and that was almost the same as guerilla, an insurgent. It had only happened a time or two before, someone coming back around after a job, looking for revenge.

"Yes, on both. She saw none of it, knows nothing about it."

"Did you recognize him?" he asked.

"I did, vaguely. He was a big black guy, dreadlocks, said that I did a hit on his brother, burned down a warehouse and sank a ship," I said.

"You think that would narrow things down," Roan said. "You've only sunk three ships. But, the Martinique Job."

"Martinique! Oh, I remember her, big hair, big breasts, had a problem with her cousin muscling in on her turf," I said.

"That's the one. Down in the Florida Keys. The warehouse was being used to smuggle drugs and of all damn things, illegal reptiles, into the States. It was just a matter of time before Kai and his guys started rivaling the Cubans in Miami."

"Well, Kai's brother is taking a really long swim," I said.

"I'll check and make sure nothing is going on, and that it was just a chance encounter. Do you need anything? I would offer to expedite something to you, but it wouldn't arrive until you were already leaving."

"No, it's okay, let's just put out some feelers, and Victoria Lake? Peek-a-boo?"

"I will take care of it, and yes on both," he said. "Is she enjoying herself?"

"I'm sure she'll tell you about it when we get back," I gave him a laugh and hung up. I relayed his guidance to the spa stylist, and the woman grinned and went off to do her thing. We spent several hours at the spa, and I wasn't able to completely resist. Getting a manicure and a pedicure was something that I routinely did anyway. Roan would give me no end of grief about it, but when the woman started rubbing the balls of my feet and someone put a Papa Doble daiquiri in my hand, my resistance was gone.

"There is something wrong with your daiquiri," Sadie said. I opened my eyes, and she was radiant and almost glowing like she was made of bronze. "No shaved ice, no strawberry, I think you're having a joke at my expense."

"This is a classic daiquiri, the sort that Ernest Hemingway drank when he wrote about killing men and fishing, something about bulls," I said. "Americans dumped a strawberry sorbet into it and decided that was an improvement."

"Papa Doble?" she asked, as I confirmed with a waiter that I did indeed want another.

"Double measure of rum, the way Papa Hemingway liked them," I said.

"Have you read any of his books?" she asked.

"As many as you have," I countered. "I have some ideas of what I would like to do this evening. There is a bottle of lube that didn't get used last night." Her cheeks picked up a hint of blush, and her lips turned up slightly. "But before that, we should enjoy the afternoon, and get you a few drinks. It'll be important to be relaxed."

"I think you should take me dancing," she murmured and threw her arms around my neck, leaning into me with a sultry little kiss. "Make up for that school dance... remember the one? You punched Ronnie Collins in the face for dancing with me after I practically begged you to and you wouldn't. Got us both thrown out and that thrashing from Dean."

"Ronnie fucking Collins, was there ever a more punchable face?" I asked. Was that the first time I knew what my greater purpose could be? Busting his nose, that had been satisfying. I barely remembered Dean and his step-fatherly beatings and yelling until his face turned red and spit dripped off of his lip.

What an asshole he had been.

I made a few inquiries and there was certainly a place on the island where I could take her dancing. It wouldn't be like a prom or school dance, but there was a reception hall. They had a live band most nights, and if you tipped them, they would play all night. There was a certain irony, one that Roan had pointed out, that the many of the people who live in places we Americans consider paradise, are poor. Poor to the point of destitution, really. Outside of tourism, St. Henri had literally nothing. It was a rock, with little farmland, barely any livestock, no mining, no industry, nothing.

I put a little cash in a few hands, convinced a few people to 'make calls' and before long I had the grand hall staffed with musicians, and catered. A few words at the dispensary and the spa and then probably a third of the tourists visiting the island came down for an open bar and live band.

I took Sadie's hand, and we danced.

She found a dress in her luggage and was able to look the part. I didn't have anything more than a single button-up shirt, and a pair of slacks. It was probably closer to what we would have worn to a dance when we were kids.

We had wine, then danced, slow and without any serious rhythm. I knew a little ballroom, it helped with high society work, and I didn't want to embarrass her by showing her that more than a decade after losing her, I knew how to do a passable if unremarkable waltz. It was touching, nice, to hold her hand, the small of her back, and do that swaying step. She pressed her head against my chest.

Roan was going to be so fucking jealous when I told him about this.

We would have to do this again, proper like, with her in a ballroom dress, and me in a fitted suit. Maybe even drag the hermit Brit out of the manse. I smiled at that thought.

By the time the band was breaking down their gear, my shirt collar was unbuttoned, and her face was flushed and she had a sheen of sweat. We grabbed a last round of drinks and made our way back to the hut. *How was I going to do this?* I knew what I wanted; it was what I took when I called up my escorts. I loved it, how tight it always was.

Was it because it was a forbidden fruit? That was too easy, and it wasn't that forbidden.

Maybe it was how they yielded, gave it to me. How they were ready to just grit their teeth and take it for the extra money and then enjoyed it.

They would have their perfectly coiffed hair, flawless make up, be so completely composed. They would make a face and then submit. Money talked. Then, when they were face down, and I took them, they would sing.

I knew the difference between real pleasure and putting on a good show.

When I was done, they would be almost shell shocked, their façades crumbled, mascara running. They would be contemplating the meaning of the universe, or half catatonic.

Seeing the effect I could have over them, that was better than the actual act. Fuck, I enjoyed it because of what it did to them.

And I wanted to do that to Sadie. To give her such pleasure, to orgasm in such a manner that she achieved nirvana. This was going to be a challenge, because normally it was simple. *Here's an extra x number of dollars, I'm going to fuck your ass and nut on your face, we good?*

I couldn't be like that with Sadie. Not my Sadie.

I kissed her on the neck and caressed her. She was warm under my lips, some from the day's sun, certainly some from the drinks and dancing. Her lips found mine, and I remembered my patience, to not rush. She wasn't a prostitute, I was going to kiss her, I was going to eat her pussy, and I wasn't going to use her as a tissue.

I eased her down on the bed, relieved her of her dress, and kissed her. Better and better. Her lips tasted like wine and fruit cocktails. I was torn, I was hard and ready to get down to business. I wanted to go straight to what I ultimately wanted.

I couldn't black credit card my way through this. I had to be calm, be patient, and I had to ask myself how Roan would handle this.

Roan wouldn't, because there is no way he would try to park his business in her ass. He was too polite.

I went down on her, with as much vigor as I could muster.

She writhed and ran her fingers through my hair, and I could feel the rake of her nails. *Don't rush, don't rush.*

I mounted her, gently and tempering myself to how Roan had taken her. Slow, measured, patient. It would work in my favor. She moaned, and we traded kisses, and I used all of my self-control, my discipline. I wanted her to cum, preferably several times.

She did, and several times I felt myself pushed to the edge of my own limit. It would have been so easy to release and let it flow through me. The hardest part was when I was going to change positions with her, and instead of getting over on her knees she took me in her mouth. She might have been showing off a little bit, and I was certainly appreciative.

I stopped her, with only a few seconds reserve left. If I hadn't stopped her, I would have lost it.

Sadie made a whimpering noise, and I pulled her up and kissed her. I needed a few moments. I had to cool off, God, I was so close.

She seemed a bit surprised by kissing again, but after that initial hesitation, she fell back into her own rhythm.

"Sadie," I said, between kisses. I gripped her ass while she gripped my shaft. "I want something from you."

"Yes," she said and all but bit my lower lip.

"Turn around, I want to take you from behind." She nodded and turned, kneeling on the bed. I grabbed the bottle of lube, while she leaned forward. When I faced her again, I saw everything: her glistening wet pink pussy, and the prize I wanted, her ass. Standing there, seeing it all, laid out like a gift for me, I felt something drip down my own leg.

Fuck I wanted her, I wanted this, I wanted to hear her sing.

I wanted her so bad.

I eased into her and fell into a very easy rhythm. She rolled her hips against me and seemed very pleased. I took some of the lube, ran a bead down my thumb, and then massaged her ass with it. She tensed, but only for a second.

"Oh!" she gasped.

I kept my pace the same and pushed until the first joint of my thumb was inside her ass. She held perfectly still, but her breath was slower, more measured. "Relax, just relax. I'll go very slow."

"Oh God," she gasped, her voice an octave lower. I pushed again, she shuddered, and then my thumb was all the way inside her.

"How is that?" I asked.

"Oh God, oh God," she panted. I gave her the business, alternating, back and forth. I would push my thumb into her ass when I pulled out, and when I thrust my cock back again, I would pull my thumb back. She was relaxing, and tensing, and I could tell she was getting there, she would be ready soon. "Oh God, Kyle, what are you doing," she groaned.

"I want to fuck your ass," I said, my voice cracking with my own need.

"My ass?" she asked.

"Yes," I said.

"Okay," she said softly.

Patience, patience, take it slow.

I used some more lube and made sure that I was as slick as possible. I pressed the head of my cock against her asshole. My heart started racing again, and excitement started building inside my chest. It felt like panic or anxiety. *Oh God.*

Was this actually happening?

She groaned, and I started sinking into her.

I heard her make the sound, the shuddering groan, and felt her ripple around me. It wasn't quick, and the strokes weren't deep. Not at first. But eventually I buried myself entirely in her. She screamed into the pillow, and I felt her fingers brush against my balls.

"Do it, do it," I said. She was furiously playing with herself, and I felt her clench. She shrieked again, and I went faster. I was less gentle, I went faster, deeper. I felt her fingering become more furious as well.

This moment was the reason I so enjoyed taking women from behind. The fact that this was my Sadie could only make it perfect beyond imagination.

"Oh, fuck!" Sadie screamed, and everything went tight. I shuddered, and I felt my self-control crumple. "Oh! Oh! Oh!" Her words trailed off into a series of groans and cries.

"Sadie…" my voice died in my throat and I almost lost my footing as my cock erupted inside her. I came to the brink of being emotional as my balls emptied into her. It seemed like something more than my jizz was spewing out of me. I held onto her hips like a like life preserver.

We didn't stay in that position long, she was trembling, and my knees were almost gone.

I put my arms around her and buried my face in her hair.

It had never been like this before. This was hardly the first time I had finished balls deep in a beautiful woman's ass. More often, I would work the backdoor until they came, and then while they were in the orgasmic aftershock I would come in their face. I was Apollo, glorious and might. I was Pan, the deviant who had pillaged their ass and turned their flawless makeup into a toaster strudel.

Except now. Now? *I was just Kyle.* I felt a contentment that I had never known before.

This was better than all the gin I had swilled, all the escorts I had railed and decorated, and all the excess and decadence I had wallowed through since doing that first job taking out the inner circle of a Miami-Cuban Cartel.

I wanted to tell her how much I loved her, but seeing her red faced and with my load running down the cheek of her ass, it didn't really seem like the best time.

"I love you." I said it anyway.

CHAPTER TWENTY-ONE

*S*adie...

"I love you."

I froze, the only sounds rippling through the ringing silence in the wake of those three words was the push and pull of the surf below in counterpoint to the push and pull of our breath filling and leaving our lungs.

"What?" I asked, barely able believe I'd just heard what I thought I just heard.

"You heard me," he said, and I searched his face, giving him a long, slow blink.

"Really?" I whispered. His smile was a careful one, edged in sadness and I uttered, "Look at me."

His night dark eyes rose to mine. "I never stopped looking for you, Shady. Not once."

"Stop with the stupid name," I chided, annoyed that he would ruin the moment with it. His eyes flashed, his nostrils flaring in his own irritation.

"Do you know why I call you that?"

"No," I said, immediately on the defensive and hating how quickly and easily he was always able to flip the script on me.

"Shady Brooks; think about it… can you honestly tell me there's nothing more peaceful than hanging out in the grass under the shade of the trees next to a nice cool brook? It's all about the context, baby. How many times have I told you that? Peace, Shady… every time that stupid ass nickname was uttered, I saw peace. That's what you were to me, what you *are* to me… *peace.*"

I choked up and searched him out, trying to decide if he was being genuine or if he was just being manipulative again.

He reached out and cupped my face, leaning forward to press his forehead to mine. Incredibly close, incredibly intimate. I closed my eyes and what he said broke the careful walls I had been trying to erect around my heart where he was concerned.

"I love you, and I am so glad I fucking found you, even though you disappeared. I *never* stopped looking…"

"Kyle…" I couldn't say more. My voice strangled with the thick rope of emotion that'd found its way around my throat.

"It's okay." He raised his lips to my forehead and pressed them there, before retreating from me and slipping off the edge of the bed. "Stay right there," he ordered, and I tried to breathe around the tears that threatened.

He didn't know, and I couldn't tell him… I hadn't disappeared. I'd had to run away. Just two months before I aged out of the system, I'd had to run or risk another beating… or worse.

In the end, it hadn't really mattered either way.

He cleaned us up with washcloths and towels and slipped into the bed beside me, silently hooking an arm around my neck and shoulders and pulling my temple to his lips where he gave it a peck. I sighed, tired, still lazing on a river of bliss from what we'd done.

"C'mere," he said, and his voice had lost its cold neutrality and I cuddled into his side. I laid my head on his chest and shoulder and hated how swiftly he could fall asleep while I lay awake long into the night remembering.

～

WHEN I WOKE, IT WAS TO THE LAZY SOUND OF THE SURF AND A COOL breeze ruffling through the hut and over my body. I pushed myself into a sitting position gritting my teeth slightly at the residual soreness in my ass, but honestly surprised it didn't hurt *more*.

I bit my bottom lip, a shiver of anxiety going up my spine when I realized that Kyle wasn't with me. I ran my hands through my hair, which was still long, just parted on the side with a glamourous sweep of bangs now, and instead of almost to my waist? It was to the middle of my back, just at the line of my bra.

It felt lighter, and cooler, and I liked the cut, but I was worried now that I'd upset Kyle enough that he'd left me here. Like he'd done in the middle of Indigo City once when we had taken the bus system from the Daughton's to the Central City Museum on its free day. We'd argued about something stupid and he'd left me there, at the museum, and I'd had to figure out my own way back. It'd taken hours and finally I had to ask a cop for help and when the police had delivered me to the Daughton's? Oh, Pricilla had been *pissed*. I'd been on food restriction for three days. Kyle had gotten his ass beat by Dean.

Truth be told, I'd rather have dealt with the beating from Dean, but they didn't hit the girls, only the boys. The girls they locked up or just stopped feeding us. Pricilla said it was doing us a favor. We didn't want to get fat, now did we?

I closed my eyes and shuddered. As I slipped out of bed and wrapped the sheet around me, the tightness in my chest loosened as I spotted Kyle down the beach. He was emerging from the water, and it ran down his perfect chest and tight abs. He was tall and lean, muscles sleek like some dark panther as he marched out of the surf, running his hands through his short dark hair, his obsidian eyes sparking and expression sour as he looked up and down the beach.

There were people today.

Modesty was in full effect – at least for me. Kyle didn't have anything to worry about. He exuded confidence, and gave no fucks, no matter what.

The more things change, the more they stay the same... I thought to myself and probably not for the first time.

He walked up the beach and up the ramp, pulling me into his arms and kissing me soundly. I made an 'Mm!' in surprise and slightly stiffened, caught off guard, his words from the night before drifting back to me…

I love you.

That was the problem, though… wasn't it? I loved him too. Despite everything… in spite of everything. I never stopped loving him and as much as I wanted to erect an impenetrable tower between myself and Kyle Lachlan to protect myself from any more hurt that loving him would bring? I just couldn't do it.

"Morning," he said, dark eyes shuttering and closing down at my stiff startlement. "How did you sleep?" he asked.

I shook my head slightly and said, "Alright, I guess…"

"You okay?" he asked, and I blinked. Had he ever asked me that before? Maybe once or twice when we were kids, but only when I think he knew he had pushed things too far.

"Yeah, no, I'm okay," I rushed out, but was I? Was I, really?

I love you…

I looked up at him and he traced a thumb along my cheek lightly, drinking me in with his eyes and it was such a Roan thing to do in a lot of ways and Jesus, I was so weak for those little touches and that look in either of my two men's eyes when they looked at me, I felt myself soften.

A slow smile curved Kyle's lips, and it was a glimpse past his diamond-hard façade. I smiled back and whispered, "Kiss me, please?"

"You never have to ask me for that," he whispered and brought his lips down to mine. He gathered me up, his hands on my ass. The sheet was trapped between us, cool saltwater soaking through the scant covering. I laughed against his lips.

"Mm, love that kiss," he said, sucking in his bottom lip. "Tastes like candy."

"Mm." I smiled appreciatively and asked, "So what were your big plans for today?"

"Flight doesn't leave until this afternoon, thought we might take a walk along the main boulevard in town, look through some of the shops, see if we can't find that big, ginger mook of a Brit back home a souvenir of some kind."

I smiled, lighting up a bit at the thought of Roan and bringing him something; honestly more delighted that Kyle had been the one to think of it and not me.

"You must really be good friends… how did you two meet up anyway?" I asked.

Kyle slapped me lightly on the bottom and murmured, "Get dressed," moving away from me to do the same.

"We were on a joint task force in Afghanistan when his Humvee got blown up. I knew right away that he would be perfect for what I wanted to do, so I faked some medical stuff and worked the system to get where I needed to be to be near him. As soon as he was recovered enough," he gave a shrug, "I did what I could to help him out the rest of the way and made him an offer he couldn't refuse."

How pragmatic and cold of him, the way he made it sound… too bad I knew Kyle Lachlan and some things about a person? They really never did change. I mean, it was one of the reasons why we were both here, right now… Kyle was all sharp angles personality wise but underneath he held such an unwavering devotion and loyalty that if you did something to catch his eye… well, that was it.

He may have been a pain in the ass to live with, but he was a loyal pain in the ass.

Knowing Roan, the way I did; I knew he had to have done something to earn that loyalty from Kyle. Otherwise, their friendship wouldn't even be a thing. I still wasn't entirely sure what it was that I had done, back when we were kids to earn Kyle Lachlan's attentions, but right now and especially after last night, I was glad I did.

I love you…

God, how long had I waited, breath held, to hear him say those words to me when we were teens?

"Something the matter with you?" he asked, and I startled slightly.

"No, why?" I asked.

He gave me a crooked grin that if I'd had panties on, would have vaporized them and said gently, "Then get dressed."

"Oh! Right!" I found forward motion and moved around the bed in the hut toward our suitcase, my train of thought derailed for the time being.

The sun was warm on my skin and Kyle, almost as mindful as Roan, insisted on spraying my pasty skin down with sunblock kissed with a bronzer again before we went out.

I stood, nude except for my sandals, dress laid out nearby, giggling and turning on his order as the spray misted my skin, the smell of coconut hanging sweet in the air.

"You're good," he declared, kissing me with a smile.

"First time I think I've ever had a decent tan," I murmured against his mouth and he grinned.

I put on the short, steely blue satin bodycon dress, the top a halter, the skirt flirty layered petals in front and hugging my ass in back. No bra or panties required, according to Kyle. 'Never ruin a good dress with panties' he had told me but I hadn't paid that much mind. He said they ruined the line of the dress and took them off of me. Kneeling in front of me and sliding the scrap of silk down my legs and over the black, strappy sandals I had on. He had such an intensity to his gaze, I half expected him to push up the short skirt and go down on me.

I was half right, he did push up my skirt, only he pressed an all too short reverent kiss over my clit and then let it drop down to cover me again, standing and flinging the panties off his finger back into our open suitcase.

I shuddered, and it took a second for me to get it together. Kyle, being the little shit that he could be, smiled in complete satisfaction at how well he could disarm me of my senses and I very nearly rolled my eyes at him. If he only knew, despite how infuriating he could be, just how much he had me wrapped around his little finger.

Me and Roan both, apparently.

He answered a call from Roan as we strolled through the island's marketplace and kissing the top of my head wandered a bit of a way off from me to take it. I was incredibly grateful that he stayed within my sight. He was like a worry stone for me, something I could see and touch to keep me grounded in this strange and admittedly somewhat scary place.

I wasn't sure if Kyle saw the things I could see. The squalor in corners and alleyways, the men licking their lips as their eyes traveled over my body in the admittedly cool, but thin dress… it wasn't any different, really, than Indigo City… except here, I wasn't in America. I didn't know my rights, and I knew in countries like this that women weren't anywhere near as 'equal' as back home which that was a joke… I knew that firsthand.

The island's marketplace was a little strange. The buildings full of upscale boutiques, little tents and kiosks full of cheap, kitschy items parked just outside. The streets were narrow, far too narrow for cars, and I realized they were even almost too small for cart and horse which told you just how *old* this place must have been.

A hand fell lightly on my lower back and I jumped, looking up at Kyle with relief.

"You okay?" he asked, eying the shop owner who had been trying to sell me an array of batik silk scarves.

"Yeah, yeah! I'm fine. Look at these…"

"You like them?" he asked.

"I don't think I would mind having one," I said with a faint smile.

"Which one?" he asked, and I considered. "I have *a lot* of purple in my wardrobe," I said with a laugh.

"Isn't it your favorite color?" he asked, and I smiled a little bigger.

"Ah, Roan's I think… my favorite color is blue."

Kyle considered me a long moment and whispered in my ear, "You should tell him that, you know… he'll get you things that you like better."

"It's okay," I said smiling. I sighed. "It's nice, you know?"

"What is?" he asked, and I bit my bottom lip, the confession a difficult one to make out loud but then I remembered… Kyle never made fun of me about the really important things. He knew. He never said anything to make me feel inferior back then… I hoped that still held true, now.

"Being cared for," I murmured. "Not having to make every single decision about every single thing and have it feel like I had a fifty-fifty chance of it being life or death."

He pressed a thumb into my trapezius and let it glide along my skin, pulling me closer into his side and pressing a kiss to my temple, above my ear… breathing me in. It was an amazing moment of stillness among the bustle of the market. The two of us, a stone in the midst of the babbling brook of humanity around us and I closed my eyes and soaked it in.

"I've got you, Shady," he murmured and for the first time, the nickname made me smile.

We bought three of the scarves. One blue, one purple, and one silver. I stopped at another stall on the street and Kyle made sure I was alright and broke from me, to wander into a shop right behind where I was at with bars on the window.

I perused some handmade silk batik neckties and smiled, holding up the charge card Roan had given me and the seller bobbing his head enthusiastically, I chose a purple one and a blue one that closely matched the scarves that Kyle had bought for me, and a hand-woven handbag that suited me to hide them in.

I took the bag back from the seller as something dropped over my head, flashing in the bright sunlight.

"What's this?" I asked, touching rippling metal with a fingertip as Kyle clasped the necklace behind my neck.

"A bit of treasure for my treasure," he said, and I could hear the grin at his cleverness in his voice. He held a hand mirror from the vendor's table out in front of me and I gasped, leaning forward for a better look.

"Is that *real?*" I asked.

"Absolutely, I assure you. Here."

He handed me a slip of paper, but I couldn't immediately take my eyes off the thick, misshapen silver coin edged in gold on its golden chain. I turned my eyes to the literature that came with it and leaned back against Kyle, his hands smoothing over my arms, as I read out loud about the piece of eight around my neck and the shipwreck it had come from.

I turned in his arms and put mine around his neck.

"It's beautiful and amazing," I murmured.

"I figured with your love of all things history and literature, it would give you and Roan something to talk about." He smirked. "That and it'll give that ginger bitch some major jealousy."

"Kyle!" I cried outraged and slapped him in his chest. "That's a real rude way to talk about your best friend."

He laughed.

"He *is* my best friend," he agreed. "And I'm sure he's said a lot worse about me."

I felt my mouth drop open, and I shook my head. "He hasn't, actually… he's never once spoken badly of you in front of me."

Kyle arched a dark eyebrow like he didn't believe me and I frowned slightly.

"We love you, you know," I murmured, and that eyebrow came down, and a slow, almost tentative and shy smile split his sensual lips.

"You love me?" he asked, and I tucked myself into his front, holding him close.

"I've loved you since forever," I said. "It never stopped. Not with time or distance. Not even when I thought you long must have stopped even thinking about me…"

He tipped my chin and forced me to look up at him, his dark eyes obsidian glass, hard and sharp as he looked at me.

"I never stopped thinking about you, Shady. Never. Not once. Don't you ever say something like that again. Don't you ever think that." I swallowed hard and nodded, struck mute by his intensity. He dipped his head and kissed me fiercely and I returned it just as ardently.

The relief that swept through me was intense. *He'd thought of me, he loved me,* all the things I'd wished for had been laid in my hands and it was overwhelming to an extent. Still, there was a frightening and niggling doubt far in the back of my mind, nibbling at the tender meat of my heart.

Could I accept it? That the Kyle of my youth, the boy I had so loved had evolved into this man? Tender, yet cruel, sharp and yet soft… it was easy to forget for a moment when he held me like this that he *murdered people for money.* It was even easier to forget that Roan helped him to that end…

What was I getting myself into? That wasn't the question so much as *how could I fall so far so fast?*

I thought I had morals, that I couldn't or wouldn't be a whore for a bit of food or comfort… but I guess I already knew that wasn't exactly true. I fought back the deep wave of shame that swept through me and smiled up at Kyle, but just like when we were kids, he knew… he *always* knew.

"What's wrong, baby?" he asked me as we continued our stroll.

"Nothing," I lied, then followed it with a bit of truth, "Just an old ghost rising back up to haunt me."

"I'm afraid ghost busting isn't one of my many talents, babe. Do you want to talk about it?" he asked.

I forced a brighter smile onto my face and shook my head.

"No, I really don't."

"Okay. You know you can tell me. I'm the last one who would judge."

My smile grew genuinely brighter at that. "Yes, I know." That was absolutely true. Always had been, and I believe always would be… especially now. How could anyone throw stones when they killed people for money?

When we returned to the resort, it wasn't back to our room. Instead, we ate a pleasant lunch and when that was through? A car was waiting for us to take us back to the airport to go home. I was surprised.

"What about our suitcase?"

"Already handled, babe. Just bring your purchases."

I smiled and nodded and slid into the back of the car, Kyle slipping in behind me. He wound his fingers between mine and held my hand on the seat between us as I watched the island pass by the car's window.

It was winding on toward afternoon and I wasn't exactly looking forward to going through the motions of security and all of that. It had been a long trip to get here and leaving this late in the day meant we wouldn't be landing until very late at night if not the earliest hours of the morning.

"Where are we going?" I asked as we drove through a back gate of the airport well away from the main terminal.

"A final surprise for you," Kyle said easily as we were taken into a hanger. "Roan chartered us a private jet, a direct flight home."

"Oh, wow, are you serious?" I balked. That must have cost a fortune! Of course, everything my two men did for me seemed to be beyond extravagant... I sat with that thought wide-eyed as we approached the plane, our suitcases being carried aboard as we rolled to a stop in front of an official looking person at a podium.

Kyle opened the car door and held down a hand for me and I took it.

I looked up at him and he smiled down at me and there he was, the boy who did sweet things and yet said such awful ones sometimes. The boy who hurt my feelings, then slipped into my room at night to hold me as I cried, making silent apologies with offerings of food and pretty bits of things.

The boy who had stolen my heart forevermore no matter how difficult he made it to love him back.

I did love Kyle Lachlan, differently and for different reasons that I was falling in love with Roan for... and I don't think I ever stopped loving him in the intervening years between when we'd last seen each other.

In some ways, that was a relief. In others, knowing what he was, how he operated now, it brought another wave of something akin to shame... perhaps because I just didn't understand. I mean, I would like to think that was what it was. I certainly couldn't talk to Kyle about it, but maybe I could speak with Roan.

"Papers," the man at the podium asked in thickly accented English.

Kyle presented our passports, and the man looked them over and looked us over. I stood silently, a bundle of nerves, waiting for questions as I had at the airport on the way here, but none came. He simply handed them back and gestured for us to walk down the actual red carpet that was rolled out beside the plane leading up to the steps.

Kyle smiled down at me and tucked my hand into the crook of his elbow leading me down that swath of red carpet to the portal to the craft that would take us home.

Home...

I felt a sudden spurt of deep emotion at the word and realized of all the gifts that Roan and Kyle had given me over the last several weeks... *months?* The greatest one they provided me was an actual sense of home.

The sensation of *excitement* filling me at the prospect of returning *home* to Roan and the mansion at Bootlegger Head was worth more to me than any dress, scarf, or pirate coin bauble. My hand in Kyle's, the knowledge that I would return to be folded into Roan's arms in one of his soothing and wonderful hugs.

That was *everything*.

Heaven on earth.

To finally *matter...* was it any wonder that tears slipped down my cheeks unbidden at how overwhelming it all was?

"Sad to go?" Kyle asked, a bit of uncertainty in his eyes.

I smiled and sucked in a shuddering breath and told the truth.

"Excited to be going *home*," I murmured and the smile that broke over his face turned him positively angelic.

God, I had missed that smile.

"Champagne?" the flight attendant asked, holding out a round silver platter with two bubbling flutes.

"Yes, thank you." Kyle handed me one and took the other. He clicked glasses with me and said, "To going home."

"To going home," I murmured and sipped. We took a pair of seats and buckled in for takeoff and I felt a knot in my chest loosen as soon as we started to move.

As we left the ground of St. Henri's behind, hands loosely clasped between us, sipping the bright champagne, I left some of my uncertainty behind with it.

"You trust me, Shady?" Kyle asked me suddenly a few minutes into the flight.

"Yes, why?" I asked, startled out of my own reverie.

"I need to know that you trust me as well as love me," he said and I think it was one of the first times I had ever heard him so... uncertain.

"I wouldn't be here if I didn't trust you, Kyle," I said softly, gripping his fingers tighter.

"I'm not Roan," he said his dark eyes traveling over my face. "I'm not good at all the hearts and flowers bullshit."

I felt my face soften and searched his guarded expression.

"I-I don't love you for the hearts and flowers," I told him, and it was true, I didn't.

"Then why do you love me?" he asked, brushing his lips across my knuckles. It was a good question. Why did I love this sharp edged, difficult man?

"Because you make me feel safe," I confessed. "Because you've never lied to me, and yes, you've said harsh things and made me feel less than sometimes, but that doesn't have anything to do with *you*, that's a *me* problem..."

He cocked his head and swept me with his gaze, like I was doing something particularly fascinating.

"You may not hold me close and whisper sweet lies in the dark about how everything is going to be okay... but you hold me close and it's what you don't say that matters." I swallowed hard. "Just like when we were teens, you didn't say much - it was always what you *did*."

He smiled brilliantly then, and I realized in that moment that Kyle Lachlan loved me so much that he invited his best friend to love me too because he knew he was broken, knew he was damaged, and knew that he couldn't give me all the things I needed to feel whole. That he would be the first to defend me, the first to extract retribution for anyone who dared try to hurt me, but that he knew I needed *more*.

He knew I needed hearts and flowers, and that sometimes I needed the sweet whispered lies and he knew that Roan was the man for that job… and he knew that Roan needed me just as much.

My heart gave a dull, fractured ache to what had led Lach here. Born drug addicted, a life spent in the system labeled difficult, labeled troubled… and yes, he was all of those things and more but those things made the man beside me, clutching my hand, sweeping my face with his eyes the *most* human male I had ever met.

"What am I to you?" I asked, quietly and his eyebrows went up in surprise.

"Everything that I lack," he said honestly, and I felt my heart throb, those broken pieces grind together.

He didn't give me a chance to say anything to that, his lips descending upon mine his hand finding the seatbelt in my lap and unhitching it.

"What are you doing?" I whispered against his lips only to feel them smile against my own, his fingers slip under my skirt, nudging my thighs apart.

"Indoctrinating you into the mile-high club – in style," he whispered and then he positively devoured my mouth with his. I arched unbidden against my seat, parting my legs to give him access as his tongue plunged past my lips and teeth to stroke against mine.

"Mm!" The sharp sound of utter surrender slipped unbidden from my mouth to his. His fingertips grazing my sex making my pussy throb with want and heat. I felt my nipples tighten beneath the thin satin of my dress as he broke the kiss, removed his hand from up my skirt and undid his own seatbelt all in one seemingly fluid motion.

"Come with me," he muttered and stood, cock straining at the front of his tan, linen beach pants, his untucked white linen shirt doing nothing to disguise things. He set his champagne flute aside and took mine from me, doing the same before hauling me to my feet.

He took us to the back of the plane and opened a door there and ushered me through before him. I blinked in surprise at the bed there. The quarters were tight, like the back of a motor home, but much, *much* nicer.

"Up you go," he said, and I crawled up onto the black satin sheets, he stepped in further behind me and shut the door.

I twisted, leaning back as he captured my ankle in his hand and slipped first one sandal then the other off my foot, letting them fall to the floor at his feet.

I watched him and he stood so full of confidence, a dark light in his eyes as he watched me, expression impassive. I reached up and untied the thin, spaghetti strap bow at the back of my neck, letting the satin covering my breasts fall away.

He smiled, a man who knew he'd won the prize as he reached down and loosened his beach pants, letting them fall. I raised my hips, and he swept my dress down my legs and let it fall to the floor and as soon as it left his fingertips in a shining fall of slick fabric, he reached up in that way that guys do and gripped the back of his button down linen shirt and hauled it up over his head.

He let his hungry gaze wander over me from head to toe and back up again before, like the predator he'd made himself into, he crawled over the top of me, kissing his way up my body to claim my mouth again like it was his ultimate prize.

I reached for him, laying back on the slick black satin, wrapping my arms and legs around him and pulling his warmth over the top of me. I kissed him until I was breathless with need for something more, for a deeper touch and I practically begged him, "Make love to me."

"Is that what we're doing?" he asked, kissing the side of my neck, sounding a bit dazed. I smiled to myself, my lip trembling.

"Always," I whispered back, and he made this satisfied little 'hm' and slid himself inside of me with a deliberate thrust of his hips. I gasped, writhing beneath him as he filled me, and he didn't hesitate, just struck a strong sure rhythm that straddled the line between possession and obsession.

I was alright with that. I understood that Kyle's version of love and loving someone had been shattered a long time ago. That things were just different when it came to him and that that was *okay*... that he had protected his heart for so long, with so many, that he just didn't know how to love anyway else.

I clasped his face between my hands as he pushed his cock deep within my pussy and made eye contact with him. I let the dark things, the light things, and everything in between swim through my gaze, showing him just how intensely I felt for him, how deeply those feelings ran and how strong I could be to take his love in whichever way he felt like showing it.

I was pleasantly surprised when he groaned aloud and covered my mouth with his, the kiss deeper, more demanding than anything we'd shared before. I buried my fingers in his soft hair, raised my hips and ground down to meet his thrusts and lost all sense of myself, of time, and let myself be immersed completely in him as we shot across the sky at however many miles per hour this private jet that we were on could go.

"Sadie." He moaned my name like it was a prayer and I cuddled around him closer, gasping, both of us panting, as we left earth's very atmosphere with how high the pleasure took us.

I kissed his chest, his shoulder, the side of his neck – just everywhere I could reach. I held him close, raked nails lightly down his back, gripped his ass and pulled him in tighter, squeezing down on him with my core muscles until he made a strangled noise of – well I didn't know what it was, but I did know it was good.

I don't know how long we were like that, how long we loved each other, how high we actually climbed, how fogged with pleasure and desire we became, I just know that when we finally came? It was together, and for me at least, it was both powerful and the most gentle thing I had ever encountered with him.

"You're a miracle made in flesh," he murmured, kissing me gently, as we both came down. I smiled and traced his sharp and handsome features with gentle fingertips.

"And you say you can't be smooth or do hearts and flowers," I whispered, and he smiled at me, chuckling.

"I can, sometimes, it's just not always my first inclination. You're different," he confessed. "You've always been different."

I raised an eyebrow slightly and cuddled closer, craving his touch. I swear, I *always* craved to be touched…

"I don't know why," I whispered.

"It's just you, babe. It's just always something that's been about you. I can't explain it. Don't need to. I just know it's real, and it's there and that is enough for me."

"Hmm," I hummed considering what he said.

"We have some hours before we land," he murmured. "You hungry?"

I laughed slightly and nodded. "Starving, actually... now that you mention it."

"Okay." He kissed the tip of my nose and pulled away from me gently. I couldn't help the pouting moan and he smiled as though it was one of the best sounds he'd ever heard.

We redressed, slipping out into the rest of the plane and he rang the flight attendant, ordering our food in a hushed tone. Coming to sit with me at the table. The meal was kind of amazing for being served on a flight, then we filled some of the rest of the time back to Maryland cuddled in one of the wide reclining seats and watching movies on the big screen set into the wall by the door to the cockpit.

We had a few drinks, watched what Kyle liked as he made comical criticisms of Roan's movie choices and I found, honestly, that I liked them both for different reasons. Roan's for the deep and emotional connections between the characters on the screen and Lach's for the bright, fast-paced action and explosions.

Somehow, the flight home from the island seemed to go much faster than the flights down had. Probably the lack of stops and layovers. I was tired and beginning to drift when Kyle nudged me awake gently and murmured, "Shady come on, let's get you buckled up for landing."

He buckled me into my seat and found my sandals, slipping them back onto my feet as I considered him kneeling in front of me. It so wasn't like him but was at the same time. He looked up and gave me one of his devil-may-care reckless grins that always made my chest loosen and I smiled back.

He kissed me, before finding his own seat and buckling up.

The landing was rougher than in a big plane, and I sucked in a sharp breath as Kyle reached out and clutched my hand in his to keep me steady. I swallowed, mouth dry as we taxied to another hangar and the plane's engine wound down.

"You're free to disembark," the captain came over the intercom.

"Um, thank you," I called out and Kyle laughed at me.

"He can't hear you, baby. Come on. I think Roan's out there waiting."

"Really?" I asked.

"Mm-hm."

I unbuckled my seatbelt and stood up, the flight attendant opening the door, the cold Maryland air blasting through the portal. I jumped and hugged myself and Kyle put an encouraging hand to my back. When we went down the steps, I turned and Roan was standing by, next to a Range Rover, his hands both resting atop his cane, his keen green eyes searching me out. His dour expression changed, his lips lifting into a smile as some of the flight crew lifted our luggage into the back-cargo area of the stylish SUV.

I went to Roan immediately and put my arms around him. He handed his cane to Kyle and scowling demanded, "Bloody hell, Lach! Where's her coat?" as he peeled off his overcoat and wrapped it around me, rubbing my arms through the thick wool, returning my hug.

"Relax, you anxious reptile. She's got us both to keep her as warm as she needs."

Roan glared at Kyle and murmured to me, "Come on, Poppet. Let's get you home." I looked up at Roan with a stupid grin and nodded tiredly as Kyle opened the back door to the car and Roan turned me to help me up into it. He insisted I keep his coat.

Kyle snuggled me close in the back seat and Roan blasted the heat as soon as he got into the driver's seat.

"Home, James…" Kyle smarted off and Roan raised two fingers between the seats. I felt my brow wrinkle in confusion as Kyle laughed.

"Do you always have to be such an instigator?" I asked, grinning and Roan jumped in.

"What she said."

"Always," Kyle vowed solemnly and I think Roan and I rolled our eyes in synch which made Kyle laugh even harder in the close back seat.

"How long is the drive?" I asked, sleepily.

"Forty minutes or so," Roan answered.

"You don't have to stay awake, babe. Sleep." Kyle pecked me on the top of my head and squeezed me a little tighter.

I tried to stay awake, I did, but I failed. It had been a long, long day.

I was vaguely aware of pulling into the well-lit garage of the mansion, of the two men murmuring to each other and of being slightly jostled. I made a noise, and they both chuckled.

"I've got her," Kyle murmured. "You go on ahead."

"Alright."

I was lifted, carried through the mansion and I felt safe enough, cared for enough, and *tired* enough that I couldn't give one whit about it.

"Sadie, gonna put you down for a minute, stand up sleepy girl."

I stood, and the string holding up the dress at the back of my neck was turned loose, the fabric slipping down my body whisper quiet.

"Arms up, lass," Roan said kindly, gently, and I put my arms up, more satin dropping over my head, slipping down my body, heavy firm hands falling to my hips.

The rustle of cloth beside me and I was turned. "Up you go." Kyle's voice. I climbed into bed and smiling, my two lovers tucked me in. Each giving me a kiss good night, first Kyle, then Roan.

"G'night," I whispered and both of them chuckled.

I slept.

CHAPTER TWENTY-TWO

*R*oan...

One of the advantages of flying chartered rather than commercial was that the private terminal wasn't attached to any of the concourses, and I could drive the Range Rover almost to the door of the plane to pick Lach and Sadie up. Bypassing the parking and regular pick up/drop off area was almost worth the cost of flying private. They both looked tired when they disembarked from the Lear, and by the look on her face and the swagger in his stride I assumed that Sadie was now also a member of the mile-high club.

She was no less beautiful to me, and the way she came to me and hugged me close was almost worth the time away from her… almost. I could have boxed Lach over her lack of coat, however.

During the ride back to the house, Sadie leaned over in the back seat and went to sleep. Lach and I might have talked about what happened, but he didn't want to talk about it front of her, even if she were dead to the world. And then there was the fact that she looked like an angel with her head pressed against his shoulder. No need to sully the moment with talk of devils and dastardly deeds.

The tensest part of getting everyone settled back in the house was helping Lach dress Sadie for bed. She still had the smell of island, travel, and sex on her, and for a moment we held her between us, naked as the day she was born.

What would it be like? I wondered, but just as soon as the idea entered my mind, I pushed it out. The coming day was her own, and there was no telling how much Lach had put on her on their island jaunt.

After she was tucked away, we retreated to the lounge. Lach dropped into his leather lounger, and I brought him a highball glass of ice, gin, and muddled mint. "How was St. Henri?" I asked.

"Rough," he said. "Between how much sun I soaked up and getting in unexpected CQC, I'm beat."

"Something's up," I said. "There's been plenty of activity and I am concerned that Chauvignon might have taken rejection as grounds to try and burn us."

"Napoleon is taking being told no as a personal affront?" Lach asked.

"Possibly, there is also a chance that this frog might have put an open contract on us," I said. "I'm not completely sure but it's pretty obvious that we've stepped into a family dispute. I didn't put two and two together, but the Death Squad leader was *le Generale's* brother."

"So, he's mad we killed his brother and aren't interested in joining his poison candy club? Fuck him," Lach sneered. "He hired us to kill his brother, double fuck him."

"I think we were supposed to fail, so that it would scare the Death squaddies to come back home to Gaffer Chauvignon, like good goons," I said.

"That's why the pay was so high, they weren't really planning on paying out," Lach said. "I bet the blonde-headed Asian bitch was setting me up to take me out."

"It's possible, she has a string of aliases and a body count that is rather impressive. Not as impressive as ours… but still impressive," I said. "Lots of close contact, and the bodies are clean, no sign of what happened, or why they died."

"She's a poisoner and uses something obscure enough that forensics doesn't know to look for it. Frog poison or some shit." He took another drink.

"It's likely," I replied. "I've started dusting some of the contingencies off and making sure that they are high and tight as a precaution."

"Good, hopefully this was just a coincidence, or we can do something to get these assholes to parley. We don't want a war with them if we can help it."

"What if we can't help it?" I asked.

"Then we remind them that France hasn't won a war since." He looked over at me and grinned. "When was the last time that the French won a war? Like on their own, not without one of us, pulling their dicks out of the fire."

"When you put it like that, I don't know." I gave a small laugh. "How was the flight back? It was a little tricky wrangling a charter flight on short notice."

His smile said it all. Sadie was indeed a newly indoctrinated member of the mile-high club, as I suspected.

"Did we buy the jet?" he asked.

"Technically, yes, but we only owned it for the duration of the flight. I had a buyer set up before you landed. They've already taken possession of it. Even made a tidy sum from it; not much, but still."

"I wonder what she's going to do tomorrow," Lach mused.

"Whatever she wants, but I've set her out a lavender and chamomile bath bomb and a thick pile robe. I remember the one time I went to St. Henri – no bath tubs, no real water pressure, and the first thing I wanted when I got back was a shower. A hot one."

"You can get that there now, but you have to book a room in the tower hotel, and if you're going to do that, what's even the point of going?" Lach asked.

"Fair point," I conceded. "She can take a bath, and then whatever she wants to do after that," he said, his gaze rather far away.

~

THEY SLEPT IN LATE, EACH IN THEIR RESPECTIVE ROOMS. I WASN'T surprised to find that neither of them had engaged in any late-night shenanigans. I wouldn't have minded a visit from Sadie, but after a three-day, two-night trip to the Caribbean with Lach? She would sleep until noon. I had plenty with which to keep myself busy.

I used the fold-down stairs, accessed the roof, and started checking some of the additions I'd made to the house. None of these features were conventional, or even rational, really. I'd had a surplus of time on my hands, and a few time-consuming hobbies. I certainly made the best use of my time investing our earnings, and making sure that we would want for nothing, but electronics and computers made that a matter of hours and required them only a few days a month. The rest of my time I gave to my post combat hobby; preparedness and building defenses.

I keyed the lock and opened the door to the cupola that over-looked the entire front of the property, turning on the light above what was easily one of my pride and joys. It had been expensive, and only very slightly illegal to get into the country. I had been in luck finding a broken one being sold in a Pakistani market, likely looted from a crashed Marine helicopter or gunship. The M134 mini-gun had six barrels, an electric drive motor, and an improvised remote-control system. I'd made a further addition of an optical camera of my own design.

I wiped the lens and checked the battery in the laser designator, regrettably one of the flaws in my design. The system drew power from the house grid, although it was hard-lined to the generator, so if the power was cut my gun wouldn't be silenced.

I cleaned and checked all the mechanisms and checked the ammu-nition belt. It almost seemed like overkill having six thousand rounds of 7.62 for it. In truth, it could empty that in a little under two minutes. But that would be a *glorious* two minutes of continuous flame from the barrels and the one note *BRRRRRRR* that gave me a little shiver just to think about it.

As much as I never wanted this thing to *ever* be used, part of me longed to see what sort of carnage it could cause.

The checks done, I locked the cupola behind me and walked over to the rookery.

The rookery was a hot rack of quadrotor drones, six held in frames that they could drop out of and take flight. My time in Afghanistan had more than taught me the value of drones, and I had already made use of this knowledge working with Lach; being his eye in the sky. These were not spy drones, however. These were larger than the normal spy drone, but they had to be to carry something heavier than a camera. I opened the crate and one by one removed the Soviet surplus S-13 rocket warheads and attached them to the drones that would take them.

I could fly these beauties from the Bat Cave, and I could either trigger the warheads manually or fly the drone into a target, where the proximity switch would take over. The former would let me turn an open space into a bloodbath. The latter could blow a hole in the side of anything shy of a main battle tank, and pulp every bastard inside in the process.

I set all six of the drones, and their warheads to *armed.*

I didn't feel the same elation with these murder birds as I had with the gun. These were ugly things, and there was nothing glorious or elegant about them. I had no desire to see these actually work. Frag-mentation weapons were dastardly things.

I retreated back into the house and went through the rest of the internal security. There were easily a dozen claymore mines hidden through the house, at doors and chokepoints. I had taken some of this inspiration from the movie Home Alone, but instead of paint cans and marbles, I had mines and grenades. These were smaller, and would cause significant damage, but wouldn't collapse the house. Lach didn't know about half of these, they would make him nervous if he did.

I was working in the arsenal when the first other person in the house found me, and to my delight, it was Sadie. She stuck her head through the door that had always been locked and her eyes bulged. "Holy shit."

"Good afternoon, Poppet," I said with a smile. I sat the P90 down.

"My God, I *know* you aren't compensating for anything, but... *holy shit*." She looked at rack after rack of weapons. "Where's the war at?"

I chuckled.

"Some of these are trophies, guns we've taken off of contracts we completed. Some are just basic prep, there isn't a single gun that's right for *every* job," I said. "Plus, tastes change, and Lach's are ever changing. He won't use the same gun very long. He likes to chase whatever the new most popular gun is, and he'll carry that. I don't get rid of the old guns, sometimes he likes to fall back to a gun he used before, and sometimes it's just a matter of controlling evidence."

"Because they've been used to kill people," she murmured solemnly, her lovely brown eyes sweeping the racks again.

"That's true. They can't be sold after they've been used on a job, because of ballistics. But there's also something just sad about taking a fine made weapon and destroying it, melting it down, to prevent a trail of evidence from building up." I said.

"That is pragmatic," she said softly, and I could tell she was struggling.

"Some, well, some were just a deal, or guns we wanted for different reasons. Collecting is collecting." I shrugged.

"Well." She came over despite her misgivings and put her arms around me. The scent of lavender was both strong and enticing. "I enjoyed the bath bomb you left me, and I missed you while I was gone." She looked up at me and went on her toes, kissing me. My breath caught, I certainly hadn't expected that. She slipped from my grasp and turning, walked toward the door, a saucy little switch in her hips I don't think she was even aware of. I didn't remember buying her the sundress she wore, an emerald batik silk. Maybe Lach had gotten it for her down there. It was tasteful. She turned to look at me, half out of the armory's door.

"I love you," she murmured softly, and then she was gone, like a mouse.

"I love you too, Poppet," I murmured, mostly to myself.

Stunning.

∼

I SAT DOWN AT THE CONSOLE IN THE BAT CAVE AND BROUGHT UP THE main screen. Six screens all synchronized and presented a single massive image. The facial recognition software pinged a screamer, and I was watching the system do the things I designed it to do.

Manuel 'Black Manny' Esposito, Giancarlo 'El Diablo' Lucasito, and Sophia 'Santa Lucifera' Rodriguez had been tagged at a checkpoint near BWI. There was no way they flew in, two of them were on the FBI's most wanted list, all three were on the DEA's wanted list, and El Diablo was wanted by the NSA and DHS, respectively. They were bad news, and all three of them in Maryland was an equally bad sign. They were all veritable nobility in the Central and South American cartels. Narcos, coyotes; cocaine lords… they had money, firepower, and we had done a number of jobs both for them and against them south of the border.

Each one of these bastards had a reason to have vendetta against us, even Santa Lucifera, who we had worked for after we took out one of her North American lieutenants.

There were a few phone calls to be made, but I needed more information. I could use one of the drones from the rookery, but it would be better to use a different drone, there were several I had that weren't for home defense. I went out, hooked one of the big quadrotors up, connected the burner phone controller, and added two battery packs in its cargo bin. I wanted her to fly long and come home without incident.

I was piloting the drone across Indigo City when Lach finally wandered in. "It's over, mate, we've lost her," he said.

"This might not be the best time for jokes," I answered.

"She found the library and your book collection," he said. He then grabbed a chair and rolled over to look at the screen. "This looks like… this looks like *here*, what are you doing?"

"Face Watch picked up some old friends, we've got at least three narco kings in Indigo City," I told him their names and watched recognition cross his face.

"Well shit," he said. "I swore I would never see *her* again."

"Why, what did you do with *Santa Lucifera?*" I asked, giving him a critical look.

"What do you think I did?" he asked, mocking innocent. I gave him a critical look. "Fine, I fucked her," he admitted.

"I guess I shouldn't be surprised," I said dryly. "Anything I need to know about her?"

"She has tattoos on her tits and gets really angry when you fuck up her makeup," he said.

"Please, for the love of God, do not elaborate on that," I said, feigning disgust. "You mentioned our girl found the library?"

"Yeah, she's going through your books like what's her name, Beauty."

"Beauty?" I asked, guiding the drone to the last known location of the trio of Narco Lords. My hand was getting tired from how long I had been flying.

"Yeah, *Beauty and the Beast,*" he said.

"Belle, her name is Belle."

"Whatever, I never watched it, cartoons are for kids," he said.

"I'm going to pretend you weren't speaking when you said that," I said. "Also, bugger, why didn't *I* show her the library?"

"Don't beat yourself up over it," he said. "You don't know her like I do. Give it time." He sighed and tipped forward from his reclining position in the office chair. "I think you've got our target; I see them on screen three." He pointed. I tapped for the camera to zoom in and the drone to move into a closer position.

"Indeed, indeed it is, looks like a meeting."

"It is, that's Oslo Jones, he's a local guy, the closest thing we have to an illegal gangster," Lach said.

"As opposed to legal gangsters?" I asked.

"Man, we live a stone's throw from DC." He laughed.

"Want to take over flight control?" I asked. He nodded, and I passed the controls to him, a video game control stick and keyboard setup. He was familiar enough with it and took to the task with the quiet skill that was his hallmark. I picked up an encrypted line and dialed out.

Affecting an American accent, I said, "Hello, I would like to talk to the Indigo City Police Field Commander, and can you conference this call with your local Drug Enforcement Agency field office?" I asked politely. There was a pause on the other end of the line, and then a confused response. "Ma'am, I have eyes on three highly wanted drug cartel fugitives and a wanted terrorist, can you make those connections for me?"

Ninety seconds later I was talking to a deputy director of DHS and the police commissioner for Indigo City. I rolled through the list of names and faces I was looking at and started feeding them addresses, and once I was able to establish a video link, I gave them that feed as well. They were very interested in this information, and I knew that they were moving as fast as their bloated agencies could get them there. They were also very interested in who I was, how I had this information, and why they couldn't trace me and my location.

"Ma'am, sir," I said. "I am just a concerned citizen, defending our nation, securing our future." The silence on the other end of the line was palpable. They stopped asking annoying questions and focused on what I was feeding them. I continued to supply information, as Lach relayed it to me. I gave them everything, where the eyes were, how many there were, how well they were armed. Lach landed the drone on a building and conserved the batteries so we could keep eyes on the scene up until the SWAT vans and black SUVs rolled up.

Even with all the information, it was a serious fight. The Narco Lords were well armed, and there were a lot of them. The black clad government agents had numbers too and had helicopters and body armor. The gunfight lasted an ungodly long fifteen minutes, and before it was over, there were dozens down on both sides, and news helicopters buzzing in the air. Lach took the drone off low and fast and took a serpentine course to bring it back home.

The last video we had was *Santa Lucifera*, bleeding from several bullet wounds, being handcuffed and dragged into the back of a SWAT wagon.

This would be on the news later.

"What was all that about being a concerned citizen?" Sadie asked. I was startled, and Lach smiled.

"That's Roan being a snake oil salesman; defending the nation, securing the future it's the motto of the NSA. The locals stopped asking questions because they thought that the spooks were involved," Lach chuckled. "The best part is that if anyone asks the NSA about this, they will automatically claim they had nothing to do with it, even before they're done asking the question."

"What's going on? You were tense earlier," she asked, looking at me.

"Does that door not lock?" Lach asked.

"It does," I said. "I tipped the local authorities off to a meeting of high-level South American cartel members at a warehouse not far from where you were previously living."

"Is there trouble?" she asked. "It feels like there might be trouble."

"Not anymore," Lach said, brushing her off. "The police and the local feds smoked those fools. They were human traffickers and drug dealers, and the ones that weren't killed are going to prison for the rest of their lives."

"So, there *was* trouble?" she asked.

"There was," I said. "I prepped the security system and have my surveillance systems on high alert. After we go, say, twenty-four to forty-eight hours without incident, I will stand it down."

"So, what happens until then? We stay all red alert and stuff?" she asked.

"No, no reason for that," I said with a dry chuckle. "Our defenses here are not just extensive, they are deep. The first layers are miles and miles from here. I'm wired into systems that let me look into local CCTV, and piggyback into other people's security. That's how I caught these narcos and alerted the authorities."

"If you can do this, why doesn't the government?" she asked.

"Because they're too busy fighting with each other, and their objective is more prestige and funding than it is getting the bad guys," Lach said honestly. "C'mon, how else does a six-foot-tall diabetic Arab hide from us for over a decade in a friendly country? Internal competition and incompetence."

"He's talking about Bin Laden again, ignore him," I said.

"So, if I wanted to spend time with one of you this evening, it wouldn't be a problem?" she asked.

"No problem at all," I said.

"What if I wanted to spend time with *both* of you?" she asked hesitantly, her lovely brown eyes bouncing between Lach and I.

"I set the system to send notifications to my phone, and still, no problem at all," I said with a warm smile.

"Okay, good," she said and Lach eyed her.

"Just what did you have in mind, baby?"

"Um, I don't know… dinner and a movie?" She made the suggestion as though she expected to be shot down. Lach and I traded a look, and he grinned.

"Sounds good."

I smiled and felt a tension I didn't know I carried ease. "What would you like for tea?"

CHAPTER TWENTY-THREE

*S*adie...

'Tea' as Roan liked to call dinner, was simple fare of soup and sandwich. Of course, Roan couldn't do anything simple, it always had to be fancy, but this dinner *was* actually pretty simple fare in its fanciness. It consisted of a Brie and butter on baguette sandwich paired with French Onion soup.

I had no idea what had gotten into Kyle but he kept busting up laughing throughout the meal and wouldn't tell me what was so funny.

"The frogs are good for some things, mate. Their food is one of them," Roan declared and for whatever reason, Kyle thought that was *hilarious*. The laughter was infectious, and pretty soon I was laughing along too, even though I didn't know why.

I helped do the few dishes, standing with Roan at the sink who made no comment about my doing them by hand. He simply took them from me one at a time, drying them with a kitchen towel and setting them in the drying rack by the sink.

"Do you know what you fancy for a film, Poppet?" he asked quietly.

"I don't really know," I said with a smile. "I just know I wanted to spend a little time with the both of you. I don't feel like we do, you know?"

"That's true," he murmured and I could feel he was just full of questions.

"Go ahead and ask, Conan," I said gently.

"Did he treat you well?"

I smiled when he finally gave in to his curiosity and I nodded. "He did. He surprised me, honestly."

"Oh?"

"He…"

I hesitated.

"He told me he loved me," I whispered.

"Did he now?" Roan sounded as surprised as I'd felt at the spontaneous utterance.

"Yeah." I gave an uneasy laugh. "I've known for a long time that he did, you know? When we were kids, I mean. Before he went off to the Army." I took a deep breath and let it out slowly. "I just never expected to see him again, let alone that I would ever hear him say it."

"And how does that make you feel?" he asked me gently.

"Blessed," I answered, nearly on the verge of tears. "Also, a bit confused, and guilty." Roan opened his mouth to speak, but the question came from across the kitchen.

"Why's that?"

I jumped and turned, Kyle was lounging against the wall just inside the kitchen door, his glass of gin refreshed.

"Because I love Conan, too," I said raising my chin in a bit of defiance, expecting his trademark jealousy or a fight.

Kyle's dark eyes sparkled, but for once, it wasn't with anger or mal-intent. His smile was… relieved, I think.

"Good," he said nodding. "That's good."

"Why?" I asked, not understanding.

He smiled at us both, enigmatically, and said, "Make sure there's popcorn for this thing, whatever we're watching." Then he backed out the kitchen door, turned, and walked toward the living room.

Conan and I looked at each other, our expressions mirroring one another's with our mutual confusion.

"Before you ask," I said, haltingly, looking after the kitchen door. "*Yes*, he's always been like this."

Roan chuckled and took the plate from my hands and dried it dutifully while I thought to myself the conversation was far from over on the topic. That eventually, Kyle would have to make his feelings known. It was our way, honestly. I just had to be patient or wait to pry. If I did it too soon, it would just end up in a meltdown. It always had; you know?

With the dishes done, Roan shooed me off to get into something more comfortable, which the sun dress I wore from our trip was plenty comfortable, but I read *comfortable* to mean sleep or loungewear, and so I went out through the kitchen door, through the dining room and made to go past the living room.

"Hey," Kyle called out softly from over by the window, the same spot as our first time. I felt myself blush as I paused in my step for him.

"Hey."

"C'mere."

I drifted over his way and he put a hand to my hip and brought his mouth to mine. I kissed him, my tense posture easing as he whispered against my mouth, "You're not in trouble with me Shady... this was my idea, remember?"

"Yeah," I whispered back softly. "I just don't know why..." I looked up at him curiously and he smiled, and that smile held an edge of something akin to sadness.

"Because, I love you *so* much. Enough to recognize that *I'm* not enough, and Roan? He's a good man, better than me, and if there was anyone strong enough to love us both, it's definitely you." He pressed a kiss to my forehead as I stood there stunned, staring up at him open mouthed.

"That has to be the nicest thing you've ever said to me," I murmured.

"Yeah, well, I'm trying," he said with an uneasy laugh. "Don't get to used to it, I'll be back to being the asshole you both know and love any minute now."

I smiled and nodded slightly. "I know that you're trying," I whispered. "And I appreciate it. So much…" My smile turned mischievous. "As for being the asshole? You wouldn't be you otherwise."

He barked a laugh, a genuine one, and I smiled. He was so achingly beautiful when he smiled genuinely like that.

"Where you scurrying off to?" he asked.

"To change; Roan suggested something more comfortable."

He looked thoughtful for a second and nodded. "Good plan." He took my hand and led me down into the living room, setting his glass on the coffee table. "Let's go."

He walked me to my room, kissed me swiftly and left me to change as he went off, presumably to his own, to do the same.

When I returned to the living room, it was to Kyle parked on the couch in his loungewear; a pair of black cotton drawstring lounge pants and a black ribbed tank top. Conan came out of the kitchen with a big bowl of popcorn and handed it down to Kyle who reached over the back of the couch opening and closing his hands like a comical toddler.

"Oh my God, yes!" he said with intensity. "I'll have some of that!"

Roan and I laughed.

"What would you like to watch?" he asked me.

"*Ever After?*" I squeaked and Kyle called out from where he'd disappeared when laying down over the back of the couch, "Oh God, no!" as though he was affronted.

"Lady's choice," Roan reminded him curtly. "Are you open to a suggestion, love?" he then asked me.

"Sure," I smiled up at him and he grinned back.

"There's quite the live action version of the animated Disney film *Beauty & the Beast* I think you'd like very much."

"Oh, do you have it?" I asked.

"Indeed, I do."

"You son of a bitch," Lach muttered, and I blinked in confusion.

"Lady's choice!" I said sternly, winking at Roan whose grin widened.

"Fine, fine! That's all I'll say," Kyle called back. Roan kissed the top of my head and limped down the hall toward his own room.

I smiled and watched him go, eyes lovingly tracing his broad shoulders and strong back feeling happier than I think I've ever been.

"Shady, come over here. Have some popcorn."

I went to Kyle and sat beside him, both of us naturally leaving room for Roan at the end of the couch, like we'd been before and I so looked forward to it, laying back in Roan's embrace, Kyle in my lap.

We threw popcorn at each other laughing, trying to catch it in each other's mouths and it was like we were teens again. Goofing off, finding a sliver of joy in the misery that'd been the Daughton's foster family home.

"Bloody hell, I can't leave you two alone for a moment, can I?" Roan asked, traipsing back to us in his blue pajama bottoms and white tee, though his smile and tone said he wasn't mad at all about the mess we were making with missed popcorn kernels.

Roan cued up the television and found the movie on a streaming service, settling in his customary spot, and holding out his arms for me. I settled, and Kyle settled on me, the big steel bowl in his lap, lazily munching away as the opening credits began to play.

True to his word, he was indeed back to being the asshole I knew and loved. He couldn't help himself. He kept making these hilarious comments about the characters and people and had Roan and I chuckling, and giggling, and pretty soon outright laughing until Roan paused the movie.

"Will you bloody well knock it off and just watch the film, mate?"

Kyle gave a mock exasperated sigh. "*Fine*! I'll be quiet" he cried, and he did, indeed, settle down for a while, setting the mostly empty bowl of popcorn aside and cuddling back into me.

It was such a *peace* being sandwiched between them. Roan, his big arms around me, fingers finding the spaces between mine, his hand covering the back of my one. My other hand I brushed through Kyle's hair as he closed his eyes and sighed in contentment. I smiled, and we watched the movie for a time, before Kyle began to grow restless, shifting in my lap, wriggling as though he were trying to get comfortable.

Finally, he turned on his stomach, shoving the hem of my short, dusky blue satin nightdress up, hooking two fingers into the crotch of my matching satin panties and pulling them aside.

"What are you doing?" I demanded with a laugh as Roan's arms tightened around me.

"Hush, watch the movie," he answered as though this were perfectly normal, and then his mouth was on me and I was sucking in a breath, as Roan held me tight and Lach's tongue parted my pussy lips. I was starting to not think of him as Kyle. Kyle was a skinny teenager. He was Lach, and I didn't know if I was just accepting this new reality or if I was just getting confused.

I watched him, engrossed, gasping, and when he slid a finger inside of me, and my hips bucked, I threw my head back to look at Roan. He was watching Kyle go down on me, just as transfixed as I had been a moment before and the naked desire on his face… I relaxed, hugging his arms around me, and secured between them both, let things play out; let them happen.

I gasped, holding my breath, as Kyle teased that place inside of me with his fingers, working me simultaneously from the outside with his warm, wet mouth.

"Hold her tight," he growled at Roan whose arms tightened around me and then Kyle slipped his hand from between my legs and fisting the material, jerked my panties, once, twice, until I cried out and stitches popping, he was able to tear them away. He shouldered my thighs apart, and laving me with his tongue, slipped his middle finger back up inside me, teasing my taint with his index and ring finger, seeking to play with my back door while he teased the rest of me to life.

Roan groaned, his arms shifting, one of his big hands slipping between the material of my nightgown and my skin, to knead my left breast, his erection stabbing me in the back, a hot, hard line as I surrendered to them both and reclined my head all the way back, offering up my lips to my other lover.

He claimed them without a second thought, plunging his tongue past my teeth, feasting at my mouth while Kyle feasted on my pussy.

Electric current swept through my body as my breathing sawed in and out of me. My heart hammered against the cage of my ribs, and I felt hot, so very hot as adrenaline or something like it coursed through me at an alarming rate. I writhed and Kyle grunted, taking his mouth off of me just long enough to demand of Roan, "Hold her."

"Mm… mm… mm!" I moaned rhythmically into Roan's mouth, and he chuckled into mine, tasting my surrender, reveling in it, and I was thoroughly trapped between them. The intensity something that I was unprepared for.

Still, I trusted them; both of them, implicitly and I relaxed between them as Kyle finger fucked my hole and sucked on my clit like it was candy until the heavy feeling grew in my body, between my legs, and I tightened down around him and clung to that ledge for as long as I could until Kyle's appreciative hum sent me over the edge a second time.

I screamed into Roan's mouth, my body bowing, his arms coiling around me holding me tight as I came, Kyle merciless in his attentions to every swollen, oversensitive part of me as my pussy bellowed and throbbed around his invading fingers and I fell into a pattern of perfect, sated, languid bliss.

I was only vaguely aware of his mouth coming off of me, of Roan's mouth leaving mine as I panted for breath.

Lach laughed and said, "Fuck, man… she's so wet. You should feel this pussy."

Roan chuckled and said, "Another time perhaps… I'd quite like not to break her."

"You okay, Shady?" Lach asked me and I looked at him heavy lidded and completely limp.

"Mm-hm…" I managed and he and Roan, I assume exchanged a look and Lach's grin only grew.

I felt Roan press his lips against my temple and ask, "You're sure."

"I'm sure." My voice sounded far away and very small.

"Good," he whispered above my ear. "That's good."

Lach cleared his throat and got up, presumably to wash his hands. "Your room?" he asked, and I felt Roan look up, hesitate, and then say, "Aye… it's closest."

"What?" I asked vaguely.

"Bed, babe. I think we're all ready for sleep; that's all," Kyle declared.

"Oh, okay…" again with sounding so small and faint, but I couldn't for the life of me manage more.

Roan chuckled and kissed me intermittently, holding onto me, holding me close and that's sort of how that happened. Lach came back, I was helped to my feet, and we shuffled off to Roan's room. The straps to my nightgown were taken down off my shoulders, the whole thing left to whisper down my skin. I shuddered, and Roan got into bed first, leaving his prosthetic and his shirt to fall along with my nightgown. Lach passed me to Roan and removed his tank and got into bed behind me and that was how we lay… me tucked tight into Roan's side, and Lach snugged to my back, spooning me.

Lips pressed to my forehead, and another set reverently to the back of my shoulder and I sighed out and closed my eyes.

"Did you guys plan this?" I asked accusingly, not one bit sorry or upset if they had.

They both chuckled.

"Not at all, Poppet. You're as surprised as I am," Roan murmured against my hair.

I was vaguely aware of Lach laughing lightly and saying, "I still got it!" in a proud sort of voice before lulled by their warmth and the glow from my orgasms, I drowsed.

____

CHAPTER TWENTY-FOUR

____

*Z*ach...

Lying next to Sadie, my cock pressed against her thigh, I was left to wonder which was the greater sacrifice. I still had some of Belle's whiny songs stuck in my ear, and after tasting Sadie, laying next to her while she slept, *hard*. The consolation was knowing that Roan was nursing a hard-on too. Her ass pressed against me, her face against his chest.

"I know," Roan said in a soft whisper, smiling over her.

"Yeah," I said.

"Reminds me a little bit of the VA hospital." He gave a soft chuckle. "Do you remember that candy striper, the blonde?"

"I do remember, she had that short, *short* skirt, and would bend over to take your vitals." I had my own laugh.

"The fishnets, I remember those." He smiled.

"She would take forever checking your leg, and man, that was a show," I said.

"You made sure she took her time making sure your vitals were okay. What was it you pretended you had to get into the medical ward?" he asked.

"Heart arrhythmia and trouble breathing," I said. "Quite hard to detect." He shook his head and stroked Sadie's hair. She made a soft sigh and shifted. When she did, I went from being wedged against her thigh to being firmly planted between her buttocks, like a fucking hot dog in a bun.

"How's the arrhythmia?" Roan asked.

"Throbbing," I whispered, and I caressed her hip. This did little to help my situation and feeling that she was completely naked made the throb a little worse.

"It is impressive, the amount of self-control you're showing," he said.

I eased my hand down her thigh, delighting with the sensation. I knew that I was working on an uncomfortable wet spot inside my briefs. I eased the waistband down and felt elation as my cock was freed from those confines. I adjusted myself until I was back where I had been before, the hot dog in her buns. I gave a sigh of contentment.

The contentment turned slowly to torture, I could move slightly, grinding my cock against her ass, feeling my own excitement turn her crack slippery. I knew she was wet too, and I was so very close to that. She pushed back against me and made a soft noise. I looked over and caught Roan's eye. I raised an eyebrow. He gave an eye roll, exaggerated for me to see in the dim bedroom. Then he stroked her hair and nodded.

I rolled slightly and lifted her thigh. It wasn't much, but it was enough to slide my cock between her thighs. I wasn't inside her, but instead of grinding on her crack, I was rubbing my head between her lips. She was so very wet, and I groaned softly. I closed my eyes and savored the sensation, the heat between her legs, the slick sensation.

She made a soft sound and shifted. She squeezed me between her thighs, her buttocks clenching and then releasing. I knew that I could do it, from her new slightly different position. I made my own small movement, and it took three gentle strokes before I did more than glance my cock off her clit. On the third push instead of sliding forward, I sank inside her. I slid all the way in, holding her hip and planting my lips against the back of her neck.

I gave her several slow, gentle strokes, and I was struck, thinking of how it had looked on the monitor, watching Roan take her for the first time. I shuddered. "Easy," I heard him whisper. "Easy." I was going to speak, but I saw his eyes flick from me down to her. She was waking up, and I felt her move her hips, and the breathless sound she made.

"Oh," she moaned softly.

"This okay, Poppet?" Roan whispered to her and kissed her on the hair. I could see her fingernails dig into his chest, and she moaned again.

"Mmmm, *yes*. Are we doing this now?" she asked.

"It would seem," he whispered to her. "Are you okay with that?" he double-checked, but she didn't say anything. She was too busy moving with me, her breathing light and fluttering, she was enjoying this.

"I want this," I heard her say, and Roan moved, and I felt her move. Then he groaned. I was able to make out her head bobbing. She had taken him into her mouth. The noises she made were subdued and sounded wet. I didn't go so gently, now that she was awake.

When she tried to take him too deeply, her entire body would clench.

I held her hips and really started giving it to her, and I could tell that I was hitting my mark. She alternated sucking him, and then laying her head on his stomach, jerking his cock while gasping and moaning in pleasure.

"You might be more successful," I said, slowing my stroke, "if we changed position." She looked at me and nodded in agreement. "On your knees, give me your ass," I told her. She did, moving until she was on her knees in front of Roan, his cock facing her straight on. Her back arched when she leaned forward, presenting me with an eyeful of glistening wet slit, a bead of her juice running down her thigh.

I took her, burying my cock in her, all the way. She took him in her mouth, and the noises she made were more sloppy sounding, and Roan started making his own moaning. I couldn't see how she was doing, but she tensed less and he groaned more. When she came up off of him, it was to gasp for air, not because she had almost gagged herself again. "Oh fuck," I groaned, my balls slapping against her. I could feel how wet she was, and I knew that her thighs were going to be dripping.

She came up off of him and turned to face me. "I want you now," she said. I gave her room, and she turned so that Roan was facing her pussy and she dropped down and took my cock in her mouth. We both moaned, her lips and tongue felt like heaven. She took every inch of me into her mouth, and I forgot to breathe for a moment.

"My God," I whispered, running my hand down the side of her face.

When I opened my eyes again, I saw Roan's hair just above her bottom. He was getting a taste of her as well. The only thing I could do was control my breathing and let myself go along for the ride. She was giving me that mind breaking good head, the sort where parts of my brain turned off.

"I can't believe this is happening." Sadie gasped, leaving my cock hanging for a moment. She grasped it and started stroking it. In the dim light I saw her look up and make eye contact with me. She teased the head of my cock with her tongue, and I felt my balls start to tighten. Without looking away, she took me in her mouth again. I groaned.

"I can't believe it either," I said.

"Have you two ever done this before?" she asked.

"No, this is the first time we've shared a woman," I managed.

Roan rose and wiped his face with his arm. "Are you ready for me?" he asked, putting a hand on her hip.

"I think so." Her eyes glittered like stars as she looked at me. I cupped her cheek in my hand as he entered her. She moaned, and after he was inside her, she went back to going down on me.

CHAPTER TWENTY-FIVE

*R*oan...

Waiting for Lach to make his move was agony, and a massive test of my resolve. All but carrying Sadie into my bedroom, and tucking her into my bed nude, had pressed my stoicism like the weight of the water behind a dam. Her breasts had been pointed and perfect, eyes soft and dreamy, cheeks pink with her post orgasmic bliss.

I thought about her kisses as she pressed her face against my chest and slept.

It would have been nice if sleep could have come that easily for me, but there was an old joke, *what was the difference between light and hard?* I could go to sleep with the light on. A good chuckle, except that I was hard, and sleep was not going to be coming anytime soon. I probably wasn't going to be either.

I saw he was awake, and he had that intent look in his eyes. He was hard too, and unlike Sadie, he wasn't likely to wait until morning, or after another date. He wasn't the sort of man who masturbated when he got turned down, he didn't get turned down. Women didn't tell him no. I didn't have that sort of internal arrogance, that drive.

He moved deliberately, slowly. He had the same sense of purpose as a man navigating a minefield or defusing a bomb. I knew what he was doing, he was doing a tactical insertion into a hot zone, and either Sadie would spread herself for him like a flower greeting the sun, or she would wake and twist away, maybe slap his face.

She woke, and then things moved much faster than I expected.

It seemed like mere seconds passed between her eyes opening and her lips wrapping around my cock. Maybe it was only because the time between putting her into the bed and her waking had seemed so long. Her desire for me was obvious and earnest as she vigorously went down on me, tackling the challenge of my size with zeal. She hit her limit several times, and I was thankful when Lach suggested she change positions. As good as it felt, feeling her start to gag on me didn't turn me on, it made me feel guilty about how large I was and how small her mouth seemed.

In their new position, Lach was freer to move, and she had a better position to go down on me. She was able to take more of me into her mouth, but still not all of me.

When Sadie decided she wanted something different, it was a delight to be left facing her pussy. There was a certain part of me that wanted to recoil from the thought of going down on her, knowing that Lach had done that, him inside her. That was a small part, one that was easily overridden by the part that loved lavishing attention on Sadie. That part of me wanted to slide my tongue between her lips and taste her.

Eating her out was a dream, but did nothing for my balls, and the ache that was growing in the shaft of my cock. I needed her again, but this time would be easier. "Are you ready for me?" I asked. I was scant inches from entering her.

"I think so," she murmured. I eased the head of my cock into her, and she moaned. After I pushed a little bit further into her, she moaned again and went back to going down on Lach. Compared to what she faced with me, going down on him was probably a breeze. The look on his face inclined me to believe that was the case.

I fed her inch after inch until she couldn't take anymore. Like when she had gone down on me, she was much better prepared this time, her orgasm, rather *orgasms*, had her much more relaxed. It was no longer her first time handling me. She shuddered, and I was able to take a less cautious pace. She sucked Lach, sometimes coming up to vent some cries and groans. I could feel her pussy clamp down on me, like I was in the world's most pleasant vice.

"I want your ass," Lach said, tipping Sadie's face to look at him.

"Please." She made a sound that was aching close to a whimper.

"Roan, back down on the bed. Sadie, you straddle him, I'll get the lube," he said.

"Nightstand, mate," I gestured to the side of the bed. It was a little strange, but we both did what he said. While he took off after the lube, I situated myself on the bed, and Sadie gave me a coltish smile.

"You've done this before?" I asked. This was probably not the best time for her first experience in backdoor action, that was something that required special attention.

"Sort of, but no. Not with two guys, but he took my... from behind, down in St. Henri," she said, biting her lip in obvious anticipation.

"And?" I asked.

"I came, and I think I peed a little when I did." She looked away. "It might happen again, but I don't know."

"Poppet." I kissed her. "That probably wasn't *pee*." I took her hand in mine.

"I'm a girl, silly. I can't come like a boy." She looked at me like I was foolish.

"That is where you might be surprised. Now might not be the best time for a biology lesson," I admitted. She nodded.

"More action, less talking," Lach said. I could imagine the look on his face, slightly annoyed but still certainly pleased with what was going on.

"I don't think the director likes our dialog, maybe we should do what he says, yeah?" She giggled.

"I did better this time, going down on you."

"I haven't words, you were amazing," I said. She smiled, gave my cock a few strokes and straddled me again. She settled down onto me, letting herself slowly slide down my cock. Her nipples were hard and her breathing was slow and deliberate. She took more and more, and she stopped almost near the base.

"Oh my God," she groaned. "God there's so much."

"I wish you could see this," Lach said with a tone of admiration. He was rubbing his erect cock, looking at us.

"Don't just stare," Sadie said.

"I need to stare for a moment, alright. I need to see how beautiful you are." He took an appreciative breath. "Yeah, are you ready for both of us?"

"Not quite, I need a minute to enjoy this." She smiled. He nodded, walked around the bed and threw a foot up on it. The view was unexpected, as he presented his cock for Sadie to suck again. She did, and I could see how easy it was for her, and then the faintest hint of her tongue as she vigorously swallowed him. As she did, she started riding me more vigorously, getting used to the new position, enjoying how I filled her out.

"I'm ready, I'm ready," she whimpered, giving his cock a few more jerks and then a squeeze that caused a ribbon of clear fluid to drip from the end of his length. He squeezed lube in his hand and I felt her move in response to what he was doing. A finger? Was the lube cold?

I felt her tense and then relax. Then there was a completely different feeling, a pressure. I could feel Lach's cock inside her, only separated from mine by the thin layer of flesh and membranes that was Sadie. When he started fucking her, I could feel it. There was something surreal about it, about being this close to him, with so little between us. My reverie was interrupted by Sadie kissing me and then biting my lip.

She barked a groan into my mouth and shrieked. For a moment I thought she was in pain, but the look on her face said I was wrong. She was lost in rapture.

I held still initially, this was something I had never done, never even really contemplated. Hell, I didn't even indulge in fantasy or porn that touched on this. There was a small window where I could move, when he thrust, I would pull back. When he withdrew, I would thrust. We worked back and forth with each other, and between us, Sadie gasped.

She made noises that were strange, somewhere between strangled sobs and almost laughing moans. I worried for a bit, but when she noticed the concern on my face, she gave me a ragged smile and kissed me with as much attention as she could spare. I could see why Lach cared so much for her, the depth of emotion in her eyes, and how she threw herself into everything she did. There was no half-assing, no cowardice or fear, she might have been small but she was *fierce*.

She wasn't daunted by my size, by his aggression, and certainly not by being wedged between us. I felt warmth, a trickle of something running down my hip, at the same time, she leaned forward and I thought she was going to kiss me, but instead she buried her face in my neck, and I felt her lips and then a brush of teeth. She used my shoulder to muffle her cry.

She was coming.

Lach pumped faster, and I wasn't able to keep up, but the harder he went, the less I had to move. She gave a sob, and I felt the wash of her coming on me again.

"Fuck, Sadie!" Lach groaned, and he thrust hard, and trembled. While he was occupied, I took over and started driving myself into her.

"Sadie," I groaned, her face was flushed and red.

"Do it," she gasped, and kissed me hard, her tongue pushing into my mouth.

It started it slow, like a guitar string of tension drawn up through the base of pelvis. It felt like a slow-moving pulse of fire moving through my shaft, and then it was so intense that I couldn't see anything. It was almost like I was on the verge of blacking out. I shuddered and suddenly my entire cock felt like it was being crushed. There was a moment where it seemed like maybe I couldn't cum, because she was so tight and there was nowhere for me seed to spill.

I rolled my hips, and I almost managed to pull myself out of her. I could feel everything, another pulse as more cum spewed out of me.

Lach's balls were mashed against mine, Sadie's own orgasm still running down my sides. I ended up thrusting back inside her, the moan I made half pleasure, and half agony.

We were still for a while, each of us catching our breath and seemingly returning to our own bodies. For that time, while we were both buried inside her, it seemed like we had become a single being. It was cliché, but the distinction between us seemed blurred. It was an incredible feeling, and I didn't want it to end.

Lach was the first to break the spell, surrendering and pulling away.

Sadie reluctantly moved, she didn't want this magic to end either, but it had to. She closed her eyes and pulled herself up off of me. As soon as I was released from her, she groaned and I saw the mess the three of us had made. Her thighs were slick and dripping with cum.

"That was amazing," she whispered, and kissed me. Before she moved away, she kissed Lach too.

"I think we've made a big mess," she said, breathless. "I love it." She covered her mouth to hide her giggle, and I sat up, pulling it away and kissing her deeply. She gasped and I smiled against her mouth to the sound of Lach's amused laughter.

CHAPTER TWENTY-SIX

*S*adie...

"Mmm..." I hummed in pleasure, shifting on the high thread count sheets of Roan's bed fetched up against his hard body as soft silken kisses fell along my exposed nude back.

"Morning gorgeous," Kyle murmured against my skin, working his way back up to my shoulder.

"Mm, good morning," I whispered, afraid to wake Roan, but when I opened my eyes, he was smiling down at me, such a reverence, love, and respect radiating from his green eyes, I very nearly shuddered from that look alone.

He hummed in appreciation and said, "Good morning, Poppet."

"Good morning," I whispered back.

"We need a shower," Kyle said then immediately asked, "You sore?" I knew he meant me. Roan wouldn't have any reason to be.

I thought about it a second, screwing up my face when I realized, *oh yeah*, I was definitely paying for it this morning.

"Yeah, sorry," I said.

"Nothing to be sorry about," Roan assured me. "You were incredible."

"I second that," Kyle said from behind me, smoothing a hand down my ribs and over my hip.

"Take a shower with me?" I asked them softly.

"Oh, Love..." Roan sounded on the brink of denying me but Kyle cut him off.

"We'll make it work; your shower is best equipped. Let me grab your crutch so your big ass can get around."

Oh. I hadn't thought about the logistics in the context of Roan's leg.

Kyle stretched luxuriously, and I took a moment to appreciate the long, lean line of his muscular body. Especially the globes of his ass, which were perfect by the way. Roan had me dying over his chest and shoulders, the power and strength with which he moved as he ushered me off the bed and scooted to the edge of it making a deeply conscious effort not to look at Kyle padding around his bedroom nude.

Kyle went over by the wardrobe and returned with one of those crutches with the c shaped collar thing on it and the jutting handle to grip and bear your weight on.

"Thanks, mate," Roan muttered softly and levered himself up onto his good leg.

"Come on, Sadie." Kyle held out a hand to me, rubbing sleep from his eyes with the other. I took it and we three went into the bathroom adjoining Conan's room.

The shower was nice, I stood between Kyle and Conan who was seated on the marble shower bench and basked in the attention they lavished on me, hands slick with soap, mouths kissing and drinking the clear water from my skin. Kyle tried to take me again, but the attempt ended on a whimper and he stopped at a terse *"Mate,"* from Roan.

"I want to, but my body says otherwise," I murmured.

"I supposed we really do need to give you a day off every now and then," Kyle whispered and turned me, tipping my face up to his gently with a hand at my jaw to kiss me passionately but slowly, driving me crazy as Roan gently bit my ass cheek.

I bowed my head, resting my forehead against Kyle's chest as I tried to catch my breath and he chuckled, looking over me down to Conan and saying, "I think we need to give it a rest, mate. Keep it up, we might break her."

"That's not funny!" I cried to their masculine chuckles.

"It's true," Roan said. "That's precisely *why* it's so funny, love."

"You're both going to be the death of me," I grumbled, meaning it as a joke, but instead what I got was a pregnant pause. I looked up sharply to catch Kyle tearing his gaze from Roan behind me. I turned and Roan smiled up at me, the smile weaker than one of his genuine ones and I heaved a big sigh.

"Well, that hit wrong," I said sardonically.

"Nothing is going to happen to you, Poppet," Roan promised.

"Not while both of us stand in the way," Kyle agreed.

I pulled away from them both, eyes narrowing and asked, "Just how deep is the shit?" I demanded.

"Do you trust us?" Roan asked, trading a look with Kyle.

"You know I do," I countered.

"Then it's nothing you need to worry your pretty little head about, baby," Kyle drew me back under the warm water's spray and between the two of them I was kissed and touched until the water *should* have run cold but didn't and we were all three all but prunes.

The next move of the day was quickly decided. Roan wanted to make us all breakfast. Kyle and I were sent to our rooms, me in Roan's big fluffy gray robe, and Kyle as naked as the day he was born, to get dressed and to meet Roan back in the kitchen.

I was told to dress to go out, so warm…

I went into the walk-in closet and clicked on the light expecting to see a cobble of the bags and boxes that had been delivered from mine and Roan's DC shopping trip, but no… instead, what I found was everything neatly arrayed and put away. Sweaters and blouses hanging. Jeans neatly stacked and boots and shoes nicely racked and standing by waiting.

He was just too much… and I sank onto the dressing bench in the center of the closet and cast my eyes around the small space, letting myself feel all the things that there was to feel. Love, gratitude, just an overwhelming number of *everything* all at once.

I rose and selected a matching bra and panty set from one of the drawers. My dresses had been moved in here, and I imagined the wardrobe out in the room now stood empty.

I chose form fitting jeans, a light tee, and a warm, thick sweater to go over it all in a light cream. I found a matching pair of tall, thick wool socks and pulled them on and up over the knee of my jeans, slipping on and zipping up a pair of knee high tall brown riding boots and shrugging the socks down artfully over the tops of them, the way the personal shopper had shown me.

I went in and dried and styled my hair and went over the array of makeup that we'd bought and actually *glad* to have such nice stuff to work with instead of whatever I could share that'd been lifted from the drugstore, I spent a bit fixing up my face. I went light, some foundation to even me out, a little natural looking deep brown eyeliner, a dusting of shadow, and a nude lip.

I finished off with a touch of mascara and leaned back from my magnifying mirror to look into the full mirror opposite the counter from me.

I looked… I looked *rich*.

I was a whole different person now, and I couldn't say I regretted it, which made me a little sad and uneasy. I stood slowly and gave myself a final going over and wondered what the boys would think…

There was only one way to find out.

I paused at the wardrobe and opened it up, smiling slightly. Purses and jackets, coats and outerwear. I smiled and opened up the straw purse I'd bought in St. Henri to hide the ties I'd bought for my men and smiled bigger when I found them undisturbed.

I went to the kitchen and Roan looked over his shoulder licking something from his thumb as he whisked something in a bowl. He stopped and his green eyes raked over me as I went over near him and unapologetically turned around, planted my hands on the granite countertop and hoisted my butt up onto it.

"Come here," I murmured, and he dropped his whisk and stepped over. I parted my knees and pulled him closer between them.

"What are you doing, Poppet?" he asked, grinning when I undid his red, gray, and blue striped tie. He looked so damned dapper in his gray suit with its fine pinstriping and vest.

"I bought something for you in St. Henri," I said with a smile and pulled his purple tie from my back pocket.

"Oh? Did you now?"

I turned up his collar and looped it over his head as he chuckled and put his hands to either side of my hips and leaned in.

"I'm afraid I don't know how to tie it," I murmured tugging his mouth to mine. We kissed, slow and sweet and he leaned back and asked, "Would you like me to teach you?"

"Yes," I said smiling. "I would like to learn, to do this for you."

"Alright."

He showed me once, twice, then unraveled his work so that I could try.

That was where Kyle found us, me on my second try, trying to get the knot as crisp as Conan could get it.

"What are you doing?" Kyle asked me and I smiled.

"You'll see," I murmured. "You're next."

I got the purple tie straight and tucked beneath Conan's vest and he smiled, nodding once.

"I think you have the right of it," he said.

He went and fetched a black chef's apron and I smiled.

"Come here." I crooked a finger at Kyle who stepped up and kissed me fiercely.

"What are you doing?" he asked again when I unknotted his tie. He was wearing a black suit, and the blue tie I'd bought him might be a little loud for it, but I didn't care.

I fixed his tie for him, giving an exasperated sound when I all of a sudden couldn't seem to get it right. With his patience of a saint, Roan came over and showed me again and I smiled and got it right. Kyle watched me curiously the entire time.

"You bought this for me?" he asked. I nodded. "When?"

"When you were in the jewelry shop," I murmured fingering my treasure coin necklace.

"Huh." He sounded surprised.

"Purple because it's your favorite color," I said to Roan, and then I turned back to Kyle, and murmured, "and blue because it's mine."

"You're incredible, you know that?" Kyle asked, and I smiled gently.

"I do now." I pulled him to me gently by his tie for another kiss.

Roan made a satisfied noise and carried on with whatever he was cooking.

It turned out to be crepes, a side of bacon from the oven at Kyle's insistence. Breakfast was a joy, and the boys decided we needed a day out of the house.

"Is that safe?" I asked.

They exchanged a look, and both laughed.

"Oh, yeah," Kyle said. "Safe as can be, especially after we stop off at the armory before we go."

"Okay, but *where* are we going?"

"Shopping?" Roan suggested, and I made a face. Kyle laughed.

"Where do you want to go, babe?" he asked.

I smiled and turned to him.

"Indigo City Museum of Fine Art," I answered, and he cocked his head. I rolled my eyes. I thought for sure he would remember.

"Remember?" I prodded, and he shook his head slowly.

"We couldn't just *go*, we could never afford it," I said. "Then you found out that the first Thursday of every month, general admission was free and you convinced me to skip school and took me."

"Right, the school called Prissy," he said, scowling darkly. I nodded.

"I was locked up and Dean whipped you with his belt," I murmured.

He nodded and said, "But the museum—"

"Was probably the best day of my life while in foster care," I admitted. "Even though we had that fight and you left me there."

He made a face, wincing slightly. "Yeah, I certainly fucked *that* up," he agreed. "What was that fight even about?"

"That part I can't remember," I said softly. "I just remember it was the greatest day of my life since my parents had died."

"Then to the museum," Conan said judiciously. "And this time, we *can* afford it and nothing will be off-limits."

"Lunch at *Chevalier*?" Kyle asked.

"Perfect," Roan agreed. "I'll make the reservation."

Kyle squeezed my hand with a wink and I smiled, happy.

Thank you, I mouthed at him and his smile grew.

"Anything for you, babe," he said, and I knew that he meant it.

"Don't start," I murmured when Kyle opened his mouth to say something sarcastic or obnoxious as we stood in front of the museum. Conan choked on a laugh, his fingers threaded through mine, his other hand on a silver tipped walking cane that held a sword inside it. He'd shown me.

We'd parked in the garage across the street, valet of course, and now we stood at the bottom of the steps leading up to the museum's main entrance. I was having a bit of a moment, the ghost of memory sending a tingling wash of goosebumps along my scalp and down my back. Kyle put his arm around my shoulders and pressed a kiss to my temple and I smiled, glad neither of them were going to get weird about being affectionate simply because we were in public.

I'd learned a long time ago it didn't matter; people were going to judge no matter what, and I honestly didn't *care* anymore. I couldn't remember a happiness and contentment like this. I think, if I had to remember, there were two places in my memory that stood out the most. When my parents were alive and the stolen moments I'd had as a teen when it was just me and Kyle and no one else and he and I could pretend the bad didn't exist for a while.

At least I could… for moments at a time.

"We going in or what, beautiful?" Kyle finally asked, and I shook myself as though waking from a dream and laughed nervously at how ridiculous I must look. Conan gripped my hand in a light squeeze to reassure me and I looked up at him. He smiled down at me and jerked his head with its fiery and perfectly styled shock of red hair at the museum.

"Nothing's off-limits today," he said with a wink of his own and my smile formed and grew on my face.

The museum was holding a special exhibition on Monet, and there was a room devoted to British fine art from the years 1560 to 1830. I wanted to see it all and to Kyle's credit, once we started looking at the art, he didn't have a single quip or comment to make, at least at first. He was just as drawn to it and enamored with it as Roan and I were. Just like when we'd been kids.

Speaking of, just like when we were kids, more often than not, I would turn away from a piece to say something to him and would catch him watching *me* almost more intently than I was looking at whatever piece was before us. It still made me color, a rush and breath of warmth coloring my cheeks.

I honestly hoped that he would never get tired of looking at me that way. I know I would never grow tired of the way it made me feel.

As for Conan, he held my hand in the crook of his arm as we appreciated what was before us, his attention as rapt as mine on the art, his thumb stroking gently over my fingers. Absently, he would lean down and murmur observations about any given piece to me and I would smile and we would discuss.

Kyle joined in sometimes, but when he grew bored with standing too long at any given display, the cutting remarks would begin. Eventually those would have Conan chuckling and me giggling, pressing a hand over my lips in an effort to contain myself until we finally moved on to get him to stop. It quickly became our favorite game as we moved from exhibit to exhibit throughout the museum.

I was well aware of the wide-eyed stares we were getting from around us. I mean, I was with two incredibly handsome men dressed extremely well in tailored suits. While I felt a bit underdressed between the two of them in my jeans, sweater, and simple black overcoat neither Kyle nor Conan seemed to care and I was sure that wasn't what the lot of the people we encountered were staring for.

No, they were staring at the light and casual touching I shared with the men. Conan holding my hand, Kyle touching my back, each of them murmuring close to my ear and pressing the occasional light kiss to my temple.

It was obvious to anyone that didn't cast just a cursory look in our direction that we were all three a couple… er… I don't know what else you would call it. A throuple? *That sounds dumb,* I chided myself.

At any rate, their open-mouthed stares and whispered comments didn't bother me, surprisingly enough. Instead, they had the opposite effect. Bolstering my confidence beyond anything I'd ever felt before. I smiled as we moved through the hallowed space filled with paintings created by countless master's hands and it was wonderful.

We saved the best for last. The exhibit of Monet's work especially taking my breath away only to have it stolen once more when I looked up and realized both of my men were staring at me the way I had stared at the painting in front of us.

We all three laughed a bit, me nervously, when Kyle said, "Whenever you're ready babe, just let us know. We're starving…" and I realized that they'd been talking over my head and I hadn't even realized it; I'd been so drawn into Monet's work.

"Just a few more?" I wheedled.

"We only have a few left," Conan said, drawing me along to the next piece.

"You do you, baby," Kyle agreed. "I'm not trying to cut things short. Just letting you know where we're at." I smiled and laced the fingers of my free hand with his as we moved along.

"Are we getting close to our reservation?" I asked.

"Yes," Conan said. "But a few moments more won't hurt."

"Okay," I said, but I did keep things in mind and while I didn't rush looking at the last few pieces, I didn't linger as long as I would have liked, either.

"Come on, Poppet," Roan said finally at the last piece. "Let's get some lunch in you, yeah?"

"Sure," I said biting my bottom lip to hide my smile. "Sorry for taking so long."

"Not at all." He raised my hand to his lips and brushed a kiss across my fingers.

"That was, surprisingly, fun time," Kyle agreed, and I didn't bother trying to hide my smile at that.

"We'll get you cultured yet, mate," Conan declared and Kyle scoffed.

"Yeah, next outing, I get to pick. Maybe get Sadie to drive a tank over something at that place out in Vegas."

"They have a place that you can do that?" I asked, contemplating it.

"They have a place for everything," Conan declared as he waved down a car to take us to the restaurant, not wanting to give up our parking space as he'd paid for the whole day.

"Sounds like it could be fun," I said and the look my ginger lover gave me was priceless. The laugh it dragged out of Kyle worth its weight in gold.

"Cheeky little monkey," Roan said, opening the car door for us. Kyle went in first to keep me in the middle.

I couldn't keep the grin off my face if I wanted to.

CHAPTER TWENTY-SEVEN

*L*ach...

Chevalier was one of the nicest restaurants in Indigo City, and a premiere destination for East Coast gourmands and Francophiles. Which meant that Roan was the one to swing us getting a table. We were slightly underdressed, this was certainly a black tie and cocktail dress kind of place, but we were saved by the fact that there was literally nothing special about the day we arrived. If it had been any sort of holiday, anything of note, we would have been turned away.

We were certainly well healed enough to be customers, so the only ruse we played was slumming. It was easy enough to pull off, It wasn't a place you walked into off the street, and everyone there knew it. There was a subset of obscenely wealthy people who took no interest in pretension, and despite having billions, still wore denim and print tees, had no interest in custom fitted suits.

Places like *Chevalier* hated them, because this place was all about pretense and being hoity-toity. They also tended to be bootstrap types and had no appreciation for Micheline Star cuisine. Hard to sell a six-hundred-dollar chicken dinner with a twelve-thousand-dollar bottle of wine sitting a table away from a guy sitting in a pair of worn jeans and a trucker hat.

That son of a bitch probably had enough money to buy the entire restaurant.

That chapped their asses too.

We were seated, and the host looked at Sadie in a serious manner, like he was trying to figure out who she was. A Hollywood starlet, an influential politico up from DC, someone so incredibly famous that it was an insult to recognize her? We were given the treatment that one would give a pair of highly capable and competent bodyguards.

"When do we get a menu?" Sadie asked, after we had been seated.

"The only menu we will get is a wine menu, and we have to ask for that," Roan said. He picked up a glass and inspected it. "It is generally better manners to ask the sommelier's recommendation and go off of that."

"How do we know what to order?" she asked.

"*Chevalier* does a prix fixe menu, you pick an appetizer, what dressing goes on your salad, and what protein you would like," Roan said. "The waitress will give us the layout, and we'll go from there."

"So this definitely isn't like an Applebees," she said, giggling.

"It would be hard to get much further from that establishment than here," I said. "And I've only been here, twice? This might make my third visit."

"Well it's my first, mister," Sadie said.

The waitress came by and gave us a quick and formal run down of the menu. The choices were short, and Sadie looked horrified when Roan made an executive decision and picked the escargot.

"Snails!" She made a face.

"Give them a chance, Poppet, we've not steered you wrong yet. Have we?" He raised an eyebrow.

"You haven't, *yet*," she said. "But… *snails*…"

"Don't worry, if you don't like them you don't have to eat any of them," Roan said.

"One," I said. "Try *one*, I think you'll like them." She nodded and gave me a dubious look. "Roan made me try them, they're alright."

"Just alright?" she asked.

"Well, yeah. But they make him do that thing with his face, and then it's just hard to say no," I admitted. She laughed.

Drinks were served, I had an Aviator: gin and crème de violette. It was a flurry of herbal, floral, and pine notes. Roan had some fancy bottle of Chardonnay and split it with Sadie. She ended up having a further treat in a kir royale, some concoction of crème de cassis and champagne. Our spirits were high as the snails in garlic and parsley arrived.

There was a certain weird little thing, eating this frequently mocked French food, sipping the nicest of spirits, while some quartet practiced their music in the corner. If I knew classical music, I might enjoy it better. Roan seemed to be pleased, and Sadie liked the escargot enough to eat a second one, but that was it.

We were halfway through the main course; they were having the duck a l'orange and I was indulging in the raw decadence that was the chateaubriand with lavender and rosemary. When I was eating it, it was like my tongue was fucking my mouth in ecstasy. And then everything turned sour.

Gwendolyn Kaijin was sitting two tables over, sipping a flute of champagne and giving me the hottest *fuck me* eyes that I had ever seen burn in a woman's skull. *What in the fuck was she doing here?* Her and the rest of the French heroin dealers were supposed to be long gone from the US. She let her eyes float across Roan and Sadie, and I felt a stab of hostility. I didn't want to fuck her, I wanted to gouge her smoldering eyes out with the escargot fork.

She wasn't alone, and the disturbing thing was that I didn't recognize the people she was dining with. Something was up, and at this point the only good thing was that there was nothing they could do here. Of course, that meant I couldn't do anything either.

I caught the waiter and had him take her a drink. It was actually surprising that he knew what a *veiled insult* was, but I wasn't surprised that they had everything, even the Benedictine liquor. It wasn't long before the drink was delivered to her table, in what looked like a very fashionable glass. It was pretty.

Her face was pretty, right up until she took a sip of the concoction. Then those perfect lips snarled in disgust. Her eyes were daggers when she looked back at me, and I lipped a kiss at her. Every horrible thing I had ever done to a woman, every self-gratifying, denigrating, humiliating thing I had done, I wanted her to feel that. I was surprised at the depth of my hostility.

What was this?

I had no reason to hate her, she was gorgeous.

She had no morals, no scruples. She would do whatever she had to get what she wanted.

Gwendolyn Kaijin was everything that I had wanted before Sadie.

The revelation hit me like an anvil dropping from the sky.

I loved Sadie. I loved Roan, too… in a different way, and I especially loved the thing we had become. I would die to protect that, to protect *them.*

I would likewise *kill* to protect that.

"Everything okay, mate?" Roan asked. "Did they fuck up the crèmes?"

"No, no," I said. I didn't want to upset anyone, this could wait. "I just thought of something that we need to talk about later," I gave him a look. Hopefully he wouldn't push the matter. He didn't, but I knew we *would* talk about it later. My steak tasted like ash, and when the dessert course came around, I passed on sweets in favor of a straight gin.

I would have stabbed someone in the head if I could have had some of the Tobacconist's battleship gin right now. I shuddered at the thought of grabbing Gwen by the back of her head and driving the point of a knife up through her jaw, into the soft palate, and then into her poisonous brain. Thankfully Roan and Sadie were far more interested in the dessert cart.

She was laughing when he showed her how to shatter the crust on the crème brûlée. He was likewise amused by the presentation of a petite croquembouche, just a foot tall instead a full three feet. We shared the pastries, and Sadie insisted that I try her crème brûlée.

It was good.

Just like the glee on her face when she shared the dessert with me.

When I looked back at Kaijin, her look could have cracked a mirror. It was pure hatred. It was more than that, it was jealousy. I felt a crack splinter through the monument of hatred I had for her. *There was jealousy.*

She was glaring venom at me, as Sadie decided she wanted to dip one of Roan's pastries in her crème brûlée and put the bite in my mouth. No one had ever done that with her, no one ever would, because she was a poisonous fucking snake, and deep down, every guy would know it.

I covered the check when it came, not letting either of them see how much the meal cost. Even Roan wouldn't know, I paid cash, so he wouldn't even see the total on a monthly statement. He would be thinking about that, and we could get up and leave without making a scene. Sated and stuffed, we were in the first group of people who excused themselves. One of the crazy things about places like Chevalier was that guests were seated in flights, so that the kitchen was able to deliver food and service that was worth hundreds of dollars per seating.

Kaijin and the rest of her cronies were in a different flight. As we were leaving, I was able to get a look at the others at the table. I recognized Ajahi, he stood out. Malmaison was harder to pick out, being a stereotypical Anglo-Germanic Aryan wanna-be.

Then I saw the old man, Guillame Chauvignon, *le Generale.* The bastard was in Indigo City, his face as hard as old oak, and an expression that would make battery acid seem sweet. Late sixties, close cropped white hair, a similar short dusting of white beard and mustache. He wasn't wearing one, he hadn't shaved recently. Long flights and jet lag would do that to a man.

He was wanted in the US, by several different agencies. Some of them large, powerful, and highly influential.

This was fucking *bad* if he was here personally.

I took the rear position and ushered Roan and Sadie toward the door. It was hard not to rush, I wanted to linger and admire her ass in the splendor of her jeans or linger over another glass of some unimaginably haute liquor.

～

I TOLD ROAN TO DRIVE WHEN WE GOT BACK TO OUR CAR WHILE I *GOT something* from the trunk. That something was a gun, an Ingram Mac-10 chambered for .45 ACP. It countered its less than stellar accuracy with a blistering rate of fire, which was fairly useful in the case of car chases. Luck was often as much a factor as skill in those circumstances.

The gun presented a small bulge when I got into the passenger seat.

"Everything okay?" Roan asked, noting it.

"Yes, it's okay. We should probably take a sightseeing tour before going home," I said, meeting his eyes. There was a flicker of recognition. He would get the details later, but he knew that I didn't want us to go straight to the manse. I wanted to make sure that we weren't followed.

The looping drive home took us across a picturesque bridge, through the oldest and most historic parts of the city, and eventually back home. Sadie took it in good stride, Roan was a stunning conversationalist, which was good. All my attention was on keeping an eye behind us, and scanning intersections, hoping to spot the ambush before it came.

None came.

At the manse Roan started the fireplace, and I prepared drinks for everyone. I could have traded the MAC-10 for a less bulky pistol, but it felt comforting at the moment. Sadie would get a sparkling dessert wine, and Roan some anise and wormwood non-alcoholic spirit of his, and for me a curious black gin from New Zealand.

While Sadie was changing from her casual jeans, I handed Roan his drink and I laid out everything. Kaijin, Chauvignon, and the rest of the Cartel Escadrille top members had been in Chevalier. He nodded grimly, and did something on his phone, and told me that he had activated something he called his Dunkirk plan. I didn't ask him to elaborate on it, but I knew it was handled.

When Sadie returned to the living room, the fire was going strong. Roan threw some wood chunks into it, so that the gas logs produced the scent of a regular fire. The effect was nice. Sadie's satin negligee was also nice. I handed her a flute of wine, and she smiled as she took it.

Roan had settled back, not picking up the remote.

No movie then, I was fine with that.

I put an arm around her and kissed her on the lips. Her kiss tasted like wine.

When my hand trailed down the front of her negligee, seeking to tease her nipples into hardness, she touched my hand. "I don't think I can, tonight."

"Are you okay?" I brushed a lock of hair out of her face.

"I am a little bit sore," she said softly. "And *Chevalier* was a large meal."

"It was," I nodded. I kissed her again, on the side of her neck. She made a soft sound. "Maybe another evening."

"Definitely," she whispered.

She sat between us, and we just talked. There were traded kisses, and the small gestures of affection we shared. It was nice. But it didn't last. Roan's phone started a vibrating alarm. He excused himself and went to the Bat Cave at a brisk limp.

"What's up?" I asked.

"Perimeter alarm," he said. He toggled through cameras, the screens filled with saturated green and black images. "Motion sensor, grid sixteen."

"What can I do?" I asked.

"Can you manage one of the drones?" Roan asked. He gestured to the control setup he had. I nodded and grabbed a chair. The drones were interesting to use, sometimes fun. "Don't grab one through six, their armed and loaded and I don't want to lose one over a stray cat."

"Aye, just call me Maverick," I said. It only took a few seconds, but

I had one of his drones out of its cradle and zipping away from the manse. "Where is grid sixteen?"

"The boat pen," he said. I sent the drone whizzing across on a flat arc across the property. There were trees, turning into a mangrove of knobby roots and then the outline of the pen. There was a powerboat inside, and that was the other end of the escape tunnel. Roan had that stocked, I was certain. Fuel, bug-out bags, firearms, the works.

"Take it across the wall, and then follow it to the drive," Roan said. I did as he instructed, gliding the quadrotor on its near silent wings.

"The middle screen," Sadie said. I looked, and she was right, there was the profile of a man, holding near perfectly still.

"Good eye, our intruder is in… grid… next to the gate," I said.

"Twelve," Roan said.

"Do any of these drones have guns?" Sadie asked.

"No," Roan said. "They are civilian remote control, and they can't handle anything but the smallest firearms, and there is no aiming them."

"Oh," she said. "But that would be useful?"

"Damn right," I said.

"I've got him," Roan said. "Swing out toward the road, go thermal, see if he has backup or a getaway vehicle."

"I'm on it," I said, and then the drone was moving again. Switching the thermal was a bit of a gamble, I had done this some, the drones could be fun to play with, but if something was the same temp, all over, then it was invisible. I had landed drones in tree branches more than once, because the cold branches didn't show against the cold air.

I avoided that particular trap and found the intruder's vehicle. "I've got a vehicle with a hot engine, hot exhaust. One passenger," I said. I flipped to the low light, and the heat map turned back to green and black. I fumbled with the keyboard trying to get the camera to grab some stills. Roan shouted the keyboard shortcut at me. "Thanks, mate," I said.

"The MMOs are good for keyboard multi-tasking," Roan said.

"This isn't a guild raid," I said. "Or whatever you do in those games."

"Ah, no, this is not a guild raid, this is a pair of idiots who don't know what they're getting into," he said.

"Should I go get a sniper rifle and put them down?" I asked. I could almost hear Sadie tense at the suggestion.

"No need," Roan said. He picked up his encrypted phone, dialed, and placed a nuisance call to the Indigo City police department, trespassers at the house on Bootlegger Head, and that the police were being politely requested to apprehend and detain the trespassers. There was a pause, some wrangling from dispatch on the other end, and then he dropped a hammer, telling them that if there wasn't a cruiser on site in five minutes, they would hear from their commissioner and the lieutenant governor, because the house is part of the state historic registry and vandals would not be tolerated.

There were a few more choice words, and then he thanked the dispatch.

A helicopter came over Bootlegger Head, coming in low across the water and circling around the property until they spotlighted the intruder. It turned out to be a woman with tightly braided hair and a black bodysuit. She bolted across the property, scaled the wall like a cat, and popped over. She attempted to make it to her accomplice in the getaway vehicle. The key word was attempted, because a police cruiser had finally rolled up behind the car, and the passenger had already been dragged from the car by several aggro cops.

Within fifteen minutes, everything was quiet, the helicopter was gone. A tow truck likewise had come and gone.

Sadie stood at the windows overlooking the front of the property, facing the distant wall and the groomed grass and bushes. Her eyes were tight, and she was tense. "Nothing else will happen tonight," I said.

"Are you sure, and who is it?" she asked.

"Some clients we recently did work for aren't taking rejection well," Roan said softly.

"We're freelancers," I said. "We do jobs, then we come back home. They wanted us to join them."

"What do they do?"

"Heroin cartel," Roan said.

"I'm a lot of things, but I'm not a piece of shit smack dealer," I said.

"We've seen the poppy fields," Roan said. "Where zealots and radicals force people to harvest the sap at gunpoint."

"Oh." She was silent for a time and then, finally, she whispered, "Thank you."

"You're welcome." Roan put an arm around her.

"What for?" I asked, mildly interested.

"For not killing them." Her voice was so quiet, shaken.

I looked at her and said gently, "It doesn't always have to be blood and body count."

"Aye," Roan followed me up. "Corpses draw attention and paperwork, especially on your front lawn."

I frowned at him and said, "Damnit, man. I'm trying to be smooth here." I turned back to Sadie who was looking from one to the both of us wide-eyed.

I shrugged and sighed. "He's not wrong."

CHAPTER TWENTY-EIGHT

Sadie...

Things were tense around the mansion, and I hated it. It was as if Roan held his breath, just *waiting* for something to happen. Spending long hours in his Bat Cave at his computer keys and when I couldn't find him there? It was typically at one of the first-floor windows, staring out as far as the eye could see at the leaden gray sky and over the steely blue waters of the Chesapeake. His keen green eyes bouncing back and forth as he swept the landscape, the gears and wheels forever turning in his skull – and I have to tell you it was driving me *crazy* watching him worry all the time but not as crazy as it drove me when he tacitly denied it every time I brought it up.

On the third or fourth day I'd had enough.

I found him in the large, formal dining room off of the kitchen, staring out the windows again and I knew it wasn't *nothing* like he proclaimed it to be... because if it were *nothing,* he wouldn't have left a pot of water boiling over on the stove unattended. Thus, was his level of distraction.

"You're doing it again," I murmured laying a hand against his back and he jumped. What happened next almost happened too fast for my mind to comprehend. I just suddenly found myself fetched up hard against the glass, Roan's big hand at my throat, his nose barely an inch from mine and his breathing sawing in and out of his big frame as though the shot of adrenaline he'd just took was never going to wear off.

"Bloody *hell*, Sadie! Are you alright?"

I half smiled, his hand on my throat firm and actually quite the turn on, my hands raised in surrender.

"I'm sorry, I thought you heard me," I said softly.

"I'm so sorry," he said. "Please, make some bloody noise next time!" He let me go and tugged down his waistcoat, and I smiled.

"I wasn't exactly being subtle, Conan," I said gently and let my gaze rove his handsome face. He closed his eyes and let out a sigh of defeat.

"At it again, was I?" he asked.

I laughed slightly and put my hands to his waist, tugging him closer to me, my back to the glass and jokingly sighed out, "Aye," before demanding, "Now come down here and kiss me."

His lips curved into that secretly pleased smile he seemed to always get when I asked him for affection and he bent, hand drifting to my chin to hold it lightly as he swept his lips across mine.

I reached up, my back arching off the glass slightly, the back of my head lifting from it, and twined my arms around his neck. I buried my fingers into his coarse red hair and pulled his mouth more insistently against mine as he made a strangled noise of surprise into my mouth.

We'd stopped with the pretenses since our threesome and all slept together now. Mostly in Roan's room thanks to its easy and convenient first-floor access. There was only one night where Roan had stayed up late and Lach had told him if he wasn't going to come to bed that Lach was taking me to his room and Roan had simply nodded without looking, waving us off. That had been *last night*, actually, and I was a little bit over this strange obsession of his.

Nothing else was happening. Nothing since the two trespassers on the property. I figured something would have happened by now if it was going to, but Roan was of a different mind on the matter, and that was okay. He was the expert, after all… Except I didn't know what to think because Kyle was of the same mind that I was.

"Sadie." Roan pulled away from me to a whimper of protest.

"Don't stop," I begged, breathily.

"*Cor,*" he muttered and lifted me up, turning me around and hooking his good leg in the rungs of the seat at the head of the table flinging it aside and almost dropping me onto the dining table's surface when his bad leg gave out.

I laughed while he cursed.

"That went so much better in my mind," he said ruefully and I captured his face between my hands, seated on the edge of the table, dragging his mouth back to mine.

He groaned, and skimmed fingertips up my thighs, massaging the tops, moving the skirt of my short, light silk dress out of his way. I felt myself get warm at the apex of my thighs, and I already knew I was wet. It was kind of a constant thing now, how could it not be living with two hot men that wanted me practically all the time?

Okay, Roan was a lot more reserved on that front than Kyle. Kyle, I swear to God, was whatever the male equivalent of a nympho was.

"Mngh!" Roan made a strangled noise when his fingertips skated across my skin at my hips, tracking back and forth, realizing there were no panties for him to remove.

He pulled back and whispered against my lips, "You little minx."

I chuckled and practically purred in satisfaction that I was even capable of surprising him at all, let alone twice in so short of a span of time. He sucked in a breath as my fingers went for his belt, working the tongue loose from its buckle.

"Sadie…" he murmured.

"Don't say no," I said softly, eyes fixed on his waist and the bulge in his slacks. He touched the side of my face and I glanced up then, my gaze trapped by his as he smiled almost sweetly.

Chidingly, he said, "Never."

He dipped his head back down to mine and claimed my mouth in a kiss that was absolute *fire.* I worked blindly to get his cock free and stroked him in my hands as I scooted my ass closer to the edge of the table.

"God, Sadie…" he murmured against my skin, his lips and breath brushing my throat tantalizingly as I wriggled closer to him. He delved fingers between my legs and groaned again with desire when he found my pussy wet and ready.

"Please," I begged, and he growled, a carnal sound of surrender that bespoke that there was no denying me, no other option. He fitted himself at my entrance and started to go slow, and I put my hands to his waist, pulling him in, wrapping my legs around him as the gap between our bodies closed and his thick, long cock stretched my body, filling me like only he could.

I was restless and had been for the last several hours, and I just wanted that feeling to go away. I wanted to surround myself and fill myself with my lover and give us both something far more pleasurable to do than just sit around, worry, and wait.

"Sadie." His voice was worried restraint.

"I won't break, Conan… please, *fuck me*."

He moaned and lost his balance slightly when I locked my legs tighter around his back, one hand catching himself beside my hip on the table, the other going to my waist.

"I hurt you, you tell me," he demanded, and I smiled up at him, biting my bottom lip.

"You hurt me; I'll tell you," I promised, even though it was slightly a lie. I wanted him to hurt me more or less. I wanted him to set a pace that rode that edge between pleasure and pain, wanted him to fuck me and make it hurt so good I came screaming his name.

Kyle had been teaching me the pleasures that could be found in that edge of pain and for some reason, my mood led me to a curiosity about what that could be like with Conan Roan.

He started thrusting, and I moaned, gripping the edge of the table and pulling myself down on his cock as he pushed into my body. God it felt so good, that zing of sensation as the head of his dick bumped my cervix was so *intense* but not in a bad way, just in… in an intense way.

"Yes!" I cried and my gasping moans of pleasure seemed to encourage him. He touched the outsides of my thighs and I let my legs fall open, he tapped his chest and said, "Put them up, lass," and I brought them together, he hugged my legs, and I held onto the edge of the table and he pushed into me once more. I gasped and the sound that came out of me was at once feral and tamed, a sultry noise of satisfaction and contentment as he moved inside of me.

It was as though the change of positioning allowed him greater reach, as though he touched every part of me, his shaft pressing out against my walls which I clenched around him tight. He rocked his hips, driving into me steadily and I panted, the only thing missing was that final spark, the one that would set us both ablaze, I think.

"Harder," I begged. "Please harder."

He didn't disappoint, thrusting harder but not faster, his eyes closing as though he listened to the symphony, turning his head, pressing a reverent kiss to the side of my calf. I panted and arched slightly my body pulled taut as he played me from the inside out and oh, God what music we made together.

The orgasm that built felt like a long time coming even though we hadn't been at it very long and when the crescendo hit, I felt blasted apart, my voice expelled from my lips in a wordless cry of pleasure that hit the high ceilings and painted the windows and walls with sound as Conan bit down on a cry of his own, his thrusts losing their careful rhythm as he shoved into me hard enough I lost my grip on the edge of the table and slid along the gleaming, polished wood several inches.

We heard a camera click and turned our heads to look at Kyle who was smiling appreciatively from the dining room entryway.

"Oh, now that was *nice...*" he said and his tone held nothing but affection and adoration.

Conan chuckled, "Have a go, mate?" he asked in jest his cock twitching inside of me.

I turned my head and smiled at Kyle in a strangely shy invitation.

"No, bro... there's no way I could top that right now. You guys enjoy yourself," and with that, he retreated. I turned and looked up at Conan who looked down at me with an arched eyebrow.

I laughed, and he grinned, laughing too.

"That was good," I murmured, and he smiled bigger.

"Aye," he agreed. "That it was."

CHAPTER TWENTY-NINE

*R*oan...

The hours of waiting crept into days. Sitting and waiting gnawed at my nerves, and it left Lach and Sadie on edge as well. We passed the time, movies and what meals I could pull together in the kitchen. We didn't dare leave the fortress that was the manse. We spent so much time together, and that was the one thing that made it tolerable, bearable.

I learned a great deal about Sadie, and how she liked it when I went down on her. How she enjoyed my attention, how it was different from Lach's.

On the third day we could no longer take the pressure cooker atmosphere that had grown in the house, so we left for the afternoon. The system was left on high alert, and all incoming schedules were deferred or even canceled. No need in having the groundskeepers show up while the mines were armed.

We took in a crab pot lunch. Even in the cold, we were surprisingly happy.

Then a swing up to the Royal Indigo Hotel for drinks and live music. Sadie and I sampled their selection of ciders, while Lach seemed to almost float with some curious apple spice brandy.

There were no alerts, no notifications from the perimeter. Nothing on the cameras, nothing for the motion detectors but a few squirrels and a large black-and-white stray cat. "I've seen him before, I started calling him Sylvester," Sadie laughed.

When we returned, the inside the house wasn't stuffy and oppressive, it was warm and welcoming, as it had been to us for years. It was nearly dark, and while Lach and Sadie were debating the pros and cons of ladies going commando, I was considering what I was going to whip up for a light dinner. The crab lunch had been somewhat late in the day, but it was also not a heavy meal, certainly not enough to carry us through the rest of the evening.

Especially if the conversation continued as it had been. Lach was likening tearing off a pair of panties, especially nice panties, to unwrapping a gift that had thoughtful paper. She was laughing at him, and there was something about how many pairs of her thoughtful paper he had ripped in his haste to get his toy.

The lights went out, there was a five second pause, and then they came back on.

"Bloody hell," I said.

"There's no storm," Lach said, looking out the window.

"Five seconds, that's the delay on the generator. The power has been cut," I said. "It's beginning."

"Sadie, get to the Bat Cave," Lach said. She nodded, and she beat me there. Lach stepped on the top of the coffee table, pressed down hard with his foot and I heard the latches release. I knew that once the top of the table was completely open, he would retrieve the rifle concealed inside it. There were easily a dozen caches like that throughout the house. I had checked the concealed top a week ago, the AR pattern rifle was cleaned and in good working order, the magazines had been inspected for broken springs, and the two pistols were likewise in good working order. The worrisome part had been bringing up the steel canister holding six of the 40mm grenade rounds that were for the launcher under the barrel.

Keeping bullets and guns in the main part of the house was one thing, having actual explosives was another. Most of the time, those, including the mines that were now packed in trap positions around the house, such things lived in an armored box in the arsenal. That armored shell was built into the wall, so that if anything went wrong and something went off, it would blow out the wall, and not collapse the house.

That armored box was empty.

It had never been empty.

Anxiety gnawed at my stomach. What had I forgotten? What had I not planned or prepared for?

"Oi House! Lights dim, red shift," I shouted. The house responded, the LEDs switched from normal sunlight white-yellow to red and the intensity dropped. We could still see, but the chances of someone getting a line of sight on us through a window dramatically decreased.

In the Bat Cave, Sadie was sitting at one of the consoles, worry etched on her face. "In that locker there, grab two of the jackets, mine is extra-large, you should be able to wear one of Lach's. I've two ordered for you, but the wait time for custom-made body armor is more than a few weeks."

"So the measurements you took weren't just for dresses, or a chance to hold me?" She gave a forced smile and laugh.

"Oh certainly, for all of those things," I said. She handed me mine, and I slipped into it and zipped it up. Lach's was oversized on her, and it wouldn't offer optimal protection, but it would be better than nothing at all. There was movement on all of the cameras, vehicles swarming up the main road, men clustering ahead of the gate, and there were so fucking many of them, so many warm bodies on the IR. I sighed.

"How many?" Lach asked, the AR slung over his shoulder.

"A lot, like, *a lot*," Sadie said.

"What was it that general guy said when he was surrounded?" Lach asked.

"That was Maverick from *Top Gun*, and we aren't surrounded, looks like a target-rich environment to me, or something like that," I said. I hit keys and the quadrotor drones in the rookery started warming up, and the explosive bolt on top of the gondola blew, dropping the plywood sides and revealing the M134 gun and in's gimbal mount. "Bootlegger Airforce and artillery corps are online."

"What about alerting the police and SWAT?" Lach asked.

"I've already triggered that call, but they've picked this time carefully. Dispatch has relayed that the chopper is on the ground and won't be airworthy for another half hour, refuel and flight checks, and its shift change. The SWAT guys are halfway home, and the evening shift is just rolling in. We won't have any local support for at least fifteen or twenty minutes."

"Well that's just fucking aces, isn't it?" Lach growled.

"Are we in trouble?" Sadie bit her lip.

"I won't lie, Poppet, maybe," I said. "I wanted to give you some time at a gun range, get you familiar with maybe a pistol, but we haven't had time. If things do go sideways, there is a full escape plan. That door over there, there is a tunnel behind it, goes about three hundred yards down to the boat pen, the boat we took out this afternoon is there. There are three bug-out bags, plenty of supplies, and the rest of that kit."

"What about my things?" Sadie asked. I could see it in her face, she had until very recently had all but nothing, and now that she had nice things, she was afraid of losing it all.

"Your photos and other things I took the liberty of scanning and putting on a flash drive in your bag, along with duplicates of personal documents, both authentic and the forgeries," I said softly.

The hammer fell seconds later when an explosion shook the house.

"What the fuck?" Lach shouted.

"That was a bloody fucking mortar," I said. I had not prepared for the house to be shelled. The roof wasn't armored or reinforced like the walls were, and one hit could splash the rookery or the gun very easily. I had only counted on an attack from the ground.

There were two more hard blasts. "We lost a camera, and a motion sensor, and it looks like the pool is full of glass," Lach said, looking up from the bank of monitors on the wall. "Perimeter and wall are still up."

"Good," I said. I brought the M134 up and swept the designator across the wall looking for the mortar team, and offering a prayer of thanks that Russian mortars were absolute shite for hitting their targets. The front gate came down as a black SUV came crashing through. I gave it a buzz of 7.62mm from the gun, shredding the front, turning the windshield into white spiderwebs, and likely turning most of the men inside the vehicle into mince.

It veered off the driveway, into the grass, and hit one of the mines buried under a cluster of hosta. The blast flipped it over, blocking the driveway for other vehicles. They would have to ram it out of the way or take their chances in the grass. I wanted them in the grass, where the other mines were.

"I'm going to the door, make sure stragglers or recon doesn't get close," Lach said. He slipped an earpiece in. "Make sure you don't turn that *Home Alone* shit on while I'm up there. I don't want a paint can in the balls or a claymore in the dick, okay?"

"You're solid, mate, go on." I said. I hooked my end of the comm on my collar. I would be able to talk to him the entire time. He went up, and I heard him hit the arsenal door. He would likely be grabbing his favorite toys for this. I looked at Sadie, and I knew I would do anything to protect her, keep her safe.

I sent the big gun into action again, raking the top of the wall, tearing men apart with a hailstorm of bullets. I saw the black-and-white striped flash of track suits, and black leather, and AK-47s, these were Russian Mafia. I swung the gun camera down and zoomed in on the first SUV that wasn't burning furiously and made out the New Jersey tags. Had Chauvignon gone and recruited all of the groups we had done work against? Was the guy in St. Henri not a coincidence, but one of those first strike wankers? The thought was chilling, we had a lot of enemies.

It would also explain the appearance of the Narcos a week before.

The cartel was going to drop everything on us, just because we told them no? It didn't make sense, that level of response.

I queued up the first drone and sent it on an arc across the property and over the wall I wanted eyes to see what was on that side. My heart stopped. There were so many, so fucking many of them. More than a dozen, more than two dozen big sedans and SUVs, guys kept coming out of them, with masks and striped track pants, gleaming AKs and other cheap easy to get guns.

We had carried out a lot of jobs taking down rogue Slavs and violent lord of war ex-Soviets and had made way more enemies that I had guessed. I didn't see any of the Escadrille cartel types, which was annoying. I dropped the drone down into the middle of what looked like their command center and detonated it.

The gun buzzed as I found it targets, and there were more house shaking explosions, some were poorly aimed mortars, others were mines on the lawn going off. It was looking like the Normandy landings, but with fewer Nazis and more azaleas.

I launched another drone to sweep the wall from the other direction. All I had found were the Russians, and I knew the Cartel Escadrille would be here somewhere. They had to be here. Lacking any other targets, I aimed the drone for the largest cluster of men and vehicles and set it off higher above the ground. The damage to the cars would be less, but the wider field would hit more of the attackers with shrapnel. I didn't let myself think about it too much, I knew what the other side of this sort of combat looked like.

I burped several more bursts out of the gun, chewing up two more vehicles that tried to force the gate. The third had enough steel in front of it that it avoided the worst of the gun. They made a hard turn, shot out across the lawn and the front of the sedan promptly exploded. It wasn't a mine, but a 40-mil grenade. Mark up a kill or six for Lach.

There was another explosion, much larger than the mortars or the mines. The house shuddered with the force of it. I searched for it, had they brought an honest to God artillery piece? How would they have gotten it into the country?

They hadn't. A section of the wall at the base of the head was gone, blasted away. A pair of heavy SUVs rolled through the rubble, followed by men on foot. These were dressed in tactical black with ARs and what looked like Uzis. The Escadrille men were here. They were avoiding the main field of fire from the gun and avoiding most of the minefield laid out in the yard.

"Lach, we've got a breach in the wall, north-west section, by the waterline." I keyed my mic. "Escadrille forces."

"Can you handle the gate?" Lach asked.

"I can, can you give them a reason to get down?" I asked. The Escadrille men made a good deal of progress across the lawn, heading toward the north side of the house. Then they weren't making any progress. The walls of the house were thick and absorbed a lot of sound. We couldn't hear Lach's AR, but we could hear him firing suppressing fire with the grenade launcher.

The French Heroin Legion grabbed turf and started shooting toward the house from prone positions. Sadie gave a sobbing noise, and we started hearing the staccato rapping of bullets hitting the walls. There was no shattering glass, but that was expected, it was all bullet resistant.

I saw the gun was starting to run low on ammo. I set the barrel speed lower, to conserve rounds, but kept it busy. Splitting my attention between two fronts was taxing. I could fly a drone, or I could guide the gun, but not both. I ran a spray across the front of the gate, sending Russians into protected positions. I grabbed another drone from the rookery and sent it skyward and was preparing to go over the wall when the entire house shook.

"The fuck was that?" Lach barked in my ear.

"The sensors at the front door are offline, and so is the door camera, I've got static," I said.

"They've got RPGs," Lach said, then there was another house rocking explosion. They were close enough to start hitting us with rounds made to knock out tanks. The armored walls weren't strong enough for that.

"Are you there?" I asked, my voice strained.

"Yeah, just a little dusty," he responded. There was more rattling of gunfire across the mic.

I grabbed the hovering drone and banked it around the front of the house and toward the north side. The front door was gone, there was only a gaping hole into the foyer. There was more damage, the upper story had been holed like a pirate ship in an old action movie. The greenhouse pool area was pure carnage, and half of the water had drained from a crack in the bottom and side.

Then the feed on the drone went out. A sharpshooter had taken it out. Apparently, they realized what the drones were. That was fine, I was almost out of them.

"Lach, you need to fall back," I said.

"You're only saying that because of…" His response trailed off into a clatter of machine gun fire, judging from the sound, it was coming from his gun.

"Sadie, I need you to close the door, but don't lock it yet. We want Lach to get in before going into lockdown." She nodded, fear in her eyes. She grabbed the heavy hinges of the door and pushed it shut, her hand on the locking lever. I engaged the gun again, and after a second, the buzz cut off and there was only silence. The ammo load indicator had clicked all the way from four thousand to zero.

I reached for another drone, and the green lights were gone, my drones were offline. They must have been still lobbing mortars at us, or one of the RPGs that hit upstairs broke the rookery. This was going from bad to worse. I got up from the chair and limped to the gun rack. This was bringing back all sorts of shite memories.

Mazar-i-Sharif was ugly. Well before I lost my leg, my first action with Lach and the rest of his Yanks. There were RPGs, half of the vehicles were blown to hell, pinned down by what seemed like half the Taliban army. They still had a few tanks left in their forces, and they had put more than a few 120mil cannon rounds through our armored vehicles.

You'll be fine, they don't have tanks, so you lads not having any isn't a big deal. They told us that the storm would keep air support grounded for a while, so no gunships, no ugly warthogs flying over with their big guns, not even air evac.

All of that would have been very useful.

There was another blast, and the room rattled.

That one was close.

I picked up the Belgian P90 and racked the bolt. The chamber was clear, the mag ready. I sighed, Lach needed to hurry. I looked over at Sadie and she had never seemed smaller, or more frightened. Well, almost never seemed so small, she was a stick wrapped in skin when Lach had first brought her to the house.

"Here," I said, and handed her one of the Berettas from the gun rack. "It's simple, this is the safety, keep that on until I tell you to click it, like this," I showed her how the safety switch worked, and made sure that the selector was set to semi-auto. It didn't hold many rounds, and it wouldn't do for her to squeeze the trigger and empty the gun with it on auto. "These are Lach's, his favorite right now. If you're in danger, point this end at the baddies and squeeze the trigger." She looked like she was going to be sick, but that steel inside her wasn't going to let that happen.

"Okay." Her voice was a mouse's squeak.

"You'll be okay," I vowed. "Nothing will happen to you. I am your shield."

CHAPTER THIRTY

*L*ach...

Everything was going as well as could be expected. Half the house was blown to bits, the other half looked like a tornado had hit it. I had to thank Roan for all of his over the top planning and fortress building. It had just seemed like a weird hobby all these years, almost comical. Now, it was going to save our lives. I was about to make a joke when I caught several rounds in the chest, slinging me into the doorframe I was using as shelter and then the ground caught me.

That hurt.

I checked, and the dragonscale armor took all of the hits, and none went through.

Yet another reason to thank the mad Brit when we got out of this.

I heard him mention falling back, and that must have meant the big gun was out of bullets, which was bad fucking news. They were coming closer to the door, there was almost no shelter across the north stretch of lawn so the Escadrille men were running. I raised the rifle and emptied the mag, sending some to their maker, most to the ground, and a few running in a zig zag. These guys, they were better than most we'd run into.

Most would have given up already, taken their losses and fled.

The AR clicked empty, and I was out of ammo. I emptied the first pistol falling back, looking for the first concealed weapon I could reach. I tried a pressure plate; the wall panel should pop open on a hidden hinge and reveal a rack of guns. It opened, but inside there were three claymore mines. I about shit, but none of them went off, they weren't armed yet.

I slammed the panel shut and backed six feet up the corridor and found the next concealed panel. Behind it there was a gun rack. I could feel my adrenaline surging, and it was messing with my perception and focus. I grabbed two more pistols from the rack, and a tactical shotgun, two tubes under the barrel, and a short bullpup build.

The first black clad person who came through the door took a twelve-gauge solid slug just below the collarbone. Their shoulder opened like a watermelon, and flaps of flesh came away all the way up into the neck. She made a horrid sound, hit the wall and fell.

There were women in the Escadrille? *What the fuck was this?*

My momentary pause was long enough for two of her companions to breach into the room, and one put a round into my chest, and shoulder. The vest stopped both, but they hurt like something else. I racked the shotgun for the other tube and fired a round of buckshot at close range. There was a thunderous roar and one went backwards to the ground while the other recoiled back against the wall.

I fell back, racked the gun again and fired half blind through the smoke. It seemed like a reprieve, so I gave further. It was a short distance from the hallway to the living room, then a straight shot back to where the Bat Cave and its armored door was. That was the objective now, slowing the assholes so that Roan had a chance to get the last-ditch defenses armed, and then we would escape.

I looked at the large window overlooking the bay, and there were three ships out in the water, close in. Certainly closer than they should have been. The window suddenly vibrated hard, and a dozen white circles, opaque, appeared. Someone on the boat was shooting at the house, and big rounds considering what it had done to the bullet-proof glass.

Well fuck.

Boats were a goddamn problem.

"Roan, are you still there?" I keyed the mic.

"Yeah, we're here. The door is shut but not locked." He sounded slightly out of breath.

"We've got boats in the water, one shot up the living room, getting out on the Rum Runner is going to be a challenge if they chase us," I said. "And they're in the house."

"Are you clear yet?"

"Almost, can you activate the north, and central sections and leave the kitchen and bedroom sections off?"

"Of course, and it's done," he said.

A trio broke into my line of sight, with more Uzies and MP5 submachine guns. I put a slug into the first person, and then another round of buckshot at eye level toward the other two. There was more screaming, more stench of blood and spent ammo. The ammo was going quick. There was commotion in the hallway, and I saw a good dozen or more coming down the hallway, stepping over the bodies of their companions.

The claymores went off, and twelve was reduced to a handful of moans and one person shrieking horribly.

This was the worst I could ever recall. Worse than when the convoy had been hit and Roan lost his leg. Worse than Mazar-i-Sharif. Certainly, worse than all of the previous jobs I had pulled, even in the worst of those I hadn't been hit so many times. That was a worrying thought, the armor could only take so many hits before it failed.

I heard other sharp barks and knew those were other claymores concealed through the house going off. How many of these assholes were there, and why were they so determined? Any sane foe wouldn't have pressed so hard for so small a gain. We were only two guys, and only had three feet between us. How many of their own were they willing to get killed for the slight of being turned down.

This made zero fucking sense.

I pumped the last round into the chamber and used it to send a man with a maimed arm to hell. He fell silently. That was good because he didn't put up any fight when I took his rifle from him.

I knew this drill, the fighting retreat. Men who turned and ran got shot in the back.

Burst fire, shelter.

Pause.

Burst fire, shelter.

Fall back.

The motions were almost mechanical. I just did them. The gun almost seemed to find the targets as they kept coming in. Body shot, body shot, body shot. They came, I fell back, they fell to the ground.

For each one I put a bullet in, two took their place.

There were more women in this group. I felt unsettled and shaken. I didn't like shooting women, women were for kissing, fondling, fucking. Not for putting bullets in.

I was hit again, and again. The armor took one, then one grazed my thigh.

Fall back, suppressing fire.

I wanted my grenade launcher back. I wanted the shotgun back.

I wanted to hold Sadie, and for the world to be just me and her again. Shady and Kyle.

This wasn't where I was going to die, that I was certain of. Fuck that. I had to get to Sadie, and to Roan. We weren't done.

Burst fire, then click as the ammo was gone. I tossed the rifle and drew my last pistol.

How had it all ended up here?

There was more gunfire, brutal and effective. My improvised barricade was shredded and enough rounds came through into my vest to knock me to the ground. That wasn't regular ammo.

"Come out you motherfucker!" Ajahi shouted. He was carrying a squad assault weapon. He didn't see me in my prone position, which was good He unloaded another long blast from SAW, shredding wall and appliances in the kitchen. This was it. If he was in the house, the rest of the leaders would be close behind.

I scooted back against the wall and raised my pistol, putting the big black man in my sites when there was a barrage of familiar gunfire and he threw himself back behind cover. I knew that sound, that was Roan's ridiculous P90. He saved my ass in that moment but I was pissed, if he was out shooting that meant the door was open and there was nothing between these assholes and Sadie.

I dragged myself back to my feet, my entire body felt like it had caught a truck head on, probably cracked ribs from that last punch. "Turn it all on, turn it all on Roan!" I shouted as loud as I could.

"You're not clear," I heard him in my ear.

"Fuck it, I might not get clear. Big dogs are in the house, arm everything."

"Everything?" he asked.

"Everything but that, c'mon, do it!" I grunted and rolled onto the floor and belly crawled into the kitchen. There was debris everywhere. Shattered glass, busted marble from the counter tops, and mangled metal and plastic. I picked up one of his precious knives.

The sounds of gunfire ceased. There was just the crunch of boots in rubble, and the wet bubbling sounds of the wounded and the dying. I waited, head down. Three people stepped into the kitchen. "Look at this set up," a woman said. She shined a gun mounted flashlight, giving her location away, but she held at the door. The other two flanked into the room.

"He is in here," an older man said.

"I saw him crawl," the other said. "Ajahi wants him alive if we can get him."

"We want him first, dead or alive," the woman said. "We have to pay out if the Ivans or the Wongs get any of them."

"Fuck them foreigners," the older man said, sniffing closer to where I was. "And this was a sharper outfit before General Snail-Eater started letting you broads in."

"Shut the fuck up, Grab-ass, and find the hitman," she hissed at him.

He came around the island and looked at me, his eyes lighting up. "Smile for the flash, asshole," I said and covered my face. He took a step toward me and the mine concealed in the island went off. For what seemed like forever there was only a painful high-pitch tone in my ears and I couldn't focus my eyes. Grab-ass was sitting against the counter opposite the island, covered in blood. He was moving slowly, his hands tangled in his own entrails. He picked up something and looked at it with his one remaining eye.

It took me a second to focus and realize he was holding what was left of his manhood.

The other two came toward me, from the other direction. I lift the gun and put two rounds in the chest of the first figure, then fired three toward the second blob I assumed as a person. Then I dropped the gun, my hand aching.

"C'mon, get up, mate."

"Conan?" I asked. He hooked his hands under my arms and pulled me up to my feet.

"Yeah, it's me, we've got thirty seconds to get to the Bat Cave, because she's alone in there." I felt my legs jerk as I forced them to move. I half stumbled; half walked back to the door. There were bodies everywhere and shouting outside. Once inside, he slammed the door and pulled the lever engaging the four steel locking arms. It would take a demolition team to get through that door.

"It's bad," I said, looking up at the two of them.

"Sadie, check him, make sure he hasn't been shot," Roan said. "I have to see what's left of the defenses."

She pulled my vest off and grimaced. "There is a lot of blood."

"Is it his?" he asked.

"I don't know!" She sounded panicked I touched the side of her face and her eyes met mine. I willed her to be still. She sucked in a sharp breath and got ahold of herself. *That's my girl.* "I'm not finding any entry or exit wounds," she said, finally.

"My arm, thigh, grazed me," I said. My voice felt like it was coming from the bottom of a barrel. She had a first aid kit and started dabbing at the wounds.

"I think it's time to start evac," Roan said gravely.

"There are three boats out in the water," I said. "The woman mentioned the Chinese, I think they are Triad ships, they have at least a fifty-cal. Damn near busted the bay window with it."

"That's not great," Roan said. "But we have a cure for that."

"What in the hell is that?" Sadie asked as he opened a hard case.

"Javelin missile launcher," Roan said. "Only slightly expensive, and four missiles."

"You two, take these, carry them down to the boat, I'll be right behind you," he said.

"You might be in better shape to carry things, bro," I said. I could feel my legs trembling, and I knew I didn't have much in me.

"Yeah, but you're in no shape to hold the rear," he said, his eyes like emerald ice.

"Goddamnit, Roan, this isn't the time," I said through gritted teeth.

"This is precisely the time, mate," he said. "The general is out there, and he has all of his goddamn wankers with him, even that blonde one, the poisoner. And I think I know why they're fired up to kill all of us." Even Sadie looked up at that.

"Why?" she asked for me.

"Because the old man in Oasis, that was Bertrand Chauvignon, Guillame's younger brother. We got thrown into the middle of a family feud where we were supposed to go down. You were supposed to be killed in Texas, and then they would come back together and get rid of me."

"Fucking frogs," I grimaced.

"Aye, bloody fucking frogs," he said. "Now here's what is going to happen. You and Poppet are going to get your asses down that tunnel, and start the boat, and then we're going to get out of here."

"Dead man switch?" I asked.

"I'm going to set that, yes. But I will set a delay on it, long enough for us to get out."

"What are you talking about?" Sadie said, her voice rising.

"Poppet, there is a Soviet surplus bomb under the house, a 700-pound fuel-air explosive warhead. When triggered it will produce a blast so big it will reduce the house to flinders, all of those bastards out there will be pulped like oranges." Her eyes were saucers.

"There's a… *Russian bomb…* under the house? It's always been there?" she asked.

"Yes, and it's armed now," he said.

"Oh my God." She covered her mouth.

"Yes, giant bomb, now that's why you need to pick up that case and go through that tunnel." he said. Sadie grabbed him in a tight hug, and I could see tears in her eyes. She whispered something in his ear and kissed him on the cheek.

"C'mon, Shady," I said. "He's right. He's professionally right." She was hesitant but started moving. Roan handed us what we needed to carry, and then shouldered the P90 again, slamming a fresh magazine home. There was a chatter of bullets against the steel door.

"They're here, now bloody well go!" Roan shouted.

"At the boat?" I asked. I could see Sadie scurrying down the tunnel, cussing as the case holding the Javelin launcher banged against her shins. I pulled the strap of the ammo bag over my shoulder, hefting nearly a hundred pounds of missile.

"At the boat, everything's been made ready."

"That's what I'm afraid of," I said.

There was another tremendous bang, and the door almost came out of its frame. The second came on the heels of the first, and then the door came crashing into the room, crushing through Roan's gaming chair and computer station.

"Go!" Roan shouted and strong-armed me back into the tunnel.

The last thing I saw, as the door to the tunnel was closing, was her. Kaijin, carrying a Steyr AUG. Roan raised his gun, and there was a roar of gunfire. Then the door slammed, and the gunfire was muffled. Then silence.

I choked back a sound and grabbed the lock bar and dropped it in place.

"Goddamnit." I turned and started dragging the missiles as fast as I could down the tunnel. I could feel tears starting to burn at my eyes.

"Where's Conan?" Sadie demanded as I heaved the missiles over the gunwale of the Rum Runner.

"He's not coming." I fell into the boat. "And if we don't go, we aren't going to make it either." Her hand went to her mouth, and I saw her eyes look from the tunnel, to the gun, and back to me. I shook my head. "Start the boat, I'll figure out how to use the missile thing."

"This is insane, Kyle, this is fucking insane."

The engine coughed to life. I was thankful for the noise because it covered the sound of me coughing out a half sob.

CHAPTER THIRTY-ONE

*S*adie...

"Don't you *dare* be a fucking hero," I whispered fiercely. "I love you too much, and I need you. *We. Need. You.*"

Roan's hands slid to my elbows, and he put me back but I saw it. I saw it in his keen green eyes, the calculations, the weights and adjustments, his precious paradigms. I saw it but I didn't want to believe it.

He's not coming... my mind whispered.

I'll die without him, without him and Kyle both... my heart cried.

"Go, I'll be right behind you, I promise," he said. I nodded.

I made my way down the tunnel cursing as the large case banged my shins and the tears burned my eyes, my vision blurring. I dug deep and deeper still for every reserve of emotional strength I had ever held as my soul rendered itself in two. Half here with Kyle, the other half staying behind with Roan.

You'll get it back when he returns to you, I swore to myself. Refusing to give up hope.

I got onto the boat, the stern reading *Rum Runner* in gilded script and dropped the heavy gun case, panting.

"Goddamnit," Kyle grated, falling into the boat behind me.

"Where's Conan!" I demanded as he dragged the ammunition for the launcher thing into the boat behind him.

"He's not coming," he grated. "And if we don't go, we aren't going to make it either."

I felt my hand go to my mouth as I choked back vomit.

"This is insane, Kyle!" I hated the edge of hysteria in my tone.

Hold it together, girl. Hold it together or lose them both, I thought at myself savagely.

"Drive!" he said. "Just like driving a car!" He was already into the cases and assembling things, loading the goddamn rocket launcher and getting ready to shoulder it.

"Not just like driving a car!" I barked, but we'd taken the boat out just the other day... *yesterday?* God no, *just hours ago!...* to go into Indigo City by water for the crab feed, and Roan had let me take the controls. Had shown me how to drive.

He wanted you to know... he knew without knowing. Oh, God...

I turned the key, the boat's powerful engines chugged to life. I nudged the throttle forward, and I looked back in time to catch Kyle severing the mooring line with a sharp hatchet.

"Go!" he screamed.

I punched the throttle. The water boiled turbulent behind us and the boat zipped away from the dock, crashing through the thin boathouse doors. We shot out into the bay faster than it seemed like a boat was capable of going.

"Kyle!" I screamed when I realized there was a blockade of at least three boats ahead of us, a chopper hovering over them.

"Just go! Straight ahead!" he screamed over the whipping wind, the boat smacking over the water's surface.

I swear I heard him grunt, and he let the first rocket fly. The rocket made a *FWOOMP* noise and looked like it was about to belly flop in the water and then vanished in a scream of fire and smoke. The thing made like a streak for the helicopter and hit it. The sound was awful and then there was fire and screaming metal everywhere. The burning wreckage fell and crashed into the front of the largest boat.

"Two birds, one stone motherfuckers!" he screamed in triumph.

"Yes!" I cried.

"Drive!" he shouted.

Oh, fuck! I realized I'd taken my attention off of the act of driving the boat, and I whipped the wheel to the right, veering around the rapidly approaching mess to a burst of gunfire from the boat that was to our right, I ducked and looked behind me. Kyle was on his knees, loading the next shot.

"Stay down!" he screamed, and I did, peeking to make sure that I wasn't going to hit anything.

FWOOMP!

The second rocket went off and the boat in front of us was blasted sky high.

"Sadie!"

I screamed and over corrected. If we were a car, we would have spun out and I guess that's what we did. Sort of, doing a complete three-hundred-and-sixty-degree turn on the water. Kyle fell sideways off balance, but thankfully I didn't bounce him overboard.

"Shit!" he screamed, and I looked over. The last boat was almost on us, and I didn't think. I kept the throttle up, I steered, and I pulled the stupid gun Roan had given me out of the back of my waistband. I pointed it and just started shooting.

Kyle looked up at me from where he was struggling to get the last rocket in place and I looked back. Something passed between us, time slowing, and he nodded and I corrected course. He popped up over the side of our boat, aimed and *FWOOMP!*

The world erupted in chaos on the water, the heat from the blast tickling my cheek, close – way close – but not close enough to burn us, thank God.

I screamed as Kyle's weight crashed into the back of me, and his hand closed over mine on the throttle lever, keeping it pushed forward.

"I got you," he uttered in my ear. "Just keep us going, babe. You did good."

"No, we have to go back!" I cried. "The boats are gone; we need to go back for Roan!"

I knew, I think, that what I was saying didn't make sense, but I couldn't make myself think of why.

"We can't, Shady."

"No! We have to," I said and Kyle's arm went around my waist, holding himself to my back, his other hand grabbing for the *Rum Runner's* wheel.

"Keep us on course, Sadie. There's no going back and there ain't no coming back!"

"Kyle, you don't know what you're saying!" I argued and then Kyle fucking Lachlan did something that he had never, ever, done before… not even when we were teens.

He screamed at me.

"Just do what I *fucking* say! He's *gone*! He's *dead*! And there ain't no going back!"

It happened then… a light lit the dusky sky, a great flash behind us and Kyle screamed, "Fuck!" His hand gripped over mine painfully hard, the wind whipping into our faces, stinging, cold, thrusting icy dread into every nook and cranny, filling every last bit of me with frozen angry hurt, my heart seizing in my breast, turning into a lump of ice and numbing me slowly from the inside out as the bomb at Bootlegger Head went off and turned the last shred of hope I had to complete ash.

~

"Look, I'm hit and we need to go to ground before I crash," Kyle said and handed me another bulky black military-like backpack up from the *Rum Runner*. I took it automatically and set it next to the two already on the dock.

He reached up, and I automatically gave him my hands, leveraging myself against the sturdy wooden timbers beneath my feet to pull his considerable weight up onto the dock beside me. He wasn't fat, but he *was* pure muscle and easily outweighed my much smaller frame by a fairly considerable amount; just how much I couldn't guess and right now, I didn't care to.

He shouldered one backpack, held out another for me to shrug into, and then picked up the third by its top loop handle.

I tried not to think about the significance of that third backpack.

"Kyle, where are we going?" I asked.

"Just follow me, the bug-out plan has more than one safe house for us to lay low."

I did, following him through the warehouses and to the chain-link fence surrounding the shipyard, or marina, or whatever you called it. I could tell he was in bad shape; he didn't move quickly and in the scattered vapor lamps I could see that his clothing was torn and some of it was bloody.

"Cover your ears," he ordered, and I did. He pressed his thumb onto a switch he held in his fist, a distant explosion thumped. I guessed it was the *Rum Runner*, and I was surprised to find that I didn't have it in me to care. I was too numb.

"Turn," he ordered, and I did and he pulled a pocket cutting torch from my bag. He turned a knob, there was a click, and then a puff of orange flame. He adjusted it until it was a blue knife and then used it to cut through the wires of the fence along one of the support poles. He leaned against it and created a gap with his body weight for me to get through. "Watch the edges, they'll be hot."

This was at least familiar. I was an old hand at slipping through fences. Kyle handed me the third pack, devoid of Roan's big shoulders to fill the straps. He stepped through and pushed the wire back together. It wasn't going to fix anything but it wouldn't be so obvious that was where we breached the fence.

"Okay, come on." He took my hand after he made it through the fence himself and we stopped at a nearby bus stop of all things. He checked the schedule, cursed, and said, "Too long to wait. Come on, we're walking. It's not all that far."

"Are you sure you can make it?" I asked, worried.

"I've been through worse," he said, glancing around without looking at me.

"I call bullshit," I said with a shudder. "There's absolutely nothing worse than what we just went through." He didn't respond, just raised the back of my hand to his lips and pressed a kiss to it, there was a pain in his eyes that I couldn't fathom. Were there worse things he had been through?

"Keep your eyes open and your head on a swivel, Shady."

"Just tell me where we're going," I pleaded. "I bet I could get us there faster and easier than you."

He stopped then and looked at me.

"I know these streets better than you, better than even..." I couldn't say his name. "With all his fancy maps and computer programs."

"Okay," he said wearily. "We're going back to the gray house."

"Not there." I drew back. He nodded without looking at me.

"Our home before all of this. The Daughton's... I bought it and had Roan flip it into one of our transient safehouses."

"Of course, you did..." I murmured. I took a deep breath. "This way."

We made it to the Daughton's, Kyle keying our way into the front door, and we shut the world out. I turned around and breathed out slowly.

The house was both completely different, and sickeningly the same as I remembered it. The Daughton's rent-to-own and flea-market furniture were gone, and the horrid cheap carpet with the cigarette burns in it too. The walls had been patched and painted, there was inexpensive but tasteful new furniture, and generic art hanging on the walls. This was a house full of demons and ghosts that he been painted for market.

I could see Roan's hand behind the renovations, and the lavender paint in the kitchen, the new clean countertops, and new handles on the old cabinets. The memories were still here, though. There was no amount of paint or new carpet and linoleum that could bury those.

"You going to blow this place up when we leave?" I asked as Kyle went to the laptop on the desk in the corner of the living room.

"Would you like me to?" he asked, shrugging out of his pack and dumping it at his feet. He hissed and stuck his leg out when he took the seat in front of the computer before he turned it on or woke it up or whatever.

"Yes," I answered, unequivocally. I hated it here. Hated everything it represented, and the fact that here... here was the start to this ravaged aching heart, tattered and torn yet still managing to beat in my breast.

"Consider it done," he said distractedly clicking at the keys.

"What are we doing now?" I asked.

"Getting medical attention, calling on Doc Max."

"I can do it," I said, and he shook his head.

"This isn't just basic first aid; I've been shot, might have a concussion," he said.

"Then I'll learn..." I protested

He looked back at me and met my eyes, finally he nodded and said, "You can't just learn to do triage like that. I need a professional, and Doc Max is the woman who pulled you from death's door when I brought you to the house. I trust her with my life," he said. "So, we can relax, take a shower, there should be non-perishable food in the kitchen."

I nodded and went for the bathroom, unshouldering the pack outside my old bedroom door, speechless.

In here, it *wasn't* new... in here, it was just as it had always been albeit dusty and unused. Right down to the ugly green and orange floral sheets on the bottom bunk bed. It seemed that Roan's efforts were solely spent in the main room and kitchen. Why had he left this? Had Kyle told him to leave it?

I sank down onto the edge of the bottom bunk and ran my hand over the threadbare tan woven blanket. It felt too 'new' so not the same, but perfectly recreated... *why?*

I closed my eyes against the hot flood of tears threatening and swallowed hard. What was I meant to do?

Shower.

Oh, right.

I went through the backpack, found a few things. A change of clothes was the bulk of it. A big manila envelope full of documents and a flash drive, and various other things that my mind was in no shape to fully comprehend right now. I took the big, oversized shirt and brought it to my nose, closing my eyes and breathing in deep.

Of course, it was his… its size, it could only be his, and it was one he had worn.

I closed my eyes and opened my mouth but I couldn't draw air or make a sound so choked up was I with the hot flood of tears that would no longer be denied.

I finally managed a gasping breath in and the *wail* that emanated from me, the broken scream… God, I'd never made any sound like it. Of course, I don't think my soul had ever shattered so completely before. Not even after the death of my parents.

I screamed, one long agonizing sound as the tears poured down my cheeks and I clutched my dead lover's shirt to my chest and it hit me with full force.

Conan Roan, my beloved gentle giant, was dead.

"Sadie?" I heard Kyle in the hall, and I couldn't stop. I couldn't keep the tide of tears at bay.

"Shady?" he asked softly, edging around the doorframe. He sank onto the bunk beside me and pulled me against him.

"It's okay," he said roughly, his own voice thick with unshed tears. I knew the sound, although I had only heard it once before when we were kids and then, he hadn't cried. At least not really.

I couldn't speak, I just let out another broken, agonizing wail. He clutched me close as I cried, despite his injuries, despite his fatigue.

"I am your knight. Nothing else is going to happen to you, baby. I promise," he said to me in a bid to comfort.

Except the worst had already happened… we had lost our shield.

Roan was gone.

To be continued…

ALSO BY A.J. DOWNEY

The Sacred Hearts MC

1. Shattered & Scarred

2. Broken & Burned

3. Cracked & Crushed

3.5 Masked & Miserable (a novella)

4. Tattered & Torn

5. Fractured & Formidable

6. Damaged & Dangerous

The Virtues

1. Cutter's Hope

2. Marlin's Faith

3. Charity for Nothing

4. Stoker's Serenity

The Sacred Brotherhood

1. Brother to Brother

2. Her Brother's Keeper

3. Brother In Arms

4. Between Brothers

5. A Brother's Secret

6. A Brother At My Back

7. A Brother's Salvation

Sacred Hearts MC Novella

Christmas with the Brotherhood

ABOUT THE AUTHOR

A.J. Downey specializes in writing real and relatable contemporary romance stories. She's from Seattle, WA and loves the Pacific Northwest. She finds inspiration from her surroundings, through the people she meets, and likely as a byproduct of way too much caffeine. An avid reader all of her life, it's now her turn to try and give back a little, entertaining as she has been entertained.

Stalker Information:

Website
www.ajdowney.com

Sign up for her newsletter at
http://eepurl.com/dkQiIH

Facebook Group - AJ's Sacred Circle
https://www.facebook.com/groups/authorajdowney/

facebook.com/authorajdowney
twitter.com/authorajdowney
instagram.com/ajdowney
bookbub.com/authors/a-j-downey

ALSO BY JARED KINGPACAL LAIN

ABOUT JARED KINGPACAL LAIN

Jared KingPacal Lain hails from the Great Smoky Mountains, a place of both beauty and dark things, where he explores strange fiction, hidden secrets, and venturing away from the main path to find hidden pleasures, wonders, and horrors.